An ex-publisher and lifelong Londoner, Natasha Cooper writes for a variety of newspapers and journals, including *The Times*, *The Toronto Globe & Mail* and *The Times Literary Supplement*. She has contributed to many radio programmes such as *Woman's Hour* and *Saturday Review*, and regularly speaks at crime-writing conferences on both sides of the Atlantic. In 2002 she was shortlisted for the Dagger in the Library, an award that 'goes to the author whose work has given most pleasure to readers'.

Praise for Natasha Cooper:

'One of the most accomplished crime writers in the country' Mark Billingham

'You know when you pick up a book by Natasha Cooper that you are going to find a literate, intelligent novel about real people . . . A complex and satisfying mystery . . . Like real life, a happy ending isn't guaranteed in this series, which increases the tension' *Sunday Telegraph*

'Ahead of most current detective fiction' *TLS*

'Strong characterisation and sense of place put Cooper among the best in current crime writing' *Publishing News*

'Natasha Cooper writes intelligent novels that manage to marry traditional English values of coppery and detection with modern storylines and attitudes . . . Cooper is a thoughtful writer about issues as well as people' *The Times*

'No matter how dark and grisly the world of her novels, Cooper never loses sight of the compassion and emotional intelligence that have become keynote elements of her work' Val McDermid

'Like Minette Walters . . . Cooper writes methodical, meticulous crime' *Daily Mirror*

'Cooper is expert at detailing the effects of emotional crossfire. She turns her penetrating but compassionate gaze on the duties of parents and those *in loco parentis*, and on the complexity of loyalty and trust – at home and at work' *Guardian*

Also by Natasha Cooper

A
GREATER
EVIL

Natasha Cooper

POCKET
BOOKS

LONDON · SYDNEY · NEW YORK · TORONTO

First published in Great Britain by Simon & Schuster UK Ltd, 2007
This edition published by Pocket Books UK, 2008
An imprint of Simon & Schuster UK Ltd
A CBS COMPANY

1 3 5 7 9 10 8 6 4 2

Simon & Schuster UK Ltd
Africa House
64–78 Kingsway
London WC2B 6AH

www.simonsays.co.uk

Simon & Schuster Australia
Sydney

A CIP catalogue record for this book is available from the British Library

ISBN: 978-0-7434-9532-5

Grateful acknowledgement is made to Faber & Faber Ltd for permission to quote from
'September 1, 1939' from *The English Auden* by W. H. Auden; and to the Coram family
in the care of the Foundling Museum, stored at the London Metropolitan Archives,
for permission to reproduce part of Margaret Larney's eighteenth-century letter.

Printed and bound in Great Britain by
Cox & Wyman Ltd, Reading, Berkshire

For
Felix Turner

Acknowledgements

A large cast of friends has helped me with information and advice for this novel. Among them are Murray Armes, Suzanne Baboneau, Mary Carter, Kate Cotton, Mark Fidler, Jean Gaffin, Jane Gregory, David Hewson, Ayo Onataade, James Turner, Anna Valdinger, Melissa Weatherill and Anne Wright. I always listen to what they tell me, just as I reserve the right to adapt the facts they offer when the needs of fiction demand it.

Author's Note

I finished writing this novel in May 2005, that is about two months before the appalling events of 7/7. When I heard the news my first instinct was to cut the scene on pages 92–96 out of respect for the victims of the atrocity. Then I came to believe that if writers start to censor themselves because of terrorists' actions we will be making a kind of surrender. And that cannot happen. So, with the deepest sympathy for everyone who suffered then, and admiration for the emergency services and all the people involved in the clear-up, I have left the scene as I wrote it.

One other scene that I might have altered in reflection of real life is that on page 308, when the judge is summing up the cut-throat rules. As any lawyer will know, they have been changed.

I and the public know
What all schoolchildren learn
Those to whom evil is done
Do evil in return

W.H. AUDEN, 'SEPTEMBER 1, 1939'

Shall the thing formed say to him that formed it, Why has thou made me thus?

Hath not the potter power over the clay, of the same lump to make one vessel unto honour, and another unto dishonour?

BIBLE, ROMANS 9:20

Chapter 1

The clay was dead between his fingers. Cold and sticky as always, but uncooperative too. It smelled of decay. He wasn't a fool: he knew it was his mind and not the stuff itself that was the problem. Even so, he felt as though it was fighting him, resisting, withholding the response he'd learned to trust. Nothing worked. Each movement of his hands made it worse and the familiar delicate modelling tools felt as heavy as sledgehammers between his clumsy fingers. What had been a promising start was now a mess.

If only he could empty his mind of the voices and the fears. Then he could focus and maybe the clay would move between his hands again, helping him reveal the idea he'd had for it. Never since his discovery of the talent he'd been given had it failed him like this. What if he'd lost it for ever, the power that had come out of nowhere fourteen years ago?

'Take your hands away before you ruin it,' he said aloud, shocking some other, less conscious, part of his brain. His voice, hoarse and a bit cracked, echoed around the big studio, bouncing off the exposed steel beams and the hard concrete floor, easily overcoming the Stones' punchy, wailing music from the CD player in the corner.

In the gap between the end of one song and the beginning of the next, he heard the whirring of the potter's wheel upstairs.

Boards creaked just above his head, and there was the sound of
exuberant female singing. Marisa Heering was having a good day.
All over the big building, potters, painters, silversmiths and
weavers were carrying on as usual: productive; successful; safe.

Sam reached for the damp cloths that kept the half-made head
workable and flung them over the hated lump. Rubbing his hands
together above the bucket, he felt thin cylinders of clay form
against his skin and watched them fall away, like a peculiarly
unpleasant species of dark-orange worm. He manipulated his own
head from side to side, trying to shrug the pain out of his neck and
shoulders. What could it be this time? Not coffee again: his brain
was already juddering with caffeine. But there had to be an excuse
of some kind to knock off work.

The CD had a long time to go before it would need changing.
Each track of the Stones' *Forty Licks* album mocked him with its
angry confidence, but he couldn't silence it without admitting failure. Which would make it worse.

Maybe the cold could give him a reason to move away. He'd
barely noticed it until he'd made himself stop hacking at the head.
Now he could feel iciness across the skin of his face, like a dan-
gerously angled razor. The old-fashioned stove in the corner could
probably do with more fuel. He shuffled across the room, moving
from concrete to boards and catching his foot in the change of
level as he always did. He managed not to fall over the tattered
Persian rug he'd once loved for its coral and lapis colours but now
ignored except when it tripped him. He pulled open the small
steel door of the stove.

Shovelling in smokeless briquettes was something he could still
do. And the extra warmth was good. He let his knees buckle and
squatted down so the heat from the tiled walls of the stove stroked
his face. At least today there hadn't been a model to witness his
incompetence.

'Face it, Sam,' he said, moving his head this way and that to give
both sides an equal share of the heat. Turning the other cheek. He

shuddered and tried to pull the real thoughts away from all the self-defensive games his mind played.

Maybe if he'd had only one fear he could have coped, but with his past and the baby and the woman in prison, all fighting for space in his mind, it was too much.

'Are you mad,' he muttered in a voice he now heard only in nightmares, 'talking to yourself all the time, you dreadful child?'

Even that was enough to force him upright and back to work. The damp cloths looked unspeakable, stained and loathsome. Like something off a slum washing line. He pulled them away, taking care not to catch sight of himself in the mirror. Instead, he stared at the lump that was supposed to become the pinnacle of his career, his entry for the Prix Narcisse, the most desirable sculpture prize in Europe. The ideas he'd had for it had gone. He couldn't see them any longer, still less feel them in the way he'd have to if the clay was to live between his fingers again. Would it ever come back, the feeling? Or the skill?

The woman's latest letter crackled in his pocket as he moved. Why didn't he just burn them as they came, without letting their words get between him and the life he'd found?

Because you're weak, he told himself. You should be able to fight thoughts of them and the baby and stop panicking.

He watched the stubby capable hands in front of him as though they belonged to someone else and saw them form fists that crashed down on the clay.

For a second he stared in shock, then exhilaration took him. He deliberately chose to raise both fists above his head this time and gloried in the way they smashed down on the lump. The edges of his hands hurt, but even that helped. His vision blurred. The music he'd chosen with such care this morning faded until he could hear nothing.

When he came to, the CD had finished. He saw he'd reduced the half-made head to a meaningless heap of mashed orange clay. Staring at the wreckage, feeling the comforting ache in his hands, he felt so much better he shouted out his triumph to the empty studio and heard Marisa Heering pause in her singing upstairs. That would teach her to sound so cheerful.

Chapter 2

The aggression in the atmosphere eased as soon as they stopped
trying to reach agreement. Trish Maguire felt her whole face relax
into a softness that told her how tense she'd been. Such was the
lottery of the law no one would know for ages which of the parties
here had lost rather than saved millions by refusing to cooperate.
She hoped it wouldn't prove to be her client, Leviathan Insurance
plc.

Hearing the chatter of seventeen sets of briefcase locks clicking
was like being let out of prison. She could stop concentrating now
and watch the others go on their way while she put her notes in
order. Moments later she caught the scent of someone's aftershave,
all musk and limes, and looked round to see one of the toughest
men moving past her.

It was an incongruous smell for such a bruiser, she thought, but
better than the stale tobacco of the old days. When she'd started
out on her career as a barrister eighteen years ago, at least half the
people at a meeting like this would have been smokers, and the
whole room would have been fogged and disgusting. Exotic scents
were a definite improvement.

This one's owner had already reached the far end of the room,
and he didn't look back, even to say goodbye to the last person still
sitting at the big glossy table. She was Cecilia Mayford, the pregnant loss adjuster, who was also working for Leviathan. She and

Trish had already agreed to let the others leave first, then have a private post-mortem.

Their case concerned the great building known as the London Arrow. Only two years old, the Arrow had already become a City landmark, loved by half the inhabitants and loathed by the rest. What most of them did not know was that within weeks of its ceremonial opening, cracks had appeared all over the structure. The horrified owners had wasted no time in making a claim against their insurance policy.

Leviathan, facing a bill of millions to repair the building and shore it up, had turned to their favourite loss adjusters in the hope that they could find a reason not to pay. When a whole range of geological tests had shown that the ground itself hadn't shifted in any unexpected way, they'd got it. The insurance policy covered subsidence but not poor design or shoddy construction.

The trouble was, no one had been able to find fault with the design, materials or construction methods either. The architect's revolutionary and breathtaking plans had been made practical by the consulting engineers, Forbes & Franks International, who had tested them with all the latest computer-modelling techniques against every possible calamity, from savagely increased wind speeds to both drought and rising groundwater. Since the cracking had begun, every part of the structure and all the materials used by the builders and their subcontractors had been checked and rechecked against the specifications. With no one else to take the blame, the building's owners had started legal proceedings against Leviathan to force them to pay.

Still determined to resist, they had briefed Trish to represent them. Her first study of the papers had told her this was the kind of case that could go on for years, involving vast costs for everyone, and possibly never coming to a satisfactory conclusion. Today she'd proposed an unusual settlement, with all the interested parties and their own insurers sharing the costs of saving the Arrow with Leviathan and so getting the whole business over in months rather than years. Her proposal had just been vigorously rejected.

She watched the pinstriped men lining up to get out of the door and thought of the fake rage so many of them had used to try to get their own way throughout the afternoon. A few looked round to nod a perfunctory farewell to the two women before they made it out of the room. Only Guy Bait, representing the engineers, bothered to come and shake Trish's hand and say how much he appreciated her efforts to broker a deal. His aftershave had a simpler smell, barely more than faintly astringent soap might leave on clean skin.

'Thank you, Guy.' She stood up and was surprised to find herself the taller by about two inches. 'We'll meet again.'

'I'll look forward to it,' he said.

He'd barely opened his mouth throughout the afternoon, except when asked a direct question. Only now did it look as though a bit more oomph from him might have helped her cause. And his breathy, gentle voice might have taken some of the heat out of the others' fury. He gave her a sweet smile, before moving on to Cecilia and murmuring similar grateful words.

She nodded but didn't speak and avoided the offered handshake by rubbing her temples as though they ached. Her face, pallid with exhaustion and anxiety, had taken on a withdrawn expression that was new to Trish. But then her only pregnancy had ended in a miscarriage at a much earlier stage, so she didn't know precisely what Cecilia would be feeling now.

When Guy had gone after the rest and the door had banged behind him, Cecilia let her head flop forwards and blew out a gusty sigh.

'At last! I couldn't have taken much more, Trish. Thanks for what you tried to do.'

'I'm sorry it didn't work. And I'm sorry it took so long. You must be worn out.'

Cecilia rubbed her eyes, then put both hands behind her

immaculate black jacket and pushed at her aching spine. Trish watched the bump in fascination as it swelled forwards. How could you lug something that big around and sit through acrimonious meetings like the one they'd just endured and still show such courtesy and patience?

Trish had always admired her, but today's performance had added a kind of awed respect she rarely felt for anyone. They hadn't yet become friends – and probably couldn't until the case was over – but she hoped one day they'd be able to meet and talk about smaller, more important, things than this claim with its multi-million-pound implications.

'How much longer?' she asked.

'Technically four more weeks,' Cecilia said, pinching the bridge of her nose. She was squinting too. The headache must be getting worse. 'But I'm so vast I can't believe it'll be that long. I'm sorry, you know.'

'For what?'

'I'd planned it all so carefully.' She took her fingers away from her face and looked at Trish. 'I thought we'd manage to get a settlement today, giving me time to clear my desk and hand over my other cases to colleagues well before Christmas, have the baby, then be back from maternity leave in time to deal with any fallout from the Arrow in the summer. Now here I am abandoning you with everything still unresolved.'

'Going for a settlement was probably a bit optimistic. There's so much at stake.'

'Even so, I hate failing like this.'

'You haven't failed. You've done wonders already,' Trish said, wanting to make her look less miserable. 'Your colleagues are good too. We'll manage to keep going while you're off having the baby. And you should be back from maternity leave long before we get to court. Now, you look to me as though you should be at home in bed. Shall I ask them to call you a cab?'

'I'd better walk.' A spasm, perhaps driven by pain, twisted

Cecilia's broad face. 'They say it helps, so I try. On days when I really can't face the flog up to Islington, I cheat and hop across the bridge to Sam's studio so he can drive me back when he's done for the day.'

'You know I couldn't believe it,' Trish said, distracted, 'when you told me that you're not only married to my favourite sculptor but also the daughter of the judge I most admire. I was up before her only last month.'

'I know. She told me. She approves of you too,' Cecilia said, but her eyes changed, as though someone had come between her and the light.

'What's the matter?'

'Nothing.' She shivered. 'Except I hate coincidences like this.'

'Do you? Why? I like the whole six degrees of separation thing, finding links wherever I look.' Trish couldn't prevent a laugh bubbling up.

'What?' Cecilia said, with an unlikely note of panic in her voice. 'What's so funny?'

'Only the words we were all using today,' Trish said, surprised into an explanation she knew would sound heavy-handed. 'Practically all of them had at least two meanings: we wanted a settlement for a building that's subject to settlement; we discussed a listed building that's listing badly; someone wanted to get cracking with the discussion about the cracks. Links everywhere, you see. I love it.'

Cecilia's frightened expression eased a little, but she didn't smile. 'I don't mind that sort. It's the personal ones I hate, where everyone you meet turns out to be friends with friends of yours, or even with old acquaintances you thought you'd never see again. They tell you stories they've heard about you and you realize everything you've ever done or said is stuck somewhere in someone's memory. Like computer data you can never get rid of, however often you hit "delete".'

She had managed to get herself upright and balanced at last.

The movement must have freed something in her, for her voice had more of its usual bounce when she added: 'Talking of coincidence: have you always practised commercial law? Something I heard made me wonder.'

'No,' Trish said, picking up Cecilia's briefcase as well as her own and following her out of the room. 'I used to do family cases but I gave up when the relentless misery got to me. But we shouldn't hang about chatting. You need to be at home. I'll phone you on Monday.'

Making her way across Blackfriars Bridge towards her flat twenty minutes later, Trish wondered whether she'd been irresponsible in letting Cecilia trudge off alone. For such a heavily pregnant woman to fight her way through the dark and cold of a December evening couldn't be sensible. But she must know her limitations, and she was an intelligent adult. No one had any right to tell her what to do.

Still uncomfortable, Trish paused halfway over the bridge, to be transfixed by her favourite view made even better by the frosty darkness. The yellow lights along the river seemed to hang in the middle of blurred halos, yet their reflections in the black water of the Thames were as sharp as ever, disturbed only by the wake of a boat chugging its way upstream. The stars were hidden by the glare of artificial lights, but the glittering city was so spectacular in both directions she couldn't regret them. To the east, Norman Foster's Gherkin stood like a brilliant sentinel, balanced by the Arrow to the north, looking as delicate as it was dazzling.

How could it be moving? What fault had there been in the design or manufacture of steel, glass and concrete that no one had yet identified?

Eventually the cold made Trish's ears ache and got her moving again. She thought of Cecilia, struggling northwards to Islington, and envied her the baby she was about to have. Not that Trish regretted anything about the way her own infertile life had taken her. With her young half-brother, she and her partner, George, had become a family. Their set-up might be eccentric but it worked, and it made her happy.

Years ago they'd devised the arrangement by which George kept his antique-filled, pastel-coloured house in Fulham and she lived in her echoing, brick-walled loft in the much edgier borough of Southwark. Each had keys to the other's place, and they wandered in and out at will.

Revelling in a security that would once have seemed wildly beyond her grasp, Trish let herself into the flat and tripped over a large, dirty trainer. As she regained her balance and stared at the offending shoe, she considered the few aspects of life with her half-brother she could have done without. Then she thought of the slight, vulnerable, silky-haired child who had found his way to the flat after his mother's death, only five years ago.

For his sake she couldn't regret his transformation into a noisy, confident thirteen-year-old, who seemed to have an inexhaustible appetite and a band of friends even bigger and louder than he was himself. Still, she was not prepared to have smelly trainers strewn around her flat.

'Daaaaavid!' she called, loud enough to reach through the beat of music that thudded through his bedroom walls. There was no response. She called again, even more loudly, without moving. The music was slightly muted, as though he'd turned the CD player down a pip or two. His tousled head peered round the edge of the doorway. Even the texture of his hair had changed into something rough and unbiddable.

'I thought you'd be later,' he grunted. 'I'll put the headphones on.'

'Great. But there's this too.' She pointed down at the trainer as if it was a dead animal brought in by someone's cat.

A wonderful smile transformed David's whole face for a second. He looked amused and tolerant and guilty and affectionate all at once. Letting his expression fade into the now familiar vacancy, he ambled out of his room. His jeans were so loose around his narrow hips they were in danger of falling down completely. The sagging T-shirt he'd put on after school had once been white but was now a muddy pink, having been washed with a variety of sports socks at much too high a temperature. His astonishingly big feet were bare and none too clean, the toes widely spaced and looking very flat against the polished wooden floor. Trish wondered where today's socks were, and indeed the other trainer.

He bent to scoop up his shoe and she caught a whiff of acrid sweat from his T-shirt. Was it time to comment or not? She'd discussed the problem with the mothers of his two best friends and learned it was a cherished mark of growing-up to have sweat that smelled. All the mothers were treading as carefully as Trish around the burgeoning masculinity of these boys, who'd been adorable, confiding children so recently and were now turning into galumphing aliens with caverns of scary vulnerability well hidden behind the mess and bluster.

'What?' said David, allowing the final consonant to dribble away somewhere unnoticeable. At least he hadn't yet had his ear pierced as some of his friends had done. 'What're you looking at?'

'Just feeling amazed at how you seem to grow every day. Are you hungry?'

'I'm always hungry, but I'm not starving,' he said, stuffing his free hand down the front of his jeans. ' 'Cos I had a couple of toasted sandwiches when I got back.'

'David, not here! You can do whatever you like in the privacy of your bedroom, but . . .'

He looked surprised, but obediently removed his hand and used it to give the back of his head a good scratch. Trish reminded herself how much she loved him, how soon he would grow out of this particularly trying stage of development, blew him a kiss that made him pretend to gag, and went up to her own room at the top of the spiral staircase.

There she indulged herself with scents of lavender and beeswax furniture polish, as well as her own expensive soap and shower gel. The poor law student she'd once been, who'd scraped together the rent for a bedsitter in Deptford, found her clothes in charity shops and subsisted on the cheapest of bargain food, seemed like someone from another world.

The luxurious sheets were crisp and white and there were fresh Christmas roses in a glass bowl on the chest of drawers beside Sam Foundling's *Head of a Horse.* She'd always loved it for its tenderness and the way the bent head curled around the neck, as though the horse was stroking its own cheek. She hoped it was a true expression of the man himself. From what she'd seen, Cecilia needed tenderness.

Trish dropped her clothes on the bed and gave herself a long shower, filling the bathroom with fragrant steam and forgetting everything except the temporary bliss of hot water. She vaguely heard the phone ring, but did nothing about it.

When she descended to the rougher world on the floor below, David bellowed from his room that Caro had phoned and wanted Trish to ring back to talk about Christmas. She smiled at the thought of her best friend, now promoted to Chief Inspector and embarking on a tough new job with the Major Incident Teams of the Metropolitan Police. Grabbing the phone, she punched in Caro's number.

'Hi. Thanks for getting back to me so soon,' Caro said. 'How are you? David thought all was well. In fact he said you were in world-beating form.'

'Your godson brings out the virago in me these days; I suspect that's what he meant. I'm fine. What about you two?'

'Not bad at all. But I'm feeling more than a bit swizzed because we've decided duty has to take us to Jess's brother for Christmas. So we're off to Scotland for three stressed days, instead of loafing round to Southwark to be with all of you. I'm sorry, Trish. We really liked it last year.'

'So did we. What a pity. But the glow of duty done might see you through the New Year glooms so it's not all bad. Have you got time for a lunch between now and then, or are you frantic?'

'Not yet. They're letting me into the new job lightly, and it's driving me mad. I never thought I'd start pining for a murder.'

Trish had to laugh at Caro's mock-tragic tones.

'I know I won't get anything except the most boring domestics for the first year or so, but even that would be better than ploughing through reports by the Murder Review Group and learning the Murder Investigation Manual by heart.'

'Poor you. But you shouldn't have too long to wait. Christmas is always crunch time for unhappy couples; there's bound to be a juicy killing in south London soon.'

'You're right, unfortunately.' Caro's voice was deeper now, and slower. 'I don't really want anyone murdered, and—'

'You don't have to tell me that,' Trish said. There were few police officers of either sex who could match Caro's instinctive compassion for the victims of any kind of violence. 'I'd better go and cook something to feed the monster. Love to Jess.'

'Sure. And ours to George. I'll phone you at work next week when we've got our diaries and fix a time for lunch.'

'Great. Bye now.'

On Monday morning, after a restorative weekend with George and David, Trish was at her desk in chambers. When she'd first decided she wanted to be a barrister, she'd found the private language as foreign as Sanskrit. Now it was second nature and she didn't even think of the oddity of naming both the building where she worked and the association of other self-employed individuals who shared it as 'chambers'.

Today she was struggling to understand some of the more complex engineering principles involved in the construction of the Arrow. There were times when she felt as though the preparation of each new case was like working for a degree in a wholly unfamiliar discipline. And when other members of chambers were in aggressive or riotous moods, concentration could be particularly difficult. Luckily the atmosphere was calm today, with all the others in court or hard at it on their own case papers.

Trish focused on her computer screen, which showed one of the working drawings for what she always thought of as the Arrow's skeleton. Because the site covered part of one of the old plague pits, where victims of the Great Pestilence of 1665 were buried, the architects hadn't been able to use ordinary foundations. The ground was too fragile and the archaeology of the place too important. Instead, they'd designed a great central core to be driven through a specially chosen part of the mass grave, down to the solid ground beneath. On to this core were hung the components of the rest of the building, suspended on steel cables. Trish sometimes thought its elevations looked more like a child's drawing of a Christmas tree than an arrow.

Her phone rang and she lifted the receiver to hear Steve, the head clerk, saying Sam Foundling was in the waiting room and wanted a private word with her.

'Send him in,' she said at once, wondering what could have happened to Cecilia.

She was on her feet by the time he came in, a short stocky man with a brooding, powerful face marked by heavy black brows and restless eyes of an extraordinarily pale blue. He was carrying a big brown envelope under one arm.

'Is she okay?'

'Who?' he said, frowning.

'Cecilia. I've been worrying about her ever since—'

'She's fine. Full of beans.'

'Great.' Trish breathed more easily as she pulled the visitor's chair nearer her desk. 'Then have a seat and tell me what I can do for you.'

She couldn't understand why he was staring at her with a mixture of expectation and something that looked like truculent misery.

'Don't you recognize me?'

'Of course.' She smiled. 'Even if I hadn't come to the private view at Guildhall last year, I'd know you from all those photographs beside the reviews of your exhibitions. But I'm amazed you clocked me. There must have been hundreds of your admirers there.'

'I didn't know you were there,' he said, even more puzzled. 'I thought you'd know . . . Maybe I should have said: I changed my name as soon as I could, but I'm Sam, Samuel Johnson.'

Trish's mental retrieval system, powering through her brain at speed, turned up only one Samuel Johnson, creator of the dictionary, hero of Boswell's masterpiece.

'You saved my life,' he said, his voice heavy with disbelief. 'You were the first adult I'd ever trusted, and you saved my life. Seventeen years ago. Have you forgotten?'

As Trish stared at him, memories of the child at the centre of the first case she'd handled on her own oozed back. Twelve years old but the size of someone much younger, with a sullenness she'd recognized as defensive even then, he'd had burns and bruises all over him.

'It never occurred to me it was you,' she said, treading carefully because she knew she trod on fragile stuff. 'One of the artists I most admire, whose career I've followed ever since I first saw the *Head of a Horse* at your degree show. I had no idea.'

He lowered his head, hiding his expression, giving her time to get her rushing thoughts under control.

'I don't know why I was sure you'd remember,' he muttered. 'But I've always felt there was this connection between us. When things got really bad, I sort of conjured you up in my mind and talked to you. Sometimes it felt as if you were answering. That's what kept me going.'

Trish couldn't have interrupted even if she'd wanted to. But soon she'd have to make him understand how a case that fills your whole life while it's happening has to be unloaded at the end to free up the mental space you need for the next.

'You never touched me, or even came too close like everyone else did,' he said, obviously well back in the past. 'You kept your distance, and you told me: "You can trust me, Samuel. I am not like them. I will fight for you. And I will never fight you. I *will* make you safe." And you did. It's all come from that moment. Everything I've got.'

Did I say anything like that? she asked herself. If I did, I was wrong. There was no way I could have guaranteed your safety. Even with the scars and bruises, your testimony and your social worker's reports, the case could easily have gone the other way. You were known as an appalling troublemaker; violent too.

Even when the judge's words had set him free from the foster parents he'd claimed had tormented him for years, Trish hadn't been able to feel triumph; only an indescribable weakness that had made her want to lie on the floor of the court until it passed.

'What happened?' she asked now, thinking of the huge obstacles the boy must have cleared to make himself what he was. 'How did you become a sculptor?'

Memories began to speed up even more, chasing each other through her mind, and she was almost back in the Royal Courts of Justice, feeling the sickness in the pit of her stomach. Even then she'd known only part of it came from horror at what had been done to him. Most was triggered by her own fear. Was she up to the job? Had she chosen the wrong career? What would happen to this boy if she failed him? What would happen to her? She'd stood up in front of a judge who'd glared at her throughout her stammering, over-worked, over-practised arguments, while she fumbled with her papers, dropped her pen, and never dared look at the child in case the sight of him removed the last rags of her competence.

'It was the art teacher at the next school I went to,' he said, pulling her back into the present. There was a distant look in his eye, as though his mind was taken up with working out how she could have failed him so.

The depth of his disillusion was a measure of the trust he'd once had in her, and that was worrying. To have had so much effect on someone else's life was a huge responsibility.

'I was angry and I hated everyone – except you – and I messed around in every class, winding the teachers up, bullying, breaking things, bunking off, stealing. One day, Mr Dixon made me wait after the others had gone. I thought it was for another punishment and I was all ready to take it, then get my own back in other ways. Like I always did. But he just gave me a lump of clay and said he had work to do in the staffroom and he'd come back in half an hour. Then he left me.'

Sam was looking less shocked, and his colour was better. Maybe he'd be able to forgive her for the lapse that had clearly rocked him to his shaky foundations.

'I don't really remember anything except the moment when the clay began to do what I wanted. And the way he came back when he said he would, and stood away from me like you'd done, and said: "I thought so. You could be very good."'

'That must have been an amazing moment,' Trish said, watching his face lose its truculence as the story developed.

'He showed me I was worth listening to. I trusted him. He was the second person. If it hadn't been for you I wouldn't have dared. You . . .'

Trish waited again. Almost the first thing she'd learned from her child clients in the old days had been that if she rushed into speech, to comfort them or ask questions, she'd risk closing them down for good. But he didn't add anything. She hesitated to turn this emotionally charged encounter into an ordinary business meeting, but someone had to move things on.

'How can I help you now?' she said when the silence had lasted too long.

He licked his lips and shrugged. His shoulders were enormous, and his hands very strong. They were dirty, she thought, until she realized the marks were bruises.

After a moment he reached for the envelope he'd brought and took out a stained, creased sheet of lined paper, which he unfolded and laid flat on the desk in front of Trish.

The handwriting was clumsy, ill-educated. She looked at the address: HM Prison, Holloway.

Sam drew in a breath so deep she could actually see his chest expand, even through the thick, dark-blue wool of his Guernsey sweater.

'She says she's my mother. The real one, the one who left me on the steps of the London Hospital in a box twenty-nine years ago.'

Chapter 3

Trish was glad her pupil was on holiday so that she could have her room to herself as she ran through everything she and Sam had said during their half-hour together. Even now he'd gone, the air still felt dank with his unhappiness. She could understand exactly why he hated the prospect of having anything to do with the woman in prison. The possibility that she might be his genetic mother was almost worse than the idea that she was an imposter, after him for the money she assumed he had.

She'd set out to find him, she had written in the first letter, after she'd read about him in a magazine one of her cell-mates had. It had been an old one, from nearly two years earlier, just after he won the Rodin Prize and became known to connoisseurs around the world. The interviewer had asked him then about the derivation of his unusual surname.

Trish pushed the letter to one side to reread the cutting he'd brought her:

> I've never known when I was born or who I am. My real life started when I was found on the steps of the Royal London Hospital on 13 February 1976. So that's always been my birthday, even though the staff thought I was about three months old. I'd been left in a cardboard box with only a thin, ragged blanket between me and the snow. And there were

bruises and cigarette burns all over my body. Who does that to a child?

There was nothing to identify me, so the staff picked a name. One of them was a literary type and she called me after Dr Johnson. So it was as Samuel Johnson that I was given for fostering. I don't want to talk about that. I was rescued twelve years later. The day I left that couple's so-called care, I decided to have a name of my own. I've been Sam Foundling ever since.

Trish had once known all about the baby's discovery on the hospital steps, but the case's details were hard to retrieve. She hated the thought that her clearest impressions were still of her own feelings. Did it matter? Maybe not, given that she *had* saved Sam from his tormentors. But she couldn't forget the look on his face earlier this morning as he'd understood she had no idea who he was, even when he'd told her his old name. The shame that was never far away made her cheeks burn.

It was bad enough that she'd given up working with damaged, terrified, battered children for the infinitely better paid, infinitely less traumatic, cases of the commercial court. But that she could make one of the few truly successful survivors of such an experience look as though she herself had hit him was awful.

She picked up the first of the letters he'd brought her and read again the pitifully ill-spelled declaration.

Deere Sam,

I di'nt leeve you without nothing. I put my weding ring in that boxe to. He hit me agen when he see my bear finger. 3 ribs and my gaw got broke. If you have'nt gote it, the nurses must of stowl it, or your foster parence. I cride till I was sick when I red what they done. First yore farther an then them. It broke my hart to putt you their, but I done it becos I din' kno what else too do. Of corse your' angry. I don expec you to fourgive me. But I wanto

*mete you. I no you won't beleeve Im' youre muther and not mad,
so Ill' take a DNA test to show you. I don neede it to no. You look
jus like my farther. Yor reel names' Giovanni Daniele. It was his
to.*

    Yore muther, Maria-Teresa Jackson

It was easy to imagine how Sam must have felt as he read the letter
for the first time, and just as easy to understand why he didn't
want to have anything to do with the woman who had written it.

'Do I have to?' he'd asked Trish.

She had seen his hands ball into fists so tight the knuckles
looked as if they might burst through the skin, which had made
the bruises look darker than ever. He'd turned his head away, as
though he couldn't bear her to see his face.

'I spent so much of my childhood longing for a mother that it
sounds mad not to want to find out now; but I've made myself
into something that works. I survived. I'm married to Ceel. My
work's doing well. Do I have to risk it all for this . . . this person?'

'No,' Trish had said at once and she still believed it. No parent
who abandoned a child had any right to demand anything from
that child in adulthood. 'Not even if she is your genetic parent.
Why is she in prison?'

'God knows! I haven't done anything about the letters, so all I
know is there on your desk.'

Now Trish examined her uncomfortably lively conscience,
aware her views on the subject of deserting parents had been
coloured by her own father's disappearance from her life when she
was seven. But she'd had a warm, intelligent, supportive mother, so
her loss was as nothing in comparison to Sam Foundling's.

Trish's father was a charming, feckless, undomesticated Irishman,
who had also tried to re-establish contact after seeing in a newspaper
article that his only child had gone on to public success. For years
she'd resisted his approaches. She'd got over that, though, and
learned to enjoy his company, even acknowledging the parts of her

character she'd had from him. Her growing affection had been stunted only by the discovery that Paddy Maguire had also fathered David and abandoned him and his mother to poverty and fear in one of the worst inner-city housing estates.

Had she given Sam the wrong advice? No, she decided, still staring at the letters. However pathetic this woman was, however cleverly she'd phrased her illiterate pleas for his understanding, she had given up her rights on that February morning twenty-nine years ago. And if she were not the woman who'd put him there in the cardboard box, with or without a wedding ring, then she was no more than a manipulative chancer in search of a free ride on Sam's earnings.

And yet, Trish could also understand why he hadn't torn up the letters or sent them back unopened. Facing fatherhood himself for the first time, he must have wanted to know more about his own parents and so about himself. But it had been hard to see what she could do for him.

'I'll pack these up again for you,' she'd said and watched his mouth tighten and his eyelids droop. Diagnosing hurt and yet more disillusion, she'd felt a powerful urge to offer amends, to do something that might justify his scary trust in her. 'Would you like me to see if I can find out a bit more about her? That might make it easier to decide what to do.'

'Yeah. Maybe. And will you keep the letters for me? I haven't told Ceel anything about them. She's got enough on her plate with the baby, so I don't want her finding them when she's tidying my stuff.'

'Does she do that?' Trish had grimaced at the thought of George or David rifling her papers. 'Even in your studio?'

'Sure. She has the run of it, whether I'm there or not.' Sam had looked oddly at Trish then and said with a quietness that was all the more convincing for its intensity, 'I trust her too. With everything. But I don't want her to see these. Not till I've decided what to do about this woman and her shitty DNA test.'

Thinking of the way he'd looked then, Trish shivered. The anger in his expression didn't surprise her, nor the bunched fists, but even the memory of them made her wish she hadn't volunteered to ask questions on his behalf. Already there were layers of potentially lethal emotional problems in store for him and Cecilia. More information about his parentage might make life even harder for them both. But she'd made the offer so she had to do something about it.

She picked up the phone to talk to Sally Elliott, the trainee clerk who was used as everybody's gofer, and asked her to resurrect Sam's old case papers from whatever archive had been used to bury them and also to find out why Maria-Teresa Jackson was in Holloway.

Chapter 4

Sam sat with Cecilia's broken head cradled in his lap. Rage had driven every thought and memory out of his mind. She was the only person he'd ever loved and she was dying. He'd phoned for an ambulance as soon as he'd understood how bad it was, then tried to keep her alive till help came. In that moment, he would have done anything, given anything – even his talent – to roll back time to the moment before she'd been hurt.

There was no peace in her dying. Snorting through a crushed and bloody nose, she thrashed around whenever he let go of her shoulders. So far he'd been able to hold her down, but if the ambulance didn't come soon, she might do herself and the baby even more damage.

It had been nearly ten minutes since he'd phoned. She was still breathing, but only just. He wanted to throw up. How could anyone do this to a woman who'd done no harm? And pregnant too? What kind of monster would you have to be?

Fresher blood was seeping now out of the corner of her split mouth. From her lungs? Was there any part of her body that hadn't been damaged? He saw her grossly distended belly move through the rips in her clothes, as though the baby was trying to kick its way out. Fluid was leaking between her legs.

The spooky two-tone sound of the ambulance siren reached him just in time, and he let his breathing become more natural.

The door was open, so he wouldn't have to get up and leave her for a second until they could take over her care. He delicately picked some of the hair away from her eyes, feeling the sticky weight of the blood that clumped it together. He could hear running footsteps and looked towards the door.

Kind voices, he thought an instant later before the paramedics had even reached her side. How can they have such kind voices when they can see this?

One of the green-suited men held his shoulders much as he'd been holding hers and gently pulled his arms away from her body.

'When's the baby due?' asked the other one, laying competent-looking hands on her belly and squinting up at him.

'Three weeks.' His voice was high and reedy. He swallowed and said it again, sounding more like himself. 'It's still moving. I saw it. Whatever's happening to her, the baby's all right. Physically, anyway. At least I think it is. And there aren't any wounds there. I don't think she was kicked in the belly. But—'

'Okay.' The kindness was still there in the paramedic's voice, but there was something else now: dislike; maybe even fear. 'That's great. Now, what's your name?'

'Sam.'

'Great, Sam.' There was a big smile on the man's lips, but his eyes were full of mistrust. 'We're going to get her on a stretcher and take her straight to A&E. Will you come with us?'

Sam nodded, watching carefully as they laid out a sheet that looked like the old picnic tarpaulins his foster parents had used. He was pushed out of the way so the paramedics could move Cecilia onto it, then lift it and her onto their stretcher. Their movements were sure but very slow until she was on the stretcher and strapped in. Then they ran with the trolley towards the door.

He'd lost his keys. He could feel the paramedics' fury at the prospect of waiting any longer. He saw the bunch in the end, in the middle of the messy table, which made them exchange more suspicious glances; then they moved out of the studio faster than he'd have thought anyone could with the weight of a pregnant woman to push.

He followed, taking only a second to look round his shambles of a studio before he locked the door. He felt as though he'd never seen it before. Blood splatters were everywhere; bits and pieces of brittle old maquettes had been flung all over the floor; and his most cherished marble piece, which he hadn't been able to make himself sell because Ceel had loved it so, had been smashed into a dozen pieces. He hadn't known blood would look so bright red against matt white marble.

Hours later Sam was aware of the voices outside the room in which he was waiting for Cecilia to die. They'd already told him there was no surgery they could perform to repair the damage to her brain and heart and lungs. The emergency Caesarian had resulted in the birth of a girl, just alive but unable to breathe on her own. She'd been put on a ventilator and whisked away to the Special Care Baby Unit. They'd told him to go along any time he wanted to see her, but he wasn't going to waste a second he could have with Cecilia.

'She might speak,' he'd said to the doctor who had so kindly and so implacably told him she couldn't survive. 'And I have to be here if she does.'

'No,' the doctor had said once more, patient as a saint. 'She's not going to regain consciousness. She cannot possibly speak and there is nothing going on in her brain, except the reflexes keeping her heart pumping and what's left of her lung function working. She doesn't know you're here; she could not hear you if you spoke to her.'

'But she *is* breathing.'

'Only just. It won't be more than a few hours. Of course you must stay with her as long as you like. The nurses will look in at intervals and if you need anything, there's the bell. I'll see you later.'

Sam hated the doctor. But not as much as he hated the owners of the other voices. They were determined to talk to him, and he knew they'd get him in the end. Whenever they'd forced their way in, they'd looked at him as if he were a wild animal that needed to be caged. It was as if they knew about every cruel word he'd ever yelled at Ceel and every single one of the times she'd made him so angry he'd wanted her dead.

He owed his temporary freedom to a tiny little Asian nurse, who'd been fighting their urge to drag him out of the cubicle to face them. She looked too delicate to do anything other than decorate a recruiting poster, but she'd been standing up to them all along and keeping them out.

'Have patience,' she said now. 'And some pity, for the love of God. His wife is dying. Give him this time with her now, whatever you plan to do to him later.'

Sam held on to Cecilia's hand and felt it growing cooler. He quickly checked that she was still breathing. For a moment he thought she wasn't, then he held the back of his own hand against her lips and felt the faintest current of air.

Curtain rings rattled behind him and he looked round, furious, to see one of the uniformed police officers. The man's pink face was eager and he took a step between the curtains.

'You're trying to stop her speaking, aren't you? Take your hand away from her mouth. Now!'

Sam looked away so that he could fall back into the old position of keeping his watch on Cecilia's eyes in case the lids lifted. He heard the Asian nurse again. She sounded even angrier than he was. The cop was forced to go. The curtain rings rattled again and the material swished. He felt her tiny hand on his shoulder.

'I am sorry. I keep moving them away and then they come back. Are you all right? As all right as you could be, I mean?'

He nodded without looking round, even though he was grateful. She must know it, he thought, so why bother to say anything? All his energy was focused on Cecilia, trying to keep her from the death he knew was coming. If she couldn't hear, then maybe she couldn't feel either, which was the only comfort he could find.

His eyes leaked more tears as he looked back at the pathetic five years they'd had together. A sixth of his life so far; a little less of hers for ever.

They'd met when she'd come to one of his first solo shows in London and bought a bronze. Only one of a planned edition of eight, it had to be cast specially, so they'd had to meet again. He'd delivered it to her flat and she'd given him a glass of wine and shown him the rest of her small collection. He'd liked everything she owned except for one painting, a meaningless pretty bit of landscape with neither depth nor atmosphere. When he'd eventually said he'd better go, Cecilia hadn't said anything about seeing him again, but she'd had his address on the invoice and used it to invite him to a dinner party only about a month later.

He leaned forward, thinking he'd seen a flicker in one eyelid, but it was only a trick of the light. There were almost no traces of her real face through the mass of blackening bruises and the raw-edged cuts. She'd never been beautiful, but he'd loved everything about the way she looked, from the broadness of her forehead and the strength of her square chin to the steady grey-green eyes and the thick mouse-coloured hair that went wriggly, as she called it, in the rain.

Rubber soles squeaked on the shiny vinyl tiles, then the curtain rings rattled again. He didn't look round until a faint vanilla scent reached him through the chemicals and disinfectant that filled the air.

'Gina,' he said, only half turning.

'Yes, it's me.' He felt his mother-in-law's hand on his shoulder, much heavier than the nurse's. In spite of the weight, he could feel her trembling. She tried to speak again, then coughed and tried once more. 'How terrible for you to find her like this, Sam.'

'It's my fault,' he said and barely noticed the withdrawal of her hand as he felt the chill sweatiness of guilt all over again. Then he understood what he'd done and rushed to say: 'If I hadn't gone out this morning, she'd never have . . . I could've saved her. If . . .' His brain was shutting down. He couldn't produce the right words. Tears were easier. They clung to his skin, sliding slowly down his stubbly cheeks until they dripped off his chin.

'I know,' said Gina, replacing her hand for a moment. 'I know. But thinking "if only" always makes horror worse.' She moved away, walking to the side of the bed so she could lay her hand on her daughter's head.

She looked as though she was establishing ownership of Cecilia's dying body. Furious, Sam forced himself to remember Cecilia was her only child. He met her gaze for a second, then couldn't bear what he saw. Bowing his powerful body over the bed, still clinging to Cecilia's hand, he tried to stifle everything in the thin torn blanket that covered her.

Every chance he'd had to love and be loved as a child had been taken away. Now he'd lost this one too.

Chapter 5

'So now you're launched, Caro,' said the chief superintendent with a friendly smile. 'Looks like a simple domestic, although the husband's trying to deny it. You've got a good sergeant in Glen Makins. Use him. And don't be too proud to take his advice. He's with your team downstairs now. Go get 'em.'

'Thank you, sir.' Caro tried not to remember her light-hearted longing for a good juicy investigation. She stood and waited till he'd left, before taking a moment to breathe carefully, check the neatness of her hair in the mirror that hung by her door, grab her phone and make her way to the office that had been designated as her incident room.

The team was waiting. She recognized Glen Makins and several of the DCs, but she introduced herself formally and shook hands with all of them.

'Now, Glen, what have we got?' she said, perching on the edge of one of the desks.

'Cecilia Mayford, guv, beaten to death in a craft studio on Bankside belonging to her husband, Sam Foundling. He's a modeller, sculptor kind of thing. He phoned the ambulance and went to hospital with her. Oh, and she was pregnant. Eight months and a bit. Death was certified at 11.05 last night.'

'I gather the husband's denying it.'

'Yup. We haven't arrested him yet. The hospital called it in as soon as she was admitted and there were uniforms there, waiting to talk to him. He gave a voluntary statement, claiming he was at a meeting on the other side of the river yesterday morning and came back to find her beaten up and dying. Been watching too many reruns of *The Fugitive*, if you ask me.' Glen grinned. 'Although he couldn't give any reason why she was there in his studio instead of at work or at home, like she should've been.'

Caro gave him an answering smile and felt the team relax. 'They didn't live on Bankside, then?'

'No, guv; he worked there. They lived in *her* expensive house, up in Islington.'

'So there's money involved, as well as ordinary domestic stress,' Caro said. 'Okay. What else have you done?'

'Sealed the studio, obviously. Two uniforms are doing house-to-house with the other tenants of the building. There are forty separate units, so someone must've seen or heard something. And there's CCTV, so we've asked for the tapes. Here are the photographs and the husband's statement.'

'Thanks. Has someone checked his alibi?' Caro asked as she put the statement to the back of the pile Glen had handed her and looked down at the first of the colour prints. The voices in the room receded in a way she recognized from childhood as a warning of car sickness.

The victim's body had been laid out on a mortuary slab. Her hair was matted with blood and the right side of her head had been completely flattened. Her face was swollen and blackened and one eye looked insecurely held in the socket, as though it might flop out at any moment. Her breasts were a mass of bruises, too, and cuts. Further down her body, the neatness of her Caesarian wound was like a mocking commentary on the rest.

Trish had no idea what was to come. All that happened was a phone call to chambers from a police station in Southwark, asking whether she could confirm that Mr Samuel Foundling had been to see her yesterday morning.

'Yes,' she said. 'Why?'

'What time would you say he arrived at your place of work?'

Trish grabbed her diary and flicked back to the previous double-page spread.

'Late morning. I suppose noon-ish,' she said, for the first time wishing she kept a time sheet broken down into five-minute slots like a solicitor's. 'Why do you need to know?'

'How long was he with you, would you say?'

'Approximately half an hour. My clerk might have a clearer idea. I didn't look at the clock as he left.'

No, she thought, there was too much else to deal with: Sam's battle against the irresistible feeling that he must engage with the woman in prison and his absolute horror of it. And her still-growing sympathy with Cecilia. Anyone who lived with an artist of any kind deserved admiration and sympathy, but to have all the ordinary insecurities and creative frenzies compounded by the baggage Sam carried must be very hard.

'Thank you,' said the cool-sounding officer at the other end of the phone line. Before Trish could ask her question again, he'd cut the connection.

She drummed her fingers on the edge of her desk, running through the likely reasons for the call. Then she shrugged. There was no point speculating. She tried to focus once more on the engineering principles behind the erection of innovative buildings on a surface as mobile as a mass grave dug in the treacherous London clay.

This too was hard. She'd have found it much easier to concentrate if she'd had some people with recognizable emotions to deal with, instead of mathematical formulae, lists of computer data, and screensful of spidery drawings, which were as hard to understand as the hard-copy versions rolled into the cardboard tubes that were stacked in her cupboard. Even the trivial question from the police about Sam's visit was more interesting. She put her hand on the phone, thinking she might call him with a witty enquiry about what he'd been up to, then thought it would be better to wait until she knew more.

The calculator should have been hot by the time she'd rechecked every sum in the first tranche of files. She still thought of them as sums, even though many were complex equations, which made her long for a sharper brain or a maths A level in her past. The phone rang again.

'Trish Maguire,' she said, in case the call had come direct rather than through the switchboard in the clerks' room.

'It's Mrs Justice Mayford,' said Sally Elliott, her usually sharp voice sounding awed. 'Can I put her through?'

'Of course.' Trish waited a moment, then heard the judge's deep, beautiful voice saying her name in a questioning tone.

'Yes, it's me. What can I do for you, Mrs Mayford?'

'Trish, I . . . Cecilia talked to me after your last meeting with her . . . and . . .'

And? Trish thought, but she didn't say it, waiting until the notoriously tough woman at the other end of the line had dealt with her strange hesitancy.

'I wondered . . . I need to talk to someone, and I think you might be the best person. I'm sitting this week, but I'd rather not do it here or come to your chambers. Is there any possibility we could meet somewhere else, in the early evening?'

'Sure. Where and when?'

'I don't want . . . I need . . . Sorry.' The judge gulped. 'What about having a drink by the ice rink in Somerset House? Six o'clock? There are always lots of people at this time of year. We'd just be two more women in the crowd.'

'Fine. Great. Six o'clock. I'll recognize you,' Trish said. 'May I just ask . . .'

'I'd rather you didn't. Not now. I've got this afternoon's session in court to get through. I'll see you later. Thank you.'

Trish quickly scanned the diary in front of her as she put down the phone. It was a relief to see there were no other post-work engagements today. David was expecting her home by six, but he wouldn't mind if she were late. He was well used to that, and it would mean he could leave his trainers all over the flat and play his vile music at ear-splitting volume for longer than usual. Even so, she left a message on his voicemail to warn him, then carried on sitting at her desk wondering what on earth Mrs Mayford could want. She hoped it wasn't anything about Sam and the woman in prison. He hadn't actually asked her to keep the letters secret, but it was clear he didn't want them made public.

Mrs Mayford ought to understand that too well even to try to pump Trish for information about him. But what else could she want? She was way above Trish in the legal hierarchy and their only connection was through Sam and Cecilia.

This wasn't the time to address any of the other questions scratching at the edges of Trish's consciousness, but they were there, as they must have been for hundreds of members of legal London for the past thirty-four years. Who was Cecilia's father? Why had Gina Mayford never named him? How had she managed to bring up an illegitimate child in a world as archaic and prejudiced against women as the Bar had been in the early 1970s? And how had she managed to pay her bills?

Looking back to her own early years in chambers, fifteen years after Gina's, Trish remembered panicking about whether she would ever earn enough to pay her rent, let alone save for a future mortgage deposit. And the hours she'd worked! There'd been times when she had been so tired she'd felt like climbing the stone stairs at chambers on her hands and knees. To have gone through all that while also caring for a baby – with its endless need to be fed and clothed and cleaned and changed, waking you up at all hours of the night when you were aching for sleep – must have been like running a marathon every day.

What guts Gina Mayford must have to have survived, let alone reached the heights of judicial eminence. Apart from the House of Lords, only the Court of Appeal remained for her to conquer, and of the thirty-five judges who sat there just three were women. So why would she want to talk to a junior barrister?

Trish phoned Cecilia's office, rehearsing a vague question she might use to get Cecilia talking. She didn't want to drop Mrs Mayford in it if her dilemma were secret.

'Hello?' said a tentative voice after Trish had asked the switchboard for Cecilia's office. 'Is that Ms Maguire?'

'Yes. May I speak to Cecilia?'

'No. I mean . . . Someone should've told you. But we've all been so shocked. She . . . She was taken to hospital yesterday. I know we'll have to do something about the case, and they're working on it here already, but just at the moment . . .' She sniffed, then sobbed and fought to speak again. 'We can't think of anything except her.'

'I'm sure. Thank you for telling me. Is it some complication of the pregnancy? Pre-eclampsia or something?'

'I don't know what I'm allowed to say.' The sound of weeping was loud now and uncontrolled. 'She was beaten up yesterday. They gave her an emergency Caesarian. Then she died. In the night. The police are here now and we've all got to be interviewed.'

The line buzzed as the voice was abruptly cut off. Trish replaced her own receiver, her mind throwing up random thoughts like rocks in a burst of magma. It would be typical of the kind of coincidence that had so upset Cecilia to find Caro in charge of this investigation. How like Gina Mayford to stick to her commitments in court on the day of her only daughter's death. No wonder the police wanted to know where Sam had been yesterday. Many cases of domestic violence start during a couple's first pregnancy. He'd had bruises on his hands. Many abused children turn abuser in their turn. Maybe he . . .

'No,' Trish said aloud. 'I don't believe it.'

*

It was hard to hold on to the certainty when she was sitting in front of Gina Mayford, with cardboard cups of hot chocolate between them, peering out through the yellowing, scarred plastic sides of the marquee at the edge of the temporary ice rink. The ice itself was filled with skaters, ugly in shapeless clothes and graceless as they fell or clung to each other and fumbled their way across the ice. The smells of coffee and chocolate inside the tent had been entirely overtaken by damp wool and the stale exhalations of a hundred pairs of lungs.

Trish turned her back on the rink. Gina looked ill, with dark crescents under her eyes and no colour in her cheeks. Her greying hair had been cut in a short plain bob, presumably for ease of cramming it under her wig, and it was thinning on top. Her hands moved constantly, turning her cup around, fiddling with the unused packets of sugar, smoothing her rough hair, or scratching at the inside of her right forearm. Exposed by the way she'd pushed up her jacket sleeve, it had long red weals all the way from wrist to elbow.

'I'm so sorry,' Trish said again, trying to submerge her own feelings in sympathy for the infinitely worse ones this woman was suffering. 'Cecilia was wonderful. Her death is the cruellest thing.'

Gina swallowed, looking away for a moment to get her face under control. Light from flaming torches around the ice flickered over her averted cheek.

'She liked you too. She told me so when she phoned on Friday evening,' she said, blinking to control her tears. 'She sounded so happy and strong I couldn't believe it. When I was pregnant with her, I was permanently tired. And frightened.'

'You were much younger, though, weren't you?'

'Twenty-one, just out of university and determined to let nothing get in the way of becoming a barrister. Not even my child. And now she's . . .'

'I wish I could help,' Trish said into the agonized silence, 'but I don't see how.'

'It's Sam.' Gina stared at the undrunk chocolate, which had cooled in her cup. 'I don't know how to be with him.'

'I can imagine. He must need so much—'

Gina held up one hand to cut off the sympathetic comment. 'The police are sure he killed her.'

Trish felt as though a cold wave was washing over her, forcing salt water up her nose and burning in her throat. The news was no more than she expected, but she hated it.

'It's true he claims he was with you when it happened,' Gina went on, sounding now as implacable as any of the old hanging judges, 'but the police have CCTV evidence that puts him in the studio within the likely time of the assault. And there's a phone message she left for him there that makes them . . . They're sure he did it. And all the statistics back them up: most murders are domestic.'

'I don't believe it.' Trish saw anger in the judge's expression and quickly added: 'Not about the statistics. I know all about them. But about Sam. He's an exceptional man. He *couldn't* have done it.'

'I wish I shared your faith,' Gina said, sounding detached now, almost distant. 'I've been afraid for her since the moment she introduced us. She kept telling me she loved him, but he treated her appallingly.'

'How? Did he hit her?'

'Most of the aggression was emotional. She hated talking about it, always tried to pretend it wasn't happening, but I could see. And sometimes she had to escape. She'd come to me then, even though she wouldn't talk. I'll never forget the sight of her face once when . . .' Gina shuddered, her own face unbearable to watch. 'When I let myself think of what she suffered, I *hate* him.'

'No one could blame you for that. But until there's proof he killed her, wouldn't it be possible to—' Trish stopped, aware Gina wasn't listening to anything but her own internal voices.

'But whatever he did, she went on loving him. Every time I protested about the way he was behaving, she'd tell me how much he needed her. He was terrified of being abandoned again. I expect she'd still be telling me to support him now, if . . .'

'I think you're right.'

Gina rubbed a hand across her flaky lips. 'So what I need to know is this: is it better to be with him and risk letting him see how much I loathe the sight of him, or keep away and make him feel rejected?' She stared at Trish with wide, hurt-looking eyes.

'Why are you asking me? I'm flattered, but I don't understand.'

'Because you acted for him when he was a child.'

'How did you know that?'

'I looked up the court records when they got engaged. I had to know what we were dealing with. So you see: you've been Sam's voice before; Cecilia trusted you; and I don't know who else to ask but you. *Can* you help me?'

To give herself time, Trish took a swig of her drink and grimaced at its tepid sweetness.

'Have you talked to him yet?' she said, putting down the cup.

'Not much. He was at the hospital yesterday evening when I got there. Sitting by the bed, holding her hand and crying. He looked desperate. But they do, don't they, brutal husbands, when the paroxysm has passed?'

'What about the police? Has he been interviewed?' Keep this practical, Trish thought, and we've a chance of getting through it to something that may help. She knew if she let her feelings go, she'd help Gina build her daughter's tragedy into something even more terrible than it was.

'They haven't arrested him, but I advised him to give a voluntary statement and answer all their questions. With a solicitor, of course. I'm not trying to make him incriminate himself. That's how I know he claims to have been in your chambers when it happened.' Gina gulped some chocolate. 'But he won't say *why* he was with you, so it looks like an excuse to let him come charging into the studio again and pretend to be her rescuer.'

'You don't have to worry about that,' Trish said quickly. 'There was a real reason. I can't tell you if he won't, but you needn't doubt his motives for coming to talk to me.'

Although, she added silently to herself, the woman in prison must have been a source of appalling pressure. Enough to make him crack?

Sam looked at the slopped tea on the table in front of him and thought of the blood splashed all over the bits of white marble that had once formed a study of Ceel's face.

He raised his head to face the two police officers and said again, 'I visited the barrister Trish Maguire, who represented me seventeen years ago, to talk about a private matter. When I reached my studio after that encounter, I found the front door swinging on its hinges and heard sounds of groaning. I ran inside to find my wife thrashing about on the floor. There was blood everywhere, but no sign of the intruder. I grabbed the phone, fell on my knees beside her, rang for an ambulance, and tried to see how badly she was hurt. You know the rest.'

This was the fourth or fifth time he'd said it. Each time they asked different questions about his feelings for Cecilia, his movements yesterday morning, how a dangerous stranger could have got access to the studio without leaving any signs of a break-in, and a dozen other questions. At first he'd answered each one with the information he considered relevant, then, losing patience, he'd resorted to this straightforward repetition of what he'd already given them.

His feelings for Cecilia were none of their business. The hole torn in his life was nothing to do with them. The fact that his only true portrait of her was the smashed white-marble one with the blood all over it was private. He tried to think how best he'd clean and mend it when they'd finished fingering everything in his studio for evidence.

Trish barely looked at the river or the lights as she plodded home when Gina had eventually finished with her. She hoped David would be in one of his more cooperative moods and that she wouldn't find herself in the middle of a domestic fight. What she needed now was quiet and a huge dose of the warmth and wordless support George was so good at giving her.

Passing one of the newsstands that punctuated her route home, she stopped to buy an *Evening Standard*, expecting to see headlines about Cecilia's murder. There was nothing, not even a paragraph inside. Instead the front page had twin photographs of the Lord Chief Justice and the Assistant Commissioner of the Met, beneath a headline that read:

> Violent Crime Up Again
> Who's to blame?

She felt something soft under her shoe and looked down to see she'd trodden in fresh dogshit. Swearing under her breath, she walked to the kerb to scrape her shoe as clean as possible. She paused there to scan the article under a street light as the rush-hour traffic coughed its way past. The latest crime figures had shown a worrying increase in unsolved violent crime. The Lord Chief Justice had blamed this on the police's failure to collect enough evidence to secure convictions. The Assistant Commissioner was now hitting back.

> Painstaking police work ends in evidence rubbished by unscrupulous lawyers, treating the legal system as a game to win at any cost. But the cost isn't theirs. It's paid by other people in ruined lives.
>
> Even when we secure convictions, woolly-minded judges hand out pathetic punishments. Dangerous criminals are back on the streets in no time, laughing at us as they reoffend. Soft sentencing sends out all the wrong messages. It's a bad example for children. It's bad for police morale. And it's bad for London.

If the judiciary doesn't get its act together, Parliament will
have to reform the legal system and train a whole new generation of lawyers. We can't go on much longer with the ones
we've got. The risks are too great, like their obscene fees.

Wow! Trish thought as she folded the paper and tucked it under
her arm. That's a declaration of war. And it's not going to go down
well in the Temple.

Four minutes later she opened her front door on to complete
silence. Delicious scents of onions and bacon frying in olive oil
reached her from the kitchen. She was about to call out when she
noticed David sitting tidily at one end of the huge black sofa nearest the door. He was reading and there were trainers on both his
feet. Looking round, he put a finger to his lips.

Combined with the smells of cooking, the gesture warned Trish
she wasn't going to get the solace she needed. She cocked her head
in the direction of the kitchen and David drew his forefinger
across his neck in a gesture of disaster. She nodded her thanks,
then, raising her voice only a pitch or two above its normal
strength, she called out: 'George? I'm back. Smells wonderful.
Have I time for a shower?'

A grunt answered her. She took it to mean there would be time.
David now gestured upwards. Trish slipped off her mucky shoes
and left them by the door, saying more quietly: 'Give me a yell if
I'm needed.'

'Sure.'

She ruffled his hair and felt some comfort when he leaned
towards her rather than pulling away.

'I couldn't do without you,' she said and took herself off
upstairs.

Typical, she thought as she stripped off her clothes, that our
tough times are coinciding.

The nearest she and George ever came to quarrelling these days
was when they'd both been too spiky with stress to read the other's

feelings or had exasperating clients at the same time. As a solicitor, George's relationship with his clients was different from hers, but both could throw up problems. With luck tonight he would cook himself out of his bad mood and she'd see what drumming hot water would do for her.

It had its usual helpful effect and, as she turned her face up to the jets, she worked herself back into the knowledge that this was her life. However awful Gina's anguish, and Sam's, whatever the pain and terror in which Cecilia had died, they were separate from the existence Trish had with George and David. It wouldn't help Gina, Sam, or Cecilia's baby to let their horrors damage this. When George was in a fit state to hear what she needed to tell him, he would provide all the care she could possibly want and almost certainly suggest ideas that would help her answer Gina's question. In the meantime she would do what she could for him. All would be well.

Stepping out of the shower onto the cold tiled floor, she reached for a scarlet towel and slipped. Her feet flew from under her and she fell, twisting, throwing out an arm to save herself. Her funny bone caught on the towel rail. With a wrench that felt as if it might pull the arm out of its socket, she stopped the fall. Awkward and hurting, she found a way to reverse the momentum and stood, feeling shock retreat in waves of prickling adrenaline.

Minutes ticked by before she was free of it. She bent to pick up the thick red towel and felt her head swim again. Straightening, she wrapped the towel around her long thin body and picked her way across the condensation-slippery tiles with extra care.

She hoped the dinner George was cooking wouldn't be too elaborate. She could never eat much when she was worried, and the adrenaline hangover was making her feel sick. Dry once more, she pulled on a pair of loose wool trousers and a long sweater and padded downstairs in her socks.

David had laid the table and there was an opened bottle of

burgundy in the middle. Surprised by the choice of wine because they usually drank basic New World stuff during the week, she reached over to pour some into the two big glasses. A heavy footstep made her look up.

George stood in the kitchen doorway, wearing a blue-and-white-striped apron over his clothes and carrying a tea towel slung over one shoulder. His firm-chinned face was tight, and the evening's stubble looked dark against unusually pallid skin.

'Hi. Good day?' he asked, not meeting her eyes.

'Not exactly. You?'

'No. Are you ready to eat? It's a cheat's *boeuf bourguignon*. There wasn't time to cook the real thing.'

'Sounds great. I'll call David.'

'He's on his way. Just washing. Sit down and I'll bring it.'

'D'you want to talk before he gets back?'

'Too much to say. Too complicated. When he's gone to bed. Okay?'

'Sure.'

They ate more or less in silence, but the atmosphere wasn't too bad, and the well-cooked chunks of meat were fairly easy to swallow in their unctuous sauce. Trish managed to finish her plateful, and David asked for more and another baked potato. As he was splitting it, preparatory to ladling in some of the sauce, Trish asked him how his day had been at school.

For once he told her in considerable detail and she recognized that his growing-up had good sides to it. He was much more articulate tonight than he'd been as a little boy, and able to talk about mistakes and fears as normal things anyone might have, instead of trying to make himself perfect to avoid disappointing her – or perhaps giving her an excuse to throw him out.

Trish joined in with questions and laughed at all his jokes. Gradually George too put aside whatever was worrying him and the atmosphere brightened into something almost normal.

'Any pudding?' David asked.

'Greedy pig,' said George, who had only recently and with great difficulty shed four stone. He had all the zeal of the convert who could vividly remember his own hunger and didn't see why the rest of the world should be let off. Or perhaps why they shouldn't share in the rewards that now seemed to him to be worth all the pain. 'There's plenty of fruit.'

'I'm a growing boy,' said David in the pathetic voice of a starving Oliver Twist. 'Unlike you, I need my calories.'

'There's three sorts of ice cream in the freezer. Help yourself.' When he'd gone to fetch it, Trish added, 'That was great, George. I wish stress made me a brilliant cook too.'

He laughed, even though his eyes were still worried. 'There wouldn't be room for two of us in your titchy kitchen. Much better to have different angst-busting techniques. D'you want to talk about your day first?'

While David was in the kitchen, she told George briefly about Cecilia. There was no point splurging out everything she felt or explaining the complications of her earlier connection with Sam Foundling.

'I heard about her death in the office today. I'm sorry.'

'What? Why? What connection did she have with your firm?'

'Too much,' he said, looking away. When he faced her again, she saw a mixture of worry and an unfamiliar hostility. 'Why didn't you tell me you'd been briefed on the London Arrow case, Trish?'

'Because neither of us ever gossips about our clients,' she said, silently asking herself why he'd asked such an obvious question. Then she saw what the answer must be and felt as though the ground beneath her was tilting. 'Are you involved too?'

As he nodded, she ran through the names of all the solicitors at the settlement meeting. None had been from his firm.

'Who's your client?'

'QPXQ Holdings,' he said, naming a conglomerate that owned property all over the world and making her heart sink. 'A couple of months ago they bought out the company that owned the Arrow.'

Trish already knew that, but Leviathan's solicitor had assured her the change of ownership would make no difference to the case or to any of the professionals involved.

'We handled the buy-out,' George went on, 'and since some disastrous negotiation last Friday, QPXQ have decided to sack the original solicitors and give us the insurance claim, along with all the rest of their work. Which means you and I are on opposing sides.' He hesitated, then swallowed a mouthful of wine as though he couldn't work out how to say the next bit.

Some of his hostility had gone, but all the anxiety was still there, which wasn't like him. Trish was supposed to be the mercurial, impulsive one, with an imagination that could show her terrors almost anywhere. George's job was to provide solid foundations of unshakeable common sense.

'We'll have to declare the conflict of interest,' he said, producing the words as though they hurt his mouth. 'But even a formal declaration may not be enough to satisfy everyone.'

'I'll take this to my room,' David said, emerging from the kitchen with a bowl the size of a baby's bath, filled with ice cream. 'That way I won't disturb you.'

'Good idea,' Trish said, then caught sight of the quantity he'd given himself, 'but put at least half that back first.'

'Tyrant,' he said, but he slouched back into the kitchen to do as she said.

'Go on, George.'

'It's not your fault. Or mine,' George went on with a dogged fairness that was much more his style. 'But it's a situation. QPXQ are our biggest corporate client.'

'Need it matter?' she said, fighting everything he hadn't put into words and beginning to understand Cecilia's hatred of coincidence. 'Can't we just carry on operating Chinese walls and not talking to each other about our cases? I'm on opposite sides from fellow members of chambers all the time and it never bothers anyone.'

'QPXQ don't like it. So much so they're threatening to remove their business. And I mean *all* their business, not just this one case. If they do, it would screw any chance of a profit this year. We could even make a loss. So no profit-share for the partners, no pay rises for the staff, and a lot of anxiety about the future for everyone.'

The muscles in Trish's face were tight enough to make her feel as though someone had slapped plaster of Paris all over her skin and it was setting hard. David walked past without a word, this time with a respectable quantity of ice cream in his bowl. She waited until he was safely in his room before turning back to George.

'Have QPXQ specified the price of sticking with your firm?'

He gazed helplessly at her, wanting her to be the one to say the unsayable. His brown eyes looked much softer now.

'They can't seriously be demanding I return the brief halfway through.' The idea was ludicrous and she let her contempt for it show.

'I got the impression today that the suggestion can't be far off.'

'Then I hope you'll explain the cab-rank rule to everyone concerned.' Her voice was crisp and clear.

She was referring to the system by which members of the Bar had to take the next case offered to them, whatever they felt about it, provided they had the time and expertise necessary. There were ways round the rule, but it existed and she did her best to stick by it.

'I couldn't possibly withdraw,' she said to make her position clear before his anxiety ran away with them both.

'*I* know that. They may not.'

'They'll have to put up with it. And don't tell me their next idea will be for you and me to split up to keep them happy,' she said, trying to make him laugh with a complete absurdity. 'Look, why have they only just started to worry about this? I got the brief nine months ago. They must have been aware of all the details from the moment they decided to buy the Arrow's owners. Why now?'

George shrugged, which wasn't enough for Trish. The timing was too pat, with this protest cropping up only just after the abandonment of the settlement talks. Coincidence might be all around, knitting apparent strangers together in weird and dangerous patterns, but this was something else.

'Could they have raised the conflict as a way of preparing the ground for an appeal if the judge finds against them when we do go to court?'

All the softness was gone from George's eyes. His face was clenched again into a frown that suggested four words he would never use to her: don't be so silly.

'Or is this more to do with your partners than the client? Is one of them trying to use it against you?'

The grimace melted into a kind of apology that told her all she needed to know. Her imagination did the rest. She saw him flung out of the firm he'd done so much to build, and all because of her. She saw him diminished and fighting resentment and herself trying to make it right, trying to go on nurturing her own career without making him feel a failure. She saw disaster for them both.

'It may never happen,' he said at last.

'Who's behind it? Malcolm Jensen?' she said, naming a young, thrusting lawyer who'd joined George's firm only two years ago and had been causing him trouble ever since.

He nodded. 'He's a prick of the first water, but he's powerful because he brought a lot of big clients with him, and they love him. He goes right to the edge for them.'

'Then we have to go further. You've got to fight this, George. We can't let him beat you.'

Chief Inspector Caroline Lyalt, facing the first murder enquiry for which she was wholly responsible, felt a passionate resentment that frightened her. Why did Trish of all people have to be the chief suspect's alibi witness?

Caro had already phoned home to tell her partner, Jess, that she had no idea when she'd be back. Jess had taken the news with all the philosophy she'd learned over their years together and merely wished Caro well, adding that she herself might nip out to see the latest *Hamlet* at the National, in which one of her friends from the Drama Centre was playing Claudius.

'Good idea. I'll see you when I see you,' Caro had said, before putting down the phone.

The report of one of the team's phone call to Trish's chambers lay on top of the pile in front of her. The rest were accounts of pre-liminary interviews with the victim's family, close colleagues from her place of work, and tenants of the studio building where she'd been killed. Caro would have to talk to Trish herself, but there was another phone call she had to make first. It should be easier, too. Checking the time, she calculated that it would now be five in the afternoon in Cambridge, Massachusetts.

'Hi,' she said when she'd got through to Harvard University, 'I'm calling from London, England. May I speak to Professor Andrew Suvarov?'

There was a pause before the operator returned to say: 'Professor Suvarov is in Europe. Can I have him call you back?'

'When did he fly out?'

'I have no information on that. Would you like to speak with his assistant?'

'Thank you.'

'Hi,' said another voice a moment later. 'This is Professor Suvarov's assistant. I understand you are calling from England?'

'Yes. I'm Chief Inspector Caroline Lyalt of the Metropolitan Police. I am anxious to talk to Professor Suvarov, who may be able to help with some background to a case I'm working on. I gather he's in Europe. Can you tell me when he left and where he might be now?'

'He flew out last Friday to Paris, France. His schedule is busy, but I'm in contact with him. Would you like me to have him call you?'

'That would be great. Or if you give me a phone number or email address, I can save you the trouble.'

'I'll have him call you.'

Caro gave her own number, then put down the phone, thinking of the stilted conversation she'd had with Mrs Justice Mayford in her library-like room in the private part of the Royal Courts of Justice. It was the first time Caro had penetrated that far into the huge building, and she'd thought it was more like a university than anything to do with the reality of crime she saw every day. Maybe it was no wonder some judges came up with such impractical ideas and pathetic sentences.

'I can assure you, Chief Inspector Lyalt,' Mrs Mayford had said, gripping a pencil tightly between her hands, 'my daughter's father has never known of her existence. Ergo, he has never made any attempt to contact her. Nor could he possibly have had anything whatsoever to do with her death. He is a professor at Harvard and is based in the United States.'

'I understand,' Caro had said, not entirely truthfully. 'But we have to look at everyone who could have been involved in her life, and I'm trying to eliminate as many as possible right away. All it would take is a simple phone call to confirm that he's there and could not have been in London yesterday. If you would just give me his name, I can do the rest. You need have no contact with him.'

At last the judge had released the pencil. She'd used it to write the name on a piece of scrap paper. 'As I said, he doesn't know he's Cecilia's father, and I would be grateful if you would merely confirm his presence in Cambridge and go no further. Is that understood?'

'Yes. If we need to ask anything else, I'll let you know before I do it.'

It had been a relief to get out of the high-ceilinged, oak-lined room and its atmosphere of sticky disdain.

Just my luck, Caro thought, that my first case involves not only my best friend, but also a highly respected judge, and an internationally famous sculptor. She had already had Sam Foundling's agent on the phone, as well as Frankie Amis, the solicitor Mrs Justice Mayford had found for him.

Both the callers knew Foundling must have done it, but they'd made it clear to Caro (as if it hadn't been clear enough without either of them) that any leaks to the press, any infringement of his rights, any slip in the gathering, collating or storage of evidence, would make the case disappear in front of her eyes, and her reputation with it. Which was why she had to be seen to be looking for every other possible suspect, however far-fetched he might be.

To make matters worse, Foundling had also refused to have anything to do with the family liaison officer Caro had chosen with such care. He didn't need anyone, he'd said, and his tiny daughter, hanging on to life by her barely formed fingernails in the Special Care Baby Unit at Dowting's Hospital, would have no use for anyone either. All he needed, he'd said with barely suppressed fury, was the right to return to his studio.

Caro had secured the services of the best SOCOs, and they'd been through the long untidy room like voracious moray eels, sucking up everything they could find. Scrapings, hairs, strips of sticky tape with all kinds of fluff and dust clinging to them, and plenty of blood samples were now in the lab, awaiting analysis. There were the ashes of some kind of textile burned in the stove, the rug that had lain in front of the tatty old sofa, an oriental throw that had covered it and was also saturated with the victim's blood, her clothes, her husband's clothes, and a whole vacuum-cleaner bag full of dirt to be sieved and assessed.

Every surface had been photographed before and after it had been searched; samples of every bit of the blood that had splashed all over the room had been taken and recorded.

Sam Foundling had volunteered to strip and be photographed for any signs of defensive wounds inflicted by his wife. There hadn't been anything except some deep scratches on his hands and wrists, which he claimed had been made while he was trying to stop her thrashing about and injuring herself still more. He'd let them take nail scrapings and he'd given reasons for the bruises on his hands before submitting to all the swabs the doctors had wanted to rub in and over different bits of his body. In every way he had behaved like an innocent man.

All of which meant there was no good reason why he should not be allowed back into the room where his wife had been beaten to death, weird though his longing for it was.

Caro needed to understand it. All she could think was that he'd hidden something there. Could the SOCOs have missed anything?

George was soaking in the bath with an old John Buchan novel for comfort, and Trish was moving about her bedroom. She switched on the bedside lamps to provide a kinder light than the harsh, blemish-revealing glare she needed when she was dressing. Twitching the heavy coverlet off the bed, she folded it and flung it in the bottom of the wardrobe, revealing the fine sheets that were as different as possible from the nasty mauve nylon ones she'd had in her first rented flat. The memory of how they'd felt against her skin made her shudder.

Unlike that damp-smelling hovel, this room was gorgeous, she thought, glowing and gentle in its muted colours. And the height and width of the great bed had just the right kind of generosity.

She heard a low buzzing sound from the direction of the bathroom, which took a moment to decode: George was attempting to sing 'The Volga Boatmen's Song' in Russian. She was glad he trusted her enough, even today, to reveal his complete tuneless-ness. Her hand rested on his pillow, sliding over the smooth linen, wondering how much longer he was likely to be.

Her pleasure in her own good luck splintered suddenly as she thought of Sam, presumably alone in his house, waiting for news of the baby. Gina's voice echoed in her mind, banishing George's attempt at a rolling bass, telling her Sam was terrified of being abandoned all over again.

His wife was dead, he had no parents he knew, and Gina herself couldn't bear to see him. Trish had tasted enough loneliness in the old days to have some idea of how he must be feeling now. He'd come to her only yesterday because he'd trusted her for so long. She couldn't ignore him now.

'I've just remembered, George,' she called as she passed the open door of the bathroom, 'there's a phone call I've got to make.'

He broke off his warbling to say he'd be out of the bath by the time she'd finished. He sounded more or less himself again. Maybe they'd get through their crisis.

Gina Mayford had ricked her back climbing up into the loft to retrieve the box of baby clothes she hadn't looked at since she'd stowed them away when Cecilia grew too big for them. All carefully washed and wrapped in tissue paper, they might be in good enough condition for the baby. If she survived long enough to need clothes.

It was a practical thing to do, Gina told herself as she tried not to cry, and not a self-indulgent wallow in grief. If she could remember the time Cecilia had had, and celebrate the way she'd used it, there might be something good to be wrested from the horror of her death. And checking over the baby clothes might help her decide what to do about Andrew Suvarov.

Dust flew up Gina's nose as she hauled the box towards the lip of the trapdoor and she sneezed, almost falling off the ladder. Eventually she got the box out of the roof-space and bumped it down as she retreated backwards, rung by rung.

At last her feet were flat on the floor again and she could let the box drop with a thud, expelling another cloud of dust. A thorough rub with a cloth got it clean enough to risk opening the cardboard lid. She washed her hands.

Inside it was better: a few sprigs of ancient lavender had crumbled into nothing, but a faint scent still hung about the tissue paper. As gently as if she were touching the baby in her incubator, she parted the first leaves of tissue. They had none of the crackle of modern paper, but felt soft and slithery, like old suede gloves.

The first thing she saw was the cobwebby Shetland lace shawl Andrew's mother had knitted for Cecilia. One fat tear dripped onto the delicate woollen lace. Without Felicity Suvarov, Gina couldn't have managed. Felicity had kept the secret of Cecilia's paternity, and her support had made it all possible.

Did babies still have shawls? Gina wondered. Probably not. You wouldn't need a shawl like this if you'd already put your infant into a stretchy all-in-one body suit. Even so, she shook it out, amazed as she'd been in the beginning by the lightness of the four-foot square. She laid it aside on her bed and bent her aching back to pick out the next package.

A voice in her mind taunted her with the threat that Cecilia's baby wouldn't live to wear any of these things. Premature, born by Caesarian while her mother was dying, and subjected to grotesque brutality in the last hour before the mad dash to hospital, what chance did she have?

'Every chance,' Gina said aloud, determined to silence her own doubts. 'The doctors promised.'

Each minute garment she retrieved from its tissue wrappings brought back pictures of Cecilia, and the unmatchable, delectable smells of milk-fed contented baby. It was probably more Johnson's Baby Powder than the child herself, Gina thought, as a guard against sentimentality.

What would happen to this child if she did survive? If Sam were convicted, there'd be no question: Gina could step in and take over. But if he were declared innocent or never tried for the crime? Would he ever be able to forgive her for suspecting him? Would he be able to let her try to do for him and his daughter what Andrew's mother had done?

And would Gina ever be able to forget her fears for the baby? Even if a jury decided Sam hadn't killed Cecilia, his background made him the least suitable man to have sole charge of a vulnerable child.

Sam knew the staff in the SCBU wanted him out of their way. They were scared of him, too. But he had the right to be here, sitting at the side of his daughter's cot, looking at her red, twisted little face under the white knitted cap. It wasn't as wizened as he'd expected. They'd told him that at only three weeks premature she was more or less the size of many full-term babies.

She still looked tiny. How could he have been so afraid of this? There was nothing in him that could have damaged a creature so fragile and unthreatening. All that fret and fear for nothing! How could he have been so stupid?

Restless as before, she rolled her head away from him, waving her fists in the air, tugging at the tubes that led from them to the machines that were monitoring her heart and helping her breathe.

He'd asked the doctor how big she'd be by the age of three months, and they'd gone together to look at a three-month-old in the next ward. This baby looked stronger, more together, but not much bigger.

How could anyone have burned a child that size with cigarettes, or hit it? Or packed it in a cardboard box with a thin raggedy blanket, and dumped it out of doors on a February night?

The new letter from the woman in prison was in his back pocket. Maybe Trish Maguire was right. So what if the woman was his genetic mother? She'd given up her rights when she put him in that box.

Even if she did it only to protect you? said a voice in his mind.

The phone hooked to his belt vibrated. He'd forgotten to switch it off. Running to get it out of the way of the machines that were

keeping his daughter alive, he found a space by the window outside in the corridor and took the call.

'Sam? This is Trish Maguire. I wanted to say how very sorry I
am about Cecilia's death. That sounds pathetically inadequate, but
there aren't any better words.'

She paused, so Sam thought he'd better say something and tried
a simple 'thank you.'

'And I wondered if there was anything I could do. Anything
practical, I mean, sorting anything out or providing company if
you wanted to talk. Anything.'

Anything? Sam repeated to himself. I wonder.

Then he remembered what she'd done for him in the past and
how she hadn't flinched from any of the things he'd told her.

'There's only one thing. The police have said I can have my
studio back. They've recommended a specialist cleaning firm, but
I don't want any more strangers in there, messing about with my
work. So I'm going to do it myself. I could use some help. But it
won't be . . . easy.'

'No.' Her voice dragged. He waited for the excuse. 'It won't. But
I'll do what I can. When were you thinking of starting?'

'Tomorrow. I'm at the hospital now. But there aren't any beds
left for parents, so I'll sleep at the studio and get going as soon as
I wake. You don't have to come that early. I know you're busy.'

'I've some phone calls to make first thing, but I could get to you
by about nine, if you give me the address.'

Sam waited while she wrote it down, then clicked off the
phone, wondering whether she would turn up. Scrubbing Cecilia's
blood away from the site of her murder was going to be hard in
every way.

Trish wondered if Sam's request were a test, designed to probe her
loyalty, or whether the true weirdness of it hadn't even occurred to
him. She didn't see why anyone would want to take on a task like
that: gruesome and most desperately inappropriate. And yet

maybe if you were an artist the idea of snooping strangers in your private space was unbearable. Perhaps if she helped him with this horrible task, she'd have done enough to show she wasn't rejecting him as everyone else had done for so long.

Back in her warm bedroom, now decorated with George's sleeping figure, she wished she hadn't yielded to the impulse to phone. But as she slid under the duvet, he opened one eye, then the other, and smiled as he reached for her.

Chapter 6

The water in Trish's bucket was red and she'd barely started to scrub. The stain Sam had directed her to clean was a broadly oval patch on the wooden floor in front of the sofa. He hadn't said anything about what he'd found when he got back from the meeting in her chambers, so it was left to Trish's imagination to work it out.

There were other, smaller splashes about two feet away, with a sharp line along the edge, as though something like a rug had once lain there. Whoever killed Cecilia must have dragged her from the sofa to this place. Had she fought back? Or been so desperate to protect her child that she'd rolled herself around her great belly, offering him only her own back to hit?

Sam himself was on his knees below a long workbench, patiently dealing with a pile of white marble pieces, cleaning the blood off each one, rinsing and then drying it, before arranging it in a pattern that must make some sense to him. He raised his head, as though alerted by the lack of scrubbing sounds.

'Is there a problem?' His voice was harsher than usual.

'No. I was pausing to get my back straight again. And I saw what you were doing. Will it mend?'

'Not really. But it was the first of her heads I ever did and the one she liked best, so I need to . . .' He looked away.

No point saying sorry, Trish told herself. Get back to work and shut up unless he wants to talk.

Trying to ignore the fact that it was Cecilia's blood she was touching, she rinsed the old-fashioned scrubbing brush in her bucket, shook the water off and leaned forward. There were plenty of women in the capital who paid a fortune to go to keep-fit classes and perform movements very like these, she told herself, swapping the brush for a wet cloth to wipe up the loosened, rehydrated blood. With the stove pumping out heat, she was soon so hot she had to pause again to take off her sweater.

Then she found a rhythm: push, pull, dip, swipe; push, pull, dip, swipe. The sound of rough bristles against the wood was like the scratching of a pack of dogs. Her back ached. Friction between her wet hands and the wooden top of the brush soon made her skin burn. When one-third of the stain was nearly gone, she broke the rhythm to examine the right palm and saw blisters, white and squishy with fluid, in a row along the side of her hand.

It took a lot to make her start again, but she did it, forcing herself to lean harder on the brush and manoeuvre it even more vigorously. Her hand slipped over the edge of the brush and one nail dragged along the floor. A splinter pierced the skin under the nail, making her gasp.

The pain was vicious; small, of course, but bad enough to make her eyes water. She examined her hand again and saw a good quarter of an inch of barbed wood sticking out from under her nail. Closing her eyes, she gripped the end of the splinter and pulled, clamping her lips together to make sure she didn't make any more noise. A few drops of her blood fell onto the newly scrubbed planks. Biting her lip, Trish shook her hand to get rid of the pain, told herself it was only a splinter and so far from everything Cecilia must have suffered that she should be ashamed to feel it, and picked up the scrubbing brush again.

Nothing else disturbed the work, except for her periodic trips to empty the horrible bucket and refill it with clean water at the sink in the corner, until there was a loud knock on the door. Trish glanced up to see Sam put down the piece of marble he was polishing. He bounced to his feet with an agility she envied.

She didn't want to pry, so she bent forward again, to push the harsh bristles into the stain.

'Trish! What are you doing here?'

The sound of a familiar voice did make her look up. There was Caro Lyalt, standing beside a much younger man dressed in jeans and a leather jacket.

'Giving Sam a hand with a hellish job,' Trish said. She brushed some hair off her forehead with the back of a sore, damp hand. 'What about you, Caro?'

'I'm the SIO on the case. I came because I need to ask Mr Foundling some questions.'

'I thought Mrs Justice Mayford had provided him with a solicitor. Why haven't you—'

'I didn't know you two knew each other,' Sam said in a voice so accusing Trish felt like rushing into apology and explanation. His face was harder than ever and his eyes showed a worrying blankness. 'I'd never have let you in here, if I'd—'

'We're friends,' Trish said, trying to sound casual, 'but I didn't know Caro was involved in this. The only person I've spoken to is a constable, who phoned to ask if it was true you'd come to see me in chambers the day before yesterday.'

He stared down at her. She'd rarely felt at such a disadvantage, scrubbing brush in hand, kneeling at his feet. They were very close to her face. And very large in thick-soled black boots. She thought of the blood tainting the water in her bucket, staining her fingernails, mixing there with that tiny speck of her own.

He looked away, releasing her. 'Well, Chief Inspector, that's your answer, isn't it? I'm not answering any more questions without my solicitor. If you want to know anything, we'll come to the police station. Otherwise, keep out of my face and my space. You can come to the house if you must, but I don't want any of you in here now you've finished collecting the evidence.'

Trish had to watch Caro to see how she took his refusal. There was nothing in her expression except cool interest, which seemed to be directed towards Trish rather than Sam. It was the younger officer who showed them a face of angry suspicion. After a moment, Caro took a step forward.

'Very well, Mr Foundling, but it seems an unnecessary waste of your money to drag your solicitor to an interview when all I want to know is whether your wife said anything to you about a man who had been harassing her at work.'

Sam produced a cruel crack of laughter. 'That's pathetic. If you really wanted to know, you'd have asked me yesterday when you had me in that interview room for four hours. Why are you here? To see if I've been trying to hide something?'

'We're on our way to a meeting and passed your door. It seemed a good opportunity to ask you about the harassment suggestion we've had from one of your wife's colleagues,' Caro said, before leaving with her junior at her heels.

Sam didn't say anything. As soon as the door had shut behind them, he made sure the latch had caught.

'It often sticks,' he said, when he saw Trish looking at him. 'D'you think that question was genuine?'

'I didn't to start with; now I'm not sure. I can't imagine someone like Caro lying about information from one of Cecilia's colleagues. It would be so easy for you to check.'

'Caro! I wish you wouldn't call her that. I hate the thought of her being a friend of yours.'

'She's a good woman, Sam,' Trish said, bending to her scrubbing again. 'And intelligent.'

'She thinks I killed Ceel. And, whatever excuse she's dreamed up, she was round here to see whether I was buggering about with evidence they'd missed. So she's a liar too.'

He was staring at Trish as though wondering whether she too

suspected him. Again she found she couldn't break the link between them while he wanted to keep it. She tried to keep her expression open and friendly. Then her phone rang, freeing her.

The call was from Steve, her clerk, telling her Leviathan Insurance had decided they didn't care about the conflict of interest that had so worried George's partners. Trish thanked him with unusual fervour.

'It's what I'm here for. The loss adjusters want to talk to you today. Can you be in chambers in two hours' time? There'll be Cecilia Mayford's replacement and some assistants. And Giles Somers, of course,' Steve said, referring to the solicitor who had originally briefed Trish on the case.

She had to work hard to avoid sounding too grateful. When she'd got Steve off the phone, she went back to scrubbing with renewed energy to make up for her relief at the prospect of escape. By the time she had to leave, she'd reduced more than three-quarters of the four-foot oval to a pale patch that showed nothing but the grain of the wood. Sam would have to colour it to match the rest if he weren't to have a constant reminder of what had happened here. But would he need reminding? How could you ever forget?

Back outside, in the crackling cold, Trish was glad she was close enough to her flat to shower and change before the meeting. But there was an uneasy sensation in her mind too.

Her own enjoyment of coincidence now seemed childish. It was uncomfortable enough to know she'd played such a big part in Sam's mind for seventeen years, during which she hadn't thought of him once. Worse was his belief that they'd been communicating in some extra-sensory way all along. She wished she could get rid of the fear that she'd been responsible for planting a kind of parasite within a profoundly damaged man, distorting all his normal relationships.

He'd lived in the studio's one room, he'd told her, until five years ago, when he'd married Cecilia and moved into her house in

Islington. He and Trish had been so close geographically for so long they must often have passed in the street, unaware of the links between them.

Steve was waiting for her in chambers. He didn't bother with any polite frivolities, such as a greeting.

'Now that Ms Mayford is dead,' he said abruptly, 'the loss adjusters need to regroup.'

'Have they appointed a successor already?' It was a question she hadn't wanted to make within Sam's hearing. 'Talk about dead men's shoes!'

'I doubt if they've made a formal appointment, but someone has to handle her caseload. Because of the size and complexity of this one, they've allocated it to her boss, Dennis Flack. His secretary says you've met him.'

'Once, right at the beginning. I didn't take to him. And he had all the short-man's Napoleonic arrogance, so I'm surprised he's prepared to have the meeting here.'

'I insisted on it,' Steve said, 'knowing you had this other private business to sort out. You've got just under an hour to review the papers. I hope that'll be enough. The tigers are getting hungry, you know.'

Faced with his habit of quoting Churchill's speeches whenever he thought she was slacking, Trish wanted to get back to the comfortable solitude of her own room as fast as possible. Steve had no need to worry: the London Arrow and its perplexing movement was in the back of her mind all the time. Now Cecilia was dead, it seemed even more important to win the case for her.

In Trish's room, her desk was piled high with papers. The sight made her think more kindly of her pupil's return. It was often a nuisance to have a scared or arrogant baby barrister with you all the time, wanting to know what you were doing, needing to be taught and given tasks to occupy her day after day until she knew enough to be let loose on a small but real case. The brighter, tougher sort could be useful, but there had been times when the current one, Bettina Mole, had made Trish think of the toddlers she'd seen clinging to their mothers' clothes so tightly the poor women couldn't even go to the lavatory alone.

Still, Bettina wasn't bad at filing and she was clever enough. No one had ever been offered pupillage in 2 Plough Court without exceptional brains. Once she'd gathered a little confidence she'd probably be useful in more ways than tidying papers. The trick would be to give her the confidence without muffling her necessary self-doubt or the urge to watch and learn. Trish had so far had her for two weeks, which meant there were twenty-two to go before she could hand her on to the next pupil master. Maybe she could ask for a break then. Presumed to be a soft touch, she was nearly always given the wobbly pupils.

She switched on her laptop and carefully reacquainted herself with all the arguments the other parties had used to explain their refusal to agree a settlement. There had been representatives of QPXQ (the Arrow's new owners), the main contractors who had actually built it, and the three separate professional-negligence insurers covering the construction company, the consulting engineers and the architects, as well as someone from each of their partnerships, and of course the crowd of lawyers.

She had all the unhelpful facts marshalled in her brain by the time Steve phoned to say that Dennis Flack was already in the library with an assistant and Giles Somers, the solicitor.

Trish arrived just as Dennis unilaterally declined the offer of tea for all four of them. She shook hands with him, holding on to his a little longer than usual as she said how sorry she was about Cecilia's death.

Dennis nodded abruptly, pulling his hand away and stepping back, as though he didn't like being reminded he was shorter than Trish. His square jowly face seemed full of rage until she looked more carefully and saw signs of misery. The pouches around his dark eyes were swollen, and his broad shoulders were slumped so that they seemed to have shrunk. 'I have to try not to think about her; otherwise I lose it completely. Can we keep this strictly business?'

'Sure,' Trish said, surprised by his unexpected sensitivity. She turned to Giles, a pleasant-looking grey-haired man in his early fifties, who'd been helpful and efficient throughout the progress of the case. 'I'm so glad Leviathan aren't worried about the conflict of interest.'

'This is the first I've heard of any conflict,' Dennis said in a voice like a barking guard dog. Trish made hers as soothing as possible and explained.

'How exceptionally inconvenient. You ought to have warned us of this as soon as the takeover was mooted.'

'Come on, Dennis,' said Giles, clearly puzzled by his reaction. 'It's a pretty tenuous connection. I've already advised Leviathan that there's nothing to worry about. And there's no way Ms Maguire's relationship could affect *your* interest in the case.'

'Great,' she said, smiling at the assistant Dennis had brought with him but not bothered to introduce. 'Hi, I'm Trish Maguire.'

'Hello,' said the assistant, without offering her own name or even a smile. She did manage to shake hands with Trish, who instantly wished she hadn't. The other woman's palm was clammy and she barely moved her muscles as Trish gripped her hand. It felt like a raw squid.

'Oh, this is Jenny Clay,' Dennis said, not looking at her. Trish put extra warmth into her smile to make up for his rudeness, resisted the temptation to wipe her hand on her trousers and set about taking control of the meeting.

By the time she had relayed all the information they could possibly need, Trish's tongue was sticking to the roof of her mouth between each word and her throat felt like the Sahara, but the atmosphere of the meeting had improved a little. She reached forwards to fill a tumbler with water from the jug. It tasted flabby and much too warm.

'That's all very clear,' Dennis said, slapping his papers into a neat rectangle. 'We'll have to run through Cecilia's calculations again, but otherwise we'll simply take up where she left off.'

Jenny sighed, then blushed as Dennis glared at her with such patronizing reproof that Trish flashed another comforting grin in her direction. A hint of gratitude showed in her eyes, before she lowered her lids again and presented an even more scared and miserable front. Trish watched and took mental notes. She hadn't expected to dislike Dennis quite so much.

'After all, Trish,' he said, with an edge that suggested he was about to punish her for her wordless interference, 'the answer to why the building is moving must be there in the files, and it's a ludicrous waste of your expensive time to be ploughing through data you don't understand and are ill equipped to interpret. We'll get back to you when we've completed our checks. I think that's it for today. When we know where we are, we can move forward.'

'Good,' Trish said, careful to hide her sense of insult.

However difficult she might have found the engineering principles and calculations, she was entirely capable of getting to grips with them. She'd learned and then forgotten far more complex stuff than this. Every barrister had to. If you didn't understand everything about the subject at the heart of an action, you weren't doing your job. And you'd never be able to cross-examine witnesses effectively.

'Before you go, Dennis, may I ask you one thing about poor Cecilia?' she asked with an entirely false smile.

'If you must.' He waved the others ahead of him. When Giles and Jenny had left the room, he added, 'I suppose you want to know whether I think her mad husband did it.'

'That wasn't what I was going to say, but it sounds as though you think he did.'

'I'm sure of it. I've known and worked with Cecilia Mayford for nine years.' He puffed out his chest and began to declaim, as though he were giving the address at her funeral. 'She was one of the calmest, kindest, brightest women I have ever known. And the most generous.'

Trish's smile became more natural. Maybe his posturing and aggression were no more than a front to cover grief.

'Watching her since she fell for Foundling,' he added, his neck and jaw tensing so his voice was constricted too, 'I've seen her good nature stretched beyond bearing. He really put her through it.'

'Yet she always talked about him as though she loved him,' Trish said truthfully, 'and he seems distraught by what's happened.'

Dennis shrugged and took a step towards the door. 'I don't suppose that would be too hard to fake.'

'Maybe. In any case, I wasn't going to ask you about him. I wanted to know about the man who's been harassing her at work.'

'Harassing Cecilia? Nonsense! We have powerful anti-sexist, anti-bullying policies in place, like everyone else these days. It wouldn't have been allowed. Where did you get such a weird idea, Trish?'

'I heard it came from one of your colleagues, but I don't know who.'

'Sounds like silly secretarial chatter to me. And wholly unlikely. I must go. Jenny will get back to you when we've been through all Cecilia's files.'

When he'd followed the others out of the library, Trish took her papers back to her room, thinking his idea of bullying might be different from hers. She quickly typed up notes of the meeting so she could return to Sam. There was plenty of work here to give her an excuse to stay in chambers, but the thought of him scrubbing away at his wife's blood told her she had to go back to help.

Before she left chambers, she picked up the phone to call Caro Lyalt, not sure whether she wanted an apology for the way Caro had treated them both this morning, or an opportunity to offer her own excuses for interfering. She and Caro had been friends for so long that it felt uncomfortable to be at odds with her like this.

But Caro could look after herself in this situation and Trish didn't think Sam could.

To her surprise, she was put straight through once she'd found the phone number of the incident room.

'Well?' Caro said, tension rattling in her voice. 'Have you phoned to offer cooperation or a complaint?'

'Neither. Come on. This is me.'

There was a long pause, which Trish didn't even try to break. She had enough faith in Caro to believe all would be well in the end.

'I'm sorry.' It wasn't a generous apology, but it was there. 'I shouldn't have been so angry this morning. It was just seeing you on your knees slaving for my chief suspect, getting between me and the truth on a case I absolutely have to solve.'

'I'm not getting between you and the truth, Caro. All I'm doing is giving a bit of support to a very lonely man at a time of maximum horror for him. You can't grudge him that.'

'Will you tell me why he came to see you in chambers the day his wife was beaten to death?'

'No.'

'Why not? He's not your client any longer, Trish, even if he was as a child. There's no privilege involved *now*.'

'Maybe not,' she said, realizing that Gina must already have told Caro everything she knew about Sam's background, 'but he talked to me in confidence. Neither he nor I have any legal obligation to tell you. If he wants it kept confidential, I can't gainsay him.'

'Gainsay? It's not like you to be so pompous unless you're trying to hide something. What is it?'

'Nothing. Caro, think what you're doing to him. Here's a man so isolated it makes my whole skin shrivel to think of it, who's found his wife dying and knows their baby may die too. He's well aware you suspect him. Are you surprised he doesn't want to tell you anything he doesn't have to?'

'If he's innocent, he has nothing to fear from us,' Caro said, pompous in her turn.

Trish laughed, with a bitterness that shocked her and silenced Caro. Into the crevasse that had opened between them, Trish dropped a reminder of some of the famous cases in which innocent suspects had had their lives ruined by the police's misguided attempts to get them convicted.

'None of those have anything to do with me or the officers working with me,' Caro said, more hurt than angry now. 'We have no interest in anything except getting to the truth. By encouraging Foundling to keep silent, you're stopping us.'

'You know perfectly well that's nonsense,' Trish said. 'In a state like his, it would be easy to say something that could be taken out of context later and used to make him look guilty, even if he's not.'

'Then it will be the job of his defence counsel to make that clear.'

'He's not on trial yet.' Suddenly what had been nasty sparring between friends became much more urgent. 'Caro, listen to me. I'm only trying to give him the kind of support you or I would automatically get from our families and he has never had. He's had more to put up with than either of us could possibly imagine and he's turned himself into someone of such creativity, he—'

'I can't bear all this, "I'm an artist so I'm too important for you to touch" stuff,' Caro said, almost spitting down the phone. 'I've had all that from his agent, from the dealer who sells his work, *and* from someone at the Arts Council. For a lonely man he's remarkably well supported. He has half the arts establishment of London fighting his corner. He doesn't need my best friend too.'

'Oh, Caro,' Trish said, half her resistance melting. 'Try not to hate him. If you do, you'll never see the truth even if it hits you in the face.'

'Has he told you about the life insurance?' Caro's voice had softened too. 'That poor woman, who married him in spite of all the warnings she was given about how dangerous he could be, took out a colossal policy when she got pregnant.'

Trish began to feel cold. 'In his favour?'

'No. In favour of her unborn child. Makes you think, doesn't it? She wrote a codicil too, to be sure the payout would go to the baby, not her husband. The will she signed on marriage leaves everything else to him, including her professional death-in-service benefit and her house in Islington. She knew her death would make Sam Foundling a rich man. This shows she wanted to be certain their child would have enough of her own money to be independent of him.'

'I've got to go,' Trish said, trying not to see what Caro was telling her.

'Back to your scrubbing for my suspect?'

'Probably.'

'I'd warn you to beware of getting too close to him if I didn't think you'd sneer. Can I trust you to tell me if you hear or see anything?'

'Don't ask me to spy for you.'

'You'd shield a murderer, Trish? You, of all people? Maybe you should see the photographs of Cecilia Mayford's body before you get too hung up on this mission to support the man who killed her. Shall I send you a set?'

Trish gripped the phone hard, as though that could help her hold on to her belief in Sam's innocence. 'When I see evidence that he *was* the one who battered her, I'll help you. Not till then.'

'Why are you behaving as though you owe him something? It should be the other way round.'

'I must go,' Trish said, thinking: I do owe him. He trusted me and believed I cared about him, while I never gave him another thought once the case was done.

When she'd cut the connection she thought of all the things she'd like to have said to Caro, explanations of why it was so important for Sam to have people on his side for as long as possible. Cecilia was now beyond help. Giving him the benefit of doubt wasn't going to hurt her any more. Even if, in the end, he were proved to have killed her, the only way he could ever be rehabilitated would be to remember that there had once been people prepared to support him.

Sam greeted Trish with a wary expression that held only the smallest hint of a smile. 'I didn't think you'd come back.'

'I hate leaving jobs undone,' she said, then winced as she remembered Cecilia's saying exactly the same to her.

'There's not much more to do,' he said, gesturing to the floor. 'You made such a good start I carried on after you'd left. And all the filthy fingerprint dust has gone. There's only ordinary cleaning left.'

'Will you be able to work here again?'

Sam shot a look at her, full of suspicion, then calmed down as though he could see the question was genuine.

'I don't know. Work's always been a refuge before; I don't know whether this will . . . I want to do another head before I forget. She . . . I've got another piece of the same marble. Carrara. I won't be able to make it the same, but there's a chance if I start now I'll catch something of how she was before . . . before it happened. Does that seem callous?'

'God, no! Brave. It sounds as though you don't need me now. I'll get off home. Look, Sam . . .'

'What?'

'I don't know whether you have plans for Christmas, but George and I are doing it this year in my flat, which is only just round the corner from here. It'll be a bit of a scrum because we're having his mother and mine, and my young half-brother's aunt, uncle and their two boys from Australia. If you'd like to come, we'd love to have you.'

He stared, as though he couldn't understand her. She hadn't meant to say anything like it and wondered whether she was mad, and whether George would go mad when he heard what she'd done. She tried to blank both thoughts with the knowledge that it was lucky Caro and Jess were going to Jess's brother.

There was no way Caro could have shared a celebration with this man.

'I was . . . I don't know,' he said. 'We were going to Gina's, but now . . . I don't know. And the baby may be out of hospital by then. I don't know.'

'There's no need to decide now. But I'll give you the address so that if you'd like to come on the day, you'll know we want you. And the baby if she's well enough.'

He put a hand over his mouth. The colour in his cheeks deepened and deepened. Trish thought he looked furiously angry again and tried to think of a way of mending whatever she'd done this time. Then she saw tears in his fierce eyes for an instant before he turned away. He'd been rejected over and over again. No wonder he didn't know how to respond to the opposite.

'We *want* you, Sam,' she repeated, almost crying herself.

Chapter 7

Sam double-locked the doors behind Trish Maguire, hating himself for showing such weakness. And for not being able to thank her for what she'd said. He hoped she'd understand. In the old days he'd have been sure she would; now he didn't know.

He could still feel the shock of seeing she hadn't cared a toss about him, after all those years when he'd held her liking between himself and the world as the one thing that made him acceptable. She'd just been doing her job, as she would have done it for anyone, even the other dishonest little shits he'd met in his years in care.

He thought of the therapist a friend at art school had recommended. She hadn't been a bad woman, just way out of her depth with him. You've got to forgive yourself, she'd kept on telling him. At first he'd said it wasn't himself he had to forgive; it was all the bastards who'd done their best to kill him or turn him into a raving loony. But she'd gone on insisting he had to find a way to let himself off.

Memories of her nagging voice echoed in his mind and he revisited the fury that had made him pick up the chair he'd been sitting on and smash it down on the floor. He could still see the pieces. And the fear in the therapist's expression, quickly masked by a cold professional smile.

Amazingly she said she'd be prepared to give him another chance, but he couldn't go back. Not after letting her see him as he really was. He'd hated her for a long time.

His head was aching again, as though his brain was swelling and swelling until it was squeezed tight against his skull. He put his hands to the sides of his forehead, rubbing at his temples with the soft circular motion Cecilia had used once when she'd tried to massage the pain away.

He caught sight of the disastrous attempt to rebuild the clay head he'd been making for the Prix Narcisse and went to twitch off the damp cloth that covered it. His own eyes glared up at him with a kind of maniacal hatred. The lips were twisted in bitter resentment, or pain. He didn't know whether it was better or worse than the first attempt he'd smashed into pulp. He only knew he hated it for the truth it showed him.

You have to learn to forgive yourself, he thought.

'How?' he shouted aloud.

Trish rounded the corner of her street and looked up towards the front door of her flat. It was open and there seemed to be something thick and round lying in the doorway. A log? Worse? She was pulling her glasses out of her pocket and sprinting towards the iron staircase that led up to the door, when she heard David's voice, higher than usual and excited.

'That's great. She won't be long. But I can sign it if you don't want to wait.'

Closer now, and with her glasses on her nose, she saw it was indeed a log: the end of the Christmas tree. She'd forgotten it was due today. Calmer, she climbed the rest of the steps, signed the delivery note and looked into David's glittering black eyes.

'Somehow I hadn't realized a two-metre tree would be quite so big,' she said. 'I wonder if George is coming this evening.'

'He phoned just now to say he wasn't. But I'm sure we can manage to put it up ourselves. And if not, we can always get Mr

Smith from downstairs. I'm sure he'll help. We must get it up tonight, Trish. *Please.*'

'Let me catch my breath first.' She unwound the red scarf from her neck. 'Did they send a pot too? They were supposed to.'

'It's here. I made them bring it in first. And it's got kind of spoke things to make the tree stand up in it.'

'Then we may be all right. But perhaps we ought to eat first.'

'Noooooo! If we put it up first, I can start decorating while you cook.'

Trish had never seen or heard him as excited as this. She could not spoil it. Together they set about erecting the vast tree. Soon she too became infected with the Christmas mood, breathing in the scent of pine needles that sent her straight back to her own child-hood.

'I had an email from the cousins today,' David said, breathless as they finished attaching the spokes to the trunk and slid the pot over them, latching them on. 'They want it to snow while they're here. D'you think it will, Trish? It *is* getting colder.'

'I know, but the forecast isn't hopeful for Christmas itself. Even so, it'll be frosty and far colder than they've ever felt in Sydney, and it may well snow while you're on holiday with them.'

'Yeah.' David's voice was less excited now, and Trish understood how nervous he was of joining his relations on their 'rellie route' around the country. Susie was his dead mother's sister, and he'd liked her and her husband and sons when he'd stayed with them in Sydney, but this trip would introduce him to other relations, English ones, who'd never shown the slightest interest in knowing him, even while his mother was still alive.

Trish dropped a casual hand on his head. 'I'll miss you horribly while you're with them, but I thought we – you and I and George – could have a private celebration the night you get back. How would that be?'

He glanced up at her with a sideways look, half suspicious, half grateful, which made her add: 'David, there's no reason why you have to go with Susie and Phil and the boys if you don't want to. We can easily sort out things for you to do here in London for the rest of the holidays if you'd rather stay with me.'

His expression firmed up as she watched and he shook his head. 'I want to go. I think. But can I come back if I hate it?'

'Of course. And you know, even if it doesn't snow, the cousins will understand Christmas food in a way they never could on the beach in the middle of summer. Have you decided what presents you're going to give them yet?'

'George said he'd take me shopping at the weekend. So we'll find something then.' He looked happier but so self-conscious that Trish deduced an intention to buy a present for her too. She wanted to tell him not to spend too much of his carefully hoarded pocket money on her but couldn't think of a way of doing it that wouldn't sound patronizing.

'And have you thought of what *you* want?' she said instead. He grinned and said what he'd been thinking was that she'd never ask. He had a list on his computer, all ready to be printed out for her when they'd finished with the tree.

'Okay,' she said. 'Let's see if this works. You stay with the pot and steady it, while I walk the thing upright.'

She had needles in her hair, up her nose and pricking her skin by the time pot and tree were firmly vertical, and several of the branches were bent out of shape. Her heart was banging uncomfortably hard under her ribs.

'We did it,' she said, pushing a bit of twig off her lips with her tongue.

'You look wild,' David said with admiration. 'Shall I get you a drink?'

'It's okay. I'll have one while I'm cooking. You go and print off your wish list and I'll see what I think of it.'

He flashed a wicked grin at her and clomped away to his room, looking his true self and age again.

*

Much later, lying under the duvet and thinking it was a pity George wasn't there too, Trish phoned him.

'Hi,' he said. 'Good evening?'

'Fine. David's in good form, and we got the tree up. Now that he's hung his decorations, it's the gaudiest thing you've ever seen. I had a fancy for some chaste white-and-silver arrangement, but I thought he should have his red and gold and purple baubles if he wanted.'

'Quite right. Adults shouldn't get precious about Christmas decorations. I'm sorry I wasn't there to help.'

'Tough day?'

'Ish. Nothing we can talk about. How about you?'

It wasn't hard to work out that he'd been having trouble with QPXQ Holdings and his partners. Trish longed to know what was happening, but knew she couldn't ask. Unguarded moments of imaginative freedom still produced pictures of him being sacked. And others of him hating her because she was still working, earning, succeeding.

'Trish? Are you still there?'

'Yes.' She made herself forget the grim future and told him a bit about Caro and Sam Foundling and how she'd been moved to invite him to share their Christmas lunch. When George didn't comment, Trish felt her neck muscles tensing all over again.

'You're not taking that Chinese proverb a bit too seriously, are you?' he asked, but he didn't sound angry.

'Which proverb?'

'The one about how saving someone's life means you're responsible for them for the rest of yours.'

'I hadn't thought of it like that,' she said, relaxing into the absurdly luxurious goose-down pillows George had imported into her flat. 'Maybe that is why I made my suggestion. I hadn't planned to; it just came popping out.'

'I think you did the right thing. Are you going to ask the judge too? She must have been expecting to spend Christmas with them.'

'I'm not sure that's such a good idea,' Trish said, remembering Gina's fear of revealing her hatred of Sam.

'Sleep on it and see how you feel in the morning.'

'Okay.'

'I must say I wish I were there to sleep on it with you,' George said, his voice deepening into theatrical sexiness. 'Last night was . . .'

'What?' Trish said, laughing.

'I don't think I should pander to your vanity by spelling it out.'

'Oh, go on.'

He laughed too. 'You know what I think. Roll on the weekend. Good night, my love.'

Trish eased her long body against the cool linen sheet and wished he'd had his way.

Caro was still in the office, fighting a sore throat as she waited for one of her officers to bring the schedule of Professor Andrew Suvarov's movements during his European trip. Whatever Trish assumed, she was still doing everything possible to find other suspects.

It was deeply unlikely that Suvarov would have sneaked to London to kill his illegitimate daughter after thirty-four years of knowing nothing about her, but it was important to eliminate him officially.

They still hadn't learned any more about the mysterious harasser. Mrs Mayford had known nothing about him, and the only specific suggestion so far was that it could have been Cecilia's head of department, Dennis Flack.

'They used to have one of those office flirtations,' one witness had said, according to the reports in front of Caro. 'But I don't think it ever went further than that. They'd go for drinks after work and she used to have him to a lot of her dinner parties before she met Sam Foundling. She dropped Dennis then, and he resented it. I don't *think* they'd ever made love or anything, but he hated the idea of her husband, although I don't think he knew him well at all.'

'Hi,' said DC Grahame, slipping quietly into her office. 'Here's the list of dates you wanted.'

'Thanks.' Caro put out a hand to take it and quickly scanned the list: Vienna, Barcelona, Paris, York. 'Why York?'

'There's a university there,' Grahame said, sounding surprised. 'Suvarov's been giving lectures in universities.'

'I know.' Caro didn't laugh at him for his literalness. 'But it isn't term time. There won't be any students in any of them.'

'Don't they have courses and things at this time of year for people who never went to uni?'

'Probably.' She smiled at her fellow degree-less officer. 'Can you find out if he flew from Paris? There must be an airport somewhere near York.'

'He didn't fly. I checked. He came in on an early Eurostar on Monday morning, reaching Waterloo at 9.51, and then took the twelve o'clock train from King's Cross to York, arriving just under two hours later.'

'Do we know what he did during those two hours in London?' Caro asked, pleased he'd taken the next obvious step and not waited to be told what to do.

'He could've just hung about the stations. Foreigners always get there much too early for trains and things. It's not such a long time.'

Someone *will* have to talk to him, Caro thought. 'Okay. Thanks. You can go home now. We won't get any further tonight.'

She drafted an email to Andrew Suvarov, reread it, then deleted it from her screen. No excuse for wanting to know what he'd been doing was going to sound credible. She picked up the phone and dialled the private number Mrs Justice Mayford had given her.

'What's the news?' she said, as soon as Caro had given her name. 'The family liaison officer was being tactfully silent this afternoon.'

'I'm afraid there isn't anything yet, but I have discovered that Professor Suvarov was in London that morning.'

'It's a coincidence. No more than that,' said the judge, although she sounded shaken. 'What possible reason would Andrew have to attack her? I've told you, he doesn't know she's anything to do with him. Please don't let him distract you from the real . . .'

'The real suspect? Don't worry, Mrs Mayford. We're doing everything we can in that area. Results will soon be back from the lab and we'll know whether there's anything on the hammer that can identify the person who, who last used it to, to—'

'To batter in my daughter's head,' said the judge. 'You don't have to worry about my susceptibilities, Chief Inspector; they've taken such a beating they're desensitized. Why did you ring? To ask permission to tell Andrew about Cecilia? I really don't—'

'No,' Caro said quickly. 'I think we should keep that in reserve. I just wondered if you knew of anyone he might have come to London to see, so that we can establish what his movements were without having to talk to him directly.'

There was a pause, filled only by the suggestion of a sniffle. But Mrs Mayford's voice sounded as strong as ever when she said she'd have a think and call back.

On Friday morning Trish found a note from Sally Elliott, the trainee clerk, on her desk.

'You wanted to know about Maria-Teresa Jackson. She's on remand in Holloway, charged with her common-law husband, Melvin Briggs, of killing their two-year-old son last year.'

Two-year-old? Trish thought. How on earth could Sam Foundling's mother also have a two-year-old child?

She unlocked the drawer of her desk and took out the stout envelope of letters he'd left with her. Picking among them, reading a phrase here and there, she found nothing to give any indication of the writer's age. She rang through to the clerks' room.

'Did you happen to ask how old the woman is?' she said.

'No, but I can find out. They may ask why we want to know. In fact they probably will. It's such, um, such an odd request.'

'Make something up if you can,' Trish said, well aware that the real curiosity was Sally's. 'I'm only trying to discover whether she's the same woman as one who cropped up in an old case of mine.'

She waited, rereading the letters, until Sally rang back to say that Maria-Teresa Jackson was forty-six and had given birth to the child at the age of forty-four.

Perfectly possible, Trish thought. It would mean she'd have been seventeen when Sam Foundling was born. Also possible.

'And,' Sally said, 'this time I asked who her solicitors are so you can go straight to them if you need more.'

'Great. Thanks. Have you got a phone number?'

Trish didn't recognize the name of either the individual solicitor or the firm, but she hadn't done any criminal cases for years and might well not know all the small legal aid partnerships that took the bulk of criminal defence cases. Contrary to the Assistant Commissioner's diatribe in the paper, few of them earned much, certainly nothing that could be described as 'obscene'. He must have been muddling them with the big commercial barristers.

Trish put down the phone, wanting to plan her approach with care. It wouldn't do to betray Sam, so she'd need a good excuse for asking questions about the woman who might be his mother.

She tried one story after another. None seemed remotely convincing. Maybe it would be better to approach the whole subject from the other end. She reached for the phone and rang the number of Sam's studio. When he answered his voice was scratchy, as though he'd been crying – or shouting – for a long time.

'Sam,' she said at once, 'it's me, Trish Maguire. I now know a bit more about the woman who's been writing to you from prison, which I can pass on to you, but I was wondering whether you'd like me to talk to her. I wouldn't be able to assess whether she is who she claims to be, but I might be able to get an idea of her real motives for writing and maybe . . .'

'It'd be great,' he said, sniffing. 'Are you allowed to do something like that?'

'I could if I wrote to her – just as a friend of yours, not a lawyer – and asked if she'd be prepared to talk to me on your behalf. There are no restrictions on the number of visits prisoners on remand can have and you don't need a Visiting Order, as you would with a convicted prisoner. Would you like me to have a go?'

'Yes.' He didn't add anything to the bare syllable, but something in the way he said it gave Trish the feeling that she had, at last, done something to make up for her failure to recognize him.

She pulled a plain piece of writing paper out of her desk and composed her letter, making it as plain and easy to understand as possible:

> *Dear Ms Jackson,*
> *Sam Foundling has your letters. He has asked me to come and see you to talk about your plans. Please let me know if you would like to see me. My address is at the top of the letter.*

As she wrote the last sentence, Trish knew she couldn't tell an unknown, probably criminal, woman where she lived. Instead she wrote the address of chambers at the top of the sheet and hoped the woman would assume that 'Plough Court' was a block of flats rather than a nest of barristers in the heart of legal London.

Her phone rang and she reached for it without looking, still rereading the letter to make sure nothing in it could frighten the woman.

'It's me,' Caro said. 'I need to ask you something. Please answer.'

'If I can.'

'Did you notice anything about Sam Foundling's hands when he came to see you the day his wife was killed?'

Trish felt her eyebrows pull together, frowning as she recreated the scene.

'Yes,' she said slowly, staring at the space in front of her where he had stood, telling her who he was. 'They looked dirty, but the marks were bruises. Grey bruises all along the sides of both hands. They didn't look exactly fresh. Why?'

'Sod it!' Caro must be pretty stressed, Trish thought; she rarely swore, even with such mild expressions as this. 'That's what he claimed, that he'd damaged his own hands days earlier.'

'Are you beginning to accept that he could be innocent?' Trish carefully kept all expression out of her voice. She didn't want to be accused of sneering again.

'Don't get your hopes up. There's stacks of evidence against him.'

'Such as?'

'Trish, I'm in the middle of a murder investigation. I can't go giving away information like that to any chance caller, particularly not one with a conflict of interest like yours.'

'You're the caller here, Caro. Blocking like this just makes me suspicious. What is your evidence?'

There was an angry laugh down the phone. Then Caro said in a deliberate voice that sounded very cold: 'I'm not going to tell you. But reflect on this, Trish: the pattern of bloodstains shows Cecilia was still lying on the sofa when the attack started. There were no signs of forced entry into the studio. Add up those two things and ask yourself who—'

'Stop there. There must be other people who have keys to Sam's studio.'

'None, except Cecilia.'

'What about the cleaner?'

'There isn't one. Which is presumably why he needed an expensive barrister to scrub his floor.'

'Lay off me, Caro. This kind of evidence is pathetically inadequate, as you very well know. Circumstantial at best, fantasy at worst. The CPS would throw it out at once. Haven't you got anything else?'

'You can't seriously expect me to tell you what we've got. But you must face it: he is almost certainly guilty.'

'I've never heard you sound so hard.'

'You've never obstructed me before.'

'I'm only trying to protect—'

'You don't have to protect anyone from me, Trish.' Caro's anger was like a nut stuck in her throat. She could hardly get the words round it. Coughing hard, she added: 'All I want is the truth. You could help, but if you're not prepared to, I must go.'

Trish was left to stare at the phone. Until this case Caro had been the most stalwart of her friends, open-minded, stoical, and very warm. Now she was acting like everyone's bad dream of a pig-headed police officer, blind to everything that didn't square with her own picture of what had happened.

She had to be stopped if she wasn't to break Sam all over again.

Chapter 8

George and David went swimming on Sunday morning. Trish didn't like submerging herself in cold chlorinated water, so she took her exercise alone and on foot. Wanting a change from her usual journey to work, she crossed the river at Southwark Bridge. Bright winter sun sparkled on the water, but the river looked odd from here, and the view was nothing like as good as you got from Blackfriars.

Up Queen Street and on past Mansion House, she soon found herself between cliff-like buildings that cut off most of the light. On weekdays these streets were full of scurrying figures rushing from meeting to meeting, with one or two loitering in doorways, hunched over cigarettes. Today there was almost no one to get in the way as she picked her route through narrow streets with the romantic names of their medieval predecessors: Bread Street, Whitehorse Yard, Love Lane. First burned in the Great Fire of 1666, rebuilt, then bombed, they'd been rebuilt and improved again and again over the last sixty years.

Streets with names like these should have beautiful buildings, she thought, seeing another monstrosity in the distance; not slabs of dirty pink polished granite like the nastiest kind of gravestone.

She turned a corner and came upon a church, one of Wren's. The stone facade was ravishing in its pale-grey simplicity, and it had a pretty red-brick vicarage still attached. There were few signs of life, even though it was Sunday, until she passed the west door of the church and a sonorous throaty rush of organ music poured out. She didn't recognize the piece but liked it and walked with a lighter step as she matched the rhythm.

On she went, aimless and at ease in her own city, until she realized she was only two streets from the Arrow. Tipping back her head, she could see it soaring above the muddled roofline. The sunlight, which didn't reach the pavements here, glistened on its pristine glass and white concrete, making it look even more ethereal than usual.

A black cab bustled past, nudging her to the back of the narrow pavement. When it had gone, she crossed the empty road and made her way to the base of the Arrow.

It stood in the centre of a square lawn, mown to the smoothness of a snooker table and edged with flat white stone panels that made it look rather like the First World War graves in France and Belgium. She thought of the hidden bodies of the hundreds, perhaps even thousands, of anonymous plague victims that lay beneath. These plain stones were more appropriate than she'd realized when she was reading the specifications.

At each of the four corners of the Arrow, narrow slightly convex ribs outlined its shape and drew the eye towards the apex, fifty storeys up. As graceful as any Gothic vaulting, the ribs looked as though they had no function but decoration, although in fact they housed the cables Trish always thought of as guy ropes, anchoring the building to piles driven as deep into the ground as the central core.

She laid her hand on one rib. The concrete looked smooth but felt rough against her palm, and very cold. There was no sign of the cracking from here, and the whole brilliant, surging structure looked as straight and strong as any other, and a lot more beautiful. What could be wrong with it?

A uniformed security guard peered out of his glass pod near the entrance, curious to see someone apparently stroking his building.

Trish pulled back her hand and made a circuit of the whole site. Still there was nothing to suggest a problem or its solution. It seemed unfair that the architects' imaginative vision should be rewarded with disaster and years of argument when the dreary rectangles of brick and granite that made the other streets round here so dull and ugly should cause no one any trouble.

A peal of church bells clattered its way through a cascade of changes, heralding twelve heavy chimes, which told Trish her swimmers would be home and hungry in less than half an hour. Turning her back on the Arrow, she hurried home.

The answer would come, as she'd told Cecilia, but would it come in time to save Leviathan millions?

Maria-Teresa Jackson's letter agreeing to see Trish came through surprisingly fast and she was on her way to Holloway five days before Christmas.

She hadn't been to the prison for years, but in the old family-law days it had been a familiar journey. There was no point taking the car, only to spend hours in traffic jams around King's Cross and then have the usual struggle to find somewhere to park, so she walked up to Holborn from chambers and caught the Piccadilly Line to Caledonian Road, almost sleepwalking the well-known route.

Today it was even more depressing than she remembered. The sky looked like mouldy white bread and as she turned left out of the Tube station it began to spit hailstones. They felt sharp as they struck her skin but bounced so high when they hit the pavement they could have been made of rubber. She narrowed her eyes against them and the cold and wished she had a hat. Bending her head, she walked as fast as she could without slipping, and turned into Hillmarton Road. The big houses gave a bit more shelter here, and she rubbed the stinging rain out of her eyes. Soon she saw the blank red-brick walls of Holloway dead ahead.

The relief of getting out of the cold was enough to ease the otherwise daunting business of queuing to get in, presenting her identification, being searched and eventually shown into the visiting room, with its huddles of weary, irritable people. The officer on duty pointed out Maria-Teresa Jackson, and Trish walked forward to introduce herself.

She had seen women like this so often her heart sank. Maria-Teresa's thin skin had the grey tinge that comes from too many fags, too much booze and too little hope. Her sharp-featured face was half hidden by lank shoulder-length dark hair, which clung to her prominent cheekbones. Her eyes were dull, as though she'd lost all sense of there being anything in the world she wanted to see. The smell of old cigarette smoke hung about her hair and clothes. Each time she moved, a new waft reached Trish, who tried not to wrinkle her nose.

It had been a client like this, she remembered, who'd gazed at her bullet-headed pre-teenage son and asked why neighbours made such a fuss about a bit of thieving and vandalism. 'He's only a boy, isn't he?' she'd said, ignoring the suffering of his terrorized victims. 'All boys cause trouble. It's not his fault.'

Trish had sometimes wondered whether the boy had been expressing the rage his mother had been too defeated to admit in herself. Now she pulled an unopened packet of cigarettes out of her bag and pushed it across the table towards Maria-Teresa. Loathe the habit though she might, Trish knew it was the only pleasure she could offer today.

'Thank you for coming,' Maria-Teresa said. There was still a faint Italian accent in her hoarse voice. 'How's Sam?'

'He's okay,' Trish said, not yet ready to hand over any more information than necessary. She smiled, hoping to evoke some reaction from Maria-Teresa. There was nothing.

Trish tried to see past the marks of hopelessness to the seventeen-year-old she'd once been. Could she really have dumped her burned and beaten baby on the steps of the London Hospital in 1975? Could her union with a man brutal enough to have tortured his three-month-old son have produced an artist like Sam?

A man so loved by Cecilia, with all her sophisticated intelligence and generosity, that she had married him and put up with his emotional violence and longed to bear his child?

'Tell me what happened,' Trish said at last, trying to see the real person behind the mask of defeat.

'When?'

'When you took the baby to the hospital twenty-nine years ago.'

Maria-Teresa scratched her left ear, which reminded Trish of the way Gina Mayford had assaulted her own forearms as she fought the urge to cry.

'I knew he'd die if I di'n' do something.' Maria-Teresa's eyes looked even bigger in her wasted face. She pushed back some of the lank hair, hooking it behind her ear, which was raw from the scratching. 'So I waited till Mick was drunk, then I put Sam's blanket on him, yeah? Then I let myself out of the house, quiet like, and took him to the hospital. We lived in Ainsley Street, near Bethnal Green. In the basement.'

'Can you remember the way you went?'

'Course. How could I of forgot? I went out of Corfield Street into Three Colts Lane, and down Brady Street to Whitechapel Road and the hospital. There was a shop, fruit 'n' veg, and there was piles of boxes on the road. I thought Sam'd be safer in one of them ones, so I took it and put him in.'

She swallowed. Trish saw her eyes were damp. It seemed wrong to take notes, but she wanted to check the story's details later.

'He was heavy, yeah? I never realized he'd be so much more heavier if I'd of carried him like that, in a box, like, 'stead of laying up against me. My arms was sore. But we got there, see. I thought of clearing the snow off of the step before I put the box down, but people was still coming and going, even though it was like four o'clock in the morning. I left the box on the step by the door, where the snow couldn't of got to him. Then I went home, yeah? I didn't have no money. Where else would I of gone?'

'You wrote in one of your letters that you put your wedding ring in the box with him. Was that true?'

'Course.' The woman's surprised expression was more convincing than any angry protestation of truth. 'He didn't have no birthmarks, so there had to be something to tell who he was.'

'Where exactly did you put it?'

'In his nappy. I didn't want it to fall out of the box, see, so I tucked it in his nappy.' She brushed the back of her hand against her eyes. Trish saw more wetness sparkling on her skin.

So maybe the hospital staff didn't steal the ring, Trish thought. Maybe it was simply chucked away with the filthy nappy.

'It don't matter, though, not now they have that DNA. The test can say who he is. Why won't he have it?' Maria-Teresa Jackson asked, her voice whiny with pain or resentment. 'It's easy. Only like a scraping in your mouth. It don't hurt.'

Memories came back to Trish of a study carried out in New Zealand, which explored the violence prefigured in a damaged or low-active MAOA gene on the X chromosome. As far as she could remember, boys with the faulty gene were unusually passive – unless they'd been physically, sexually or emotionally abused, in which case they were likely to be violent. Abused boys who didn't have the damaged gene were no more likely to be violent than the rest of the population. Girls with the damaged gene were less at risk because of their second X chromosome. If Sam did have the DNA test this woman wanted, maybe the lab could also check his MAOA gene. An undamaged one wouldn't prove anything, but its existence would be reassuring.

'It'd be the best Christmas present in the world,' said Maria-Teresa, twisting her left hand in her straggly hair. 'Every time I go to mass, I ask for it. At the Protestant service too. You know what it says in that carol they have? "Unto us a child is born. Unto us a son is given." It's what I want. Just to know Sam'll take the test, like, and see he's mine.'

'Why is it so important *now*?' Trish said and watched a fanatical light flash in the woman's eyes. But she didn't answer. Her greyish lids dropped over her eyes, hiding whatever they might have revealed. 'Because of the trial that's coming? Do you want the court to know how you saved the life of one baby boy all those years ago so they'll find it easier to believe you might be innocent this time?'

'I di'n' kill Danny,' Maria-Teresa said with quiet dignity. 'I tried to protect him, like I tried to protect Sam, all them years ago. It's not why I want him to know he's mine. I don't want him in court, giving evidence, like. Only to say he knows why I done it and left him at that hospital. That's all.'

'Fine,' Trish said, more curious than ever. There was more to this woman than her pathetic looks suggested. Unfortunately neither her increasingly obvious intelligence nor the hints of spirit that were sparking like an engine about to ignite meant she was honest. 'But just tell me . . .'

Maria-Teresa Jackson stood up, stiffening her spine so that she looked much taller.

'I don't want to talk no more.' She turned and stalked away.

Feeling thoroughly rebuked, Trish gathered her belongings and made her way towards the exit. As she left the visiting room, she heard a long agonized scream and shuddered. In the old days that had been the sound of Holloway for her, more even than the endless shouts and banging doors. Designed to give the impression of a hospital rather than a prison, it had confounded all its creators' intentions and become a place of horror for many of the inmates.

Mentally ill, addicted to drugs, incapable of seeing the outside world or its inhabitants as anything but hostile, they were confined in cells and dormitories that made recovery unlikely. Weeping, screaming, cutting themselves, they infected each other with their own particular breed of distress. Like the wildly multiplying bacteria of MRSA, misery ended up devouring all the healthy emotions it touched. Trish shivered again, then checked her watch.

It was a gesture David had recently shouted that he hated, so she tried to do it as little as possible. The trouble was that time ruled her life. There was never enough. At least today he was having tea with one of his friends and wouldn't get back until nearly six. Even so there was no incentive to linger, either in the prison or on the depressing walk back to the Tube.

Minutes after her train had left King's Cross, it screeched to a halt, making much more noise than usual. Mildly surprised, Trish raised her eyes, expecting to see Russell Square station. All that met her gaze were the dingy brick walls of the tunnel. Careful not to contravene Tube etiquette by catching the eyes of any other passengers, she went back to her paper. Five minutes crawled by. Everyone in the carriage was becoming restless. Trish recrossed her legs and turned to the foreign news.

There was still trouble in the Middle East. She couldn't remember a time when there hadn't been and wasn't sure she could imagine how it would be if all the killing and kidnapping stopped. A croaking noise from the loudspeaker distracted her and she tilted her head to hear better.

'Erm, well, folks, sorry about this delay,' said a disembodied male voice. 'I've been informed that there's a signalling problem. Should be sorted out soon and we'll be on the move again. Sorry about that.'

Grimacing, Trish found herself catching the eye of the woman opposite. Now there was a problem, it seemed reasonable for them to communicate.

'It's a right pain, isn't it?' the woman said. 'I've got a meeting in ten minutes.'

Trish offered a sympathetic smile, then went back to her paper. The tension in the carriage increased as the long minutes dragged on, and there were sounds of much fiddling with packages and luggage. No more information came over the loudspeaker. She didn't look up again until a different woman's urgent shout disturbed her.

'Kayleigh, come here! You come back here. *Now.*'

A wail told Trish Kayleigh couldn't be more than a toddler. She tried to hide her loathing of mothers who yelled at their children with that kind of cruel edge, but she couldn't stop herself looking up to see who they were.

A small dark-haired child in a pink parka was being hugged so tight it made no sense of the woman's harshness. Puzzled, Trish followed their frightened gaze and looked further along the carriage until she saw a sallow young man with a dark beard, sweating heavily into his long beige robe and paler overshirt. He had a crocheted cap on his head. A canvas bag rested on his knees, tightly gripped between his hands. As she watched, he started to shake, looking first one way then the other, as though for sympathy, or perhaps a means of escape.

A European man, several years older, got to his feet to take a seat right at the opposite end of the carriage. Two teenage boys exchanged glances and crashed open the door connecting theirs to the next. Several of the women, looking steadfastly at the floor, collected their bags together and sat on the edge of their seats, clearly not sure whether to follow the teenagers' example.

'Sorry, folks.' The same disembodied voice made Trish jump. 'The signalling problem seems more serious than we thought. But it shouldn't be too much longer. Just relax and we'll be away as soon as we can.'

The heating seemed to have been turned up. There wasn't enough air. Trish pulled at the polo neck of her sweater, swallowing with difficulty.

It's ludicrous to think he's got a bomb, she told herself. Ludicrous, racist and disgusting.

She caught sight of a poster opposite, informing her that cameras had been installed on the train for the greater safety of passengers. Had they picked up the face of a wanted terrorist? Was the voice lying about the signals?

It was impossible not to look at the bearded man. He stared

back, apparently terrified, then down at his watch. Was the bomb on a timer? Had he planned to leave his bag and get out at the next station? Or was he a suicidal martyr to his cause, ordered to wait with it until it killed everyone within reach?

Either way, Trish did not want to be caught in a tunnel with an explosion. It wouldn't do much good to get further down the train, but the possibility of being out of this particular carriage was becoming so attractive she was twitching in her seat like most of the others.

The lights went out. Darkness sharpened the menace. Further down the train people were moving. Someone sobbed, probably a child. Someone else swore sharply.

The engine began to whirr and the lights flickered back on. Another crash of the door at the far end made them all turn to look. Two uniformed police officers came through from the next carriage with a man in plain clothes and a ticket inspector.

'No need to panic,' said one of the police officers, with the kind of cheerfulness that was more worrying than any severity. 'We won't be long.'

They walked steadily along the carriage, looking carefully at all the male passengers. Trish waited for them to reach the Middle Eastern man and was amazed when they passed him without comment. She saw a woman pull at the sleeve of the plain-clothes man and point to him. The official shook his head.

A tall brown-haired man in jeans got up from the seat next to Trish's and moved casually to the doors, heaving his rucksack with him and leaning against one of the glass panels, as though he could barely stand. Sitting at right angles to him, she could see he was pale, and his fleshy face was damp. In a way she wasn't surprised – the airlessness and tension were enough to make anyone feel faint – but he was a big man, and his loose, scuffed, black leather jacket did nothing to conceal his powerful shoulders. He looked too tough to be overcome like this.

The uniformed officers closed in on him. The plain-clothes

man said something too quiet for Trish to hear. He struggled. One dirty trainer connected with the shins of one of the officers, who grunted and bit back an insult. Handcuffs snapped and the tall man was still again.

'Okay, ladies and gentlemen,' said the plain-clothes officer, relief making his voice breathless. 'Sorry for the delay. Would you now like to make your way along the train. You'll find the front coach is already in Russell Square station and you can make your exit there. No need to panic now, but move on as fast as you can.'

Trish didn't wait. She had no luggage and was on her way before most of the others had even stood up. Conscience-stricken, she looked back from the doorway to make sure there was no one old or frail enough to need help, then she hurried along the train, eventually reaching the end of the queue to get out.

On the platform, she found a phalanx of officers, instructing all the passengers to move straight up to street level.

'What's the problem?' she asked. 'What did that man have in his rucksack?'

'Don't you worry about that, madam,' said a woman officer, not meeting her eyes. 'Just make your way up to street level. We're evacuating the station. Please keep moving. Fast as you can.'

Oh shit! she thought. If it's not a bomb, it's chemicals of some kind.

The robed man had caught up with her, still hugging his canvas bag to his chest. 'What did they tell you?' he asked in a clear British accent.

'Nothing,' she said, meeting his eyes. 'Except that they're evacuating the place.'

Together they waited for the lift, both longing for escalators that would have got them out quicker. Eventually they were up, breathing in the sweet petrol-scented air.

'Goodbye,' he said to her. 'Good luck.'

'Thanks. Same to you.' She wanted to apologize for her

suspicions, but that would have made the injustice worse. She compromised: 'That was horrible, wasn't it?'

He nodded and hurried away. A taxi passed with its light on. Four separate people claimed it and started to argue. There were no other taxis in sight. Trish could have caught a bus, or even walked back to chambers from here. It wasn't far. But she needed time to get rid of the taste of fear, and the shame that she'd made such a misjudgement of a wholly innocent man. It wasn't his fault he shared his appearance with a few genuinely violent terrorists.

Over the heads of the agitated, curious crowd, she saw the trees of the Brunswick Square garden and thought she might sit there for a few minutes and recover her common sense. Even chilly drizzle was welcome after the stultifying fifteen minutes in the Tube.

Sitting on the damp bench, she let her head fall back and her eyes close. She felt light-headed, quite unlike her usual efficient self. After a while, she sat up straight again and looked around. There were few people here, but she could still see the crowds on the pavement outside the Tube station. There were police vans too and a couple of ambulances standing by.

Had it been a bomb in the rucksack? Or poison gas?

You'll know soon enough, she told herself, looking round for distraction. A big double-fronted building stood at the far end of the square. She'd never spent any time here before and had no idea what it could be. A few people walked up the steps and disappeared inside. Curious, she followed them and found a sign announcing the Foundling Museum.

Intrigued by yet another coincidence, she decided to go in. When she'd paid her entry fee and bought a guidebook, she discovered the museum was devoted to Thomas Coram's eighteenth-century hospital for abandoned children. The place was so quiet she felt as though a shutter had fallen between her and the quarrels of the modern world.

Starting at the top, she found a lot of the museum taken up with the artists and rich men involved with the charity. The attic belonged entirely to Handel, one of the earliest benefactors. But on the ground floor were exhibits that brought home to Trish the reality of life for some of the foundlings.

Her own reaction to a few minutes of alarm on the halted Tube this afternoon felt ridiculously exaggerated as she listened to the recorded voices of men who'd been sent to the hospital as children nearly a hundred years ago. Awed by the stoicism with which they described their frightening, comfortless lives, she moved on until she came to a long, narrow glass case. This held tokens left by some of the mothers who'd handed over their babies in the earliest years of the hospital's existence.

A small notice described how its policy of giving anonymity to the women meant none of their children ever knew they had arrived with a brooch, a lock of hair, a seal, or a scrap of paper that might one day identify them to their birth mothers. After the loneliness she'd heard in the recordings, she could hardly bear the thought of how much it would have helped the foundlings to know their mothers had cared enough to leave these pathetic objects with them.

Raising her eyes, Trish saw a row of letters written by or for desperate women, begging for their children to be admitted to the hospital. Clearly, whatever its privations, it had offered a better life than any other available to them. One letter in particular made her stop breathing for a second. Signed by Margaret Larney, it had many crossings-out and read:

I am the unfortunate woman that now lies under sentens of death at Newgatt. I had a child put in here before when I was sent here his name is James Larney and this his name is John Larney and he was born the King Coronation Day 1758 and Dear Sir I beg for the tender mercy of God to let them know one and other.

Human nature doesn't change, Trish thought, whatever else happens. I wonder what she'd done to earn her death sentence, poor Margaret Larney. How bad could she have been if her overriding thought as she faced the hangman was that her two fatherless boys should be allowed to know each other after she was dead?

Trish stared at the letter, trying to decide what to say to Sam about the woman she had just met in Holloway; how to advise him now.

Chapter 9

On Wednesday Trish was sitting in the Temple Church beside David, listening to the first line of 'Three Kings from Persian Lands Afar'. In spite of the stone vaulting and the muffling effect of the huge crowd, the sound of the solo voice was pure and literally thrilling. She shivered and could feel hairs on the back of her neck stiffening. The other voices of the choir joined in and the effect became a lot more ordinary.

She looked away from the singers, around the rich crowd, and thought how odd it was that they were only a twenty-minute Tube journey from the miserable, impoverished world contained within Holloway's red walls. To her left she could see the life-sized effigies of supporters of the order of Knights Templar, which lay only inches above floor level under the dome. Long legged and digni-fied in their chain mail and surcoats, they were images of stoicism in suffering.

They reminded her of the voices of the foundlings she'd heard in the museum, which in turn reminded her of how she still hadn't decided what to tell Sam about Maria-Teresa. Would it help him to meet her and see that, even if she had been the woman who'd abandoned him, she was no monster? Or would it stir him up even more? After all, this must be just about the worst time to take any risks with his fragile stability.

Thinking of him, and what he would face if Caro went ahead and charged him with his wife's murder, Trish lost all sense of the music around her and was back in the original court, telling the judge what had been done to Sam and why he had to be rescued from his foster parents. Could you ever get past something like that? He'd done so well, achieved so much. If he had to go back to court now, to stand in the dock and wait to hear whether the jury thought him guilty of killing Cecilia, he'd lose it all. No more than justice if he had done it, but Trish still believed – still fought to believe – he hadn't.

David was tugging at her shoulder. She looked round to see the whole congregation standing to sing the last carol. There weren't many other children here, packed as the church was with the grandest members of legal London, but she'd wanted him to see it now that he was old enough to appreciate it – and to join in the carols. Unlike her and George, David could sing in tune and she tried to give him every opportunity to exercise a skill that still seemed unearthly to her. As usual, she kept her mouth shut, not wanting to embarrass him or herself.

She could see Antony Shelley, her head of chambers, a few pews ahead with his beautifully dressed wife at his side. Another thing Trish still hadn't decided was what to do about their Twelfth Night party. Always one of the most glamorous evenings of the year, this time it clashed with George's office party. Normally she'd have cut that short without compunction, but now he wanted her support, to show Malcolm Jensen and the other partners there was nothing to be ashamed of in their relationship and no genuine conflict of interest for anyone at QPXQ Holdings to fear.

The congregation subsided for the final prayer and she leaned over her knees and shaded her eyes.

'Amen,' bellowed the congregation a few moments later, and it was all over for another year.

As Trish and David waited their turn to move away from the

pew and join the shuffling queue to get out into the cold, she heard someone say her name and looked back to see Mrs Justice Mayford smiling at her.

The judge looked older than she should have, but there was a little more colour in her cheeks than there'd been the day they met at Somerset House and her smile no longer made Trish want to burst into tears of sympathy.

'It's lovely to find you here, Trish,' she said. 'I've been trying to telephone to say that I won't be able to accept your really kind invitation to join you for Christmas lunch. I couldn't just leave a message because I wanted you to know how much it means that you asked me.'

'I'm glad. But it's a pity – for us – that we won't be seeing you. How's the baby? Is there any news?'

'She is doing better. She's off the ventilator now, which is definitely something. But . . .'

'I'm glad,' Trish said again, wishing she'd thought of another phrase. She was like an old-fashioned vinyl record that had got stuck.

'They're keeping her in over Christmas. Which is just as well. The thought of Sam learning to look after such a tiny creature on his own is . . . tricky.'

Trish would have given a lot to know whether Gina had actually asked the doctors to pretend the baby needed a longer stay in hospital than necessary. She looked up to assess the other woman's sincerity and saw an expression of such penetrating intelligence, she felt herself blush.

'Happy Christmas, Trish,' Gina said with a kind smile. She turned towards David. 'Is this your son?'

'We're brother and sister; we live together. David, this is Mrs Justice Mayford.'

'How do you do?' she said.

To Trish's relief David shook hands with aplomb. She wished the judge a happy Christmas, then moved away. It took five minutes to get from their pew to the outside world. Too many of the congregation had too much to say to each other for any faster progress.

'I liked that,' David said, tipping his head back to look up at the sky. Here in the Temple garden, it was just possible to see one or two stars.

'Good.' Trish knew better now than to hug him to share her pleasure with him. They walked side by side, with two feet of safe space between them, down towards the river and so home. 'I've never asked if you'd like to do some extra music at school, learn the piano or something. Listening to you sing just now, it struck me that I should have.'

'I've got enough to do as it is. *Are* we going to be able to go to Heathrow tomorrow to collect the cousins?'

Trish smiled inwardly at the connection between the two remarks. Luckily, for once, she had enough time to give him what he wanted.

'Yes. The courts have closed for Christmas. Chambers is already emptying, and I've told Steve I'm not available till after New Year. So I'm all yours and the cousins' now.'

'And George's.'

'Yes. George's too.' And Sam's, she added to herself. But this was David's time, so she made an effort to forget Sam and added aloud: 'What I thought we'd do tomorrow is take the car out to Heathrow, pick them up and drive them to their hotel so they can get some sleep, while you and I go on to buy the food. George has given me a shopping list that's about two metres long. D'you want to help?'

He looked round, his face bright in the lamplight. 'Yeah. I need to make sure you get a big enough turkey. Is that bloke you told me about, the one whose studio's round the corner, going to come on Christmas Day?'

'I still don't know. But I've got a present for him in case he does. When we're back with the shopping, if we're not too knackered, I thought we could start to wrap. How would that be?'

'Great.'

They were knee-deep in boxes, torn-off price labels, clumps of useless but viciously sticky tape, and heaps of wrapping paper offcuts the next day. The phone rang for the fifth time since they'd unloaded what looked like enough food to keep three armies supplied for weeks. Trish sighed.

'I'll get it,' David said, leaping to his feet.

Trish's knees were aching so much she couldn't work out whether it was better to go on kneeling on the rug to wrap her share of the parcels or to perch on the edge of the sofa, bending to the task.

The huge dining table was out of operation at the moment, covered with wire trays of mince pies George had baked before work and the marzipan-covered cake he was planning to ice as soon as he got in. He seemed determined to recreate in Southwark the kind of elaborate ritual with which he'd grown up in the English countryside.

Trish's very different childhood had entailed far less ceremony, and the Christmas food had been restricted to a roast turkey breast and bought plum-pudding with brandy butter. In George's world there seemed to be special menus and recipes for every meal from breakfast on Christmas Eve until supper on Boxing Day. He was contributing the skill and effort, and a ludicrous array of wines, spirits and liqueurs, while she was supplying the ingredients he'd specified. She still couldn't get over the sight of the trolley she'd filled at his instruction. Even with David's appetite and the presumably similar hunger of his cousins, it had to be far too much.

Still, the scents of spice and pastry, combined with the pine needles, made an intriguing change from the usual furniture polish and flowers.

'Trish,' David called. 'Sam Foundling on the phone.'

She heaved herself up from the floor, grimacing at the pain in her knees, and walked to take the receiver from him.

'Sam. How are you?'

'Okay. Trish, I've just heard from the hospital.' His voice was buoyant enough to tell her the news was good. 'She's now off all the tubes and things and as soon as they're sure she can manage, she'll be out of the SCBU and on an ordinary ward. They say I should be able to have her out and home by the New Year.'

'That's fantastic news, Sam. I'm so glad.'

'So, I can come to lunch on Christmas Day after all. If it's still okay with you.'

'We'd love to have you. David, my brother, and I are just back with the shopping.' She laughed. 'There's more than enough. Come any time after one. We'll probably eat about half past. See you then. Oh, by the way, Gina told me yesterday that she won't be coming.'

'I know. I just phoned her about the baby and she said she's going to some old friends in Dorset.'

'Fine. Have you decided on a name for your daughter?'

'Not yet. Gina wants me to call her Cecilia, but I want her to have a name of her own. She mustn't grow up to think she's only a substitute. She has to know who she is as herself, right from the start. But I don't know what I want for her yet.'

'You probably need to get to know her a bit before you decide,' Trish said almost at random, just for something to fill in the conversational gap, but Sam sighed.

'You see, you always do know what I'm thinking. You don't get it wrong, like everybody else.'

'Good. But I ought to go now. See you on the twenty-fifth.'

'Before you go, Trish . . .'

'Yes?'

'You were going to the prison to see that woman. What happened?'

Trish looked towards David, happily wrestling with an

intractable parcel and showing no interest in her conversation. She still didn't know whether he'd realized that the Sam Foundling who phoned her was the same Sam Foundling in the news because his wife had been murdered. David occasionally read the papers and had a knack of picking up the most gruesome stories from school friends, but he'd made no mention of it. The reports had been surprisingly minimal so far and the press hadn't yet suggested Sam had anything to do with it.

'I can give you all the details later,' she said casually, keeping her eye on David, 'but my impression is she almost certainly at some stage left a box like that outside the hospital. There was too much detail, trivial but telling, for her to have invented it entirely. And the route she described fits the map. I checked.'

'But the baby needn't have been me. That's what you're saying, isn't it?'

'Yes. If it was, she'd have been just seventeen.'

'Do you think I should take the DNA test she wants?'

Trish paused to make sure she was going to say what she meant. 'In many ways it would clarify things, but it wouldn't help with your original dilemma of whether to have anything to do with her.'

'I suppose not. So that's probably it for now. No. Sorry. What I wanted to ask is: did you *like* her?'

Another pause let Trish examine her memory, recreating the moment when Maria-Teresa's air of defeat and misery was lightened with intelligence, dignity and hints of lifesaving stubbornness.

'I didn't have long enough to decide. But she didn't make my skin crawl, as some people I've seen in prison have. And I'd say she was considerably more intelligent than her letters suggest. I'd have no problem going back to see her again. So, as far as it goes, I suppose there was more liking than disliking, if that makes sense.'

'It does, but it's not helpful.'

'I'm sorry.'

'Not your fault. I just meant it doesn't get me any further, except in the wrong direction.' He stopped. Trish waited. 'I suppose I wanted you to hate her so I could write her off. Thanks. See you on Christmas Day.'

Gina Mayford finished wrapping the presents she would take with her to Dorset and tried not to look at the glowing semi-abstract seascape she'd bought for Cecilia or the batch of sweaters for Sam. They were a bit pedestrian, but she didn't understand enough about his taste to buy him any kind of picture or object, and he always wore sweaters rather than jackets. She hoped he wouldn't feel short-changed or insulted.

She longed to phone Chief Inspector Lyalt and beg for news of the investigation, but she knew she couldn't. The family liaison officer had told her everything she was allowed to know.

Sam's innocence had still not been disproved. Trying to believe in it, trying to forget all the times Cecilia had arrived at her house in tears or looking white and strained to breaking point because of something he'd done, Gina stared at the parcel she was making for him.

Once he'd spent nearly a whole weekend without speaking, giving Cecilia nothing but furious glares and increasingly impatient grunts whenever she asked a direct question. She hadn't been able to tell whether he was angry or unhappy, and the only response she'd had to any of her attempts to comfort him had been snapping and criticism of everything she said or did or cooked or ate or wore. It had sounded like hell.

Now Gina remembered listening to Cecilia's tears and trying to help. The trouble was she'd had so little experience of close relationships herself. She'd considered sharing some of the stories she'd heard in court, then thought better of it. In the end she'd fallen back on the old method of cooking something special to take the place of words. Unlike Sam, Cecilia had known exactly what the beautifully presented soufflé meant and had absorbed the intended comfort with the foamy cheese confection.

'And she loved him,' Gina said aloud. She reached for another sheet of thick, grey-and-silver paper and folded it around the box containing the first of Sam's cashmere sweaters. 'She *did* love him, however bad it got.'

She was a little comforted until she thought of the poor judgement Cecilia had shown in picking earlier boyfriends.

There had been a parade of them, from her last years at school all through university and her first ten years on her own in London. All of the men Gina had been allowed to meet had shown signs of being wounded in one way or another and all of them had soon overstepped some undisclosed mark, making Cecilia dismiss them before they got too close. Only Sam had lasted more than a year or so.

Was that because his wounds were obvious? The trickiest of his predecessors had been the ones who presented themselves as perfectly normal, functioning human beings, only to end up playing bizarre emotional games neither they nor Cecilia had understood. Sam's verbal aggression and sulks might have been uncomfortable to live with, but at least they weren't devious.

What did I do to her to make her need damaged men? Gina wondered. Was it only bringing her up without a father? Did I lay her open to this kind of horror from the beginning simply because I was too wet to lay claim to Andrew Suvarov?

The questions in her mind became more personal, more selfish, as she wondered whether it would have been easier to face being in the same house as Andrew over Christmas if he'd known he was Cecilia's father. And with that question came another: what if she did, at last, tell him and find he hated her for depriving him of the pathetically inadequate thirty-four years of their daughter's life? And what *had* he been doing in London on the day she died?

Gina speeded up her rate of wrapping and bent her mind to the task of finishing the parcels with ribbon and miniature berried wreaths. There had never been any easy answers in her life and she should have known better than to expect them now.

Thirty-four years ago, she'd been sure the refusal to name her baby's father had been principled. She'd needed to protect him from knowledge of what had happened, to leave him free to find his utopia in the New World. In spite of all her own need and longing, she'd been determined not to cling or hold him back and make him settle for less than he wanted from life. But he'd never married and from what his sisters had told her he hadn't found utopia either, or even ordinary contentment.

Was she mad to be putting herself in his way again after so long? Wouldn't it be better to hole up in the flat for Christmas, not letting anyone know where she was or that she was alone, to watch television, listen to music, and eat stupidly luxurious delicacies packaged for the rich and lonely? Or even join Trish Maguire's eccentric-sounding household and risk falling into the black pit of suspicion and misery at the sight of her probably murderous son-in-law?

On Christmas Eve Caro was sitting in her glass-walled cubbyhole at the far end of the incident room, feeling as though all the contradictory pressures were closing in on her. It was like being permanently stuck in a rush-hour Tube train with the hot bodies of angry strangers pressed right up against you. When her phone rang and she saw Trish's name on the screen, she was tempted to leave it unanswered. But she'd never be able to forgive herself if it turned out later that Trish had finally decided to cooperate.

'Yes?' she said into the phone, trying to forget how angry she was. 'What can I do for you?'

'I just wanted to let you know I'm having Sam Foundling to Christmas lunch.' Trish's voice was unusually breathy, as though she knew she was behaving badly but couldn't bring herself to acknowledge it. 'I didn't want you finding out from someone else and being angry again. The poor man's on his own and grieving. I had to do something.'

'You must do whatever you want,' Caro said, a whole new outrage latching on to the old. She thought about pointing out the risks Trish was taking, then saw her chief superintendent appearing at the far end of the incident room. 'I've got to go.'

She vaguely heard Trish wishing her a happy Christmas and murmured a reluctant echo before she put down the phone. The chief super was stopping to speak to each officer. He looked like an old-fashioned industrialist tipping his workers at Christmas. Was this common practice in the Major Incident Teams? Surely not. Even such a senior officer couldn't imagine they'd close down an enquiry as important as this just because the rest of the working world was about to stop for ten days.

Some of the team were taking Christmas off, but there'd been more than enough volunteers prepared to carry on collecting information, collating and then analysing it to see if there could be anything they'd missed. The surveillance boys would continue to watch Sam Foundling too, even though their overtime was going to screw the budget.

The chief superintendent was only two desks away from Caro's door when he looked up to catch her attention. A big man, he had a jowly face and usually looked as though he needed at least one extra shave a day. Now she saw his expression was much too serious for this visit to be part of any Christmas courtesy. She was relieved.

'Morning, sir,' she said, standing up as he closed the door behind him.

'Caro. Sit down.' He pulled out the visitor's chair. She saw coarse dark hairs poking out from under his neat cuffs; others grew right down on to the backs of his hands. 'How's it going?'

The tone of voice told her this was no casual friendliness. He couldn't have come for a report either; she was producing those at regular intervals. This had to be the preamble to a reprimand.

'I'm sorry we haven't got a result yet,' she said.

'It is a pity. We need one quick. This isn't a case we can leave with everyone knowing who did it but no evidence to bring the suspect to court. What are your principal lines of enquiry?'

'The husband's movements and motives,' she said, ticking them off on her fingers. 'The still-unidentified harasser. And the visiting professor from the US, Andrew Suvarov, who's been confidentially named as the victim's father.'

'What about her work? Anything there?'

'No. For one thing: who'd try to kill a loss adjuster, even if they didn't get the insurance payout they'd expected? For another: how would disappointed insurance claimants have known she'd be in her husband's studio? And why would they have done it there? I did check that out with the shrink when I was talking to her, and she said it was psychologically highly unlikely.'

'So the best prospect is still the husband?'

'Definitely. Although the father has been identified as the owner of the newly bought mobile phone from which the last text was made to the victim's BlackBerry, about half an hour before she left the office for the last time.'

'What's the significance of the text?'

'The victim's mother—'

'The judge.'

'Precisely. Mrs Mayford has insisted that Professor Suvarov did not know he was the victim's father and had never met her, which makes him trying to contact her suspicious.'

'What are you doing about it?'

'He's in the country with his sisters for Christmas, but he will be staying at the Heathrow Hilton on the night of the twenty-sixth, before catching an early flight back to Boston the following morning. I have an appointment to talk to him there at 7 p.m. on the twenty-sixth.'

'Why you, Caro? You're in charge; your responsibilities are managerial. It's members of your team who should be rushing about interviewing people.'

Caro blinked at his tone, then collected her thoughts at speed. 'In view of the sensitivity of the case, and the unlikeliness of Suvarov having anything to do with it, I thought I'd . . .'

'Ah, I see. Kid gloves. Not a bad idea.'

'That's right, sir. Mrs Justice Mayford has asked me to be particularly discreet and there's no reason – no evidence – to override that yet. It's possible some of the hairs and fibres we've found in the studio belong to Suvarov, but we're still waiting for results from the lab. They're taking even longer than usual because they're short of staff in the run-up to sodding Christmas. We can't get much further till we've got the results. And we certainly can't keep Suvarov from flying home.'

'Could he be the owner of the gloved smudges on the hammer?'

'He could. But there's no way the scientists will ever be able to prove that unless we can get hold of the gloves and match the oil traces we think were left by the leather. And we won't. Those gloves will have been destroyed long ago.'

'Pity,' he said again. She still didn't know why he was here. There was nothing he'd asked that hadn't already been included in all her reports. 'Where are you with the husband?'

'He's stopped cooperating, but the original statements he gave us contradict the evidence we've got from the CCTV outside the studio building. Those show he left at 11.20 a.m., returned at 11.23 and did not emerge through that door again until he left with the ambulance at 1.10, giving more than enough time to quarrel with the deceased, who was logged on the CCTV as arriving at 11.45.'

'Any other exits from the building?'

'There's a basement back door without CCTV coverage. We have no evidence to show he used it, but he must have if it's true he went to see the barrister, Trish Maguire, in the Temple. We just don't know when.'

'What does Maguire say?'

'She has confirmed he was there that morning; so has the head clerk at her chambers. But she won't say what Foundling wanted. And neither of them can give precise times for his arrival or departure, which is why the whole thing looks like an attempt to muddle the evidence and so establish an alibi.'

'Who else have you identified from the CCTV?'

'Not everyone. There's a lot of coming and going. We've put names to several of the other tenants of the building, but not all. It's not a particularly high-grade system, and there are quite a few people whose faces are simply not clear enough on the film, even with the enhancement technology. Some were looking away from the camera; others moving too fast; others had hoods or scarves that make it hard to see their features clearly. It was a cold day.' Caro tried a smile, but it didn't arouse an answering one.

The chief superintendent looked like any employer of a new manager, hoping for signs of success but wary of failure.

'We recognized Sam Foundling,' Caro went on in a more formal tone of voice, 'because he wasn't wearing any kind of hat or scarf and he has a distinctive build and gait. His wife's pregnancy makes her easy to spot too.'

He took a small leather-backed notepad out of his pocket and reached for one of the pens on her desk to make a note, adding without looking up: 'Is there anything you need from me?'

'What happens if I go over budget, sir? I've still got Foundling under surveillance, and it's costing . . .'

'That's less important than you may have been led to believe at the start of this enquiry.'

Caro's surprise sent her head jerking up. She'd never heard anything like this.

'Why?'

'Word has come down from on high that it's essential to get a result on this one.' The chief superintendent looked over Caro's head. His chin was tilted so far up that the usually slack skin of his neck was stretched tight. His continuing refusal to meet her gaze suggested either shame or suppressed fury. Knowing what she did of his record, she thought she'd go for fury any time.

'She's a popular woman, the judge,' he went on, still looking at something way up the wall. 'It's been decided that a satisfactory outcome to the enquiry into her daughter's murder could go some way to mending our rift with the judiciary.'

The formal phraseology and sluggish delivery were enough to tell Caro her analysis of his temper was correct.

'After the Assistant Commissioner's unfortunate public reaction to the Lord Chief Justice's attack on our ability to solve crime, we are thought to need some of the judges back on our side.' He lowered his chin so for a moment their eyes were on a level again. At last he looked more human. 'Don't let me down. It's not just your career that depends on this one now.'

'I am doing my best, sir.'

'Good. I wish we'd known who the victim was when I gave you the case. I assumed it was a straightforward domestic.'

Caro swallowed rage at the insult.

'I've been asked more than once whether I'm happy keeping such an inexperienced SIO in charge.' He hesitated, now staring at her as though he expected her to cringe or crumple. She stood her ground and kept her eyes steady. 'I've backed you so far, but I'll need something to give them soon.'

'Thank you, sir. One relief is the lack of press interest. I'd expected with such a high-profile group of people we'd have them on our tails from Day One.'

A short sharp laugh made her wonder what she'd missed.

'That too will be because of the saintly Mrs Mayford. I'd lay a sizeable sum on her being best mates with the most important editors, or at least someone influential at the Press Council. But it's a two-edged benefit.'

Caro raised her eyebrows at the weird metaphor.

'Although it may be keeping the dogs off you,' he said with the air of a man deigning to explain the obvious, 'it also means less pressure on the husband. You might have had more luck getting him to talk if he'd been all over the pages as the prime suspect.'

Caro waited. She was sure there was more to come.

'And it wouldn't be *sub judice* because we haven't charged him yet.'

Chapter 10

Christmas lunch had taken more than two hours so far. Trish, who felt as though she would have to sit very still for a long time to allow her body to deal with the quantity and richness of the food she'd eaten, looked down the long table to where George sat and raised her glass to him. The whole feast had been his triumph, a miracle of cookery, timing and generosity. No one had wept or shouted, or been sick; the brandy poured over the pudding had burned with blue and orange flames for longer than Trish had ever seen; and David's face was still bright with excitement as he chattered to his big blonde Australian Aunt Susie.

Sam was sitting next to Trish's mother and seemed to be confiding in her. Trish read interest in her mother's expression and concern in the way she was leaning towards him. As tall as Trish and even thinner these days, Meg looked as though the slightest push could knock her over, but she had more guts than anyone Trish had ever known; and more instinctive sympathy for anyone in trouble.

There were those who said Trish had an uncanny knack of getting people to talk, but with her it was a matter of asking the right questions and interpreting often unspoken aspects of the answers to get at the truth. Meg was different: she had only to enter a room for the most troubled people in it to come and tell her the story of their lives. Whatever talent Trish had was undoubtedly part of her genetic inheritance from her mother, to counteract, she sometimes thought, the tendency to fury and other even less appealing traits she had inherited from her father.

It was lucky, she decided as she let ideas meander without direction or censorship, that his current girlfriend had grown-up children from her first marriage and that they were happy to include him in their Christmas plans.

'One tradition in my family,' George announced, breaking into her musing, 'is to make a toast at this point in the festivities.'

David's cousins exchanged mocking glances at the prospect of yet another strange English custom, while Susie frowned them down. Sam looked away from Meg for a second, his eyes flickering in Trish's direction. From her side of the table, his expression looked odd. There was a faint smile on his lips, but his eyes were bleak. Trish couldn't work out what the funny little smile meant and hoped it held some pleasure, or at least amusement, rather than pure bitterness.

'Absent friends,' George said, raising his glass. Everyone else followed suit, even Sam after a tiny hesitation, the children making their toast in soft drinks.

'That was nice, George,' Meg said, pushing back her chair. Perhaps she'd had enough of Sam's confidences. She definitely didn't look happy. 'A good tradition. You've worked so hard you ought to let some of us clear now.'

'We don't do the washing-up yet,' he said, sharing smiles with his mother before blowing a kiss to Trish. He looked comfortable and serene and quite unlike the worried butt of office politics. 'The light's already going, so if we're to have our walk, we need to go now. The dishes can wait.'

'Walk?' said Susie. 'After all that food? I'm only good for lying down now.'

'You must walk.' George was definite. 'Otherwise you won't sleep tonight. We needn't go far. I thought we could stroll along the south bank to the Millennium Bridge, cross the river there, carry on down Queen Victoria Street, back over Blackfriar's Bridge and so home. Just to get some air and see London as the daylight goes completely and the lights make the sky look dark blue. You'll like it, I promise. Come on.'

Groaning, laughing, they all pushed themselves up from the table, littered now with tangerine peel, broken crackers, nutshells and chocolate papers, and found their coats and scarves. The weather had done them proud, avoiding the snow that always turned into dirty slush in London but providing a crisp frost that made the air feel like champagne as it prickled against their skin. George hung back to hug Trish.

'Was that all right?' he said.

'It was amazing. Everybody loved it. I've never seen nine people smile so much. I just hope no one collapses in the cold.'

'They won't. D'you want to go ahead, while I give the mothers an arm each?'

Trish wriggled through the small crowd, fished her keys from the bowl by the front door, nodded to Sam, who was waiting there, and pulled it open.

Cameras flashed in her eyes, making her fall back and grab the door. Sam put a protective arm around her shoulders and steadied her.

'What the—'

'Sam Foundling? How does it feel to know the police aren't looking for any other suspects in your wife's murder?' shouted one coarse voice.

'Sam, this way!'

'Is it true your alibi's bust?'

'What would you say to—'

Trish got the door shut and unbuttoned her coat. Fury that their perfect day was spoiled churned in her gut with dread of what the others might say or do. Very conscious of Sam at her side, she turned first to George's mother.

'I'm really sorry, Selina. If I'd had any idea this might happen, I would never have staged Christmas here. Are you all right?'

'Yes,' she said, but she looked shaken. With an obvious effort, she added: 'I'm sure it's not your fault, Trish. And we have been having a lovely day.'

George took her arm to steady her, leaving Trish to make more apologies to Meg and the others. She could see Susie wanting to ask questions and knew she couldn't answer honestly with the children listening.

'I don't think we should all walk,' she said quickly to forestall them. 'It's too provocative. George, would you like to take the family out, while I'll make a cup of tea for Sam?'

'Sure.' His eyes looked worried in spite of the wide smile that pinned back his lips. 'I'll go out first. Meg, will you bring up the rear?'

Trish watched her mother nod, then look at her with questioning eyes.

'Unless Trish and Sam want company?' she said.

'We'll be fine,' Trish said, trying to put all the necessary reassurance into her voice. 'You'll have the toughest time getting through them, but when they see Sam's not with you, they should let you pass. And you can always remind them they're trespassing on my stairs.'

'They'll only retreat to the street,' George said, before turning to Susie to offer his free arm. 'You know they're unlikely to get bored and go away.'

'I know,' Trish said. 'But I'll do what I can to take down the tension by making tea for them too. They must have been out there for hours and will probably be freezing.'

She hoped George would be able to explain what was happening in a way the others would forgive. She had considered warning them about Sam, knowing news of the murder was most unlikely to have reached the Australian press, but decided it would be easier for everyone if they came to him without preconceptions. The risk of someone's saying something hurtful was less than the likelihood of stiffness and embarrassment if they were circling round the subject no one must mention. The door clicked behind them all.

'Bastards!'

At the sound of Sam's explosive voice, she turned to see him standing only a couple of feet away, his fists balled at his sides and his face reddening.

'How the *fuck* am I supposed to cope if everywhere I go people accuse me of killing her? And how the *fuck* did they know I was here? Your *fucking* friend the chief inspector, I suppose.'

There was no answer, so Trish went silently into her narrow kitchen to make tea. She had to guess the number of photographers and journalists outside and took ten mugs down from their shelf. There were plenty of mince pies left; they might help too. She filled two plates and waited for the kettle to boil.

'Sam,' she called over her shoulder in a gentle voice designed to take some of the tension out of the atmosphere. 'I think the best thing to do now is for each of us to take out a tray of tea and mince pies and offer them round. When you get to the end of the line, you can either give me the empty tray or dump it on the ground and simply walk through them. Okay? That way, their hands are going to be occupied with hot mugs, so they're unlikely to take any more photographs as you go.'

'They've already got plenty of shots. And if anything I felt shows in my face they'll be corkers.'

Trish understood, but she felt a stirring of impatience too. She was doing her best to help. If he chose not to cooperate, he was going to make things worse for himself with the press.

'Sorry,' he said abruptly. 'Your mother-in-law's right: it's not your fault. But the way people see me now matters.'

'Of course it does, Sam, but . . .'

'Because of the baby. I'm not stupid; I know they're keeping her in hospital longer than they need. I know how close I am to losing her for good. I can't be shown up as a violent thug in the papers as well as the minds of the police and my mother-in-law or I'll never be allowed to have her home.'

Trish knew it too. There was no comfort to offer and she wasn't going to pretend.

'Which is sodding ironic given how hard I tried to persuade Ceel to wait before we tried to get pregnant.' He looked away, but the tightness of his shoulders and the way he'd curved his back to protect himself were eloquent enough. At last he faced Trish again. She flinched from the pain in his eyes.

'She wanted children, you see, but I didn't think we were ready. I didn't think *I* was ready. She said I needn't worry, that with her history, and being so far past the peak of fertility, it would take years before she got pregnant. But it happened more or less straight away. And we were stuck with it. At least that's how it seemed then.'

'Her history? What history?'

'Oh. Well. You know. She'd been on the pill for years.' Sam wasn't looking at her. 'Your water's boiling over.'

The over-full kettle was pouring out so much steam its lid was wobbling. Trish made the tea.

'Are you up for another sortie, Sam? There's too much for me to carry out on my own.'

'I suppose so. If I'm holding a tray, I can't hit any of them.'

'That *would* be a mistake,' Trish said, trying for a light-hearted tone. 'So, here we are. You take this one and I'll follow with the other. Have you got your keys?'

He nodded, gripped the tray and strode to the door. Trish followed, wishing, as she'd often wished before, that misery didn't make some people aggressive.

More camera flashes and shouted questions greeted them as Sam stepped out. But the mood changed with comic speed as the enemy saw they were to be fed. Hands reached out for George's overflowing pies and the hot mugs.

'You must be freezing,' Trish said with her biggest smile. 'How long have you all been out here?'

'Hours,' said one man with a camera hanging around his neck. Crumbs of rich pastry flew out of his mouth. 'There's been no other news this Christmas. Not so far anyway.'

She watched the dirty looks his colleagues directed his way. Sam quietly walked down the iron staircase, propping his tray at the bottom and was away down the street before they noticed. A few of the photographers took shots of his back view then.

'Just leave the mugs on the step when you're done,' Trish said, turning to go back inside.

'How will the judge feel next time you're in front of her,' said one quiet female voice, 'knowing how much support you're giving to the man who killed her daughter?'

Trish looked at the woman. She was young and fair, as unlike the accepted image of a reptilian hack as possible. But that didn't make her question any less dangerous. Trish took a moment to plan her answer.

'First, Mrs Justice Mayford would never allow any personal consideration whatsoever to affect her in court. Second, there is nothing to suggest Sam Foundling had any part in what happened to his wife. It's outrageous to talk as though he could be guilty.'

Without waiting for a reaction or any more questions, Trish went back inside, hoping she hadn't said all the wrong things. Like most other barristers who'd conducted big cases in the London courts, she had often been filmed by television news cameras as she'd emerged on the steps with her clients. But she'd never been interviewed or had to justify any of her actions to the press. It was nearly always the solicitors who read out clients' statements.

Still troubled, she surveyed the wreck of George's triumph and was glad to know this was one mess she would be able to clear up. Housework could be remarkably soothing, especially when it involved hot water. As soon as she'd loaded the crockery into the dishwasher and set it going, she filled the sink, added a slug of detergent and set about the glasses, glad to know a pile of silver waited for when they were done, and greasy pans after that.

Through her own clattering and splashing, she heard the journalists clomping down her iron staircase to the street. Car doors banged and engines revved. It could have been a decoy departure, but with Sam gone there wouldn't be much point in their staying. George and the others should have a free passage when they returned.

Much later, when the Australian party had gone back to their hotel, David was getting ready for bed and George was desultorily chatting to his mother on the sofa, Meg asked to have another look at the latest painting Trish had hung in her bedroom. Together they climbed the spiral staircase. At the top, Meg ignored the new canvas, plumping down instead in the spoon-backed chair in the corner.

Trish recognized the signs and obediently stretched herself out on the big bed, piling George's pillows on top of her own so that she was still semi-upright.

'What?' she asked, watching the serious expression on Meg's lined face.

'You obviously like Sam,' she said slowly, 'and I can see why. He's very appealing.'

'But?'

'I think there's more to him than he shows.' Meg brushed her thin cheek with one hand in a troubled gesture long familiar to Trish. 'He was telling me how guilty he feels.'

'About what?' Trish felt cold in spite of the efficient radiator coils in the corners of the room. She tried not to recognize her own fear.

Meg looked as though she knew exactly what was going on in Trish's head. 'His actual words were, "about so much to do with my wife".'

'Did he tell you he'd killed her?' Prayer didn't form part of

Trish's life, but if it had, now would have been the time to give it her all.

'Not in so many words. The guilt he was actually admitting was about not being in the studio to protect her when she was attacked.'

Trish felt her neck muscles let go and she lay more comfortably against the pillows. But Meg hadn't finished.

'What's worse, he said, is knowing how his jealousy of her past lovers stopped her talking about any of the other men she had to deal with at work. He's afraid that's why she never said anything to him about the bloke her colleagues say was harassing her.'

'I can see how a man who'd been abandoned as a baby would hate the idea of other men. Can't you? At some level, he must always have been afraid one of them would pop up again and make her abandon him all over again.'

'He thinks if he'd been able to listen to her stories of old boyfriends,' Meg said, paying no attention to Trish's speculations, 'she might have told him something the police could use to identify the harasser. Sam's convinced himself the same man killed her.'

'Why are you sounding so doubtful? Isn't it the likeliest possibility?'

'I don't think so.'

There was so much pity in Meg's voice that Trish shivered again and pulled George's half of the duvet over herself so that she felt like a silkworm in its cocoon.

'We had a man in the surgery once who told us his wife had been beating him up,' Meg said, still in the kind, regretful voice. 'He came again and again, always with injuries. We were all worried, I mean the receptionists as much as the doctors, and we persuaded him to go to the police to report his wife. Eventually they set up video surveillance and what that showed shocked us all.'

'How did you come to see police videos?'

Meg's face crumpled a little. 'It was the only way they could persuade us to believe what they'd seen. Every time the man was
injured, the fight had started with him hitting his wife. She was
just hitting back, Trish, trying to defend herself. The reason he'd
convinced us he was her victim is that he'd convinced himself first.
He wasn't consciously lying. He genuinely believed it was her
aggression not his own that led to the injuries.'

Trish nodded without speaking. This wasn't an alien concept,
but she didn't want to get into a conversation about spousal abuse
with her mother. She'd only witnessed one occasion on which her
father had hit Meg, but she was sure there had been others. Even
now, more than thirty years later, Trish found it impossible to deal
with the mixture of rage, pity, helplessness, and guilt for not
having stopped it.

'There's no need to look so tragic,' Meg said. 'Just remember
that things are very rarely as simple as you'd like them to be. What
does your mate Caro think about this Sam?'

'She's the senior officer in charge of the investigation and she's
sure he's guilty. We're not speaking at the moment.'

'She's got good judgement. And unlike either of us she'll have
seen all the evidence.' Meg looked kinder than ever as she added:
'Don't let him break your heart, Trish.'

At the end of Boxing Day Caro drove into the car park at the
Heathrow Hilton with fifteen minutes to spare. She took her
portable tape recorder from the glove box and slipped it into her
bag, adjusted the driving mirror so she could check her appearance, and tucked a few stray hairs behind her ear.

It shouldn't be too hard, she thought as she walked across the
car park, taking care not to slip in the icy puddles. Just a matter
of establishing his movements on the day his daughter died and
making sure I have contact details in case we need more from
him.

If there hadn't been the problem of the influential Mrs Mayford

and her secret past, Caro could have sent a couple of junior officers to get the information and saved herself the journey.

A tall, slim man was waiting in one of the few chairs in the
reception area. He looked at her over the top of his newspaper,
assessed her and then nodded.

'Chief Inspector Lyalt?' he said in a quiet American accent.

'Yes.'

He pulled himself out of the chair and came towards her with
a devastating smile on his face.

'Shall we talk here or would you rather come up to my room?'

'Here's fine by me, if you don't mind.'

'Not at all. I've only just managed to get rid of Gina, who drove
me back from my sister's in Dorset. She showed signs of wanting
to stay – presumably to defend me from interrogation – but I told
her I could manage.'

'It may be that or it may be that she was afraid I might . . .
shock you.'

'You couldn't, Chief Inspector. And that's why I wanted to be rid
of her. I've known for thirty-four years Cecilia was my daughter.'

Talk about shock, Caro thought, angry that Mrs Mayford
should have had to fight all the battles of a single mother while
this man turned himself into a world expert on international relations. What about personal ones?

'Now I've shocked you,' he said. 'But it's not as simple as it
looks. At some level Gina must know I know. I'm no mathematician, but I can count. I was already in the States when I heard
about the baby from one of my sisters. I wrote and proposed right
away, without mentioning Cecilia because I didn't want Gina to
think I was offering to be the sacrificial victim of a shotgun wedding. She said no. So here we are.'

Why is he telling me this? Caro wondered. Do I need to hear
his excuse?

'Does all this mean you did see your daughter that last morning?' she said aloud, quickly trying to reorganize her mind to avoid

hurting him now she knew he knew who Cecilia was. 'And do you mind if I record this interview?'

'Go right ahead. The one thing I have to hold on to is that I did have an hour with her. If I'd known I'd never see her again, I—' He broke off, looked away, then fiddled about tidying the newspaper.

At last he coughed and looked back at Caro, before saying clearly, almost as though he was dictating to his students: 'You'll want to know my movements that day, Chief Inspector. I picked up a cheap pay-as-you-go phone when I arrived at Waterloo, as I always do when I come here – it's more economical than using my US phone account – and texted her BlackBerry to find out if she could see me in her office before I caught the train to York.'

'And did she?'

'She texted right back to suggest we meet by the ice rink at Somerset House. I thought it could be risky with Gina at work on the opposite side of the road, but Cecilia assured me she'd be stuck in court. So I walked over the bridge from Waterloo. Cecilia walked up the Strand from her office. And we had a cup of coffee together.'

'What did you talk about?'

'Nothing much. How she was. What sex the baby was. How she felt about becoming a mother. How I thought we should maybe tell Gina we knew each other.' He closed his eyes momentarily, then opened them to offer the same dazzling smile. Only now could Caro see the sadness behind the glitter. 'It was something we nearly always did talk about and we always came to the same conclusion. We'd left it too late. And that was my fault.'

'Hard to pick a moment for something so emotional,' Caro said, managing to find a little sympathy for him.

'I know. Think of the hurt of being told by your only child that she's been lying to you all her adult life. But now . . .'

'And yet they were so close.'

'In everything except this. There are a lot of things I regret, but this . . .' Again he hesitated. 'This situation is one of the worst. And now I can never put it right. When I think of the waste of it all, the time the three of us could have had, I . . . It's too much. I can't deal with it yet.'

'I'm sorry. And I'm sorry to press you, but I need to know everything that happened that morning. When did you part from Cecilia? Can you remember?'

'Sure. My train for York left King's Cross at twelve o'clock. I walked out of Somerset House at 11.15, as I'd planned all along, and took the Tube, the Piccadilly Line, to King's Cross. You know, I could have told you all this over the phone.'

'Is there someone in York who could . . .'

'Establish my alibi? Sure. I was met at the station by the woman who organized the seminar. Here.' He pulled a pile of old envelopes out of his jacket pocket, tore the back off one and scribbled a name on it, before consulting his diary and adding a couple of phone numbers. He looked up at Caro. 'You'd better have my phone numbers in the States too. There may be more questions later.'

'Thank you.'

As he handed over the grubby piece of paper, he said: 'You won't tell Gina, will you? You don't seem malicious.'

'I'm not,' Caro said. 'But I have learned that nothing good ever comes from secrets. If I were you, I'd tell her myself and try to make her see that you and your daughter only wanted to protect her all these years. I must go. Thank you for being so frank.'

'Selfish bastard,' she muttered as she reached the chilly car park again. Protecting Mrs Mayford indeed! Protecting his own chance of a big career in the States, more likely.

It was convenient for him that there were no living witnesses to the fact he'd always known he was the victim's father. Still, there was CCTV at Somerset House and it would be better than the system outside Foundling's studio. It should have logged his departure and it would tell her precisely when he and Cecilia left the place.

It wasn't until Caro had bleeped up the locks of her car that she thought of a question she hadn't asked.

Back in the hotel, she found no sign of him in the foyer. But the receptionist recognized her and directed her to the bar. There she found Professor Suvarov drinking Stella from the bottle.

'Hi. Thought of something else, Chief Inspector?'

'Did she talk to you about her marriage?'

'Not a lot. It was clearly tough, but I'd say she genuinely loved the guy in spite of that, which is what makes this so . . . so unbearable.'

'So you think he did it?'

'It's the obvious answer, isn't it?' He sounded sad. 'I never met Sam, but I know she was afraid of what happened when he was angry. She once saw him smash the phone to pieces in front of their friends merely because a call-centre salesman phoned and interrupted them at dinner. By all accounts, he's a violent man, who deals with his feelings by hitting out.'

'What about the man who was harassing her at work?' Caro said. 'Did she say anything about him?'

He shook his head.

'Then what about Dennis Flack? Did she ever mention him to you?'

'Nope. Who's he?'

'Her immediate boss at work.'

'Never heard of him. The only thing she said was bothering her, apart from how tough it was dealing with Sam's problems, was that she'd become spooked by coincidence. But that was only because I told her the name of the woman organizing the York seminar, and it turned out Cecilia had known her at university. Not in the same league as his violence.'

'Thanks. Sorry to disturb your drink.'

'Not at all,' he said, sounding more and more English. 'Can I buy you one?'

Caro shook her head, thanked him again, and headed back to

the car. She tried to make the coincidence mean something but couldn't. Even Trish would have to admit there was no way a lecturer from York University could have a bearing on Cecilia's murder, however well they'd known each other as students. All she'd got from Suvarov was more support for her own suspicion of Sam and absolutely none of the evidence she needed to do anything with it.

The newspaper that flopped onto the doormat on Boxing Day was pitifully thin. The lack of weight mattered not at all to Trish, once she'd seen there was nothing in it about Sam. She embarked on her round of treats for David with more zest than she'd dared contemplate.

While George drove his mother back to her Suffolk house on Monday, Trish took David to a dry ski slope she knew to practise for their half-term trip to the French Alps. He was in fine form, unhampered by the immense amounts of food he'd consumed over the last few days and apparently no longer fazed by the thought of meeting some of his distant relations, who had treated his mother so badly. But his confidence leached away over the next twenty-four hours and on Wednesday morning his face had a pallor and tension that took Trish back to his first weeks in her flat.

'Got your mobile?' she said with a breeziness she didn't feel. 'I'll have mine switched on wherever I am, so you can always . . .'

'I'll phone if I need to,' he said, then clamped his lips together. It would have been cruel to make him say any more or probe for exactly which ingredients made up his particular fear. He forced a smile that didn't reach his eyes. 'Look after yourself, Trish.'

'You too.' She looked over his head and met Susie's sympathetic blue eyes.

'We'll have a great time, Trish.' She pushed her chunky gold bangles up her smooth, tanned arm. 'There are so many things I want to see and places to go. We've got Stratford and all the

Shakespeare stuff first, then Warwick Castle. We'll have fun, and we'll see you in a fortnight.'

'Thanks, Susie,' Trish said and kissed her.

Watching them drive off in the hired car left Trish feeling surprisingly deflated. In the mad rush to get everything done before Christmas, she'd looked forward to having time to herself with David away and George already back at work. Now she wondered what she'd expected to do with all the free hours.

London was still and cold, and apparently empty except for a few gulls shrieking on the river, and the usual scavenging pigeons. A big dog fox sauntered down the road towards her, looking far cockier than he should and sleekly plump from raids on well-filled dustbins. Trish had never seen a fox out in the open like this in broad daylight. They usually confined their excursions to what passed for darkness in the city. He walked so close his pungent smell filled the air between them.

A mile or so away in Oxford Street, she knew there would be crowds of shoppers, hoping to take advantage of huge reductions in the sales. Some of her friends were probably available too, although the best of them, Caro, had barricaded herself behind her certainty of Sam's guilt. There was still clearing up to do in the flat and plenty to read. Trish could write her thank-you letters, or even see how Sam was.

None of it appealed, and the empty spaces of the flat she'd only just left felt threatening in a way she'd never known. Chambers was probably the best place to be. There might be some company to be found there, refugees from too much family, just as she was trying to escape too little. And she could always work. She'd never known a time in the last eighteen years when there'd been nothing to do in preparation for one case or another. In fact this would be the perfect moment to have another crack at the engineering principles behind the erection of revolutionary buildings on slippery London clay.

Turning east, she walked along the Embankment towards the

Temple. It was impossible to forget everything Meg had said or to ignore everything she hadn't said. Last night, waking in the early hours, Trish had been aware of the answer to a question that had been nagging at the back of her mind: why had the wife-beating man Meg had described gone to the surgery in the first place?

Somewhere in his subconscious he must have known he was guilty. Unable to bear the knowledge, he'd invented the story of his wife as aggressor. When it had stopped convincing him, he'd taken it to an independent audience, pretending to ask for help. The same hidden intelligence must have known the doctors would uncover the truth. Which had to mean he'd wanted to be found out.

Had Sam's description of his own jealousy been the same kind of coded confession?

'Lovely day, innit?'

The cockney voice made Trish's head flick up. She was surprised to see the newspaper seller at his usual stand on the corner of Arundel Street. He couldn't have much custom on a day like this. No wonder he'd wanted to tell her he was there. She smiled and put a hand in her pocket for change, only to see her own face glaring at her from the *Daily Mercury*. The newspaper man didn't seem to have recognized her, but she hurried through her purchase of all the papers she hadn't already read in case he noticed the likeness. He tried to keep her by asking if she'd had a good Christmas, but she said it was too cold to stay and chat. She wished him well and tucked the bundle of newsprint under her arm.

Chambers was still double-locked and the alarm beeped its warning as soon as she pushed the door open. Once she'd punched in the disabling code, she shook out the *Mercury*, keeping the rest of the papers jammed between her left elbow and her ribs, and turned on the passage light with her right shoulder.

The front page had two photographs side by side. One was of Gina Mayford, looking distraught; the other, of Trish, glaring over Sam Foundling's shoulder. His face showed nothing but shock, while hers was a mask of undiluted rage. She'd rarely seen any picture for which the term harpy was better suited. The headline made her tighten her hands so hard that one fingernail broke right through the page.

Barrister and Judge at War over Murder Suspect

But we're not, she thought, walking into her room and sinking into the chair behind her desk. All I said was that Mrs Mayford was far too professional to let any personal consideration affect her in any way whatsoever. How *could* they print this?

She let the other papers drop and read every word of the article below the photograph. There was hardly anything in it about Sam, beyond the fact that his late wife was the daughter of Mrs Justice Mayford and the police had him on their list of suspects. The editor's legal advisers had clearly filleted the piece to remove any libellous allegations, but the impression given was that the *Mercury* agreed with the police. Not that there was anything odd in that. The editorial line had always been that the police were perfect and incorruptible and anyone they suspected must be scum.

Today the paper had also provided a potted history of Trish's career, including the time when she briefly came under suspicion in a case of child abduction and her later private involvement in a notorious case of a woman unjustly convicted of the murder of her father. Trish's domestic arrangements were described in the kind of detail that made them seem bizarre.

Once again she could see evidence of the lawyers' involvement. David wasn't mentioned by name, but there was a general reference to her fostering the child of a murder victim. Even worse was a trailer for a feature on 'The Passion for Justice' by the paper's tame psychiatrist. With a hollow feeling in her head, Trish turned the pages until she found it.

A frantic skimming sweep told her that her name didn't figure in the article, which allowed her to read it more calmly. The tone was cooler than usual in the *Daily Mercury* and the sentences considerably longer. She was mildly interested until she came upon the last two paragraphs.

> Ambulance-chasers are driven by profit, and ghoulish sightseers by an addiction to adrenaline thrill, but there are plenty of people whose altruistic involvement in the aftermath of violent crime is the product of childhood experiences. For some, the motivating factor is a sense of rage at injustice done to them. Their identification with anyone accused of crime is that of a fellow sufferer, determined to punish the parental accuser. For others, it is a sense of guilt, sometimes misplaced.
>
> Children who believe themselves to be the cause of parental unhappiness, or who witness violence at an age when they're powerless to intervene, are particularly prey to such feelings.

'How *dare* he?' Trish said aloud. Her jaw tightened and her teeth clamped against each other as though someone was trying to force-feed her. She was well used to journalistic conjecture, but this insinuation was too acute to take easily. She needed coffee.

Ten minutes later she was back at her desk with a covered cardboard cup holding four shots of espresso. She swallowed some. The caffeine hit at once and she let the pumping sensation in her head and heart banish everything else for a while. She could almost feel the drug pushing the walls of her arteries apart, opening them, making them work better and so feed her brain with all the blood it needed. Her thoughts moved faster. She felt more intelligent. More powerful. Then she caught sight of the headline again and took another gulp of coffee. This time she didn't get the same rush, and she was left with a whole lot of unanswerable questions.

Why was she of interest to any journalist? She'd assumed it was

Sam the pack had been after. But this malice was directed at her, merely hung on his story. Who had known he was to be with her for Christmas?

She tried to collect her scattered thoughts as she pushed the sleazy paper along the desk with one shaking finger. Gina had known about her Christmas plans, but she wouldn't have gone to the papers. George knew too, but he had never been leaky. And it couldn't have been Sam himself. Which left Caro.

Had she taken advantage of Trish's attempt to safeguard the shreds of their friendship with that one warning phone call? Had she told the press where her main suspect would be eating his turkey and plum pudding on Christmas Day? Did she think publicity would put so much pressure on Sam that he'd confess?

It was hard to believe. But then Caro's appearance in his studio on such a lame excuse had been pretty hard to believe, and that had definitely happened. So maybe this was down to her too.

Trish thought of David and how he might react to these articles at a time when he was already dealing with emotional problems no child of his age should have to face. With luck Susie and Phil wouldn't bother to buy British newspapers, but it was ludicrously over-optimistic to assume David would never know what had been written about his sister.

She stared down at the loathsome photograph of her scowling face and hated it.

Chapter 11

The first thing Antony Shelley said to Trish when he phoned later that day was, 'You must reschedule whatever it was you were supposed to be doing on Twelfth Night and come to my party after all.'

'I can't,' she said automatically. 'It's George's firm's annual do. I have to be there for the duration. Ordinarily it wouldn't matter if I left early, but there's stuff going on that makes him need support just now.'

'Whose career is more important?'

Trish hadn't heard Antony's voice as steely and precise for a long time. She couldn't answer.

'Come on. Be honest, Trish. Whatever you feel for him, you've got to look after yourself. If your practice is to survive, let alone thrive, you need to be seen to be untouched by all this publicity. Gina Mayford has promised to play, so you get yourself into your best frock and be on my doorstep no later than eight o'clock on the sixth of January. Is that understood?'

'Mrs Mayford?'

'Luckily she's on your side. I phoned her to ask for help and she was generous enough to agree at once. She's going to get the *Mercury* to print a retraction tomorrow, so you don't need to do anything about that, and she'll show everyone at the party how much she trusts you. You have more friends than you realize,

Trish, and you need to use them all now before any real damage is done.'

'I don't suppose she feels much like partying with her daughter's body stuck in the mortuary.'

'Of course not. But she's coming anyway. So the least you can do is tell George you can't be his arm candy for once.'

'It's kind of you – and her – but I'd rather fight my own battles.'

'Don't be silly. This isn't only yours. It's mine and the whole of chambers' too. What you do affects the rest of us. No excuses, Trish. Be here promptly on the sixth, stay until at least half the other guests have gone, and smile for God's sake. Gina and I will do the rest.'

'Okay,' she said with unexpected meekness. 'It's very kind of you both.'

'Yes, it is. I'm sticking my neck out for you. I hope you won't be so damn silly as to get yourself publicly involved with a murder suspect again. And particularly not at this time of year when the editors of the legal directories are scouting around for gossip on all of us for their nasty little paragraphs.'

He put down the phone, as though he had no interest in anything she might offer to excuse herself. Everything he said made sense. But it wasn't going to be fun explaining to George that she wanted to renege on her promise to help him face down the sharks in his office.

Unless she could at least put in an appearance at his party. He hadn't sent her a formal invitation and she'd never asked what time she was expected to appear. The party would go on half the night, of course; they always did. But if there were any chance that she could look in for an hour or so before fighting for her own future, she'd do it.

She picked up the phone to speak to George's secretary. Only when she'd had the assurance that the Henton, Maltravers party was due to start at seven did she ask to be put through to George himself. He listened without interrupting until she'd finished her explanation, then merely said how generous of Antony and Mrs Mayford to be so concerned to help.

'See you tonight,' he added in a brisk tone that told her he must have clients or colleagues in the room with him.

'Work,' she said into the empty room, when she'd put down the phone. 'It's the only thing.'

She pushed the pile of papers to one side and switched on the computer, opening the file of notes on the Leviathan case.

Sam heard the letter-box flap, which released him from the trap of staring at his clay head to try to see what was so wrong with it. He flung the damp cloths back over its ugly proportions and staring eyes and went to see what the postie had brought. There was only one letter. The writing on the envelope made even the thought of more work on the head alluring.

For a while he couldn't make himself bend to pick up the letter, then, cursing his own cowardice, he did, ripping the envelope open before thoughts of its author made him freeze again.

Deere Sam,

I di'nt know yore wife had been kiled. I'm sory. It must be terable for you. Speshly with the police thingink yore guilty. I hope yo'ur baby wil live.

No wander you dont' want to have the DNA. Do'nt worry now. You have to much too put up with. I unnerstand. I can wait.

With love from yore muther,

Maria-Teresa Jackson

PS The preest here sais God cees not what you are nor what you bin but what you want two bee. Remembre, son.

Sam shouted and punched the wall so hard he broke the skin over his knuckles. There was a heavy stamping from the floor above:

Marisa Heering wanted him to know how much she disliked the noise. Well sod her.

Sucking the blood from one of his knuckles to look at the wound, he saw it wasn't nearly bad enough. He stuffed the letter into his pocket with his other hand and sucked again.

How could the woman in prison do this to him? After all those years of longing for a mother, of needing someone to protect him from all the bastards around him, it was vile to be offered the kind of comfort he'd never had and didn't need. Not any more. He'd grown a skin tough enough to deal with anything, even Chief Inspector Caroline Lyalt.

For this woman to try to peel back the skin now was vicious. A continuation of the old cruelty. Like Cecilia's in the days when she'd tried to scrape away at everything he'd fought to build around himself for safety. She'd wanted to make him remember and talk about it, when all he'd needed was to forget.

He hated the thought of her probing. So why were his eyes damp all over again? He sagged as though someone else had punched him.

The sensation of more and more blows to come had him shrinking against the wall in a way he hadn't for years. The knowledge flayed away his rage to lay bare the whimpering boy he'd fought for so long, even harder than he'd fought his enemies. This time the boy was winning. His knees gave way and he cowered in the angle of wall and floor, pulling his knees up under his chin and lowering his head until he could hide his eyes against his knees.

Trish picked up the phone. She had to know whether Caro had sent the press. The only answer was the automatic voice of her message service.

'It's Trish. I need to talk about what happened at Christmas. Ring me when you can.'

She didn't have long to wait. There'd been time only to reread the original brief given to the Arrow's architects before her phone chimed out its familiar jingle.

'What did he tell you?' said Caro, sounding almost gleeful.

Trish kept the frown at bay with pure will power and tried to be as effective in controlling her voice.

'He didn't tell me anything. I wanted to ask you how the press knew he'd be with us.'

'Are you accusing me of selling you to the papers, Trish?'

Was the outrage in Caro's voice genuine? It was hard to tell. Trish needed more.

'No,' she said. 'I'm asking. I don't know how they got on to me, and I don't know why they wanted to. They distorted what I said, and I don't understand the agenda behind it. I'm of no interest to them. I thought you might be able to help.'

'Sorry. Nothing to do with me. If that's all, I've got to go.' There was no more outrage in Caro's voice; only coldness. 'I thought you were going to pass on some information I could use.'

'I haven't got any. Caro—'

'Pity. See you.'

Sam had picked himself up, aware of pains in every joint. He staggered over to the sink to hold his face under the cold tap. He let the water run until it felt icy, making his skin contract and, with luck, removing all the evidence of his snivelling collapse.

It had been mad to let himself look back to the dead years. Nothing good could come of that – just as he'd said to one of the shrinks years ago – only more anger. The one way to make any kind of decent life, especially now he had the baby, was to go forward. Draw a line and go on. With enough grit, he could do it.

Water had splashed all over the sink and draining board, as well as down the front of his jersey. He stripped it off and found a spare in the dwindling pile of clothes he kept here. He'd have to get more from Islington soon, even though he hated the prospect of facing Cecilia's space, the house she'd bought and decorated long before she knew him, where he'd always felt like an interloper.

Pushing away the thought, he made a mug of strong tea to help force himself to reread Maria-Teresa's letter.

Go forward, he thought. Trish is right: there's no obligation here, even if this woman is who she says she is.

But memories of longing and isolation told him he had to answer the letter. He couldn't leave her waiting for an answer she would never get. He grabbed the big sketching pad and tore off a sheet. Trying to think how to say what had to be said, he made a start, then swore and ripped up the paper. Maybe he'd have to do it face to face. He tore off another sheet and quickly wrote to ask if he could visit her. He would go and explain why he wouldn't take a DNA test. That way, surely he would have done enough and it would be over. There were stamps in a little brass box somewhere on his drawing table. He found it, stuck one on and went to post the letter before he changed his mind. He could go on to the hospital after that.

Trish felt her steps dragging as she took her favourite walk across the bridge. George should be waiting in her flat, both of them released from family obligations. She'd looked forward to these two weeks for so long it seemed cruel to have had them spoiled before they'd even begun. The views up and down the river didn't give her the usual lift, so there was no reason to hang about in the cold.

From the top of the iron staircase that led from the street to her front door, she could smell the familiar scent of onions stewing in olive oil. George must already be home.

Be cheerful, she ordered herself as she brought a wide smile to her lips and squared her shoulders. The key turned easily in the oiled lock and she pushed open the door, calling his name. He emerged from the kitchen, familiar in the butcher's apron tied around his waist. Such was the transformation of his figure that the tapes now went twice round and could be tied in the front, like a professional chef's.

He held out an arm without speaking. She leaned against him and felt the arm come round her shoulders. His lips brushed her hair.

'We'll get through it,' he said. 'And Antony's right. You need to show yourself as untouchable in the right circles.'

She pulled back to look into his face. He was only a few inches taller so she didn't have to lean far back. There was no tooth-gritting determination in his expression or suppressed rage. He really meant it. They had become a unit, facing the world and each other's enemies together. Recognizing the security made for a strange sensation. Trish was trying to find words to say why it meant so much when his arm was hastily withdrawn.

'Shit,' he said with uncharacteristic fervour. 'The sodding onions!'

Now she could smell it too, the bitterness of burned sugar. She followed him into the kitchen to see her most cherished pan, one he himself had given her, with a thick charcoal coating. He wrapped a cloth around his hand and picked up the pan to hold it under the running cold tap.

'That makes it smell even worse,' she said. 'Shall we eat out?'

'I think we'd better. What would you like?'

She ran through the mental list of their favourite restaurants and didn't find any one that seemed right for tonight. Besides, there might be other people there, people who would recognize her and George and might have read the papers.

'Or shall we make toasted sandwiches like David's and eat them in bed?' she said at last.

He took her face between his oniony hands and kissed her. 'Sounds perfect to me. Except for the bed bit.'

She stiffened.

'Let's keep that crumb-free,' he said, stroking her cheek with one finger. 'I'll do the sandwiches while you open the bottle and tell me about your day.'

With the conflict of interest over the Leviathan case, she could not talk about her work, only about Sam and the journalists' malicious interpretation of her interest in him.

'Am I *so* neurotic?' she asked.

George put back his head and produced the biggest gale of laughter she'd heard for a long time.

'Of course you are, my only love. But you know that.'

'I suppose so.'

'Come on, Trish: don't sound so tragic. We're all bonkers in one way or another. You know that too. It's just that some people's oddities are nearer the surface than others'. For what it's worth, I don't think any of the suggestions in the shrink's piece apply to you.'

'You read it.' She didn't know whether she was more relieved or revolted.

'I read it. As you know, I loathe the *Mercury*, but once I knew our mini-ratpack had it in for you I wanted to know everything they were saying. I tried to think of a way you could sue, but there isn't one. It was a neatly judged operation.'

He poured some claret into a large glass and handed it to her.

'I thought so too. D'you suppose that's the last of it, or should I get an injunction to stop them printing anything more specific about David?'

'I doubt if they'd risk it, and taking any legal action, even just getting an injunction, would intrigue them and could make them look more closely at us. Have you talked to him today?'

'I phoned just before I left chambers. He sounded fine, much better than when he went off this morning. He didn't mention anything about the papers to me.'

'Nor to me, which suggests he hasn't seen anything. Let's wait and see. Better than wading in with things we may regret. Now, am I going to be allowed to come to Antony's Twelfth Night party with you?'

'Could you? I mean, don't you have to stay at your own?'

'Don't see why. I'm not senior partner any more. So long as I'm seen to be there it ought to be enough.'

He'd started slicing bread and cheese so she couldn't see his face, but he sounded as though he meant it. She moved sideways until they were in contact again. He shot a quick glance in her direction. 'What?'

'I just wondered where you'd got to in your fight with Malcolm Jensen. I know I shouldn't ask, but I need to know. I'd like . . .' What she wanted was to do for him what he'd just done for her.

Putting down the bread knife, he held her for a second. 'I followed counsel's advice by telling the bastards I was going to fight,' he said, making her smile, 'but that wanker Jensen has been fighting back. There's to be a final decision at the partners' meeting on January the eleventh. Then we'll know.'

'Only five days after the party,' Trish said. 'I'm really sorry this mess in the *Mercury* has come out just when you need me to look faultless and incorruptible.'

He finished laying the last slice of cheese on the bottom slices of bread, added the top ones and slid the sandwiches into the toaster.

'I'm sure there's a comforting comment I could make, but let's not bother. We both know what we're facing. No point saying any more about it until after the partners' meeting. Let's take our comfort from unhealthy food and concentrate on getting through this with the least possible fallout for both of us.'

'You have got guts,' she said, fighting her own urge to produce the kind of verbal solace that wouldn't change anything.

Later, when they were eating the last drips of molten cheese and making New Year's resolutions to avoid anything so delicious and artery-clogging for the next twelve months, he said: 'What was Cecilia Mayford like? I know you had a lot of time for her, but I can't picture her married to Sam Foundling now I've seen him at close quarters. What made the relationship work?'

'If it did,' Trish said, sobering. 'I keep trying to picture it myself.
I mean, I like him . . .'

'So do I. An interesting chap in lots of ways, but spiky I'd have
thought, and not just because of what he's had to handle these last
few weeks. Difficult to deal with. Rough trade, too, for the likes of
Cecilia Mayford.'

Trish opened her mouth to answer, then saw the psychiatrist's
column once more and kept quiet.

'What?'

'I was about to pontificate about the way people who grow up
feeling unwanted latch on to lame ducks to give themselves a
reason to exist – which is about as impertinent as this morning's
piece of press garbage.'

'Perhaps. But it could be true. D'you know anything about
Sam's predecessors in her life?'

'Not a lot,' Trish said. 'But there's a suggestion she was having
to fight off a senior colleague she may or may not have had an
affair with before she married. Although,' Trish said, thinking of
the few times she'd met Dennis Flack, 'I can't say *he* comes over as
a lame duck.'

'Her mother might know more.'

'She might, but I doubt if she'd pass it on to me. She did tell me
she'd been appalled that Cecilia chose Sam, but that's as far as it
went. And I can't exactly ask her—' She broke off, remembering
the scared face of the assistant Dennis Flack had brought to the
consultation in chambers. Maybe *she* would be able to fill in a few
of the gaps.

Chapter 12

For form's sake Trish asked the switchboard to put her through to Dennis Flack's office. She was pretty sure a man of his seniority wouldn't be working between Christmas and the New Year, but she didn't want to look as though she was going behind his back if he was there.

'He's on holiday at the moment. Can anyone else help?'

'I think so. Is Jenny Clay in?'

Trish waited for only a few seconds before a tentative, slightly squelchy voice said: 'Is that Trish Maguire?'

'Yes. Jenny?'

'Yes. How did you . . .? I mean, I'm glad you phoned. I . . . I need to ask you something.'

'Sure,' Trish said, putting confidence-boosting warmth into her voice. 'D'you want to go first or shall I?'

'I . . . Could I come and see you? There are things I need to show you. It would be easier face to face.'

'OK. Come to chambers. Most of the clerks are away so the door may be locked, but if you bang on it, I'll come down and let you in.'

'I'll be about twenty minutes. Bye.'

Surprised by the haste, Trish fired up her laptop so she could check through her latest notes on the Leviathan case, hoping to fire up her brain too. If she had only twenty minutes she'd better get a move on.

In fact Jenny didn't arrive for nearer half an hour, by which time Trish was reasonably confident of being able to understand whatever information was coming her way. She ran downstairs as soon as she heard a knock on the door and pulled it open. Jenny stood there, dark hair sticking up all round her head, as though she'd been running her hands through it. She was dressed in jeans almost as saggy as David's and a very old CalTech sweatshirt, and she carried a slim dark-green folder.

'Hi. Sorry I'm not dressed for work. I'm supposed to be on holiday. It's just that I was working at home when I realized I've . . . Oh, God! Somehow I seem to have cocked up the calculations. And I don't know what . . . I've been over and over them and I can't work out what's wrong. I daren't tell Dennis until I can find out how it could have happened. And I—'

'Hey, Jenny. Calm down.' Trish gestured to her own loose grey trousers and ancient raspberry-coloured sweater. 'No one in the Temple is dressed up at the moment. Come on in and tell me what's happened.'

Jenny rubbed her right eye. It was red and sore-looking. Her lips were bitten too.

'Whatever's happened, there'll probably be a way round it,' Trish said gently, as they went upstairs to her room. 'And if there isn't, it's much better to know now than to have it chucked at me unexpectedly when we're in court.'

'Okay. Well, look here.' Jenny dumped the folder on Trish's desk.

Trish whisked her papers out of the way and put them on one of the shelves behind her desk, before bending to look over Jenny's shoulder.

'Here's the series of wind-stress tests on all the components,' she said, pointing to a sheet Trish recognized as part of a print-out listing the preliminary work done before the final specifications had been produced. As Jenny turned the pages, Trish saw she bit her nails and had chewed one so far down that the nailbed was bleeding. She used the finger to point to a line on the printout.

'This is the one that won't work, the stress test on the outer cables.' Jenny looked up at Trish, frowning. 'You know the ones I mean?'

'The ones that act as guy ropes at the four corners of the Arrow.'

'That's right.' She pulled another sheet of paper from her folder. It was a hard copy of one of the test results, and it had little sums in red ink scribbled all over the page. The numbers at the top were neat and tidy; lower down they sprawled and some were crossed out with wild hatching.

'Here.' Jenny pointed again. The nailbed was oozing fresh blood, exactly the same colour as the red ink. 'I've been checking the figures again and again, rerunning the test, and the answer always comes out wrong. I don't understand how it can because everyone involved would have checked it before they accepted the results. And both Cecilia and I went through *all* the tests when Leviathan first handed us the claim to investigate. So it must be me doing something wrong. And I just can't see where.' Tears spilled from Jenny's eyes. She looked half demented and wholly terrified.

'Sit down a minute,' Trish said, gesturing to the visitor's chair. There were more important aspects to this than an inability to get the right answer to a series of sums. 'How long have you been working for Dennis?'

'Since I left university, three and a half years ago.' She sniffed and rubbed the back of her hand under her nose.

'And has he always frightened you?'

More tears spilled over, dripping down her pink cheeks. Trish offered her a box of tissues. Jenny took one, shaking her head.

'It's not Dennis. It's me. He's been under tremendous pressure, and I can't help making mistakes and losing things, which makes it all so much worse for him. I don't know why. I've never been like this before. I used to be quite efficient, but now I put things in the wrong order and even when they're not, I can't find them. My calculations keep going wonky like this. I can't seem to get the same answer twice, whatever calculator I'm using. Which is why I started to do them by hand, too. But that doesn't work either.'

Trish remembered how much she'd disliked Dennis Flack's bullying air when he came to chambers. Even then she hadn't realized how destructive it was. She pulled her own calculator out of the top drawer and whizzed through some of the red-inked sums on the photocopy.

'I get the same answers as you,' she said, looking up with a smile. 'The original mistake will be buried somewhere in the files. It'll take time to find it, so there's not much point looking while you're here. I'll have a crack at it later. Did things go wrong like this when you were working with Cecilia?'

'Sometimes. Not so often. But then she was more patient than Dennis.' Jenny looked away from Trish, biting her lip. 'I know I must sound like a pathetic five-year-old, but I really miss her.'

'So do I.' Trish watched Jenny's head come round until they were face to face again. 'You shouldn't give yourself such a hard time. It sounds to me as though Dennis is taking his own grief out on you. He was particularly close to Cecilia, wasn't he?'

'Not as close as he wanted,' Jenny said, perking up a little. 'He was always trying to pretend they were a kind of unit and she'd pull back every time. It was quite subtle, but anyone watching them would have seen it.'

'Was she scared of him too?'

'Cecilia?' Jenny looked astonished. 'She wasn't afraid of anything. She'd have known exactly how this happened and what to do about it now, unlike me. I just can't . . .'

'Don't beat yourself up,' Trish said, thinking of the shadows she'd seen in Cecilia's expression. 'Everyone's frightened of something. And fear makes all of us less competent than we really are.

Being a bit more detached from all this than you I may be able to see what's gone wrong. In any case, I'll get back to you. Will you be in the office tomorrow?'

'Yes. I've got to work out what's going wrong before Dennis gets back on Monday. I can't . . .' She was back to staring out of the window, chewing her lip again. 'I found the problem on Boxing Day and I haven't been able to sleep since, except with pills. Even then I wake at dawn, wondering if I should resign now, or . . .'

'You should be wondering why no one else has noticed that the figures don't work,' Trish said, letting herself sound tougher. 'You've had the guts to bring the problem to light, so there's a big mark in your favour. I'll let you know what I track down.'

'Okay.' Jenny pushed both hands through her hair and licked her lips as she faced Trish again. 'Sorry to have banged on so. You wanted to ask me something too.'

'I just wondered whether you saw Cecilia on the morning she died.'

Jenny nodded. 'She looked tired, but I wasn't surprised: she'd been working really late the night before.'

'On a Sunday night? How d'you know? Were you there too?'

'The last email she sent me was timed at just before 11 p.m., so she was still at her desk then. She was trying to get everything finished before she went on maternity leave.'

'So why did she leave the office on Monday morning? It can't have been normal for her just to waltz out like that, particularly when she was so busy.'

'She was always having to go out to site meetings and client meetings.' Jenny's surprise at Trish's obtuseness was making her sound more confident. 'And doctors, of course, being pregnant. She was too senior to have to ask anyone's permission. Like Dennis.'

'Did he go out that morning too?'

Jenny nodded and sniffed. 'Luckily. He'd had a real go at me because of some papers I couldn't find and then he got even crosser because I couldn't stop crying.' She brushed her eyes again. 'When I'd got hold of myself and washed my face and come out of the loos, he'd gone. Which meant I could get stuck in to doing the stuff Cecilia had emailed about.'

'Had there been any phone calls for her just before she left?'

'Of course. Her phone hardly stops; that's why sometimes she used to work at home. They all do when there's a lot of documents and stuff to get their heads round. Then they come in at weekends or evenings to work while the office is quiet.'

'Thanks.' Trish smiled, even though she hadn't got what she wanted. 'Now, if I were you, I'd knock off for the rest of the day and go to the gym or swim or something. Forget all this, let your brain relax. It'll function much better if you do.'

A quivering smile made Jenny look a bit less defeated. 'That's not a bad idea. I'll give it a try. You will tell me if you find anything, won't you?' She fished a card out of her wallet and handed it to Trish. 'This has my mobile number. You will ring me, won't you?'

'I will.' Trish escorted her safely off the premises and sighed in relief to be rid of her fears and misery.

Before Trish went back inside, she looked round the empty courtyard, as always enjoying the sight of the fountain in the centre with its neat octagonal grey-stone balustrade and elegantly planted flowerbed. Now, in mid-winter, it was filled with glossy evergreens. Turning her back on it, she hoped Jenny's news would provide the spur she'd needed to make herself concentrate on the Arrow's problems.

A rolling clatter made her look over her shoulder to see the postman pushing a red trolley so stuffed with letters and packages they stuck out at all angles. Trish waited until he'd reached her steps, before putting out a hand.

'I can take anything for 2 Plough Court,' she said.

She needed both hands to hold the four thick bundles. Some

must be Christmas cards, sent too late or delayed in some over-burdened sorting office. She took the load to the clerks' room and handed them to dark-haired Sally, the long-suffering trainee clerk, who was the only one not allowed an extended Christmas break. She too was wearing weekend clothes, in her case a flippy pink corduroy skirt barely covering her knickers and a low-cut purple sweater that showed off not only her incredible cleavage but also a diamond S suspended on a gold chain.

Considering Sally's usual all-concealing dark-grey or black suit, Trish had to admit this rebellious mufti was a more cheering sight. She had to hide a smile at the thought of Steve's likely horror. As she waited for her post, she saw a copy of the *Daily Mercury* in the wastepaper basket.

'May I borrow that?' she said, pointing to it.

Sally blushed until her cheeks almost matched the skirt, which told Trish more than she wanted to know. She took the offered paper and tucked it under her arm while she waited to be given her letters.

There were only two: both stiffened brown envelopes, one with a typed address; the other handwritten by Caro. Trish checked the postmarks. Caro's had been sent only two days ago, but the typed one had been franked on 23 December and sent by second-class post.

'Thanks, Sally,' Trish said and ripped open Caro's as she walked back to her room. She didn't want to look at the paper until she was alone. There was a pile of glossy photographs in Caro's envelope, with a Post-it stuck to the top one.

You ought to see these, Trish, as a corrective to your idea that it's better for nine guilty men to go free for ever than one innocent to be put through a bit of anxiety while we get at the truth.

Trish caught her foot in a rip in the carpet on the threshold of her room and tripped, dropping the paper and spilling the photographs as she fought to stay upright. Looking down at the prints, she saw a body laid out for autopsy. The scar of her Caesarian, a wide smiling shape at the base of her belly, was raw, with the few clumsy stitches very obvious. Presumably the surgeon had known she was dying and hadn't spent any longer than absolutely necessary as he worked on her suffering body. But it was the wounds to Cecilia's head and face that made Trish gag.

The features were just about recognizable, even through the red-and-black bruises and the cut under one swollen eye. Cecilia's dark-blonde hair was matted with dried blood and the right half of her skull looked quite flat under it. The weight of the blows must have been tremendous.

Hating Caro for making her look at these, hating the knowledge that Cecilia had lived nearly a day with these injuries, Trish gathered the photographs together, shoved them back into their stiffened envelope and put them in her desk. She hadn't needed to see them. The horror, the sympathy she had always felt for Cecilia, did nothing to loosen her determination to protect Sam for as long as she could.

She shook out the *Mercury* and turned the pages, looking for her own name or that of Mrs Justice Mayford. Neither appeared until page eight and only then in a small paragraph at the bottom of a list of trivial news items.

> Contrary to the report in yesterday's edition, Mrs Justice Mayford and barrister Trish Maguire are not in conflict. Ms Maguire's support for the husband of Mrs Mayford's late daughter is a source of reassurance for Mrs Mayford, who is extremely grateful for it. We are happy to make this clear.

It wasn't hard to imagine the negotiations that must have gone into that bland paragraph. Hardly anyone except the individuals concerned would even notice it, but it was there, and for that Trish was grateful.

She stuffed the *Mercury* into her own wastepaper basket, where it belonged, and opened the second envelope. Its typed and official-looking address gave her the instant sense of relief she always found in word-heavy documents. They were safe, however scary the information they might contain. Subject to rational analysis, they could not destabilize her as pictures like the ones of Cecilia's body might.

The envelope contained a batch of letters, handwritten by the same person, with a covering note typed on the loss adjusters' thick, headed paper.

> *Dear Trish,*
>   *You asked about a stalker who could have been scaring Cecilia. We found the originals of these in her desk. Maybe they explain the rumour.*
>   *We've obviously given the originals to the police, but your questions make me think you might like a set of copies.*
>   *Yours ever,*
>   *Dennis*

The photocopies were clear enough to see that the originals had been written on lined paper ripped from a shorthand notebook. Trish could see the imprint of the scalloped edge at the top of each page. The writing was the sloping-back kind often produced by lovers of the green ink that usually signalled someone with iffy mental controls and an overflow of spite. The first letter addressed Cecilia formally and went on to say:

> *How can you be in any doubt about the forces making the London Arrow move? You must know as well as I that when the resting places of the dead are disturbed, their ghosts will walk.*
>   *Go to the Arrow tonight and listen. If you have any sensitivity*

*at all, you will hear echoes of the crunch of bones as the pile
drivers did their evil work. I had to listen to them for real as I
stood on the edge of the pit they dug to raise their impious
monstrosity.*

*If you care enough you will also hear the cries of the plague
victims themselves and smell the stench of the suppurating buboes
on their rotting flesh.*

*How can you pretend the building is not cursed and everyone
involved in its wicked construction consigned to hell for ever?*

'Wow,' Trish said aloud, as she swapped the first letter for the one
beneath. She rather liked 'impious monstrosity'. All eight letters
were written in the same hand and the same high-flown language.
None was signed.

There was nothing in any of them to make Cecilia afraid, even
if she hadn't been the sensible, intelligent woman Trish had
known. As a loss adjuster, she'd had nothing to do with the
choice of the Arrow's site or its construction. She'd probably
never given the building a thought until it had become part of
her caseload. And as an admirer of common sense, she'd have
had no truck with ghost stories. Like Trish, she'd probably
believed the only ghosts were either minute, localized climatic
effects or memories, generated within the minds of the living by
their own emotional needs.

There was nothing in any of the letters to suggest someone
capable of wreaking the kind of damage Caro's photographs had
shown. In Trish's experience effusions like these provided the perfect creative outlet for their authors' bizarre impulses. They rarely
needed any other satisfaction.

It crossed her mind that Dennis Flack might have sent them
himself, as a way of diverting attention from whatever pressure
he'd been putting on Cecilia. Could he have the imagination necessary to write of the stench of buboes?

*

Sam got Maria-Teresa's letter agreeing to his visit on New Year's Eve. He'd been so sure the post would take even longer than usual at this time of year that he was shocked. There should have been more time to get used to the idea of confronting her. He thought of phoning Trish and asking her to take over and make the visit for him, but that would have been cowardly, and whatever else he was, he wasn't a coward. Never had been. The whimpering boy might be, but Sam had him safely back behind strong mental bars where he belonged.

When the phone rang, he picked it up automatically and said his name.

'This is Dowting's Hospital. My name's Anita Matthews. I'm calling to let you know the doctor has said your baby's now well enough to go home. Have you got everything ready for her?'

Sam pulled his mind back from the woman in prison and considered everything he'd been told to buy. Most of it was already in the house, efficiently laid in by Cecilia over the past few months.

'I've got it all. But I can't come straight away. There's something I have to do first.'

'When will you be here? We need to make arrangements for the health visitor to come by and make sure you've got everything you both need and that you can manage her.'

'I'll pick her up this afternoon. Say about four?'

'We'll expect you.'

It's just as well to see the woman in prison before the baby comes home, Sam told himself. That way we can both go forward and forget the rest.

He doused the stove, switched off the lights and let himself out of the studio, taking one last look before closing the door on his past. He still wasn't sure how he would incorporate his daughter's needs into his own routine, but he'd find a way. Gina kept trying to make him hire a nanny, offering to pay the wages herself, but he wanted to see what he could do first. A nanny, particularly one hired and funded by his mother-in-law, would be a spy.

It wasn't until he was sitting in his van at the traffic lights controlling the junction at Camden Town that he realized he ought to give Gina the news. He waited until he saw a parking space, then pulled over and took out his mobile. He wasn't going to take any risks with even the smallest of laws that might give Chief Inspector Lyalt an excuse to haul him into her interview room again.

'That's wonderful, Sam,' Gina said. Her voice sounded odd, strained. 'I know you've been sleeping in the studio, so would you like me to look in at the house, turn the heating on and things like that? I could buy some food for you too.'

'It's okay,' he said, failing to sound grateful. He didn't want to have to explain his plans. 'I can manage.'

'It would be easy, Sam. I've got to go to Sainsbury's anyway this morning. Why don't I just get in some basics for you both? I'd like to.'

'Fine, then. Whatever you want.' Forcing himself to sound kinder, he added: 'I'll talk to you when she's settled so we can sort things out. I've got to go now.'

He clicked off the phone without waiting for more, aware that he was as uncomfortable with their new relationship as she was. He wished he'd remembered she had keys to the house. She'd always had them and it had never occurred to him to ask Cecilia to take them back after the wedding. In a way it had been reassuring to know she could get in if something happened to the house while they were away. Now, with their relationship so strained, it was different.

If she was going to drop in later this morning, he'd better go to the house now to collect the carrycot, nappies and all the rest. Otherwise Gina would try to bring it to the studio herself and start interfering there too. He was only about eight minutes' drive away.

In and out of the house in little more than half an hour, he stowed everything the baby could possibly need in the back of the van and retraced his earlier route. Following signs to Holloway and The North, he expected the journey to last for ages, but in fact he was there, facing the low red-brick building, long before he was ready for it.

Once through the prison gates, he had to go through a whole series of searches and demands for identity. His feelings were all over the place. One minute he was spooked, the next relieved. At first he couldn't understand why the searches made him feel a bit safer. Maybe it was because they showed he was an outsider here.

Waiting at the plastic-topped table, he lost the weird sense of comfort. If the police had their way, he'd soon be in a place like this for real. He looked round, trying to get used to the idea, but all he could feel was a shrieking 'no' in his mind.

A woman appeared in the further doorway. Thin and scraggy, like the stray cats he and Cecilia had seen in the Greek Islands last year, she hesitated, but she looked straight at him, undistracted by the other groups of remand prisoners and their visitors.

It's because you're the only one on your own, Sam told himself.

'Sam?' she said, standing behind the orange chair on her side of the table. 'It's you, isn't it?'

Photographs, was his next thought as he nodded to her. She's seen magazine photographs. Even if she is my mother, there's nothing in how I look now that she could have seen when she dumped me on the hospital steps.

'Thank you for coming,' she said in a husky foreign voice. 'I know how hard it is. And I'm sorry about your wife. How's the baby doing?'

'She's fine now. I—' He only just stopped himself giving her the news that was none of her business. 'I didn't come to talk about her. Or myself. I came because it didn't seem fair to say what I have to say in a letter.'

'You're not going to have the test,' she said, slumping in defeat. 'You don't even want to know if I'm your mother.'

Fight back, he wanted to shout at her. Don't just take it. You'll be a victim for ever if you don't hit back.

'What you wrote to me may well be true,' he went on, answering the protests she should have made, 'but I can't deal with it, okay?'

She shook her head, gazing down at the scars on the table.

'I've got enough to do to keep going and make a life for the baby now. I can't go back. Whatever the truth is, it's in the past, and I don't want to go there. There's too much . . . I can't go back.'

She didn't raise her head or answer.

'D'you understand?'

A faint shake of her head was the only response, but still she didn't protest.

'Maybe I should have done this on paper,' he said, putting both hands on the edge of the table so that he could push his chair back and stand up. 'I'd better go. I hope things go okay for you at your trial.'

She did look up at that. Her deep-set eyes were very dark. There were no tears in them. And no hope.

'Nothing won't go well now,' she said.

Get away now, Sam told himself. The longer you stay the worse it'll be. You can't do anything for her, and she can only drag you down. Leave. Save yourself and leave. He walked away, towards his route out into the free world, but he had to look back.

She too had got to her feet. Moving as though every step was painful, she stuffed her hands into the central pockets of her fleece and bent her shoulders round and down. Her head hung down, as though her neck was too spindly to support it. If she was his mother, she'd been only sixteen when her first brutal bloke made her pregnant. Sam tried to remember how he'd felt at sixteen, thirteen years ago. He wasn't ready to be a parent now. Then he'd barely been able to look after himself. How had it been for her?

Four steps took her across the path of another woman, stronger-looking and much younger, who took a swing at her, catching her chin with a vicious upper cut.

He heard himself shout as she went down. Officers started to move towards her. In his mind it took minutes, but it can have been only seconds. Even so it gave the thug enough time to kick her hard in the head, then in the belly. She lay there, the woman who might have given birth to him, taking it. She didn't move or try to protect herself, as though she felt she deserved the punishment. Some of the children around them screamed and the adults shouted protests.

At last two officers grabbed the other woman, while one knelt beside Maria-Teresa, and a fourth talked urgently into her radio.

Fighting an impulse to rush forward, to agree to anything she wanted, Sam waited until he saw the officers help her to her feet. Once she was standing again, she turned to look over her shoulder and stared at him through a slick of blood, which dripped untouched down the front of her pale-grey fleece.

It was as if she was saying, 'See. See what's been done to me all my life. Can't you understand? Can't you forgive what *I* did? Can't you believe me? Can't you save me?'

He looked back at her, not sure which of his feelings he could trust now. Her bloody head dropped even further towards her chest and she turned away from him. All Sam could do was stand and watch until she was removed from his sight. Then he let himself stumble out into the cold.

A man sitting in the front seat of an old dark-blue Fiesta illegally parked in the street just outside the gates glanced away as Sam went past looking as though evidence of everything he'd ever done wrong was plastered over his face. For a while Sam couldn't remember how to open the van door and just leaned against it, breathing huge gulps of air, trying to subdue the acid surges in his gut and deaden all his thoughts.

The man in the Fiesta kept his head averted until Sam had walked out of sight. Then he activated the phone pinned to the dashboard and heard the dialling tone. He pushed in a one-button code and was through to Chief Inspector Lyalt's direct line.

'It's me again, guv. Foundling was inside for nearly half an hour. On his way now. D'you want me to follow the van or go in and find out what he was up to? He looked shaken.'

'We'd better know who he was visiting, what she's in for. Get all that and anything else interesting and report back.'

'Okay, guv.'

He switched the phone off and pulled himself out of the car. It was too small for a man of his size. Even so he'd have preferred to stick in it than penetrate Holloway. Most officers loathed the place for the misery you could smell the minute you were through the door. Still, it had to be done and the quicker the better. This trip of Foundling's was the first surprising thing any of the watchers had seen him do.

Trish decided to call it a day. She'd used her personal password to log on to the extranet that had been set up in the earliest stages of the Arrow's design to allow architects, engineers, quantity survey-ors and all the other groups involved to exchange and keep track of all the drawings and information they needed. Everyone involved had a different password, and there were innumerable different levels of access. Hers allowed her only as far as the final drawings and specifications, but that was all she'd needed. She'd wanted to see whether Jenny's printout of the stress test had been corrupted in some way. But it was precisely like the one on the extranet. She still couldn't understand why no one had spotted the discrepancy before, and she'd been staring at the unworkable results for hours.

She'd recalculated all the figures, first on the computer; then by hand. Neither method produced the right answer. Jenny's inabil-ity to balance them was justified and not part of some subconscious fight-back against Dennis's bullying. Trish wasn't yet sure what effect – if any – the discrepancy had on the building's cracks. But it was the first oddity, so she'd have to pursue it until she was satisfied there were no more questions to ask.

She couldn't leave Jenny hanging on for reassurance any longer, so she made a quick phone call to explain the little she'd found and what she still needed to establish. Jenny sounded breathlessly grateful and rang off.

Putting down the phone and looking back at the figures on her computer screen, Trish felt as though her eyes were blurry with strain and her brain fogged with too much irrelevant information. The advice she'd given Jenny applied just as much to herself. Knock off now and come back with clearer eyes and a fresher mind. Which was lucky because she was supposed to be dressed up and in Fulham in less than an hour's time.

Neither she nor George had ever liked elaborate New Year's Eve parties, but this year they'd agreed to go out to dinner with his oldest friends, who lived within walking distance of his house. It wasn't going to be formal, but Trish would have to change into something tidier than her sagging grey trousers and comfortable old sweater.

The phone rang. Presumably George wanting to know where she was.

'Hi,' she said. 'I know it's late, but—'

'This is Caro, Trish.'

'Ah. Great. I'd love to talk, but now isn't a good time. I'm late.'

'I won't keep you long.' Caro's voice had never been so formal. 'Provided you tell me now why you went to Holloway to visit Maria-Teresa Jackson on the twentieth of December.'

'I thought remand prisoners were allowed unlimited and un-supervised visits,' Trish said, while her mind churned through the only information her private and professional ethics would allow her to give away.

'Don't play games. Sam Foundling was there today, so I'm assuming you went on his business, which suggests it could be why he came to see you on the day his wife died. That being so, I need more from you.'

'Caro, we're back with the same point. Until Sam himself gives me permission to tell you why I went there, I can't. It's true I went on his behalf, but Sam's interest in Maria-Teresa Jackson is irrelevant to his wife's death. You must accept that.' She paused, then added with unusual bitterness, 'Just as I had to accept those gruesome photographs you chose to send me. I told you I didn't need to see them.'

'They were to make you take this seriously.'

'Oh, I take it seriously, Caro. Believe me.'

'Has he spoken to you since he got back this afternoon?'

'No.'

'So you don't know that Maria-Teresa Jackson was attacked while he was there?'

Trish felt her heart jolt, as though someone had thumped her chest. She kept quiet, knowing Caro would get to the point soon enough.

'She was attacked by another inmate, as she's been before, because she's thought to have killed her two-year-old child last year. She was kicked in the head and trunk. One rib is cracked and she has a black eye. Why is Sam Foundling interested in her?'

'Caro, you'll have to ask him. There's nothing discreditable about it. But it's private.'

'This case has already shown me one example of how cruel well-intentioned secrecy can be,' Caro said slowly. 'Talk to me, Trish. I need your help.'

Trish had never found it easy to resist that particular plea, but Sam's needs were more urgent than Caro's.

'Ask Sam. There's no reason for him not to tell you now. But it has to come from him. I've got to go, Caro. I do want to talk, not to the SIO but to my friend. Will you be at home over the weekend?'

'I doubt it.' The angry edge was back in Caro's voice. 'There's too much to do. Goodbye.'

As soon as the phone was back in its cradle, Trish swore with the kind of violence that would have shocked her in anyone else.

A picture slid into her mind of Cecilia, still working after eleven at night just before she was killed: Cecilia, whose files were always in perfect order, checked and rechecked. What if she *had* seen that the figures didn't work and wanted to know more?

Reopening her laptop, Trish typed a message for Giles Somers, the solicitor who had briefed her on the case and was in charge of garnering all the files and any other evidence she might need.

Did Cecilia email you the night before she died, asking for copies of any original documents or computer files relating to the Arrow's construction or components?

Another possibility struck her as she watched the email disappear from her screen, and she reopened the file containing the final specifications for the Arrow. The cables listed there conformed precisely to the ones tested. Frustrated, she searched for the letters that had been sent out to all the contractors who had been invited to tender for different parts of the building and double-checked the documents attached to each of them. All specified the same cables.

She heard echoes of Cecilia's voice in her mind, saying: 'I know there's a reason; I just wish it had been me to find it.'

Maybe you did, she thought as she caught sight of the reference at the top of the tender documents: VF59687/F&FGB/JMcS.

VF stood for Verity Farnell, the architects' practice, and the number was the file reference for the whole project. F&F were Forbes & Franks International, the consulting engineers. And GB had to be Guy Bait, the partner who had attended the abortive settlement meeting on his firm's behalf.

Trish should already have been on her way to Fulham, but with curiosity pricking her on, she had to dig deeper. In the library were all the relevant professional directories, as well as *Who's Who*, and *Debrett's People of Today*.

It was the work of only a few minutes to establish that Guy Bait had been at Brunel University at precisely the same time as Cecilia Mayford. Was *this* the coincidence that had worried her so? Had she too been wrestling with a professional conflict of interest?

A clock somewhere in the Temple boomed out seven thudding strokes. Trish crammed the books back into their shelves and ran back to her room to close down her computer, lock her desk and beg the fates to send a free taxi to the Embankment.

Chapter 13

Without David to look after, Trish moved into George's house in Fulham for the whole of the New Year weekend. The friends who'd given them dinner shared their dislike of making a fuss over something as arbitrary as a change of date, so they'd been encouraged to leave well before midnight, even though Trish had arrived three-quarters of an hour late.

Now she'd had a shower and was tucked up in George's antique bateau bed while he bathed. The central heating had gone off an hour earlier and the air in the room was freezing. It smelled faintly of the rosemary he'd learned to keep in the linen cupboard. 'More masculine than lavender,' he'd once explained, 'and just as good at keeping mustiness at bay.'

She sniffed appreciatively and pulled the duvet closer. Filled with Siberian goose down, it was like a warm cloud billowing around her. She wriggled down the bed until it covered everything up to her nose, and thought about a city in which some people were free to care about precisely which species of bird provided the feathers in their duvets, while others had so little they slept on newspaper and cardboard in the street.

George emerged from the bathroom, untying the cord around his frayed dark-blue wool dressing gown, which he'd had for thirty years.

We're not extravagant in everything, she thought and felt a bit better.

'You look very serious,' he said, as he dropped the dressing gown on the end of the bed and inserted himself in beside her. 'Ouf, it's cold. Come here.'

Her body had warmed up enough to feel the shock of his cold legs and feet. It took some time before they were both comfortably the same temperature. Big Ben's gong-like chimes echoed from a neighbour's radio and there were cheers from out in the street, then breaking glass and a lot of raucous laughter.

'Hmmm,' Trish said against George's shoulder. 'Who'd have thought that Slummy Southwark would be so much quieter and better behaved than Fancy Fulham?'

'You don't know what they're doing in Southwark tonight, so stop throwing aspersions on my streets. And concentrate.' He trailed his now-warm fingers down the length of her spine.

That first evening set the pattern. They idled about in dressing gowns until lunchtime, filling the days with food and drink, and sex and Scrabble. It was a quite different game between two adults, without David to be placated or educated. The spats they had about whether a word was acceptable or not added just enough spice to stop them breaking their resolve to avoid talking about their professional conflict and what George's partners might decide at the forthcoming meeting. Trish couldn't keep it right out of her mind and she was pretty sure it still took up quite a lot of George's, but they never mentioned it.

Even so, by Sunday evening Trish felt as though someone had combed out most of the tangles in her spirit, and George had lost the tightness in his jaw that had begun to worry her. He smiled more often and could hardly keep his hands off her. She couldn't remember this ease of touching between them, even in the early days of quite irresistible lust.

On Monday they decided they needed a little bracing before the re-entry to work next day and set off in Trish's car for Richmond Park. There was so little traffic they were there in less than quarter of an hour, and it was easy to find space in the first car park they tried. Pulling on gum boots and Barbours, winding scarves around their necks, they were behaving, said George, like any traditional couple from the country. All it needed to complete the picture was a dog.

They set off towards the ponds and Trish listened in admiration to George's ease in naming all the species of waterfowl skittering along the surface of the water or zooming across the low white-and-grey sky. That was probably the kind of knowledge you picked up without even noticing when you were brought up deep in the country, part of a family who'd lived in the same place for generations.

A noisy group with a clutch of children trying out new bicycles and roller blades soon sent them away, to tramp around the Isabella plantation. It was duller now in its winter barrenness than it would be when the red, pink and orange azaleas were in flower and looking like thickened sunlight pouring along the banks of the curling stream. Even so, it was pretty and empty of every other human being, which was what Trish and George wanted. They stopped in the shadow of a big beech to watch a thrush systematically smashing a snail on a flat stone until she could get at the meat within the shell.

George turned and backed Trish against the smooth trunk of the tree and kissed her cold bright face.

'If anyone had told me when I was young that the love of my life would be a skinny, black-haired barrister with a mind like a razor and an independence so impenetrable she'd never let me look after her in even the littlest ways, I'd have . . .' He paused.

'What would you have done?' Trish was trying not to laugh at the least romantic, but most heartfelt, compliment she'd ever had.

'I'd have sent him to a shrink.'

She did laugh then and asked what kind of woman he'd expected to love.

'Oh, blonde, you know. And little, and a bit round. Slim but a bit round. And blue eyes. Grander than me, coming into money one day from a grandfather or a godfather or something. And no ambition beyond beating her mother at her own game.'

'So what went wrong?' she asked, not sure if he was serious. 'With the life you led, you must have met dozens of women like that.'

George leaned back, keeping his arms locked around her waist. 'I suppose I did. Luckily – for them as well as me – my subconscious must have known that sweet passivity wasn't my thing.'

'Sweet passivity sounds like a plant,' she said, laughing again as she looked over his shoulder at the woodland undergrowth all around them. 'Low-growing, evergreen ground cover with tiny little scented white flowers in June.'

'Positively inviting trampling. Give me soaring spikes any day. What about you? What were your girlish dreams made of?'

'I'm not a romantic like you,' she said. 'All I wanted was to prove to my bossy stepfather that I could make it at the Bar in spite of everything he thought about my intellectual and social shortcomings.'

'No dreams of love *at all*?'

'A few, I suppose.' She had to smile at the memories he was stirring up. 'But they were all wound up with the rest. My fantasy bloke was definitely a star of the Bar: much, much cleverer than me, but dazzled by my amazing insights and staggeringly brilliant advocacy. I'm not sure I ever really got past the approval bit into any actual love.'

George tightened his arms, kissed her again, then let her go. 'I'm well and truly dazzled, so I qualify there, if nowhere else.'

'You qualify,' she said. 'In every way that matters.'

They walked on, with Trish thinking about the generosity of a man bruised and worried about his career who could still reveal himself so clearly. She let her shoulder touch his as they strode across the scrubby remnants of bracken towards the car park and hoped she would be able to contain her rage at what his young partner was trying to do to him at work when she came face to face with him at the Twelfth Night party.

Chambers was much fuller after the bank holiday, but the atmosphere hadn't yet tightened into the mixture of aggression and cynical humour that would set in once the courts started sitting again. All Trish had had in answer to her email to Giles Somers had been an automatic response to say that he would be out of the office until 10 January. Hoping one of his juniors might have read his emails and decided to help in advance of his return, Trish checked her email for the tenth time at the end of Thursday afternoon, just before leaving to dress for her two important parties. Still nothing.

Back in the flat, she set about her preparations with as much care as she took when robing for court. Dressing well was part of the job. And she had the perfect clothes to do it in, including an apparently plain dark-red Jean Muir jacket, which moved in ways she'd never known clothes do. She put it over black silk trousers and camisole, knowing it would show off the triple-row choker of baroque pearls George had given her for Christmas. She was reasonably satisfied as she stood in front of the long mirror in her bedroom.

Never beautiful, she thought she looked better now than she'd done in her twenties. Part of it was that she could afford more expensive clothes, and the dark-red collarless jacket warmed her pale skin and dark hair; and part was simply that she was more confident and met the rest of the world as an equal, instead of an angry outsider. Tonight she looked as different as possible from the mad harridan of the *Daily Mercury*'s photographs, or the violence-obsessed neurotic of the editorial.

A quick spritz of a new fruity Jo Malone scent round her neck and on her wrists and she was ready. She collected her heavy overcoat, made sure she had enough money and left the flat to find a taxi.

'You look fabulous, Trish.' James Rusham, the new senior partner of George's firm, was standing with his back to a lusciously decorated Christmas tree in the biggest meeting room at Henton, Maltravers. He bent to kiss her cheek and his boyishly shaggy fair hair tickled her skin. 'I've never understood why George should have had the luck to find a woman like you.'

'Perhaps you don't appreciate him as you should,' Trish said with what she hoped was a flirtatious smile. She'd love to have told him precisely what she thought of his weakness in the face of Malcolm Jensen's plotting, but that would have been counterproductive. She glanced around the crowded noisy room, recognizing some of the clients and most of the older solicitors. 'How are you liking being senior partner and in charge of this lot, James?'

He reached towards a passing waiter to grab a glass of champagne for her.

'To tell you the truth, Trish, I'm no longer surprised George decided to jack it in. I don't mind the strategic responsibility or the ambassadorial stuff, or even the extra financial headaches. What I can't bear is the *moaning*.'

The stress he'd put on the last word was enough to make anyone laugh, so Trish had no difficulty joining in. He offered her an urchin's smile in return. It went well with the absurd hair, but it had none of the gravitas most senior partners tried to show.

'It's true,' he said, pinning a more serious expression on his big face. 'Until I was the target, I'd never realized what the effect of one person's perfectly legitimate complaint is when it's multiplied by fifty or more. You start to feel as miscreants in the stocks must have felt in the Middle Ages, stuck with your head and hands stuffed through a board while the populace threw rotten veg at you.'

Which explains why George was often so tetchy during those years, Trish thought, as she sipped her champagne. She let her eyes gleam as she looked up at his successor.

'He says you're doing a wonderful job, James. Look, with all the

formal hostly stuff you've got tonight, I'm sure I shouldn't mono-
polize you, but do tell me: which one is Katey Wilkins?'

'Why?'

Trish put the flirtatious smile back in place. 'Because last year
she kept phoning up, wanting George at weekends and in the late
evenings. I'm curious to know what she looks like.'

'Jealous, dear?'

'I'll tell you when I've seen her. Just point her out.'

James jerked his ample chin in the direction of a stocky, freck-
led redhead, standing beside a man of such pristine smoothness
that Trish automatically mistrusted him. 'She's that one. Talking to
Malcolm Jensen. Shall I introduce you?'

'That would be really kind.' Trish was intrigued to see that
Jensen showed every physical aspect she most disliked, from the
sleekness of his dark hair to the width of the pinstripes in his suit
and the ostentatiously heavy gold cufflinks. She'd prefer George's
wild hair and crumples every time. Or even James's mixture of
schoolboy and baby elephant.

Don't prejudge, she told herself as she stood demurely at his
side. As soon as James had performed the introductions, he
tramped off in the direction of the boardroom table, which had
been pushed to one end of the room to serve as the bar.

'So, you're the famous Trish Maguire,' said Jensen.

'Famous? For what?' Trish looked away from his smugness to
smile at Katey and was surprised to see a blank expression on her
plump face.

'What do you mean?' Jensen asked, looking disconcerted.

'Never having thought of myself as famous, I merely wondered
what had led you to pick that adjective.'

'We all know you live with George,' Katey said, rushing in to save
Jensen's possible embarrassment. 'I think that's all Malcolm meant.'

'Really?' Trish looked from one to the other, like a spectator at
a tennis match. 'I like to know what people say about me, however
difficult it may be to take. Honesty all round makes life so much

easier than whisperings and plottings in the corridors, don't you think, Malcolm?'

For a second, he looked positively murderous. Trish wondered if she'd gone too far. George had wanted her at the party to smooth his way and show all his clients and colleagues that her presence in his life was no danger to anyone. The last thing he'd expected was to have her throwing down a challenge to his biggest enemy. Still, she didn't think it would do Jensen any harm to know she wouldn't be a walkover.

'Very well,' he said, his jaw so tight she could see the muscles quivering beneath his skin, 'you're as famous in certain circles for your emotionalism as for the way you allow personal likes and dislikes to distract you from the work you're paid to do.'

'Wow!' Trish said, reeling at the insult and determined not to show it. 'Emotionalism? How interesting. Who could have given you that idea? Specifically?'

'I don't know what you're talking about. You wanted to hear what I knew of your reputation. I have told you. Now, if you'll excuse me, I must talk to a client I see arriving.'

Trish inclined her head like a Victorian dowager and resisted the temptation to watch his progress across the room – or trip him up as he went. She felt as though he'd stripped her of not only her clothes but also most of her skin. It would be typical of all the coincidences piling up since she'd first met Cecilia if Malcolm Jensen were the man invited to assess her skills for the next directory of British barristers.

'How are you enjoying partnership, Katey?' she said, making an effort to concentrate on the plain, inexpressive face in front of her. 'You've done well to achieve it so young.'

'Thank you. Like everything, it has its ups and downs.'

'D'you get much help from the oldies? Or do they fight to guard their territory?'

'Some are better at helping us up the ladder than others,' she said, taking a step backwards.

Trish didn't understand until Katey made a forty-five-degree turn, which took her into the shade of a large ficus growing in a huge coiled pot, which had been incongruously decorated with swags of tinsel. Trish followed her and waited, out of sight and earshot of the rest of the crowd.

'George was sweet to me last year. Please don't think I'm not grateful – or let him think it. I couldn't have managed without him. But I'm only thirty-two. I should have fifteen, twenty years ahead of me here. I need to look to my own future. I can't afford to let gratitude blind me to the alliances I have to make. Sorry. I've got to go.'

'Hold on.' Trish managed not to grab her arm, but only just. Luckily Katey paused and looked back. 'Why does Malcolm hate him?'

Katey shrugged. 'Maybe because George is so much more successful, more . . . what's the word? Secure in himself, I suppose. Maybe he humiliated Malcolm in a meeting once, or with a client. I don't know. I can't . . .'

'Okay. Just one more thing: is Malcolm's wife here?'

'I doubt it. She usually has to work at the paper later than this. I *have* to go.'

This time Trish did swing round to watch her cross the room. Jensen was laughing sycophantically at something a tough-faced woman in a black Armani suit had said and Katey was threading her way through the crowd in the direction of the bar. When she'd refilled her glass, she took a sip, before surveying the room. A moment or two later and she was heading for a knot of men by the door. She had to hover on the edge of the group for a while and Trish was impressed to see she neither pushed her way in nor cringed, watching and waiting until there was a gap in the talk she could fill. She obviously knew exactly what she was doing.

Poor George, Trish thought, remembering the efforts he'd put into saving Katey's career last year.

All his partners were deep in conversation and looked unlikely to welcome interruptions. He too was concentrating hard as he talked to someone who had his back to her.

She moved towards them and brushed past George, murmuring: 'I ought to be on my way to Holland Park. I'll see you there later, if you can make it, but don't worry if you can't. Okay?'

He nodded, but his expression was worried. Trish looked more carefully at the man opposite him and recognized the finance Director of QPXQ Holdings. She made herself smile, wondering how to deal with the situation. If QPXQ were as angry as George believed that she was acting for their worst enemies on the Arrow case, this man could be hard to placate.

'I—' she began, but was interrupted as he leaned forward to kiss her cheek.

'How *are* you?' he said far more cheerfully than she could have expected. 'George was just telling me how much he enjoyed spending Christmas in Southwark. You must be some kind of genius to have got him to like anywhere as edgy as the Borough.'

Reassured, but puzzled, Trish laughed and stayed for a few minutes of polite chat about how he'd spent Christmas and what he thought the new year would bring the economy. George looked a lot happier by the end, so she was able to leave without feeling she'd abandoned him. Either his partners had exaggerated QPXQ's reaction to the conflict of interest, or the finance Director had unparalleled diplomatic skills.

A taxi was depositing a couple on the pavement as she emerged from the building and she took it over, giving the address of Antony's big white house. As the cabbie set off, she repaired her make-up and combed her hair, hating Malcolm Jensen even more than she'd expected.

Emotionalism, she thought, forgetting QPXQ completely. Letting my likes and dislikes distract me from the work I'm paid to do. How dare he? And where did he get it? Or did he make it up there and then to rile me?

Checking her face in the flapjack mirror, she saw how memories of the small battle had added a glitter to her dark eyes. No bad thing for the next campaign.

Antony's double-fronted house was set back from the road, protected by austere black railings and fronted with a deep terrace of black-and-white hexagonal tiles. The great bay windows on both sides of the door were lit. No curtains or shutters hid the party from curious onlookers in the street. Both rooms were still decorated with Christmas swags of fir and dark-green ivy leaves studded with gold and crystal baubles, and white-jacketed waiters carried silver trays of filled champagne flutes through the crowd. The lavish picture was as far as possible from the standard neighbourhood Christmas party. From out here the Shelleys' collection of devastating paintings was barely visible, but Trish knew them to be of the same museum quality as the furniture and the antique carpets that filled the great rooms.

These days there were few houses she visited that could still make her feel like the clumsy law student from the wrong kind of university, but this one did. She breathed carefully, reminded herself she was happy in her life and adequately successful in her profession and stalked up the five steps to ring the front-door bell.

As soon as she was launched into a conversation, she knew she'd be fine. Even so, hovering on the edge of the room was hard. She inhaled the heady scents of fir, spice and wine and wished this were a dinner party, where at least she would have a chance to build up a conversation with her neighbours as they ate, instead of having to make a witty pitch in the first few minutes of each encounter.

She recognized Antony's wife and headed towards her across the room. Liz Shelley had never been one of her greatest fans and was distinctly withdrawn tonight, but their polite questions about each other's families bridged the gap and soon Trish moved on.

A glass of champagne was thrust into her hand and she caught the familiar smell of Antony's eau-de-cologne soap.

'Glad to see you look like a world beater,' he whispered into her ear.

She turned, kissed him, and said, 'Do *you* think I'm over-emotional?'

He laughed. 'You know I do. You care far too much about who wins your cases. I keep saying you need to be more cynical to protect yourself.' His lively face softened. 'But I'm glad you're not. Now, come on and talk to Gina. She's looking very shaken and she could definitely do with some of your TLC, overemotional or not.'

Feeling better at the prospect of doing something for someone else, Trish followed him to the fireplace, where Gina Mayford stood chatting to the most entertaining of the Lords of Appeal. At first sight, Trish couldn't understand what Antony had been talking about. Gina was better dressed than usual, and since they'd last met her short straight hair had been cut and coloured by the best of the best into a mixture of honey and caramel. Her make-up was as unobtrusive as it was perfect. She was somewhere in her mid fifties, Trish knew, but tonight she could have passed for much younger.

'Ah, Trish,' Gina said, leaning forwards to kiss her. 'How lovely to see you. Do you know Benjamin Malton? Benjie, this is Trish Maguire. I don't know whether she ever appeared before you in your days in the High Court.'

'Probably not,' he said, holding out his hand. 'But I know of you, of course.'

My overemotional style, no doubt, Trish thought as she smiled up at him with what she hoped would look like eager pleasure.

'I particularly remember your work on the MegaPerformance Bond Fund case,' he said. 'Most impressive.'

'Thank you,' Trish said, now feeling everything she had faked in her smile. His approval reminded her that this was her world and she had a legitimate place in it. 'I'm not sure I've ever worked as hard in my life as I did mugging up everything about junk bonds and the European money markets for that case.'

'All of which, presumably, you've now forgotten. It's Leviathan now, isn't it, and the Arrow?'

'It is. How amazing that you should know.'

'Gina was telling me. I must go and have a word with Sniffer over there. See you, Gina.'

'Absolutely, Benjie. Lunch on Friday. I look forward to it.'

He patted her shoulder and eased his way between the noisy groups of revellers until he reached the Lord Chancellor's side.

'Coo,' Trish said, forgetting herself. 'Sniffer? I've never heard him called that before. Where does it come from?'

Gina's face broke into a smile. 'An old joke from his early days at the Bar when he was known for nosing his way through documents looking for suspicious gaps, like a sniffer dog in search of hidden drugs.'

'I don't suppose many people dare use the nickname these days.' Trish caught sight of the Prime Minister's wife and added: 'This is probably the grandest party I ever come to. I'm very grateful for what you're doing here.'

'Don't be, Trish. It's my fault you got involved with Sam. I know that. If I hadn't dumped my dilemma on you that day in Somerset House, you'd never have felt obliged to invite him for Christmas, and you wouldn't be in this mess now.'

Trish was so surprised it took a while to remember that Gina knew nothing of her much deeper involvement in Sam's life and problems.

'As I said before, I am really grateful you're giving him the support I still can't bring myself to offer.' She sighed and looked down into the illicit log fire. 'I wish to God that nice Chief Inspector Lyalt would get a move on and find enough evidence either to charge him or to arrest someone else.'

'So do I,' Trish said with feeling. Gina looked up and Trish saw there were tears in her eyes, swelling up over the lower lids. She really couldn't cry in here, however awful the circumstances of her daughter's death. 'Let me get you a drink.'

'That'll only make it worse. I'll be fine so long as I keep looking at the flames.'

'Is it the thought of what Sam—'

'No.' Gina pinched the top of her nose, which made her look more like Cecilia than usual.

'I find biting the tip of my tongue often works,' Trish said, moving so that she could shield the other woman from the few people who were beginning to look curiously in their direction.

'Thanks,' Gina said a moment later. 'I hadn't tried that before. It does help. No, it's not Sam that keeps making me do this. It's knowing that Cecilia and Andrew knew all about each other for years, and I wasted . . . wasted the chance to . . .' She gave up the attempt to say what she meant.

'You've lost me,' Trish said gently. One of the logs crackled, throwing sparks right out of the grate. 'Look, I think we ought to move back if we're not to burn holes in our clothes.'

'What?' Gina sounded dazed. Trish pulled at her arm and pointed to the embers glowing bright orange on the grey marble of the hearthstone. 'Of course. Sorry. You're not hurt, are you?'

'No. Only puzzled.'

'I assumed you'd know. I can't think why. Sorry. I really am losing my mind in all this. I don't know how I'll concentrate when I have to start sitting again.'

'Who is Andrew?' Trish said.

'Cecilia's father. He lives in America. I never told him about my pregnancy. And I never talked to Cecilia about him. I thought the only bearable way of managing it all was to keep silent. But we spent Christmas together at his sister's house in Dorset and although we didn't talk much then we made contact of a kind. Which must be why he phoned the other day and came clean.'

Trish opened her mouth to ask a question, then shut it again when she saw Gina had no need of any prompt.

'So now I know he wrote to Cecilia decades ago to introduce himself,' she went on, almost tripping over the words in her haste to get them out. 'Apparently he'd always known about her but thought I didn't want to have anything to do with him.' The tears welled again. 'What a mess! She could have had a father; I could have . . . Instead, she's dead and he and I have nothing. Except regret.'

'I'm sorry.' There was nothing else to say.

'He was with her on the morning it happened. They met at Somerset House. Somehow that makes it worse. I don't know why.'

'Somerset House?'

'Yes.' Gina sounded impatient. 'You know, the ice rink, where you and I had our hot chocolate that day.'

'I know that. I did . . . I just don't get the significance.'

Gina twitched as the firelight leaped, throwing shadows over her face, which made it look collapsed and crumpled, like a very old monkey's. 'It's all so vivid in my head I assume you can see it too. Every winter since they first brought skaters into the court-yard, Cecilia and I have used the place to meet for coffee or a quick bite at lunchtime. We both loved it. I thought no one else knew we went there. Now I find it's where she met Andrew too.'

Trish was still not quite sure what the significance of this was. Surely Gina didn't suspect the man of killing their daughter.

'Why did she lie, Trish?' The tears were back. Trish found her own tongue clamped between her teeth in sympathy. 'What else did she keep from me? I thought I knew her. Everything about her. But if she kept this secret, how much else? Like this man Chief Inspector Lyalt thinks harassed her. Why didn't she tell me about him?'

Trish thought about her own relations with her mother, easy and communicative as they had always been. 'There are always some things one doesn't want to tell: sometimes out of protectiveness; sometimes just because there are times when one needs privacy.'

'You're right, of course. Trish, I'm sorry. What's happened is making me question everything.' Gina too looked around the room at the groups of impervious confident people. 'I feel as though I don't know anyone any more. As though they're all strangers. I can't reach anyone.'

'You were doing pretty well with Benjamin Malton,' Trish said, smiling.

'It was a performance.' Gina staggered slightly and covered her mouth with her hand. Above it, Trish could see yet more tears welling in her eyes. This time they overflowed. 'I can't do this any more. I need to go home.'

'Have you got a car, or shall I come out with you and find a taxi?'

'Would you?'

'Of course.'

While Gina retreated to Liz's bedroom to blot her tears and find her coat, Trish went in search of Antony to explain.

'Good idea, Trish,' he said, 'but you must come back – and hang on until the midnight disposal of the decorations. You've never stayed that long before, but it's worth it. Fun.'

Out on the street, it took ages for a free taxi to appear. Trish stayed with Gina until they saw one and waved him down, shivering as the icy wind blew through her thin clothes. The handle felt freezing as Trish opened the door.

With one foot on the step, Gina looked back to say: 'You make it very easy to confide, Trish. It's a dangerous skill. If Sam did kill Cecilia, he'll tell you sooner or later. If he does, will you . . .?'

Trish held her breath, hoping Gina wouldn't put the question into words.

'Perhaps that's not fair. But if he does, will you at least try to make him go to the police? I . . . I need to know who killed her.'

'I know you do,' Trish said, aching with sympathy as much as cold. She was still holding the door and longed for Gina to get in and go before she tried to extract any promises.

'It's not only for my satisfaction.' Gina's face quivered again and she visibly bit her tongue. 'I need to know whether it's safe to leave the baby with him.'

Nothing could have made Trish more uncomfortable. Her natural sympathies were torn three ways. Holding on to her belief in Sam was getting more difficult. If he ever did confess he'd killed Cecilia, she would have to make him tell Caro. Until then, she'd go on fighting for him as though she were sure he was innocent. There was no one else to do it.

Gina pulled herself into the taxi with an ungainly movement that made her seem much older. She didn't look at Trish again, merely gave the cabbie her address and sat back in the seat, looking out of the far window. Trish was left on the pavement. The cold pressing against her skin had reached every bit of her body, and her blood moved as sluggishly as her mind.

'What on earth are you doing out here?' George's voice pulled her out of her miserable dream.

She watched him pay off his own taxi and let him hug her.

'You're freezing. How long have you been out here? Was someone horrible to you?'

'Quite the reverse. Everyone's been incredibly kind, particularly Gina Mayford. I was out here to keep her company while she waited for a taxi. If I'd known how long it would be, I'd have got my coat. Come on in. I'm under strict instructions to stay until the pulling down of the decorations at midnight.'

Antony was right. The best bit of the party definitely came with the chimes of midnight signalling the end of the traditional twelfth day of Christmas. While Liz produced stout boxes for the crystal drops and golden balls, Antony noisily shook out extra-strong black bags for the ribbons and bigger swags of greenery, but he instructed Trish to lay the first three branches of fir across the logs in the fire. The smell of boiling, then burning resin burst out among the guests. Antony turned off the lights and they watched the flames surge up the chimney, casting flickering yellow light all over the room. Only when the last flames died down did he turn the lights on again.

With fourteen people at work, the decorations were quickly stowed. Four of the men wrestled the bursting black bags into shape, twisting their tops ready for wire ties. The bags, with prickly branches already bursting through the plastic, were slung down beside the bins outside the basement door. Dusting their hands the men came back. Liz produced a tray full of delicate china cups of old-fashioned beef tea, hot and savoury.

'May this year be better for us all than last,' Antony said.

'And may we all be back here in twelve months' time,' Liz answered in what sounded like a familiar exchange.

Nearly everyone downed their beef tea, although Trish noticed Benjie Malton quietly putting his cup down on the mantelpiece, and they began to murmur about finding their coats. Malton stopped on his way to the door to tell her how glad he was he'd met her and how interested he would be in the outcome of the Arrow case.

'It's such an extraordinarily beautiful building it ought to be allowed to survive,' he added.

She was so grateful she nearly kissed him and saw from the glint in his eyes that he could tell.

'Fulham or Southwark?' George said as they descended the steps.

'Up to you. I'm happy.'

'I can tell,' he said, putting his arm around her shoulders. 'Let's go to Southwark. We don't often have it to ourselves. Taxi!'

There was a message from David when they got back to the flat. To Trish's relief he sounded happy, full of news of what he'd seen and what the cousins had said and how he'd been explaining some of the highlights of English history to them. Trish smiled, knowing how much he enjoyed telling other people things they didn't know, and replayed the message twice to make sure there were no hidden undertones in any of it.

'He's fine,' George said, lifting the red woollen scarf from around her neck and kissing the soft skin of her neck. He unbuttoned her heavy black overcoat and flung it on the nearest sofa with his own. 'It's a long time since we've had a shower together, Trish . . .'

'Sex maniac!' she said, pulling down the knot in his tie so that she could lift the whole thing over his head. She felt his thumbs stroking her nipples through the soft material of her camisole and the flimsy bra beneath.

'That makes two of us,' he said, gasping as she moved against him. 'D'you think we'll make it upstairs?'

She laughed and, hooking her fingers into his belt, towed him towards the spiral staircase.

Later, lying with his head between her slight breasts, idly stroking his hair, she tried to keep her mind quiet, but the questions Gina Mayford had planted in it wouldn't stay down. And with them sprouted a whole lot more about the true reasons for Malcolm Jensen's campaign against George.

Chapter 14

Caro found a note from the chief superintendent on her desk on Monday morning.

> This has to be wound up, fast. If there's no progress by the end of the week, I'll have to give in to pressure and bring in the Murder Review Group to oversee your work.

'Shit!' Caro said in an unaccustomed burst of rage. Her landline phone rang and she grabbed it, shouting, 'Yes?'

'Hey, Caro. What's up? This is Trish.'

'I can still recognize your voice, you know. What do you want?'

'This is obviously a bad moment. I was phoning to offer you a pair of alternative suspects. May I come and explain? Or would you rather come here? It would be easier face to face.'

'Is this a joke?'

'Don't be silly, Caro. Both are still only hypotheses because I don't have the facilities to gather evidence. You do. So I want to offer you what I've got.'

'Give it to me now.'

'Too complicated. We need to be face to face and I need to be able to show you something.'

'The evidence Sam Foundling was trying to hide in the studio?'

'This has nothing to do with Sam,' Trish said through her teeth.

Forcing herself to relax, she added more calmly: 'I told you, they're *alternative* hypotheses.'

'All right. But I'll come to you. I've got a meeting in five minutes. It shouldn't take much more than an hour. I'll be with you after that.' Caro was determined to keep Trish well away from the incident room and any secrets she might pick up from it.

Putting down the phone, she nodded to her sergeant, Glen Makins, who was beckoning from the other side of the glass partition, and moved through her industrious team, all heads down and working as hard as anyone could, on to the interview room. There one of the force's approved psychologists had been watching the CCTV films taken outside Sam Foundling's studio, and the video tapes of Caro's interviews with him.

'Hi,' she said, closing the door behind her. The shrink, an intense-looking woman in her early thirties, glanced away from the screen for a moment to smile. 'What have you got for me?'

'There's nothing definitive,' the other woman said in the west country accent that seemed out of kilter with her thin face and sleek dark hair and made her sound as warm as a batch of farmhouse baking. 'But the artificiality of the body language outside the studio is interesting. Look at this section.' She pushed the remote control towards the television and wound the film back. 'Here.'

Caro watched the unmistakable figure of Sam Foundling emerge from the studio's double front door, look up towards the camera, as though making sure it was recording his features, then down at his watch.

'Now.'

Sam looked up again and slapped the flat of his right hand against his forehead, before turning back the way he'd come.

'I haven't seen anyone acting out that kind of "how silly of me" moment since I watched the film of *The Day of the Jackal*,' said the psychologist. 'Have you?'

'I don't know. But you're right: it does look theatrical. What else?'

'Moving on to the video of your interviews with him, there are several moments when he displays marked aggression and hostility. Both would be characteristic of your killer.'

She switched the tapes and showed Caro what she meant over and over again, until Caro's restiveness got the better of her discretion.

'As you say, none of this is definitive.'

'I was invited to express my opinion about your suspect,' the psychologist said with an unexpectedly patient smile, which ratcheted up Caro's own impatience by several notches. 'My opinion is that you have a man here whose violent impulses are not well controlled, who is probably frightened by his own anger and what he knows it might make – or may already have made – him do. You also have him giving an exaggerated show of his departure from the building and re-entry, which goes to support your idea that he could have been setting up confusion in order to distract you from the imprecision of his alibi. That's all I've got. If you haven't anything else for me, Chief Inspector, I ought to go. I'm on a tight schedule today.'

'Thank you,' Caro said, recovering her temper. 'You're right. You've done precisely what I asked. I just hoped you'd be able to provide me with the certainty I need.'

'You know where to find me. If the CPS want me as an expert witness at his trial, I'll be happy to appear.'

'So you *do* think he did it?'

A wide smile revealed perfect teeth and an even more attractive personality.

'Listening to that interview and watching the films of him all morning? Added to what we know of his childhood? Of course I do.'

The burning sensation in Caro's eyes eased. At last!

'But that's not evidence either,' said the psychologist.

Strong black coffee, Trish's favourite stimulant, was keeping her mind buzzing. She reread the message that had at last come through from Giles Somers on his return from the extended Christmas holiday:

> You're absolutely right. Cecilia did email me at about midnight the day before she died. She wanted any hard copies I could get of the original documents relating to the external cables. She was very specific about that. It wasn't the internal ones on which the components are suspended; it was the four you always call guy ropes. I'm afraid I quite forgot in the horror of her death. I'll get on to it now and forward anything I can get as soon as it reaches me.
>
> D'you want to tell me why you want them? Giles

Trish had decided to wait for the evidence before passing on to Giles any of the speculations that had been teasing her brain. Now she had to get them organized. It was lucky, she thought, that her pupil had developed 'flu over the Christmas break and was still in bed. She didn't want any witnesses to her forthcoming meeting.

'Chief Inspector Lyalt is here,' said Sally Elliott over the phone fifteen minutes later.

'Thanks, Sally. I'll come and fetch her.'

They didn't kiss each other as they would normally have done. Caro, dressed in her usual dark-grey suit and flat shoes, looked more tired and strained than Trish had ever seen her. She also had deep vertical lines between her flattened eyebrows, and her hostile eyes were almost covered by the overhanging lids.

It's only a frown, Trish told herself, understanding now why George so hated it when she glared at him.

Caro waited until they were safely inside Trish's room with the door securely closed before she said: 'If you're wasting my time, I don't think I'll be able to forgive you.'

'Sit down and listen,' Trish said, making her own face as friendly as she could. 'And really listen because it matters.'

'Fire away.'

'The day we met in the studio, you told me someone had been harassing Cecilia at work.'

'So?' Caro's tone was obstinately unforgiving.

'It's pretty clear to me it had to be her immediate boss, Dennis Flack.' At the sight of another impatient scowl distorting Caro's good-looking face, Trish hurried on to describe the way Dennis had treated his assistant, Jenny Clay.

'It would be unlikely for there to be two men bullying younger women within one office, so I suspect the rumours you've heard came from the way Dennis tried to exercise the same kind of power over Cecilia.'

Caro neither softened nor said anything.

'He also sent me photocopies of anonymous letters Cecilia had about the ghosts of the plague victims buried under the Arrow,' Trish went on, feeling as though she were ploughing the stoniest ground. 'He said you had the originals.'

'Again, so what?'

'Don't you think he might have written them himself? As a way of distracting you from your suspicions of him?'

'No. We know where they come from and we've eliminated the writer from our enquiries.'

'Did you know Dennis Flack went out of the office around the same time as Cecilia on the morning she was killed?' Trish asked, suppressing her curiosity about the letter-writer. 'And that he'd been her favoured walker until she met Sam? And that he kept trying to make people believe she was his property, while she did everything she could to show she wasn't? And that he's talked to all kinds of people, including me, about how much he loathed Sam?'

'None of this makes him a killer, Trish.'

'If he was angry enough to want her dead, he'd have had a real incentive to throw suspicion on Sam, wouldn't he?' Trish went on, refusing to be deflected. 'Maybe he somehow discovered Sam wouldn't be in the studio that morning and faked a message from him, asking Cecilia to go there, followed her and beat her up just before Sam got back from his meeting with me.'

Caro was silent, but she looked a little shaken. This time it was Trish who said, 'Doesn't it at least make you think?'

'You said you had two possible suspects. Who's the other?'

'An engineer called Guy Bait, who worked on the designs for the Arrow, is involved in the insurance battle, and must have known Cecilia at university.' Trish pushed forward the photocopied pages of the reference book in which she'd found entries for both of them. 'See: they were both at Brunel at the same time.'

'Trish, no one is going to murder a loss adjuster because of an insurance fight. Anyone with half a brain would know the company would simply put someone else in her place. And partners in consulting engineering firms have a lot more than half a brain. I can't believe you got me out of my office for *this*. I don't have any more time to waste.' Caro's voice sounded tired now.

She blinked and the horizontal line of her eyebrows broke. She rubbed her eyes, then massaged her forehead.

'If I don't get a result by the end of the week, they may take the investigation away from me,' she added, looking up.

Trish felt the tendons in her neck soften. This was more like the old Caro: human, honest and a lot less angry.

'Better to take time to get the right result than make a case that goes tits up,' Trish said, but Caro didn't smile. 'Even if you won't consider Dennis Flack, you must look at Guy. The insurance case is going to turn on the precise causes for the failure of the Arrow's structure. For reasons I can explain if you want, this is likely to be down to the engineers and the work they did to make the architects' designs practical. Guy Bait is probably implicated in whatever went wrong. The fact Cecilia knew him at university could be the coincidence that was haunting her.' Trish waited for a response, thought of all the half-formed ideas in her mind and added: 'Part of it anyway.'

'Likely; probably; maybe; and you think,' Caro said as the ugly frown snapped back into place. 'You've no evidence against either of these men, have you?'

'No, but . . .'

'But nothing.' Caro reached for the squashy shoulder bag she'd allowed to flop on the floor. 'As you're always reminding me: without evidence, the most convincing speculation is worthless.'

'Don't go yet. Please.'

'I must.' Caro was on her feet and halfway to the door when she looked back over her shoulder. She tried to smile and failed. 'Next time, Trish, wait until you've got something that will stand up before you pull me away from my team during an enquiry as urgent as this.'

'Why is it okay for you to be convinced of Sam's guilt on no real evidence but monstrous of me to suggest Dennis Flack and Guy Bait could be worth a look?'

Caro produced a sound between a sigh and a growl, before muttering something about a psychologist. Before Trish could ask any questions, she'd slammed the door behind her.

Trish felt her back itching as she thought of all the other ways she could have handled the meeting. Would any of them have been more effective? Probably not. She shoved her hand painfully up between her shirt and her back to scratch and thought of Gina Mayford with those red weals up the inside of her forearm. Why did worry make you feel as though you had microscopic insects hopping about on your skin?

Filing Dennis for later because she had an almost direct line to him through Jenny Clay, Trish tried to see a way of approaching Guy Bait so that she could get something that would make Caro look harder – and might save Sam from more fruitless but destabilizing interviews.

If Trish hadn't been involved in the Arrow case she could have arranged to meet Guy herself and used her supposedly miraculous skill to make him talk. Had Cecilia faced the same dilemma and come to a different conclusion? Had she risked her own professional ethics by sharing her doubts about the cables with him? Or even by asking him about the wind-speed tests with the inexplicably wrong calculations?

Or had he been trying to influence her findings? As Caro had suggested, no one would set out to kill a loss adjuster in order to avoid the embarrassing outcome of an insurance claim, but was it so impossible to believe Guy Bait could have been trying to persuade Cecilia to soften her report, only to lose his temper when she refused, and then lash out at her?

Trish could just about picture it, but she couldn't see why it would have happened in Sam's studio. She definitely preferred Dennis and the idea of his faking a message from Sam to get Cecilia to a place where he could take whatever revenge he wanted on them both.

Even so, neither he nor Guy was as likely a suspect as Sam himself. Trish could see that as well as anyone, however hard she fought it, but she wasn't going to allow herself to believe it until she was faced with evidence. Hearing a mental echo of her mother's warning not to let Sam break her heart, she picked up the phone to call the Royal Courts of Justice and asked for Mrs Mayford's clerk.

This time it seemed the judge had no inclination for another session beside the ice rink in Somerset House. Instead, the clerk said she would come to Trish's chambers on her way home at the end of the day.

Gina Mayford's hair still had the good colour Trish had noticed at the party, but the cut was already looking ragged. Her skin was dry and flaking, and she had the thinned-out appearance of someone who'd been forgetting to eat or sleep.

'Dennis Flack and Guy Bait?' she said in answer to Trish's first question, as they sat on opposite sides of the desk with cups of tea in their hands. 'I'm afraid I don't remember ever hearing either name.'

'Pity. Did Cecilia socialize much with people from work?'

'I don't know. She never introduced any of them to me. But then we never lived in each other's pockets.'

'What about the other engineering undergraduates when she was at Brunel? Did she do things with them?'

'A fair amount, I suppose, although her best friend was a mathematician. Jane something. Jane Frant, I think. Another lost soul: she had that intense inwardness of so many mathematicians, which looks a bit like Asperger's to the outside world.'

'What happened to her?'

'No idea, I'm afraid. I'm sorry I can't help you.' Gina had her hand over her mouth again, so Trish couldn't hear what she was saying. But her misery was clear enough without words.

'How is the baby?' Trish asked, trying to help.

Gina's eyes darkened as though the pupils had widened in shock, but she took her hand away and spoke easily enough.

'She's out of hospital and Sam has her living in the studio with him. He says he's coping and wants her there to keep her from feeling she's got to fill her mother's place.'

'At less than a month old?'

'I know, Trish. The health visitor's going in as often as she can manage, much more often than new mothers get, because everyone can see Sam needs support. I've volunteered to babysit whenever he wants to go out, but he hasn't let me do it yet.'

A shadow fell across her face as she raised her hand again, this time to pick at the loose skin between her eyebrows.

'What am I going to do, Trish? It isn't safe. Even if he didn't kill Cecilia, he's not the man to have uninterrupted charge of a small baby. When he's working he gets so absorbed that all idea of time disappears and with it any hint of an obligation to anyone else. But I can't . . .' Her voice faded.

'You can't use the law to try to get her away from him,' Trish said, unable to hide her loathing of the idea. 'Of course you can't.'

Gina winced and went on scratching, staring at the flakes of skin that fell into her lap. She picked one up and absent-mindedly rolled it between her fingers. 'Last night, I even found myself wishing someone would come up with enough evidence to convince a jury he killed Cecilia, even if he didn't, because at least that way I'd be able to save the baby. There's not much further down to go.'

'I wish I could help.'

Gina's mouth quivered, then firmed up again. 'You're a bridge to Sam. That does help. And I'm grateful.'

She stood up abruptly and left without another word. Remembering the smoothness of her social skills, Trish knew she was at the very edge of what she could bear. The only thing that could help now would be proof of who had killed her daughter.

Trying not to think what would happen to Gina if the case were never solved, Trish opened her emails in case Giles Somers had sent her the documents she needed. There was nothing.

Silently swearing in the filthiest words she could think of because she couldn't get any further until she had the information, Trish clicked her way out of her email and on to a search engine, typing in the name of Cecilia's university friend. There were pages of references to people called Jane Frant, but only one looked promising, the author of papers on fractals and chaos theory. An email address was given so Trish clicked on that and quickly typed in:

Dear Dr Frant,

    You probably know that Cecilia Mayford died just before Christmas. I am trying to contact people who knew her, and believe you and she were friends at Brunel. I'd very much like to talk to you.

    Yours, Trish Maguire

It could take a while before she got an answer. Most people, deluged with spam and schoolboy hacking attempts at this time of year, put off answering unsolicited emails from anyone they didn't know.

The ease of finding the list of Jane Frants tempted her to search for both Dennis and Guy, and she flicked through a selection of the hundreds of links listed, frustrated and disheartened, until she found her way to reports of two big construction cases on which Guy had acted as an expert witness. In itself that wouldn't have meant anything, but the instructing solicitor in each case was named as Malcolm Jensen, working at the firm he'd left two years ago to join George's.

Another coincidence? Or something more significant?

Trish scrambled her way from website to website until she learned that Jensen was married to the news editor of the *Daily Mercury*. With links like these in front of her, she was pulled away from her ideas about Cecilia's death and deep into a much more personal quest. At last she saw one possible reason why the ratpack had been sent to her flat on Christmas Day. And why the finance Director of QPXQ Holdings had shown no hostility to her and George at the firm's party. She'd been wondering why, if his company was genuinely afraid she represented a dangerous conflict of interest, he'd been so friendly.

A beep announced the arrival of an email. With all her instincts pushing her to see Malcolm Jensen as publicly humiliated as she had been in the post-Christmas newspapers, Trish clicked back to her email inbox to see that Jane Frant had answered.

Hi. I didn't know Cecilia had died. How awful. I haven't seen her for years.

When's the funeral? What do you need to know?

Trish tried to ignore everything she wanted to do to Malcolm and tapped away:

Sorry to be the one to give you the news. No funeral can be
organized because she was murdered and the police still haven't
charged anyone. I need to know the names of people she was
close to at Brunel. Any advice wd be v. welcome.

She thought for a moment, then added her phone number. It would
be much easier to drop Guy Bait's name into an oral discussion than
anything written down. Ten minutes later, she was talking to a
woman with the soft adenoidal accent of the Midlands.

'But who are you?' she said.

Trish explained her interest in the case as unexcitedly as possible, mentioning her growing friendship with Cecilia's mother and
her long-standing connection with Sam Foundling.

'Right,' Jane Frant said. 'And what exactly is it you want to
know about her friends at uni?'

'Her mother has talked about the way Cecilia tended to fall in love
with men who had problems of one kind or another. She doesn't
think she ever knew all their names. We wondered if you could help.'

Is that 'we' fair? Trish wondered as she waited for an answer,
then decided she didn't much care. Sam's safety was too important
for little niceties.

'There was Guy, but Cecilia's mother must know about him.'

'Why?'

'They were engaged.'

'What's his full name? Mrs Mayford hasn't mentioned any
engagement to me.'

'I'll get the surname in a minute; it's on the tip of my tongue.'

'Great,' Trish said. 'D'you know what went wrong with the relationship?'

'I didn't know anything had. They got engaged in the last
summer term, just before finals. I assumed they'd gone ahead with
the wedding.'

'Wouldn't you have known? I mean, you were her best friend;
you must have expected an invitation.'

There was a brief sigh down the phone. 'I didn't like him much, and when I said so we quarrelled. I went to see her just before finals to wish her luck. She looked awful, ill, but she said she'd been working all night. I tried to tell her she was wasting herself on Guy and she told me to bugger off because she was committed now. I always meant to get in touch after the exams, to make up, but something always got in the way.'

'Like what?'

The laugh came again, a defence presumably against anything too personal. 'I thought she ought to apologize.'

'What didn't you like about him?'

There was a long pause. 'It wasn't just that he always came right into your face to talk – you know, pushing you back into a corner as you tried to keep your distance. He had a scary voice. He always talked very quietly, sounding kind and breathy. I hate it when people do that. It makes me wonder what they're hiding.'

'You've been very helpful,' Trish said, thinking of the moment when Guy Bait had finally spoken after the unproductive settlement meeting, and she'd appreciated the gentleness of his voice after the manufactured aggression of the others.

'Except that I can't remember his surname.'

'If it comes back to you, would you email me?' Trish was determined not to make any suggestion that could lead her witness to a false memory. The phone emitted the beeps that told her she had another call waiting. 'I'd better go. Thank you for taking the trouble to get back to me.'

'When you know about the funeral, will you tell me? I'd like to make peace, even now it won't do her any good.'

'Of course I will.' Trish scribbled a note, then switched to take the new call. It was David, still sounding happy. She tilted her chair back, swung her legs up onto the desk and prepared to listen to his adventures.

Sam couldn't work. It wasn't Felicity getting in his way. She was lying in her carrycot on the floor near the stove, breathing easily with a kind of wuffling sound he liked. It was his own clumsy hands again. And his brain. Again.

Stare into the mirror though he might, he couldn't see anything in his own face he wanted to reproduce in the clay. Even if he had, he wouldn't have been able to do it. Each piece he tried to add looked more like a huge bubo than any ordinary piece of flesh.

The only things keeping him going were the baby and the knowledge that she was happy here – so far anyway – and the sight of the Carrara marble head he'd mended and replaced on its rudimentary MDF pillar by the sofa. Even with the cracks, the face looked like Ceel's again. It helped him remember there had been times when she'd been happy here too. Not always, but often enough to make it possible to ignore the worst of his unbearable thoughts.

He tried to reconstruct what she'd said once when he'd been unable to work like this. Something about it being him she loved, not his skill or the brilliant reviews he'd been getting in the French art press. Nor the price he'd just been paid for his *Head of a Man*. At the time he'd thought it patronizing. Now he'd have given anything to be able to replay the words she'd spoken in that deep, kind, confident, steady voice he would never hear again.

It was exactly five weeks since he'd sat on the floor here with her battered head in his lap, waiting for her to die.

Chapter 15

Caro looked at the grey-suited man on the other side of the desk and wished the winter sun wasn't quite so bright behind him. All she could see was a shadowed face and the outline of impressively square shoulders and very short hair.

'I don't understand why you want to talk to me,' he said, sounding entirely unworried. 'But I'm more than happy to tell you anything I can.'

On his desk was a tangle of thin stainless-steel rods and curves standing about ten centimetres high and mounted on a black plaque. He put one stubby finger on a protruding corner and set the whole thing rocking. Caro instinctively put out a hand to stop it collapsing. He laughed as he saw her register its paradoxical stability, each piece pulling against the stress of the next so that, rock though they did, they held together and remained upright.

'My version of all those 1960s executive toys like Newton's cradle,' he said. 'More original and all my own work. But I distracted you. Sorry. You were going to tell me what I can do to help your enquiry into poor Cecilia's murder.'

'We're trying to talk to everyone who had any contact with her in the weeks running up to her death.'

'But why? Didn't her husband do it?'

'It's a question of evidence,' Caro said, hoping this meeting would produce enough incontrovertible facts to establish his non-involvement and so justify hating Trish for her endless interference. 'Did she ever talk to you about him?'

'I can't help you there.' Something in his gentle voice suggested he was smiling, but the dazzle behind him made it impossible to see. Caro felt like a prisoner interrogated in front of a spotlight. 'We had no opportunity for any kind of personal stuff because we're on opposite sides of a big insurance case. I don't suppose I saw her more than three times, and then always at big meetings.'

'But you had a personal relationship with her once, didn't you?'

'You *are* having to dig a long way back, Chief Inspector.' He sounded a little less friendly, but still untroubled. 'I don't envy you trawling through the past fifteen years for evidence of her husband's brutality. Yes, when we were at university, Cecilia and I were close. But I never knew Sam Foundling. Was he there at the same time?'

'No; he's younger than you. He was at the City & Guilds art college in Kennington and then worked with a sculptor in France. How close were you and Cecilia?'

'Very close indeed – for a while,' he said, wistful now. The stainless-steel tangle had come to rest and he set it going again. This time Caro repressed her urge to hold it together. 'But it didn't last. To tell you the truth, I'm amazed she ever did get married. Was she happy with her sculptor?'

'I hoped you'd be able to tell me.'

'We'd had no contact since university until the day she turned up as the loss adjuster for Leviathan Insurance on the Arrow case.' He got up to show Caro a large matt black-and-white photograph of the building set against an angry sky. It looked even more magnificent than in reality, and sinister.

'It's about this building, Chief Inspector, which has been showing signs of cracking none of us can understand. It's giving us all a lot of grief. The one good thing in the whole sorry mess was finding myself on the opposite side of the table from Cecilia. And now she's dead.' He turned his head away, swallowing with difficulty.

Now they were away from the dazzling sun-filled window, her eyes worked better. When he looked back at her, everything she saw in his expression squared with her idea of a man whose old friend had died in a brutal attack.

She stood up, her mind full of everything she wanted to say to Trish. She must be really frightened for Sam Foundling to have set up a red herring like this. Guy Bait was an even less likely suspect than the victim's colleague Dennis Flack.

'Are you sure there isn't anything else I can tell you?' Guy said, taking a step towards her.

'I don't think so.' The phone in Caro's pocket vibrated against her thigh. She couldn't break off the interview to answer it. 'Unless you know of anyone else who could have been involved in her life and who we might have missed.'

He shrugged, his shoulders almost filling the small gap between them. Caro stepped back.

'I've read about her husband's work, and I believe her mother's a judge. That's all I know.'

'Not even the name of the man who was harassing her at work?'

His easy smile disappeared behind a mask of surprise. 'Harassing Cecilia Mayford? Chief Inspector, I don't want to sound rude, but do you know anything at all about the woman? She was astonishingly tough. Think Boadicea and double it. No one would have dared harass her.'

Caro smiled and shook his hand. 'I keep wishing I'd met her. I think I'd have liked her.'

'I think you would too. In Yorkshire, where I grew up, they'd have called her grand; a grand lass.' He laughed, then added in a thick northern accent: 'And *gradely* with it. Good to meet you. Don't hesitate to phone if you think of anything else you need from me.'

Caro heard echoes of Trish's voice in her mind, taunting her with having no idea what this man had been up to at the time Cecilia was beaten to death.

'Thank you,' she said. 'Maybe as I'm here you could tell me what you were doing on the morning of December the sixth.'

'Hang on while I have a look at the diary,' he said, apparently quite happy with the question.

Like everything else in his office the diary was simple in design and beautifully made. He flicked through the pages.

'We had an internal partners' meeting,' he said, with one finger resting on the relevant page. 'It started at eight o'clock. I haven't got a note here, but they're usually over in about half an hour. My next appointment wasn't till lunch. So . . . I remember. I went out to look at a site in the City. We're working to make the architect's weird ideas practical at the moment. I can get you the details if you want. Then what happened? I know: I have a feeling I bought my Christmas cards. Hold on.'

He opened his door and went out to talk to one of the secretaries who worked at a four-person station in the corridor. Caro watched his back view, impatient at the waste of time and at her own weakness in coming here at all. Friendship had made her cross her own boundaries before, but never as stupidly as this.

'Lucy agrees,' Guy said on his return. 'It was that morning I came back with the cards. She printed off the address labels while I was at lunch and had the cards ready for me to sign when I got back from the afternoon meetings.'

'You don't have official cards?' Caro said, while at least half her mind was still on her own weakness.

'As a firm we give a donation to charity instead, but there are still some clients and colleagues I feel should have cards, so I send my own. After buying them, I had my lunch engagement. Then . . .' He looked down at the diary again and swung it round so she could look. 'Then – as you see – solid client meetings all afternoon. I hope that helps.'

'Thank you, sir. It's very clear.'

I can't risk phoning Trish, Caro thought as she waited for the lift, or I'll shout at her. She entered her PIN into the phone to listen to her messages.

'Guv! I've been trying to get you all morning,' said the voice of Glen Makins. 'We've got a witness.'

She stuffed the phone in her pocket and drove back to the incident room, reining in her impatience all the way and muttering each time a mad pedestrian stepped out into the road without looking or a van carved her up. She was sweating when she drove back into the car park, but it didn't stop her flinging herself up the stairs at speed. She found her team steaming with excitement.

'Tell me, Glen.'

'The witness saw Sam Foundling let himself into the studio, guv. Only minutes before Cecilia Mayford started shouting and there were sounds of crashing.'

'Why didn't she intervene?'

A smile spread over Glen's face like melted butter. 'Because it wasn't the only time there'd been rows and broken china and hammers chucked across the room. The first time this woman – Marisa Heering – heard it, she did try to intervene and had her ear chewed off by Cecilia herself. So she kept quiet on December the sixth. Now she can't forgive herself.'

'So why haven't we heard this before?'

'Because she went on holiday the next day and missed our house-to-house enquiries. She's been back for weeks, though, so I don't know why she waited to come forward till now.'

'Bring her in and give me the notes of your interview.'

Caro retreated to her own office, sat in her high-backed chair and let her head rest against it. She was breathing more deeply than she had for a long time, and her fingers relaxed out of the claw shape they'd been in for days. Now she'd get somewhere.

'Trish?' Sam Foundling's voice was rough and demanding over the phone. Trish levered herself up from the sofa, where she'd been lying half asleep with a mug of tea on the floor beside her.

'Sam, what's happened?'

'Can you help me with the baby?'

'What d'you need?'

'Someone to look after her. Can I bring her round?'

Trish looked wildly about the echoing spaces of her flat. 'What about your mother-in-law?'

'I can't go to her. It's not safe. Please, Trish.'

'How long will you be away?'

'I don't know. The sodding police are here. I'm being arrested.'

Trish felt as though the floor had tilted suddenly, throwing her off balance. She grabbed the back of the sofa and hung on, trying to find something to say that might comfort him without sounding idiotic.

'So I need someone to look after the baby,' he said into the silence. 'Will you help?'

'Yes.'

'Great,' he said, sounding like any impatient angry man. 'We'll drop her off on the way to the fucking incident room.'

Trish heard the rumble of male voices and knew the arresting officers must be standing very close to him.

'Don't forget to bring nappies and bottles,' she said quickly. 'And formula if you've got some. I haven't anything here to feed a baby.'

'It's all ready. Be with you in ten, Trish.'

Why had Caro done this? Hadn't she listened to a single thing? Or was this punishment at one remove for the way Trish had told her to look at Dennis and Guy? How was Sam going to cope with the assault on his fragile personality of a pair of aggressive – or manipulative – detectives trying to make him confess?

Only minutes later, Trish heard at least two pairs of feet on the iron staircase and pulled open the front door. Sam stepped across the threshold, holding the straps of a pale-blue carrycot in one strong hand. From the other dangled a scarlet nappy bag of the kind that unrolls into a changing mat. A uniformed police officer behind him was holding a rucksack. He offered it to Trish and she nearly dropped it, not having expected such a weight.

'I don't know how long they'll keep me,' Sam said, gently lowering the carrycot onto the nearest black sofa. 'So I've brought all her bottles and the sterilizer and the biggest tin of formula I could find. You've got nappies for three days and if you need more, I'll obviously reimburse you. There's a big pot of nappy-rash cream. I can't think of anything else. She sleeps most of the time and is . . .' He gritted his teeth, then produced something that sounded like a cough but could have been meant to be laughter. 'She's the easiest baby I've ever had to deal with.'

Trish laid her hand on his arm, knowing this was the only baby he'd ever dealt with. How much longer would he be allowed to keep her? He stared at Trish with an intensity she found unbearable. Looking down at the baby was the only way of escaping his gaze.

'Don't go handing her over to Gina now, will you?' he said, the effort to sound casual making his voice even scratchier. 'I don't want to risk a messy legal fight to get her back. If this nonsense goes on for more than a day or two I'll have to think again, but if I come out of it I have to know I'll be able to pick her up straight away. Can I rely on you to keep her with you until we've talked? Whatever happens?'

'Yes.' Trish forced herself to look back at him, hating her own impotence. 'You can trust me, Sam.'

There was a long pause. The police officer said they had to go. Sam looked straight at her. 'I know. She's called Felicity.'

Trish nodded. Memories of what had been done to him when he was barely older than this baby, and of what had happened once he'd been handed over to the care of foster parents, made it easy to see why he couldn't bear to let her out of his reach. Even to someone as honourable as his mother-in-law.

'I didn't do it,' he said.

Trish wanted to repeat the words he'd just used, but she couldn't. She didn't know whether he had killed his wife or not. She could only hope, so she nodded and smiled. Felicity cried, with a sound like a mewing kitten. Sam's face clenched. The copper took his elbow and tugged.

'We've got to go,' he said urgently. Sam didn't move.

'I'll look after her,' Trish said, trying to make it easier for him. 'Do you need me to phone your solicitor?'

'I'll be allowed to do that at the station, I assume,' he said, glancing at the policeman.

'Of course, but we have to go now.' The officer nodded to Trish and it struck her that he'd shown real humanity allowing this visit. There were plenty of men who'd have taken the baby with Sam and handed her over to the duty social worker, in which case she would have ended up with Gina. Trish hoped he wouldn't get into trouble for it. Or had he got permission from Caro? It would be good to think this morning's intervention had had that much effect at least, but it didn't seem likely.

Trish saw them out, then came back to sort through the equipment Sam had brought. Felicity seemed minute and terrifyingly breakable; the responsibility of looking after her, mountainous. As was the trust Sam had put in Trish.

The phone rang, making her jump.

'Trish?' said the familiar voice of her accountant, sounding much more aggressive than usual. She tried to focus her mind on him, but the baby's expression kept changing. Her face crumpled as though she was about to wail, but no sound emerged.

'May I remind you,' he went on, 'that we're now well into January and you promised me the figures for your tax return by the New Year at the very latest.'

'Shit!' Trish looked away from the sleeping face of the baby, towards the towers of paper on her desk. 'I'm sorry. There's a lot going on and I've been distracted. It's almost all ready.'

'Almost isn't enough. Have you any idea how many of my clients leave it this long? Why d'you think I'm still in the office, when I should be eating a delicious dinner at home? Send me the figures tomorrow and I'll do my damnedest to get them processed in time to avoid you having to pay a fine. Okay?'

Felicity opened her mouth and another small cry escaped. Her eyes opened too. So far she didn't look too worried. But that cry was followed by another, then another.

'All right,' Trish said, more meekly than she'd spoken to anyone for years. The tax authorities had always spooked her and for ages her accountant had done the same. Only recently had she allowed herself to believe he was both competent and aware of precisely what the Inland Revenue required of them both. He'd already sent her a list of paperwork for this year's tax return. It was lying somewhere on her desk. 'I'll get down to it as soon as I've fed and changed the baby.'

'Baby? What—' he was asking when she put down the phone to answer Felicity's increasingly frenzied mewing.

Trish was clumsy as she performed the unaccustomed tasks, but eventually Felicity was changed, fed and back in her carrycot, and apparently content. Breathing almost as heavily as George during his daily run, Trish turned her attention to the pile of financial papers that had been gathering dust in a brushed-aluminium tray at the back of her desk. Once she'd got going, the whole process would be logical, not remotely difficult, possibly even pleasurable in the way washing-up could be. But it was hard to start.

The first stage would be to dig out her copy of last year's accounts and tax return to have a model to remind her of what she was supposed to be doing.

Don't be pathetic, she told herself in silence to avoid worrying Felicity. It's not difficult. And it'll stop you imagining what's happening to Sam. You can't do anything to help him now, so you might as well get on with it.

Once the files containing her private financial documents were sorted in front of her, she laid the chambers accounts beside them, then tugged open the drawer that held her bank statements. Beneath that was the one where she kept her old chequebook stubs. There had been fewer of those for the past five years or so, since she'd taken to using credit cards or phone banking to pay her bills, but she'd never thrown any away. The old inability to trust anyone, including herself, meant that for ages she'd had a nightmare fantasy of some Revenue inspector demanding documentary proof of a figure she'd entered in a tax return twenty years ago.

Trying to mock herself out of the silliness, she took out an old set of cheque stubs and saw the ink on the counterfoils had almost faded. She could just make out the date – 6.9.83 – and saw she'd spent twenty pounds on something at Miss Selfridge.

Who on earth is ever going to need to know that? she asked herself. And what would the revolting *Daily Mercury*'s tame psychologist make of my keeping it?

Child of a broken home, she decided, desperate for security of any kind and unable to believe she'll ever find it.

I wonder, she thought, switching from her own neurotic habits into contemplating Cecilia's. Who was it who said the truth of the past lay not in accounts of what had happened but in account books?

Unable to talk to Sam, she grabbed the phone without thinking too hard about what she was going to do and called Gina Mayford again.

'Cecilia's financial records, Trish?' she said a few moments later, sounding puzzled and a bit affronted. 'What do you want those for?'

'It's just an idea I had. I know you want to know the truth, so I've been trying to think of any alternative suspects. Something struck me, which could be absurd, but might answer a lot of questions – if I could check. *Did* she keep all her bank records?'

'I've no idea.' Gina's deep voice was slow, as though she was having to force herself to talk. 'But what's the point anyway, now they've arrested Sam?'

'What d'you mean?'

'I thought you knew. I was told he'd brought the baby to you on the way to the police station.' Gina's voice was rising now: urgent, almost panicking. 'Haven't you got her, Trish?'

'She's here. And fine. I was only questioning the idea that his arrest means the police have got it right. Have they said why they've taken him in?'

'All I heard was "new evidence". That's what the family liaison officer told me. No details. Now we need to make arrangements. You shouldn't be burdened with Sam's babysitting. I assumed that's why you were phoning.'

'I'm happy to do it. Until we know what's going to happen to him, it's more sensible if I—'

'I'm afraid we already know what's going to happen, Trish. You must be realistic. And the baby's place is with me.'

'Gina . . .' Trish hesitated. 'I just can't help thinking of all those cases in which the police were sure they had the right man, only to find years later that the killer was someone else entirely.'

There was a chilly pause, before the judge said: 'No one could deny that has happened. Occasionally. Very well, I won't interfere for the next forty-eight hours, but please tell me if you need help with my granddaughter.'

'I will. Thank you.'

'Fine. Then what is it you expect to find among Cecilia's financial papers?'

'Something to tell us more about her university friends,' Trish said, making it as general as she could. '*Did* she keep her papers?'

'It's possible. She was immensely methodical. If she did they'll be at her house.' There was a pause that Trish worked to stop herself from filling. 'I have keys. Would you like to have a look? It's not a police scene because the crime didn't happen there. And I'm one of her executors. I can let you in, if you really think it'll help. D'you want to go round now? We could meet there.'

'You are kind.' Trish heard Felicity moving in her carrycot, snuffling. 'But I can't do it yet. I . . . I have some urgent work I have to finish here. It could take me all evening. Might I perhaps collect the keys from your clerk tomorrow?'

Another pause, which again Trish had no impulse to shorten. Then came Mrs Mayford's voice, colder still: 'I suppose that would be feasible. What time?'

'Eleven o'clock,' she said and was given reluctant assent.

Trish's next call was to her mother, begging her to come to London tomorrow to take care of Felicity, to avoid any possibility of being made to leave the baby with someone on Mrs Mayford's staff.

Court should start sitting at ten, Trish thought, glad the Christmas vacation had ended a week earlier than usual. So Gina will be well occupied and untouchable from then till at least half-past twelve. I don't want her there while I dig up evidence that could explain so much, including her daughter's terror of coincidence, even if it doesn't identify her murderer.

'Of course I will,' Meg said at the end of Trish's explanation. 'How's it going so far?'

'Fine, but I've only had her for about forty minutes.'

'Good. I hope the night's all right. Just remember, if she starts crying: confidence and a slow, quiet, sure voice from you will help. As well as firm hands. Not tight, but firm.'

'You sound almost scared.' Trish tried to laugh.

'Infants this small can be a nightmare in a strange place with strange smells and sounds and handling. She hasn't had an easy start, which may make her more jumpy, and she's a bit young for Calpol. If it gets bad, Trish, phone me, whatever the time. Promise?'

Does she think I'm completely incompetent? Trish wondered.

'Okay,' she said into the phone. 'In any case, I'll see you tomorrow. About ten o'clock?'

'Sure. Unless you'd like me to come over now and spend the night.'

'I think I'll manage,' Trish said.

By three o'clock in the morning, Trish wished she'd accepted the offer, but she was determined not to call for help. There was no anger in her, just a feeling of hopelessness. She couldn't understand what the problem was that made Felicity cry with this terrifying intensity. There were moments when Trish thought her breathing was about to stop as the noise pumped out, louder with each second, and her tiny crumpled face grew redder and redder.

She'd had clean nappies; she'd had a bottle; she'd had clean bedding; she'd even been taken into Trish's bed.

Thank God, she thought, George hadn't planned to be here tonight.

The only thing that kept Felicity quiet for more than a few seconds at a time was being walked up and down the living room, with Trish's tuneless voice singing snatches of half-remembered folk songs or chunks of Gilbert and Sullivan to her. She only hoped the downstairs tenants couldn't hear any of it.

'Take a pair of sparkling eyes,' Trish croaked, remembering the Losey film of *The Go Between* rather than any performance of *The Gondoliers*. 'Take a pair of ruby lips.'

Felicity turned her face towards Trish's chest and sighed a little as she relapsed into sleep. Trish stopped singing with relief, but she didn't dare stop walking for another ten minutes. By then the baby's breathing was regular enough to give her a little more confidence. With great care, Trish ascended the spiral staircase and laid the child back in her carrycot. Hardly daring to breathe, Trish waited, staring down at the tiny face, terrified the eyes would open and the cheeks clench all over again. Nothing happened. Walking backwards, she moved away until her legs touched the end of her own bed. She crawled into it and let her head touch the pillow. Breathing became possible again. She let her own eyelids close.

An urgent, unhappy, angry sound forced its way into her brain. With her mind screaming protests and obscenities, she dragged her eyes open and saw a pale-grey streak outlining the blinds that covered her dormer windows. She lay, watching it for a few seconds, unable to believe it could possibly be daylight, while the cries became even angrier.

Running her tongue around a mouth that felt and tasted disgusting, Trish flung back the duvet and padded over to the carrycot. There she saw the expected crumpled face. With all her mother's advice in her mind, she made herself smile and put a firm but gentle hand on the baby's chest. Like a miracle the sound stopped. Felicity's eyes opened and she started to suck at her bottom lip.

'Good heavens,' Trish said aloud, leaning down to scoop her up. 'It works in the daytime.'

She found the sling Sam had left, then had to lay Felicity on her bed in order to strap it on. The cries started up again at once. Resisting a momentary temptation to swear, Trish finished tying on the sling, picked Felicity up again and awkwardly deposited her in it. Once there, her cries began to dwindle. Trish hurried down to the kitchen to heat water and make up a bottle, while also brewing a pot of seriously strong coffee.

Meg's arrival was nearly always an event to be cherished, but this morning, when she rang the bell at ten, Trish practically fell into her arms. Meg laughed.

'I thought it might be harder than you expected. You look like hell, Trish. Go and have a shower and get dressed. Whatever work you're planning to do this morning won't succeed if you embark looking like that.'

Chapter 16

Gina Mayford's clerk looked pretty frosty when she came out into the huge stone hall of the Royal Courts of Justice to find Trish, but she handed over the keys, adding: 'The burglar alarm code is 9158. You have to punch it in when you hear the running beeps. When you've finished in the house, Mrs Mayford would like you to reset the alarm. You have to punch in the number again, then press button A, then press the white button on the lintel outside the front door when you've shut it. Then you must double-lock it. Do you understand?'

'Perhaps you'd better write it down for me,' Trish said, not wanting to antagonize this woman.

'I can't do that. You might drop the note somewhere it could be picked up and used to burgle the house.'

Trish summoned her reserves of patience and asked for the instructions to be repeated. She thought she could probably remember them between the Strand and Islington. As she stood on the steps a moment later, she saw a passing taxi with its light on, hailed it and was in the pretty early nineteenth-century street in less than fifteen minutes.

No one approaching the neat white-painted house would see anything amiss, she thought. Its stripped-pine shutters, probably original, were all closed, but so were many in the other houses along the street. Inside, she managed to silence the alarm's beeping without trouble and put the keys down on the radiator shelf so she couldn't lose them.

The house felt empty in a different way from the big spaces of her flat, which had an invigorating kind of energy. In this house the atmosphere was heavy and bleak, almost as though someone had been very unhappy here.

Old-looking parquet covered the hall floor, and the walls were painted a sunny yellow, presumably in an attempt to add light. There was a thin veil of dust over everything. Looking back towards the door, she saw her own footprints. No one else had been inside for days.

With no map or information to guide her, a systematic search seemed like a good idea. She started in the basement, where she found a traditional dining room, papered in a Regency stripe and furnished with antique mahogany and a lot of silver, which was already tarnished. Surprised by so much formality, Trish opened the sideboard doors and found nothing but bottles and flowered china. There were no other places where files and documents could be stored.

The kitchen had all the unlikely high-status contents that had become desirable in areas like this: an Aga, still belting out heat even though there was no one around to use it, as well as innumerable machines for making bread and ice cream, rolling pasta, and reducing vegetables to uniform slices or juice. Even if Sam and Cecilia had been the kind of obsessive cookery enthusiasts George could be, they wouldn't have needed all this. Trish thought of the double gas ring in Sam's studio, the cracked pottery sink, and the few battered pans.

Again the cupboards held nothing unusual and certainly no papers. The only oddity was a collection of full supermarket plastic bags in the centre of the kitchen table. Already powdered with dust, they proved to contain both dry and tinned food and more or less the same baby kit Sam had brought round last night. Beside one was a package wrapped in crisp white tissue paper and pink ribbon. A folded note with his name on it lay on top.

Trish looked at it. There was no envelope, and no staples or Sellotape sealed it. Giving in to temptation, she flipped it open with one finger, as though physical gentleness made her curiosity less offensive:

Dear Sam,
    This was Cecilia's when she was a baby, knitted by my dearest friend. C always looked especially serene when wrapped in it. I would love it if it had the same effect on your daughter. Please let me know as soon as you need anything. I want to help, Sam.
    With love to you both, Gina

Ashamed of prying, Trish replaced the letter, using the dustmarks as guides and retreated upstairs.

Two ground-floor rooms had been knocked through to make one reasonably light drawing room, decorated in a style of slightly countrified elegance that added to the stultifying effect of the dining room and made Trish understand Sam's less than enthusiastic attitude to the house. It reminded her of George's place and the way she'd felt imprisoned in its chintzy softness in the early days of their relationship. She knew Cecilia had owned this house for several years before she'd met Sam. Perhaps he too had felt he could only breathe safely in his own studio in Southwark. Even so it still seemed odd that he was happy to live in a place where she'd been beaten to death.

A pretty walnut bureau standing where the back fireplace would have been yielded nothing more than old Christmas cards and the records of any busy woman's life. Trish pulled open each of the four drawers below the flap and found nothing useful. There were bookshelves in each of the alcoves beside the chimney breasts, with solid cupboards beneath them. The pair nearest the window held outdated hi-fi equipment, CDs and vinyl records. The next had a television on a complicated swinging arm that would bring it up to eye level for anyone seated on the sofa. And tucked onto a lower shelf was an old-fashioned computer with the kind of stout rounded screen not seen in any office for years. Clearly Cecilia couldn't bear to throw away anything. The third cupboard looked more useful. There were neat rows of box files on both the shelves.

Trish sat cross-legged on the floor and began to look. She found it much sooner than she'd expected: two box files full of cheque stubs, just like her own. To her delight, she saw Cecilia had kept her account with Coutts, who provided more information on their statements than any other bank. The statements must be somewhere close by. It would be easier to search those than the cheque stubs.

Here they were, filed in the bank's own dark-red leather folders. It wasn't hard to work out which years Cecilia had spent at Brunel, or to chart the pattern of her spending: university bills, credit cards, the odd restaurant, and plenty of entries for small amounts of cash. She'd owned a tiny share portfolio, Trish discovered, which generated dividends of a few pounds every quarter, and there was a regular sum from Gina, which must represent her allowance, as well as the termly grant cheque.

She had obviously been a careful student, rarely straying into overdraft and ticking off each entry as though she balanced her chequebook at regular intervals. The amounts hardly fluctuated. In some summers there were extra payments, presumably the proceeds of temporary jobs. Then, just after her last term at Brunel had come a large sum paid to her by Guy Bait.

Bingo, Trish thought, before turning the page. If the story she had dreamed up to explain everything she'd heard from Sam, Jane Frant and Cecilia herself was accurate, there should be a balancing payment somewhere.

She found it on the next statement: a payment for precisely twice Guy's amount had been made to the Primrose Clinic, with a neat tick beside it to show that Cecilia had checked the figures as usual.

No wonder she made such a good, clear-minded loss adjuster,

Trish thought. If she kept her own papers in this kind of order it must have been second nature to ensure she never lost track of anything in her case files.

Directory Enquiries provided the phone number of a Primrose Clinic near Brunel University and a call there confirmed it had been in existence fourteen years ago and that it existed to provide abortions.

Which of them wanted the termination? Trish wondered as she clicked off the phone. Did the engagement break down because Guy wanted children and she wasn't prepared to take on such a responsibility before her own adult life had begun? Or did he decide she'd agreed to marry him only because she was pregnant and demanded she have an abortion to prove she loved him? Or did they fall out over something else and she refused to bring a child into the world, knowing how it felt to be fatherless?

Trish was never likely to find out. Even if she ever found a legal way to question Guy Bait, she wouldn't be able to trust his memory or his reasons for saying whatever he chose to tell her.

She tried to bring back into her mind an accurate picture of the only moment when she'd seen the two of them together, at the failed settlement meeting. Cecilia had looked ill and withdrawn, and she had avoided the risk of touching him by covering her face with her hands. But that was all. And it wasn't enough.

At what point in her work on the Arrow case had she become aware that one of the crucial members of the engineering team was her old fiancé, the father of her aborted child?

And what had the sight of her, pregnant by someone else, done to him?

The phone rang, a sharp urgent sound in the silence. Trish looked round and saw a combined phone and answering machine on a flouncy table near the window. She waited until she heard Gina's voice:

'Trish, are you still there? If you are, please pick up. This is Gina Mayford.'

She pushed the files to one side and stood awkwardly, almost falling as the pins and needles in her right leg made it give way beneath her. Hobbling, hopping, she reached the phone and said her name.

'I'm glad you're still there. Have you found what you wanted?'

'I think so.'

'I've been worried all morning: where's the baby? Have you got her with you?'

'I left her in my mother's charge.'

'Trish!' For the first time in her life, she heard Gina sound angry. 'How could you! She's *my* granddaughter. I told you to telephone me if you needed help. Why didn't you?'

'You were sitting today,' Trish said with care. 'I know you want . . . I'm sorry. Sam left her in my charge, so when I knew I had to come here, I called on my mother, who's the most reliable, kindest woman you can imagine. She's retired, so she has more time than either you or I. Please don't worry. She'll take the best possible care of Felicity.'

'What? How d'you know that's her name? Sam told you, I suppose? That man . . .'

'Gina . . .' Trish gazed up at the ceiling in despair. Who else was she going to piss off in her determination to stick by Sam for as long as she could? 'Whatever happens in the investigation, even if they charge him, he ought to get bail. I'm not laying any kind of claim to Felicity. God forbid. I'm just babysitting her while her father is . . .'

'Unavoidably detained,' Gina said, pulling back with audible effort. 'You're right of course, and it's not fair to be angry with you. May I come and see her at the end of the day?'

Trish hesitated.

'You invited me to your flat for Christmas.'

Trish didn't need the reminder. She was aware of everything they'd tried to do for each other, including the generosity of Gina's support over the *Daily Mercury*'s malice and the threat to her own reputation. Why was it never an easy choice between good and bad? Why did fighting for Sam entail hurting this woman?

'What time would you like to come? You could meet my mother too. You'll like her.'

'I'll be there at five. You'd better give me the address again.'

I only hope Sam doesn't arrive while you're there, Trish thought, as she gave directions to her flat. Or he'll think I've sold out.

She put down the receiver and took her own mobile from her jacket pocket, pressing in the code for Caro's number. She'd be questioning Sam now, so Trish didn't expect to be answered by anything but the voicemail service.

'Trish.' Caro's real voice, clipped and cold, almost made her drop the phone. 'Don't send me on any more wild-goose chases. I trusted you enough to spend an hour with Guy Bait yesterday morning, and I can assure you, he—'

'Don't go any further, Caro. I know you're busy, but there's something you have to hear. I'm in Cecilia's house at the moment, with her mother's permission. Let me tell you what I've found.'

'Go ahead.'

Trish's well-trained mind organized the facts and the inferences she'd drawn without conscious effort. She laid it all out for Caro, who kept quiet until the end.

'That makes her fear of coincidence wholly credible,' she said at last. 'But no more than that. This discovery of yours is interesting, but it's even less of a motive for your man than the possibility that he made a mistake in his work on the London Arrow and killed her because of it. You keep telling me my evidence against Sam Foundling is circumstantial. It's nothing to this fantasy of yours. I'm busy. I've got to go.'

Caro flipped her phone shut and fought her own anger. At last she felt her heart return to the steady slow beat she needed. Some of the heat left her skin. Maybe Trish's intervention wasn't all bad. The abortion story could help her crack Sam Foundling open.

So far he'd done no more than repeat the information given in his first few interviews. Neither she nor any of her officers had managed to get more from him, and they had limited time left to question him before they'd have to decide whether to charge him or let him go. The story was more fluent now he'd had time to practise it, or been coached, but so far there had been no gaps Caro could use to insert any kind of emotional chisel to lever out the rest.

His solicitor had had nothing to do as Sam explained over and over again, sounding more tired than angry with each retelling, that on the day his wife died he hadn't seen her. He'd been working so late the night before that he'd slept at the studio, as he often did. He'd then left to visit Trish Maguire in her chambers some time after eleven o'clock in the morning, only to remember a moment later that the dustbins were due to be emptied during the morning. Not wanting to miss the rubbish collection, he had turned back, collected two black bags for disposal and carried them out of the back of the studio building, unbolting the basement door from the inside in order to do so. He had then taken a taxi to Trish Maguire's chambers and spent some time with her, perhaps twenty minutes or half an hour, returned to the studio building on foot and entered through the basement door so he could rebolt it from the inside. He had climbed the back stairs, where there were no CCTV cameras, because that was easier than walking through to the front of the building to take the lift.

He had found his own studio door closed but not double-locked and guessed his wife had come to see him, she being the only other person to have keys. He was worried because this kind of visit was odd in the middle of a working morning and she was within weeks of her due date. He unlocked the door as quickly as he could and heard her moaning from the doorway. He sprinted across to where she was lying, bleeding in front of the sofa, and called an ambulance, using the mobile from his pocket.

When Caro had told him they had a witness to his return to the

studio at least fifteen minutes earlier than he claimed and only just
before sounds of banging, shouting and screams could be heard,
he had merely said: 'They're lying. If this witness heard screams
why the fuck didn't they intervene and save her?'

Not even a betraying pronoun to suggest he knows who the witness is, Caro had thought, while she'd said aloud: 'Because it wasn't
the first time the witness had heard sounds of argument and things
being thrown in your studio. On previous occasions it had been
you. The witness assumed it was you on this occasion too, having
only just seen you letting yourself into the studio.'

Sam had tightened his right hand as it gripped the left. Beads of
sweat had burst out of the skin on his forehead. But his voice had
been as tightly controlled as ever.

'Any artist worth anything loses patience with his work and so
shouts and throws things. That's all your precious witness can ever
have heard from me.'

On the brink of losing patience, Caro had decreed they all
needed a bathroom break. She had parted from the rest and taken
five minutes in her own little office, imagining some barrister with
even less conscience than Trish making Sam's points for him and
persuading a witless jury he had no case to answer.

'God, how I hate lawyers!' she'd said aloud. Then the phone had
rung and she'd seen Trish's name on the little screen.

There was a water cooler just outside her cubbyhole. She filled
a plastic cup with cold water and sipped, listening to the glopping
bubbles as the water level readjusted and trying to think herself
back into the kind of calm determination that was the only state
in which she'd get what she needed from Sam.

'Right, Sam,' she said as she walked back into the interview
room, while Glen Makins told the tape who had entered the room
and the time at which the questioning was resumed.

'Tell me about your wife's abortion.'

The solicitor's head snapped up. Clearly this was news to her.
Unfortunately it was just as clearly no news to Sam.

'Why? It happened over a decade ago. Long before I knew her.'

'But she told you about it?'

'Of course.' He looked puzzled and more reachable than at any time so far. Maybe this would do it. 'She told me everything.'

'Everything?' A sarcastic edge in Caro's voice made Frankie Amis, the solicitor, twitch. It didn't seem to worry Sam. 'I doubt that.'

He didn't respond.

'Did she talk to you about her father, for example?'

'Andrew Suvarov? Of course.'

'You mean to tell me she talked to you about him, even though she never said a word to her mother, even about knowing who he was? Why?'

'Because she didn't need to protect me.'

'I don't understand.'

'That's because you won't *listen*, Chief Inspector.' His voice throbbed and he looked like a man in the middle of a marital row. Caro smiled and waited. This was looking more hopeful.

'My wife and I . . . Oh, what's the use?' He sighed. 'Listen: she grew up with the knowledge that her very existence was a threat to her mother's well-being, so she had to learn to be quiet and tidy and good and hard-working and never to say anything that might add to her mother's burdens.'

Caro glanced at Frankie, who had been provided by Mrs Mayford, and wondered whether professional etiquette would stop her passing any of this back. She was impressed to see no change of expression on the solicitor's face.

'I thought you told me you liked your mother-in-law, Sam.'

'Even though she shares all your suspicion of me, I both like and respect her. That doesn't mean I want her interfering in my life, but—'

'How can you like her if she put this kind of pressure on the woman you loved?' Now Caro was genuinely puzzled.

He laughed at the question, with a cackling sound that made

her wince. 'That's nothing to what some parents do to their children. Gina's a good woman and absolutely straight. I've never caught her out in a lie. And she never plays emotional games.'

At least he's talking, Caro thought, even if it doesn't make sense. 'Did you trust your wife?'

'Yes.'

'In spite of her abortion?'

'What the hell's that got to do with me?'

Come on, Caro, she told herself: get down to it. She fixed an even smugger little smile on her lips and said casually: 'Only that she'd been in contact with that baby's father, who paid half the cost of the termination. That must have made you pretty angry. Jealous too. After all, you didn't like hearing her talk about your predecessors, did you?'

Sam tightened in front of her. She could see his bulky chest shrink as though he was pulling all his muscles in, a kind of shutting down that also had the effect of shutting out everyone else in the room.

'Sam?'

'I don't know what you mean,' he said after a long pause. He was no longer looking at her, but picking at a rough patch on the edge of the table. 'I had no idea she'd been approached by the man and so I was neither angry nor jealous. How could I have been?'

'Guy Bait, wasn't that his name?'

'I've no idea. She didn't volunteer his name and I never asked.'

'He's another engineer.' Maybe Trish's interfering digging really would be useful. 'They were at the same university and it seems that work has recently brought them together again. They'd been seeing each other.'

'Is he the one you talked about before? The man who's been harassing her?'

Sod it, Caro thought, feeling punished for her smugness. Why did I ever tell him that?

'We don't know. It seems unlikely.'

'But . . .'

'A lot less likely, in fact, than that the sounds of banging and shouting your studio neighbours heard so often had nothing to do with your work and everything to do with your anger and jealousy of your wife. When did she tell you she'd been seeing Guy again?'

He was silent, back to laboriously picking a long splinter of veneer off the edge of the table.

'You had a fight, didn't you? And it got out of hand.'

'We never had fights.'

'Come on, Sam.' Caro laughed. 'Are you really trying to make me believe you never rowed?'

He looked up. 'Of course not. All couples argue. We yelled at each other often enough and made each other unhappy – just like you and your partner do – but no more than that.'

Damn Trish Maguire, Caro thought as her next set of prepared questions flew out of her mind in a surge of fury. Damn her to hell. How *could* she tell him about Jess and me? How am I supposed to get anywhere with her coaching him in the best way of blocking me?

Felicity was beginning to feel more at home in the flat, or perhaps it was just that Trish was better at keeping the baby comfortable and at exuding the necessary confidence. She'd given Felicity her last bottle of the day and watched her fall asleep upstairs in the bedroom about half an hour before George's heavy tread sounded on the iron staircase outside the flat and then his key crunched in the lock.

'Hi,' Trish called from the sofa, not getting up because he didn't like her making a fuss of his arrivals and departures when he was stressed.

There was no answer, so she shifted her bum along the sofa, then craned her neck to look round the great double-sided fireplace to see what he was doing. He was standing beside the front door, head bowed, slowly unwinding the scarf from his neck.

Unusually for him, he let it lie where it fell and plodded towards her, unbuttoning his overcoat as he came.

'Hi,' he said, leaning down briefly to kiss her. His cheek felt cold and rough with the day's stubble.

'You okay?' she asked, frowning because it was obvious that he was far from happy. He was pale too, and his normally smiling mouth looked pinched. His thick, dark-brown hair was wilder than ever. This was no time to introduce him to the sleeping baby. 'What's happened?'

He blew out an angry-sounding breath. 'Those bastards at work have sent me on a six-month sabbatical.'

'But it's your firm, George. Henton, Maltravers. And Maltravers went years ago. How can they?'

'Because we're a partnership.' He plumped down at the end of her sofa and absent-mindedly rubbed one of her stockinged feet. So vigorous was he, and so repetitive the movement of his hands that it soon began to hurt. She pulled her foot away, smiling to mitigate the rejection. 'I suppose I could have fought, but it might have broken the firm completely. And they were so revoltingly reasonable.'

'Who were?'

'James Rusham mainly.' George looked at her and she flinched from the mixture of sympathy and resentment in his face. 'The man I worked so hard to make the others take seriously enough to accept as senior partner when I stepped down. At least he kept making jokes at the meeting and didn't join in when the rest had a go at me because of you.'

'What did they say about me?' she asked, mostly to give him permission to tell her if he wanted to.

'You don't want to know. It was insulting and inaccurate.' His lips jammed against each other so hard the blood was driven out and a white line ringed his mouth.

'George . . .'

'Don't try, Trish. I'll only lose it. James did his best to shut the bastards up, then he pointed out that with QPXQ Holdings still threatening to withdraw all their business, it was only politic for me to absent myself from the office until the Leviathan case is over.'

'I'm sorry,' Trish said at once, even though it wasn't her fault QPXQ had bought the company that owned the Arrow. Or that someone – presumably Malcolm Jensen – had stirred them up to make this protest. Should she tell George what her internet searches had suggested about the link between him and Guy Bait, even though she still had no proof? Or wait till she had some and George was calmer?

The sight of him so angry and defeated sent her back to some of their difficult early days together. Their combined insecurities and weird expectations of what the relationship would be like had made them hurt each other over and over again. They'd both moved hundreds of emotional miles since. She couldn't bear to go back. She'd do anything to give him the contentment they'd shared over the last year. Then she heard Antony Shelley's mocking voice in her mind: 'Whose career is more important, Trish? Yours or George's?'

'I know,' he said, making her wonder what on earth he was talking about. 'At least James managed to hold the rest of them to nothing more than a sabbatical – and paid at that. My profit share won't be affected, nor my standing when I go back in July. Or that's the theory.'

She waited. This was just the kind of moment when you could say too much too soon and cause yet more hurt.

'But, you know, I just sat there and thought how I half killed myself to qualify and do well enough to become Maltravers's partner, then to build up the practice into what it is today. I've given more than a quarter of a century to the firm that provides those ungrateful shits with their living. I've put my own life on hold over and over again because of work. Why? What did I do it all for?'

'Money,' she said drily, reminding herself of his preference for spiky women over sweetly passive ones. 'Money and status and interest – and an occupation. Come on, George. It's unutterably bloody, grossly unfair, and completely unnecessary, but it wasn't only altruism that's kept you working so hard. And besides—' She broke off, watching his face harden to shut her out. Had she taken the wrong tone with him this time?

'Worse things happen at sea,' he said, heaving himself off the sofa as though he still carried the excess stones he'd shed last year. 'I know. I just feel as though they've kicked me in the gut. Is there any food in this place?'

'Plenty of raw materials in the fridge,' she said, knowing how he used cooking to get rid of unbearable emotion. 'Shout if you need an assistant.'

He nodded, the recently revealed bones of his cheek and jaw looking sharp beneath the skin. Maybe she had made it worse. The only thing to do now was wait, without trying to comfort him, until he found his own way out of the humiliation his partners had visited on him.

Caro couldn't understand how Sam managed to look and sound so calm. They'd been at it in this session for four hours now, as she'd felt around for gaps in his mental armour. Each time she thought she'd found one it closed up on her before she could use it. He'd shown anger sometimes and plenty of misery but he'd never betrayed himself. All she had to show for the effort was a crunching headache and the kind of circumstantial evidence any good barrister could argue away.

And the witness, she reminded herself. At least I've got my witness to the fact that he returned to his studio long before he claims and just before the witness heard the banging and screams.

'Chief Inspector,' said Frankie Amis, her voice stiff with lack of use and tiredness. 'This is going nowhere. You're talking round and round the same issues. My client has answered all your questions and given you satisfactory back-up to every piece of information you have demanded. It is nearly eleven o'clock. Everyone needs to sleep. Please bring this to a conclusion.'

Caro exchanged glances with her inspector and thought of the chief super upstairs, waiting to hear that she'd done what he wanted. She thought of the highly paid shrink and *her* belief in what Sam Foundling's body language and choice of words had betrayed. She thought of the CPS gatekeeper, who'd already sanctioned a charge of murder. And she thought of all the hairs, fibres, fingerprints and blood splashes the lab had proved belonged to Sam. His lawyers might claim they'd been deposited in the most innocent way possible as he tried to save his battered wife's life, but for Caro they added to all the rest to tip the balance. Just.

Bracing herself against all her own doubts, she said: 'Samuel Foundling, I am charging you with the murder of your wife . . .'

Sam let himself go at last and slumped forwards, letting his face hit the table with enough force to hurt. Caro winced as she continued to recite the formal wording of the charge.

'And so, Trish, the hearing will be at Southwark Mags tomorrow,' Gina Mayford said, referring to the magistrates' court. 'The case will automatically be sent to the Crown Court under the provisions of S51 of the Crime and Disorder Act 1998, and—'

'I know,' Trish said, holding the phone hard against her ear to make sure the noise didn't disturb George, who was fast asleep at her side.

'Of course you do. Sorry. I'm all over the place,' Gina said. 'I imagine he'll be in police custody until then, but it's just possible he'll get bail. If so, I expect he'll want to collect Felicity from you tomorrow afternoon. In the circumstances, Social Services will have to be involved, unless he's prepared to hand her over to me. I hope he'll see that's the better way. So it makes sense really for me to collect her direct from you. Shall I come now?'

Trish, reeling from the news, noticed Gina's studied fairness and was grateful for it.

'It's kind of you,' she said, trying to sound polite as well as keeping her voice quiet enough to prevent George waking. 'But I can manage till he gets here. Or till we know he won't. Why have they charged him? There wasn't any evidence.'

'The lab has come up with enough hairs, fibres and prints to convince the CPS to go for it.'

Trish felt her breath stop, as though a plug had been put in her throat. Police officers and juries loved scientific evidence, even though it was often ambiguous.

'And there's the witness I told you about,' Gina reminded her, 'who saw him return to the studio moments before the sounds of battery and screaming.'

'I'd forgotten. Is the witness reliable?'

'It'll be up to defence counsel to test that in court.'

'D'you know who that'll be?'

'I thought probably Jake Kensal.'

'He'd be ideal if you could get him,' Trish said, thinking: You really are an extraordinary woman. There can't be many people in your position who would use your professional knowledge and contacts to provide the chief suspect in your daughter's murder with the best possible legal team. Maybe that'll help Sam hold on until his trial. And maybe it'll help him agree you should have the care of Felicity till it's over. But if he doesn't, I can't give her to you.

Gina put down the phone, wishing she'd asked what Trish had found in Cecilia's house. Her own attempt to track Trish's footsteps had turned up nothing but dust. It hurt to see that Sam hadn't unpacked the baby kit and food she'd so carefully bought to ease Felicity's first few days with him. He hadn't even touched the parcel with the Shetland lace shawl, although it looked as though he'd moved the note she'd left. It didn't quite fit the dust marks.

Or had that been Trish?

Gina wished she'd thought more carefully before asking for support and a bridge to Sam. She should have known she was laying herself open to this kind of invasion. Trish had one of the best forensic minds of her generation and Gina had let it loose on Cecilia's life. Was she scuffling around now to find information to discredit Cecilia so Sam's counsel could run a defence of provocation?

Her ears hurt as her teeth ground together, shutting out her own feelings. The image she'd had of her daughter – over-scrupulous, intelligent, kind and generous – was being overtaken by someone else.

An anger she could neither understand nor bear kept trying to make her hate Cecilia. It was as though a malign force from deep in the most primitive part of her brain was throwing up pictures of a secretive woman who'd lived two quite separate lives: the superficial life in which she would never give her mother a moment's worry; the other, wilder, bigger, more free, and belonging to people and places she should never have known.

Chapter 17

Sam fell fully clothed onto the sofa in his studio. He didn't have the energy to pull it out to make a bed of it, or to light the stove. All he wanted now was oblivion, even if it was freezing here.

Sleep wouldn't come. In spite of feeling as though his skull was full of wood shavings instead of grey matter and his legs so weak they couldn't bear his weight, he couldn't lose consciousness. Eventually he got up, put a match to the kindling sticks already laid over the briquettes in the stove, turned on all the lights and examined the marble head he'd worked so hard to repair.

The joins were like scars and just as obvious. They always would be, even when time had faded them, but it was recognizably Cecilia, as she'd been in the beginning when his need to be with her had been so strong it had hidden everything else.

He stroked the white marble head as it stood on its pillar, then stepped back to see it more clearly. In her own way, she was beautiful, his wife, his love, his life. His rescuer. Beautiful in spite of the breadth of her face that had worried her so. He took another step away, liking the way the light fell slantwise across her cheekbones, making the head look almost alive, moving again. Another step brought him up against the modelling plinth, which rocked at the impact. He swung round to catch the swaddled clay head just before it fell.

Leaving the cloths on the floor, he stared at his own hated face and drove his thumbs into the eye sockets, pulling the clay away from the chicken-wire core. There was no way he could make this head work.

Echoes of Cecilia's pleas during the worst of their times together sounded all around his mind: 'Don't be so afraid of showing your real self, Sam. You're safe now. I love you. Why can't you let me in?'

He'd nearly hit her then, as her deep, kind voice bored into the shell he'd grown to cover all the things he couldn't bear to remember. The impulse had so shocked him he'd crashed out of her tight, pretty house, and spent the next five hours walking along the canal. First he'd gone east to Canary Wharf, then when he'd run out of canal, he'd crossed over and come back on the opposite towpath, striding on right through Islington and reaching the Paddington basin before he'd walked off his rage.

Cecilia hadn't been there when he'd let himself back into the house. Later he'd learned she'd gone to her mother's. But when she came home, she didn't mention the quarrel or his departure or whatever she'd done to try to heal herself. She'd just been ordinary, carrying on as though they were a normal couple with nothing to hide or fear. He'd loved her for it.

Now he had most of the clay torn off the core, which he squashed under his heel and threw into the gaping black bag of waste. The clumps of clay were probably still workable, but he'd handled them too much and they must be impregnated with his sweat as well as the hatred that had filled the studio on the day she died.

Hot water pouring over his hands stung in dozens of small cuts. He didn't know how he'd got them, but the small hurt helped. When he was sure he was clean again, he levered a fresh chunk of orange clay off the huge plastic-wrapped block and began again.

He was so tired the usual defences were down. He didn't even think about where he was going or what this head would look like and he never once glanced in the mirror. His hands could do the thinking for him, and the talking too.

Three hours later, he knew he mustn't do any more. His legs were as useless as a pair of stuffed stockings and he could hardly drag himself to the sink to wet a new set of cloths, but he forced himself to do it. With the head protected, he let himself go and blessed sleep rolled over him, shutting out every memory and all the biting fear.

The phone woke him on Wednesday morning. Lying with his head bent at an extraordinary angle, he heard someone banging on the door too. The phone seemed less urgent. After all, there was an answering machine. Wincing as he stretched his cramped muscles, he made it to the door and dragged it open. His solicitor stood there.

'I've just come from the Mags. You were supposed to be there at ten o'clock. You *promised* when I was arguing with Chief Inspector Lyalt last night and she wanted to keep you in the cells. What are you thinking of? I'd never have fought so hard if I'd realized you could be this irresponsible. What—'

'Shit! I forgot,' he said, dragging yesterday's smelly shirt over his head. He hoped she wasn't going to mind the sight of his hairy chest. An itch halfway down made him scratch, hard. She looked away.

'There's a taxi waiting downstairs. Put on a suit and tie. We can do the rest in the cab.'

Four minutes later, he was following her out of the door and tying his tie at the same time. He hoped no one would get too close to him today. He needed a long, hot shower and a lot of soap. In the cab, she handed him three pieces of extra-strong chewing gum and a battery-driven razor from her handbag.

'As fast as you can,' she said to the cabbie. 'We're late and it matters.'

'I'll do what I can. But look at this traffic.'

They were in a narrow road, lined on both sides with the red-and-white barriers utility companies erected to protect their workmen as they dug up the roads. Cars were hooting. A large lorry was reversing at the cross-roads.

'Wouldn't we be quicker to run?' Sam said, at last facing the truth of what he'd risked by forgetting to set the alarm clock.

'No,' she said. 'Once we're past this crossing, it'll go quicker. At least I hope it will.'

Trish had risked bringing Felicity to chambers and so far it was working fine. The baby slept and evoked only sentimentally admiring attention in the few people who came into the room. Bettina was back, looking pale enough to justify her long absence with the flu, and she seemed more than familiar with babies' routines, which was an unexpected bonus.

'Shall I change her again?' she asked, as Felicity produced another wail.

'Would you? It's hardly suitable work for a pupil barrister, but you're much better at it than me, and she should be picked up soon. One way or the other.'

Bettina smiled and looked transformed into someone intelligent and attractive and confident. 'I've got a much younger half-sister. I'm used to it.'

She slid one hand under the baby's head and lifted her smoothly. Felicity's cries stopped at once.

Trish turned back to a comparison of the hard copy and computer files of detailed specifications for the cables that held the Arrow upright. The few paper versions Giles Somers had managed to find had at last arrived. They all described cables of the precise type and diameter listed in the specifications, on the suppliers' invoices, and on the results of the tests Cecilia had had done once the cracking had become visible.

'Shit!' Trish said, then heard the email beep and clicked to see it on screen. It was from Giles.

Did you get everything? Did it help?

She typed back a yes/no response and watched it leave her computer. A half-formed idea teased the back of her mind.

Pushing her chair away from the desk with such vigour that the wheels spun, she shot to the shelves under the window where her bag lay and in it her phone. She grabbed it and punched in the code for David's mobile. As expected, she was answered by the automatic voicemail.

'Hi. It's Trish here. I don't want to disturb you, but I need some help. Techie help. When you've got a minute.'

She put the phone back and picked up a pencil and a torn-off piece of scrap paper, sketching something that could have been a maypole or the Arrow's central core with the cables hanging off it. Her phone rang.

'Trish?' David's voice was excited. 'What can I tell you?'

'Am I interrupting anything?'

'No. We're in the car.'

'Okay. Is it possible for someone to monitor someone else's laptop and see exactly what she's typing into an email?'

'Of course.' His voice was puzzled. 'It's easy. You'd either put in a key logger, so that every keystroke she used popped up on your computer, or you'd open a back door.'

'A what? How?'

'You'd send her an email with the name of someone she often had in her inbox, and an attachment.' David was speaking patiently and very clearly, as though to a confused inhabitant of a geriatric ward. 'When she tried to open the attachment, there wouldn't be anything there, but by clicking on it, she'd have opened a back door into her computer, so that whenever she was online you could get in, do anything you wanted.'

'How easy would it be? I mean, could you do it?'

'Are you asking if I'm a hacker?' he said, suddenly wary.

'Heaven forfend!'

'Fuckin' hell, Trish. What does forfend mean?' he said, his voice now bright with laughter.

'Doesn't matter.' She thought this wasn't the time to explain the taboos she hoped he'd accept before too long. It was weird, she'd decided a while ago, that words you used yourself without even thinking about them could sound seriously offensive coming from the mouth of a child. 'How easy would it be to open a back door?'

'Easy for anyone with the right stuff. I haven't got it, but it's not hard to get and some of it's even legit . . . for companies and things to use. Of course she could stop it if she had good spyware and kept it up to date and used it properly. But lots of people don't. And if she was using wireless technology, you wouldn't even need to open a back door, you could just get everything that went in or out on your own laptop.'

Of course, Trish thought. Why didn't I think of that?

'We've got here,' David said. 'D'you need any more? Or can I go with the others?'

'I don't need anything else. All okay with you?'

'I'm fine. We're having a great time. Bye.'

Could it be as simple as this? she wondered. Did someone who'd opened a back door into Cecilia's computer panic when he read her email to Giles Somers, asking specifically for any hard copies of documents relating to the external cables?

And if he had done that, what else might he have done? Trish looked for another piece of scrap paper, always finding it easier to think or to demonstrate her thinking with written words and diagrams. Computers were wonderful – her work would be infinitely harder without them – but pencil and paper still felt right for some aspects of it.

'Idiot,' she muttered, just as Bettina walked in with Felicity draped against her shoulder.

'I'm sorry,' she said immediately. 'What—'

'Not you. Someone involved in the engineering of the Arrow. We're going to need Giles to get us a computer whizz. When you've put Felicity down, I'll show you what I mean.'

Bettina settled the baby, then came to stand at Trish's shoulder and listen to her explanation.

'And so you see,' she said at the end, 'what I think must have happened is that when Guy Bait signed off on the drawings, specifications and letters inviting contractors to tender for the project, he didn't notice that a decimal place had gone astray in the diameter of the outer cables. Look, the actual figures are the same for both inner and outer cables. It's just that the outer ones should have been ten times the size.'

'And no one else noticed either? Is that possible?'

'Why not? Think about it: all the double-double-checking that went on before the drawings and specifications were finalized would have been done on the correct diameter. Then somehow the mistake was made – human error presumably. Probably someone, late at night and fuzzy-brained, thought they were making a crucial correction to ensure consistency with the other cables. And Guy, the only partner around in mid-August, signed off on it all without noticing what had happened.'

'Wouldn't he have been rather young for that kind of responsibility?'

'Absolutely.' Trish smiled up at her. 'But, as I say, the invitations to tender went out in August, when most of the more senior partners would have been on holiday with their children.'

'But it was a huge project. How could they have—'

'It's only huge to us. Forbes & Franks International deal with buildings and dams and motorways on a far bigger scale all over the world all the time. This would've been fairly run-of-the-mill for them.'

'And no one would have had any reason to check back through the paperwork Guy had signed,' Bettina said, at last thinking through all the ramifications in a way that pleased Trish. 'Unless there was a problem. Which there wasn't until the Arrow had actually been built and started to crack.'

'Exactly. But at that stage, when everybody started looking for the reason for the cracking, they tested the actual components that had been used. So they'd have done it against the specifications, not against the original calculations – which means the cables would have looked right. The decimal point must have slipped – or been changed – during that one small gap between the final approval of the scheme and the printing of hard copies of drawings and documents sent out for tender.'

'But . . .'

'And then, I think,' Trish went on, 'someone must have realized what had happened and tried to hide it by altering the diameter of the outer cables in all the original files too, so that they matched.'

'Who?'

'The obvious suspects are whoever actually made the mistake in the first place and Guy Bait, who didn't notice. But it's dangerous to rely on the obvious.'

Trish thought of Sam, and of the man on the Tube who she'd been so sure had had a bomb. She ran her fingers through her hair as vigorously as though she was washing it, rubbing away the memory of the shame she'd felt then.

'Guy certainly ought to be far too clever to have done such a half-arsed job.'

'What d'you mean, Trish?'

'Look, whoever did it changed the diameter of the cables in all the documents and drawings *and* in the stress tests, but didn't bother to change the other figures in the tests to make the sums work. If he had done that, we'd never have spotted it.'

Light dawned in Bettina's eyes, and with it an anger that pleased Trish even more. 'How do we find out who it was?'

'How do I know?' Trish said, sounding as frustrated as she felt. 'It shouldn't matter as far as our case goes. The building was erected with cables only one-tenth of the size they should have been – which means that Leviathan cannot be held liable for the failure.'

'Don't you care who it was?'

Trish had to laugh. 'Of course. Who wouldn't? But we must be practical. If Giles produces good enough computer experts they may be able to show how it was done and when, which will probably throw up a name. But it doesn't matter to us.'

'You know, altering those figures would be very hard to do,' Bettina said, with a frown nearly as forbidding as Caro's.

'Would it? I thought hackers could do anything with computers.'

Bettina shook her head. 'There was an extranet for all the different professionals involved in the Arrow's design.'

'So?'

'Extranets are set up so that no one can change anything without it being absolutely clear to all the others. Once a file has been uploaded, it's effectively locked and can only be changed by uploading a revised version. The extranet audit trail logs anything like that and keeps a record of all the changes, who made them, and who received them.'

Trish looked at her pupil with a mixture of astonishment and awe. 'Are you sure there isn't a way round the audit trail?'

'I can't think of one.'

'Then I'll have to see if Giles can come up with someone who knows even more about computers than you.' Trish chewed at her lower lip. 'There *must* be a way. Nothing else explains why no one noticed there were figures in the stress tests that didn't add up. Will you get Giles on the phone for me?'

'Sure.' Bettina's expression suggested she was truly engaged in her work for the first time since Trish had known her.

The whole story had to be explained to Giles, who was even less ready to be convinced than Bettina. Trish wondered whether she should have gone to his office to draw it for him. Patiently, she went through it all again, and once more for luck. Then she put down the phone and waited for him to get back to her. She knew it would take some time.

Sam stood in the dock, listening in disbelief. The magistrate wanted to overrule the CPS, who'd said they were prepared to see him get bail until his trial. Just because he'd been three-quarters of an hour late this morning, the old bags on the bench wanted to stick him in a cell for the next ten months or more.

Was Gina behind this? It would give her the chance she needed to get control of Felicity. His hands curled into fists and he had to fight to keep from banging them on the smooth wooden edge of the dock. The only way was to force them down against the grain, grinding his skin into it.

Frankie Amis was on her feet now, arguing for his right to bail to be restored, even if it had to have conditions attached. He could feel blood pouring into his face as he clenched every muscle to control himself. A vein pumped in his temple too. He was sure the magistrates must be able to see it. Would it make them think he was dangerous?

It wasn't possible to relax. If Frankie didn't win this, he'd be taken into a police van and driven straight from here to whichever hellhole they'd picked for him. He thought of his trip to Holloway, and the hate and violence he'd had to watch.

He hadn't locked the studio properly. The stove was still alight too. They'd never let him go back to sort it all out. Would Trish help? Even if she turned off the stove and locked up, she couldn't do anything about the new head for the Prix Narcisse. It would dry out under its cloth and crumble into nothing. And Felicity would be taken away. She'd be another child growing up without a father. Gina would never mistreat her, but what if Gina lost interest or died? What guarantee was there that Felicity would be safe? Who could be trusted to make sure? And how would it be when he was let out in the end? Would she scream at the sight of him? Or hate him?

Then the killer thought hit him: would he even want her back?

The women's voices clacked in his ears and didn't reach his mind.

*

Gina nodded to the claimant's counsel, who'd just finished his closing speech on his client's behalf. She couldn't stop herself looking up at the clock. Sam's appearance before the magistrates must have finished. Had they given him bail? What was going to happen to Felicity? How should she set about finding the best nanny? It would have to be someone young but with impeccable references, who'd be prepared to live in and could be trusted to do everything Cecilia would have done for her daughter. It would be easier this time round, now that Gina had all the money she'd need for every kind of permanent help. And . . .

'. . . my lady?'

Gina looked up. Defending counsel must have been talking for several minutes. She had to focus. Whatever was happening in Southwark, she couldn't let these people down. But for a moment she couldn't remember who they were or what their argument was.

Trish was still waiting for an interim response from Giles Somers. To keep her impatience under control, she tidied up the digital files and relabelled the copies so she couldn't get muddled about which was which. She phoned Jenny Clay to tell her how her perception and honesty might have broken the case, and promised to get back to both her and Dennis as soon as there was more information. Bettina was back at work and Felicity chuntering peacefully, sucking at her lower lip.

Trish's phone rang. Watching the baby's face, she answered the call. The junior clerk told her Sam Foundling and his solicitor had arrived.

'We can hand Felicity over now,' she said to Bettina as she put down the phone.

'I'll miss her.'

'Me too, but she's too much of a distraction.' The door opened and Trish got to her feet. 'Sam. How're you feeling?'

And that's a stupid question, she thought as she took in his hollow eyes and bitten lips. He needed to wash too.

'I'll live. In the end they gave me bail, thanks to Frankie here, so it's over for the next ten months or so, before I hear whether I'm to spend the rest of my life in prison.'

'It won't come to that,' the solicitor said, taking on responsibility for comforting him. Trish was grateful. Lie though she sometimes had to, she hated it.

'That being so,' Sam went on, pretending he didn't care, 'I'll take Felicity off your hands. How's she been?'

'Amazing. We kept to your routine, and apart from the early bit of the first night, she's been really good. I've got some of her stuff in my car downstairs. I'll come down with you.'

Trish noticed that Frankie Amis didn't join them. Sam wanted to know whether Gina had been in touch and Trish relayed everything she could remember of their talks and Gina's visit.

'Will you be all right, loaded down like that?' she asked as he hefted the carrycot off the ground by her car.

'Yeah. I'll catch a cab if there is one. It's a bit cold for her out here like this. But we'll be fine. Don't worry.'

'You will phone if you need me, won't you?'

He nodded, raised a hand and wheeled round to leave the Temple by the Embankment gate.

Back in her room, Trish found Frankie waiting and heard a fuller version of the morning's proceedings.

'Mrs Mayford talked of briefing Jake Kensal for the defence,' Trish said. 'Do you think he'll take the case?'

'He already has. I wanted to have a word with you before I talk to him.'

Trish felt Bettina's curiosity like a kind of mist settling over her skin. She wished she could think of a good excuse to get her out of the room. Trying to ignore her, she smiled at Frankie.

'Sure. Look, sit down and tell me what you need.'

'Mrs Mayford tells me you're convinced of Sam's innocence. Why?'

Trish stamped on all her doubts and spoke as confidently as

though she were giving a closing speech in court. 'I don't believe in this elaborate set-up to provide an alibi, with confusing timings and so on. It's ludicrous in the context of the overwrought violence of what was done to Cecilia. Far too well planned. And then because the day he came here to talk to me—'

'The day his wife died?'

'Exactly. He was completely obsessed with the question that brought him here. Cecilia wasn't anywhere in his mind. Has he told you why he needed to talk to me?'

'Yes. And I can understand why he didn't want anyone else to know. It's good of you to have kept it quiet.'

'There's nothing else really,' Trish said, 'except my feelings about him – not *for* him, but about him. I do not believe he is violent. Not now. Whatever he was like as an adolescent, I believe he's got past it.'

'Your feelings are not susceptible to proof,' Frankie said with all the casual disdain so many solicitors used without even thinking of the effect it might have.

Trish had taken years to break George of the habit and even now stress could bring it back. She hated it.

'Jake Kensal may want to call an expert psychiatric witness to testify to his ability to overcome his old violence,' Frankie went on, 'although that can be dangerous with juries these days. They're more and more reluctant to trust experts after those cot-death cases. But apart from that, we haven't got a lot.'

'There are some bits of evidence that might throw doubt on the prosecution's allegations,' Trish said, working far harder than Frankie to avoid trampling on other people's sensibilities. 'I think the police have been studying CCTV tapes of the Somerset House ice rink on the morning Cecilia died. Could you get hold of them?'

'Of course. But it may take ages.'

'I'd like to see them. If they show what I think they may, that would be something you could use.'

Frankie shrugged, not looking remotely convinced, then nodded. Trish wasn't sure what either gesture meant.

The post had been delivered while Sam was in court. As he swung the carrycot across the studio threshold, he saw the letter on top of the sprawling pile. It was from Maria-Teresa Jackson.

He did everything Felicity could possibly want before settling her in the crook of his arm to give her a bottle, then put her down for her afternoon sleep. At last he could have the shower he so badly needed. Clean again, and warmer, he wrapped himself in a bathtowel the size of a Roman toga to heat some tinned meatballs and baked beans on the old Baby Belling's double rings.

Spooning the food into his mouth as though he'd been starved for a week, he stared at the untouched pile of envelopes by the door. He decided to get dressed first. Only when he'd run out of excuses did he rip hers open.

Dere Sam,

Im' sory you sore that beeting. I'd never of wanted you too. Im beter now. Just bruised stil and my eye looks badd. Wourse than it feles.

I heard what you sed when you come here and Im' not going to try and change yore mind. I unnerstand. Its only write after what I done for you too be free of mee now. But think of mee now my trile's come up. Its' at the Old Baylie. I'm scard. I do'nt mind what they do too mee, not now I have'nt got you nor Danny no mor, but Im' scard of standing thare in that dock heering what they say about me.

He's in the dock two, neere enough to tuch, and I never wont to see him agen after what he dun to Danny.

Think of me, Son. I'm so scard. Maria-Teresa Jackson

Sam lit a match, but he couldn't make himself set fire to the letter. When the flame reached his fingers, he cursed and blew it out.

Felicity woke, crying with an urgency that was new. He stuffed the letter under a pot of orange sticks on his desk and ran to pick her up. It took nearly half an hour to get her calm enough to lie down. She started crying each time he put her in the carrycot.

Kissing the top of her downy head when he'd picked her up yet again, he noticed the way the brain pulsed between the bony plates of her skull under the thin skin. Or was it just her blood pumping? He could fit her whole skull into one hand. The most vulnerable part of her body had no protection at all. His own survival from birth to the moment he was discovered on the hospital steps was taking on a miraculous aspect. Maybe he hadn't been uniquely unfortunate.

He strapped the sling around his body and levered Felicity in. She felt warm against his chest. The weight of her made him aware of his heart as it beat with a steady thud. Could he work like this? Encumbered but warmer than he could remember feeling in his life, he flexed his arms. They still moved freely.

He'd never know unless he tried. Still afraid of her presence, needing to protect her, feeling weird with her small body between him and his work, he put his hands on the clay, and let ideas about fragility flood his mind.

The next day, Trish was sitting in Frankie Amis's office, with the Somerset House CCTV tape running. She was amazed at how quickly the police had disgorged it. Was it a sign Caro was feeling so guilty about what she was doing to Sam that she wanted to bend over backwards to help his defence? Or was it evidence of her absolute confidence that he was guilty?

Cecilia was easy enough to spot with her great pregnant belly taking up the space of two ordinary-sized people. Beside her walked a man of medium height. At first his face was fuzzy, like Cecilia's, but as they neared the camera their features were more visible. He looked rather like Chekhov without the beard. She looked troubled. Trish searched the crowd behind them, peering forward as though she could make the tape reveal what she needed. But she couldn't see anyone else she recognized.

'What did you expect?' Frankie said, seeing her droop.

'One of the two other men who I think could have killed her,' Trish said.

'I can't believe you made me get it for that. It's not our job to show who did it, only to maintain that the police haven't proved it was Sam Foundling.'

'I thought . . .' Trish hesitated. She'd seen Guy Bait only once and couldn't conjure up a very precise idea of his appearance, except that he had not been as tall as she was and he had a pleasant roundish face and short hair. And a very quiet voice, which wasn't relevant to his appearance. But, allowing for the difference in age, he did look rather like Dennis. They were the same physical type at least. And so was Sam.

Trish thought of all the people she knew, both men and women, who'd divorced their first spouses, only to choose replacements so like the first they could have been clones. Even their affairs had been with men or women of the same physical and emotional type as the ones who'd proved so unsatisfactory.

'I thought we might get a full-length picture of him, which could explain why the witness in Sam's studio believed she saw Sam coming back at least half an hour before he did,' she said.

'That's more like it. Who is he? Or they, if there really are two of them.'

Trish sketched in what she knew about Dennis and Guy and why both of them could have been in pursuit of Cecilia on the day she was murdered.

'It's all supposition,' Trish said at the end. 'But supposition based on fact and reasonable logic.'

'I'll see what Jake Kensal thinks he can do with it,' Frankie said. She looked more friendly now. 'And whether he thinks it worth getting an investigator to dig for evidence of misidentification. Thank you.'

'Let me know if there's anything else I can do.' Trish was aware that she stood on delicate ground. Anything she did or said to help Sam now could be taken as trespassing on Jake Kensal's territory.

'I will. Thanks again.'

Walking back from Lincoln's Inn to chambers, passing plenty of people she knew and stopping to talk to a few, Trish knew her only permissible role was to support Sam emotionally as he spent the best part of the next year worrying about what would happen at his trial.

She should have been feeling triumphant now her own work was going well and she and Jenny Clay had uncovered a possible reason for the Arrow's cracks. But all she could think of was Sam.

Plenty of adults had felt unwanted in childhood, yet managed to deal with most crises in later life. Sam was different. For him, there could be no question of distant feelings or vague memories. He knew the facts. He'd been thrown away as a baby, then spent twelve years with foster parents who had systematically tortured him.

Trish had no difficulty calling up the feelings he must have fought all his life: the anger, the guilt, and the inability to believe he would ever be acceptable to anyone. It would undo any of the healing he'd achieved for such a man to stand in the dock at the Old Bailey and hear witnesses testifying to his violence and lack of control, his inevitable moments of mistreating his wife, his identification as the man who had smashed her head in with a hammer and killed her. And if he were convicted . . .

She shuddered. It mustn't happen. If he hadn't done it, the injustice would be terrible.

Meg's gentle warning echoed in her head. 'Don't let him break your heart.'

I have to know, Trish thought. Either way, I have to know.

Chapter 18

Trish shoved a pound coin into the slot to release her trolley. It seemed no time at all since she'd last been here, at the biggest supermarket in the area, and stocked up with enough food for the inhabitants of a small country. She had George's list for the welcome-home supper he'd planned for David in her pocket. Her own list was in her head.

'Trish!' A familiar, beautifully modulated voice made her whirl round to see Caro's partner with a trolley half full of food.

Jess was a slight woman, several inches shorter than Trish and about five years younger, with a charming face fringed with feathery blonde hair. She looked and often sounded fragile, but Trish had come to realize she had her own strength and an obstinacy of astonishing power. You probably couldn't bear the uncertainty of life as an actor without it, she thought. Today Jess was wearing blue jeans so tight they looked painted on and a short soft cardigan of a slightly darker blue, which showed the lacy top of her white bra at the point of the V-neck.

'Jess,' Trish said, leaning over the trolleys to kiss her cheek. 'How are you? Is Caro here?'

'No. Which is lucky. She'd probably throw a wobbly at the sight of you. I've never heard her so angry with anyone.'

'Why?' Trish gripped the plastic pushbar of her trolley. 'What have I done *now*?'

'Betrayed her,' Jess said, wide-eyed with surprise at Trish's stupidity but matter of fact in her speech.

Trish reminded herself that Jess's profession sometimes spilled out over into her private life.

'How, precisely?'

'By coaching a suspect in the best way to resist her questions.'

'That's rubbish, Jess. As Caro must know.'

'I don't think she does. She's never talked about what goes on at work before. But this time she was so hurt she couldn't hold it in. I heard the whole story last night: all about how she'd told you everything about our life together and how we nearly broke up last year, and how you've passed it all on to this wife-killing psychopath she has in the cells.'

'I didn't,' Trish said, but Jess wasn't listening.

'After hearing you bang on about loyalty and law for years, I could hardly believe it. How can you live with yourself?'

'You can't believe I'd do anything like that.' Trish was grateful she had the trolley to lean on. 'And if Caro does, she must have gone mad. Jess, you've got to make her see I'm not capable of it. Will you tell her?'

'She can't bear the sound of your name right now.' Jess looked like someone delivering the diagnosis of a terminal illness.

Trish opened her mouth to protest, but Jess wouldn't wait.

'All that's happened,' George said later that evening, with a gritty edge to his voice, 'is that I've been given a present of six well-paid months of freedom. They'll mean that I can take over responsibility for David and let you give your all to the Arrow case. It has to be a good thing.'

Trish pushed all her feelings about the three-way row with Jess and Caro to the back of her mind. She laid her face against George's shoulder, feeling the smoothness of his sweater against her cold cheek, as he cooked David's welcome-home supper. He wasn't here yet, but it couldn't be much longer. She had to use this time to shore up George's sense of himself, without behaving like a soppy adorer who'd say anything to please. He'd loathe that as much as she would.

They knew several couples whose relationships had foundered on the mismatch of power that came with a career blip for one or other. It shouldn't be more difficult for men to play the less powerful role, but it nearly always was.

One good thing was that she and George weren't going to have any financial worries. Some women's much greater earnings sent a message to their husbands that said: 'My time is worth more than yours; therefore I am worth more than you; therefore you should not have the cheek to contradict me or demand of me anything I don't already give. How am I supposed to defer to you when I'm responsible for paying the bills?' However much those women would hate the message if it had been spelled out to them, it was the one they often transmitted.

Trish tried to think of something to say that might help. She was fairly sure the only guaranteed way of bolstering George's mood would be to persuade him to tackle something he found seriously difficult.

'You've always talked about learning to sing,' she said, remembering the rumbling bass monotone that occasionally issued from the bathroom. 'Why not use this bonus time for that?'

She felt his tension all through her own body and hurried to take away any sense of criticism. 'Or something else. Anything. Kayaking, playing poker, macramé. Whatever. But don't turn yourself into David's nanny. He doesn't need one these days, and you'd end up hating him and me and probably yourself, as well as Malcolm Jensen and the rest of the stinking crew at Henton, Maltravers, who deserve to be hated.'

'Anger management would probably be the most useful lesson. And I could pass some on to you.' George managed to laugh, which helped, even though there wasn't a lot of humour in the sound. 'You'll have to move. I need to start beating this sauce.'

Trish stepped back. 'I'll go and make sure my mother didn't leave any of her stuff in David's room when she was here looking after Felicity.'

Not surprisingly Meg had tidied away all evidence of her presence. The television with its integral DVD player, which was David's second favourite possession, was neatly squared up on the desk beside his computer. The wide bed, almost a double, which was his all-time best thing, was shrouded in a handwoven blanket with broad stripes of scarlet and kingfisher blue. Over the head of the bed was a poster of his swimming hero, rearing up in mid-stroke, looking like an insect with a gigantic wingspan, his eyes covered in narrow black-edged goggles, his hair in a smooth white cap, and fountains of water drops falling either side of him.

In spite of the insect-look, it was a picture of masculine youth and strength and power: everything in fact that George felt had been taken away from him by Malcolm Jensen's malice and the spinelessness of all the other Henton, Maltravers' partners.

Trish straightened the blanket over David's pillows so the stripes ran evenly. There was no doubt her family would survive the next six months, and George would probably be fine once he went back to work. But she didn't want him just to survive. She wanted him strong again and happy, powering his way through life, shaking off malice like these water droplets.

With one more look at the poster, she left David's room and was halfway back across the acres of bare wooden floor in the living room when she heard him on the iron staircase outside. Longing to fling open the door and grab him, she made herself wait and heard him thank Susie for the holiday and for driving him home.

Go on, she thought. Invite her in.

'Come in and have a drink,' he said, as though he'd picked up Trish's cue. 'Trish and George will want to see you.'

'They'll be busy. Tell Trish I'll phone her in the morning.' There was the sound of a smacking kiss. 'Thanks for coming with us, Davy. It wouldn't have been half as much fun without you.'

He waited until the sound of her steps had dwindled and a car door banged; then he let himself in.

Trish watched him close the door behind him with a casual kick, then stand looking around his home, pausing occasionally as though to check off particular items. Satisfied, he let his parachute bag drop to the floor. She watched his eyelids close. She had to hold her hands tightly together behind her back to stop herself reaching out to him.

'Hi,' she said when the silence had gone on too long. 'You okay?'

He opened his eyes and sighed. 'Yeah. It's best here. I liked the trip, but it's best here.'

'Good. George is cooking spaghetti carbonara and caramel pancakes with toffee ice cream and butterscotch sauce to celebrate. It'll be ready in about fifteen minutes. D'you want a shower?'

'Why?' he said, trying to sound cocky and untouchable. 'Do I smell?'

'I always like a shower when I get back after something difficult, as you know.'

He stumbled forward, tripping over his trainers, so Trish had to hold out her arms. He seized her and rammed his face into her shoulder. His voice was so muffled she couldn't make out what he was saying, only feeling his hot breath through her clothes and the vibration of his voice in her bones.

'What, David?'

He moved his head a few inches from her shoulder. 'How did you know it was difficult?'

She put one hand on his head and pulled his face back against herself. 'That kind of trip always is. I've missed you.'

He moved further away this time, tilting up his face to look into hers. 'Really?'

'Every day.'

'Great.' His face lost its intensity and his arms relaxed, soon dropping away from her. 'Really really?'

She laughed. 'I *really* did, and judging by his bad temper so did George. Hence the carb, sugar and fat-fest tonight. He knows the menu's your all-time fave.'

David left her to fling himself down on one of the black sofas. He levered off his trainers, without bothering to untie the laces. One lay where it fell; the other he kicked out of his way. He swung his huge feet up on the sofa to lie full-length, with his hands behind his head. He looked as though he'd grown another inch at least.

'I'm home,' he said.

'You are.'

His eyes closed again, so she could gaze down at him without fear of showing too much.

There was a curious atmosphere in chambers when she arrived at a leisurely half past nine next morning, having taken time to walk to school with David on his first day of the new term. The usual buzz in the clerks' room stopped as she walked past. Looking down the corridor, she saw one of the other junior barristers scowling before shutting his door on her.

Take your time, she thought, running through every possible disaster as she walked to her own room. Bettina was hanging over a file on her desk, fingers in her ears as though to cut out every noisy distraction. Unnoticed, Trish hung up her coat and went back to the clerks, straightening her jacket as she went.

'Hit me with it, Steve,' she said. He looked up to reveal a face like a well-fed wolf's. But he didn't speak. 'What?'

'There's a note in your pigeonhole.'

Her gaze flicked across the room to the row of wooden racks, where briefs and letters were left for all the tenants. Hers had the usual mass of paper, as well as a pink-tied brief.

'What's that? You know I don't want to take on more until I've got Leviathan under control.'

'Have a look.'

'Stop this, Steve. Just tell me.'

'QPXQ have withdrawn the action against Leviathan, offering to pay all their costs to date. There's a note for you from Leviathan.'

Trish understood David's stillness and closed eyes last night. Relief was better savoured like this than with any kind of sigh or cheering. After a moment, she collected the papers from her pigeonhole and said: 'Tell me about the new brief.'

'Just a little one to bridge the gap. It's right up your street. And a really good fee. I know you can do it in no time. There'll be lots more big stuff once word gets out about how you cracked the Arrow case.'

His phone rang. Without looking away from Trish, he reached for the receiver.

'Two Plough Court. Yes. Yes. She's right here. Hold on a moment while I see if she can take the call.' Eyes popping, he pressed the mute button on the phone. 'It's Giles Somers. Wants to pass on the personal thanks of the managing director of QPXQ Holdings. Can you take it?'

'In my room,' she said and saw disappointment washing away some of his pleasure. 'Sorry, Steve.'

In the old days clerks had been able to listen in to their principal's conversation. Modern technology had, as far as Trish knew, stopped all that. Although now she'd learned a little about what someone might have done to files held in the supposedly secure extranet set up for the Arrow, she'd never trust any kind of privacy again.

'Bettina,' she said as she pushed open her door. Her pupil wrenched the fingers from her ears.

'Yeah?'

'Could you nip out and get me a large latte? And whatever you'd like for yourself.'

Looking cross, Bettina accepted the heavy handful of two-pound coins Trish held out and stomped out of the door. Only then did Trish pick up her receiver and tell Steve he could put Giles through.

'Hi. Sorry about the delay.'

'Too busy receiving accolades and envy, eh, Trish?'

'Wanting to engineer a bit of privacy. Was Steve right? Are you really phoning to pass on compliments from QPXQ?'

'Absolutely. With your discovery of the attempt to hide the cock-up in the cable specifications, they know they'll get a settlement from the engineers and their professional-indemnity insurers and won't waste any more time or money pursuing Leviathan. I don't think I've ever had a call from the opposition solicitors in a case like this before. It sounded as though their clients' admiration for what you've done will result in something tangible like a good fat brief for you in due course.'

'The only thing I want is the removal of suspicion that George Henton and I were trafficking in confidential information.'

'What?' The word exploded down the phone in a mixture of surprise and irritation.

Trish reminded him of the supposed conflict of interest and added a little about the mess George had been stuck in at Henton, Maltravers, apparently driven by someone at QPXQ, adding: 'It's not only that it was so insulting; it was silly too. He wasn't working on anything to do with the Arrow, and we never talk about our clients anyway. Even if we'd both been on the same case, we'd manage to keep ourselves honest.'

'Leave it with me.'

'Thanks, Giles. Of course, George may decide not to break off his sabbatical now, but he should be given the option.'

'Right. Bye.'

'Before you go, Giles.'

'Yes?'

'Has your computer whizz found out *how* the data were altered in the locked files of the extranet?'

'It was done at the ASP.'

'The what?'

Bettina arrived with the coffee. Trish pulled off the lid of her cup and took a swig.

'Application Service Provider,' Giles said down the phone. 'The company that hosts the extranet on its server. We've been on to them. At first they were highly resistant to the idea that anything nefarious could have been done. But eventually we managed to persuade them to have a proper look. They've found evidence of alterations made on the Arrow extranet just under two years ago. They think it must have been done by a member of staff who left around that time, claiming to have had a big lottery win.'

'Bribed, you mean?'

'That's the inference they're making now. Since he left they've lost all trace of him.'

'How convenient – for someone.'

'Precisely, Trish. Obviously the ASP company would like to keep it quiet – the last thing they need is publicity about such a serious security breach – but QPXQ Holdings will be pushing for more. There may well be a criminal investigation in the end.'

'I hope so. Did you get anywhere with finding out whether someone had opened a back door in Cecilia's computer? It could easily have been the same person.'

'We've checked her computer and you're right: someone did open a back door. It was done from a computer at Forbes & Franks International, the engineers. Unfortunately it's one of a batch of out-of-date laptops awaiting reformatting and resale to any member of staff who wants them. So we're not much further on.'

'Can't they tell who used it?'

'Nope. Until there's some kind of biometric version of a password, you'll only ever be able to track hacking back as far as the computer that was used, not the person who did it.'

'Sod it!'

'Indeed,' he said, sounding amused. 'But this is huge progress, Trish.'

'You're right. Thanks, Giles. Let me know if you hear any more. Bye.'

When she'd put down the phone, Trish thought about phoning Caro to give her the news. Surely with this kind of evidence of criminality it was no longer so unlikely that Cecilia had been killed because of the Arrow case. Then, remembering what Jess had said, Trish realized she'd have to get more than suspicion and logical supposition to make Caro listen to her.

The trouble was, she was no private eye and she had no resources for collecting the kind of evidence a court would accept.

Trying to stop her mind playing around ways and means, she slid the pink tape off the new brief Steve wanted her to take and began to read, glad to see it was another case of building failure. At least her brain-aching work mugging up the structural principles holding up the Arrow wouldn't be entirely wasted.

'What do we do with all the Leviathan files?' Bettina said later, as she threw her empty cardboard cup into the bin.

'Giles will send someone to collect them. It would be a good idea for you to tidy them all together and make sure everything's there. Then when I've absorbed this, I'll go through it with you and we can discuss the issues.'

'But I've got a brief of my own,' she said. 'I need to ask you . . .'

'Give me the morning to absorb this; then I'll take you out to lunch and we can go through your brief together. Okay?' Trish said kindly.

Lunch, she thought, realizing there was one way of getting some evidence that might connect Guy Bait and Malcolm Jensen and so help to overturn George's suspension. She pushed the chair away from her desk and stood up in one easy movement, feeling as though her joints had been elasticated by the possibility of doing something useful for him.

'I'll be back in a moment, Bettina.'

Trish was almost past the clerks' room when Steve called her name.

'I knew it,' he said, when she leaned back to look round the door jamb. 'I've already had a call from James Rusham, the senior partner at Henton, Maltravers, to say QPXQ Holdings want to brief you in their upcoming case against Forbes & Franks International, the consulting engineers involved in the Arrow.'

'Stall them.' Trish's voice was urgent. 'Give me till next week, if you can.'

'It'll be a pleasure. Negotiating the brief fee can easily take us several days. It's almost certainly a pre-emptive strike in any case, to stop you being nabbed by anyone else. Where are you going?'

'To deal with some personal stuff. I'll be back soonish.'

Outside, the air was tingling with sunny chill. She was amazed to see fat green spikes of daffodils already fighting their way out of the soil in one of the window boxes as she hurried through the Temple to Fleet Street, where there were still a few public phone boxes. She did not want this call easily traceable to any of her own phones.

Somewhere in her wallet was an old phone card. Miraculously, it still worked and she was through to Forbes & Franks in no time.

'May I speak to Guy Bait?'

'Who shall I say is calling?'

'Maggie Jones,' Trish said, making up a name at random and injecting an all-purpose London accent to her voice. She hoped this was going to work. 'I'm a temp'ry secker*tary* working for Mr Jensen at Henton, Mal-travers.'

'Guy Bait,' said a recognizably gentle voice a moment later. 'What does Malcolm want this time?'

Yee-es! Trish thought and fought to keep the triumph out of her voice, as she said aloud: 'He's out this morning, but he left me a note saying he wants to meet you for lunch at the usual place and time today. Can you do that?'

'I suppose so. All right.'

'Where shall I book then? And what time? He didn't say, but he's always really cross if I don't get him the right table.'

For the first time, Trish heard Guy laugh: a great gale of cheerful amusement.

'No need this time. We bring sandwiches and sit on a windswept bench overlooking the Globe Theatre.'

'That sounds like a long way.' Trish made her voice rise on the last word. 'He's got a meeting at two. Will he be back in time?'

'It's not so far: this side of the Thames,' he said. 'Okay. If he phones in to check, tell him I'll be there at 12.30.'

'Thank you very much, Mr Bait.'

Pressing the button for a follow-on call, Trish repeated the pantomime with Malcolm Jensen and secured his promise to be at the bench by 12.30. She went more slowly back to chambers, thinking up excuses to offer Bettina for making their own lunch late. Back in her room, she searched the bottom drawer of her desk for the digital camera she'd bought in an access of enthusiasm a couple of years earlier and used no more than about four times.

The weather was still ideal when she set off half an hour later, with enough sun to make any kind of photography easy and wearing dark glasses natural. It was also cold enough to justify the felt hat she bought in a souvenir shop. Decorated with a cockade made from the union flag, its ugly shape made her shudder but no one who knew her would dream she'd wear anything like it. With luck, it would make her look like a naive sightseer.

It wasn't easy to find a bench that could be described as overlooking the Globe Theatre, but she identified it eventually, unoccupied except for a tatty-looking supermarket carrier bag. There was a convenient niche between two neighbouring buildings, where she could be sheltered from the wind. She settled down to wait, gazing across the river.

Brisk-sounding steps disturbed her. Their owner must have metal edges to the heels of his shoes. She turned idly to see

Malcolm Jensen, looking pissed-off in his velvet-collared overcoat and well-polished black brogues. A sharp gust of wind blew his hair across his forehead and he shoved it back with an audible curse. He flung himself down on the bench and ripped the cover off a plastic packet of sandwiches. Picnicking like this seemed unlikely for a man so concerned with his appearance. As he gobbled, Trish worried for the effect on his digestion as well as his image. He'd finished both halves of the sandwich before Guy Bait hurried towards him.

'Sorry,' he called. 'As you can imagine, all hell's broken loose today.'

'I don't know what you expect me to do about it,' Malcolm Jensen said, standing up to brush the crumbs off his lap. Neither of them paid Trish any attention. There were always tourists here, on their way to the Millennium Bridge and Tate Modern.

With the two men standing facing each other, Trish couldn't get a clear shot of them as a pair. Would they discover the scam before she could get one? Just in case, she took a picture from behind Jensen, which showed Guy Bait clearly. Twiddling the zoom, she saw his face bloom to twice the size. There was unmistakable fear in his expression. She took four more shots.

The wind flung itself around the small paved square again, picking up grit and throwing it in their faces. Both men sat down. Jensen smoothed his hair again. Trish turned her back on them and the wind, to lean against the parapet and photograph the Globe and the Millennium Bridge before wheeling round again and taking several shots above their heads. When neither man so much as glanced in her direction, she lowered the camera and took a series of ten photographs of the two of them obviously talking to each other. One must come out. Surely this would help persuade everyone that there had been something nefarious in Malcolm's campaign against George.

Time to go, she thought, before these two start asking each other for the reason for this morning's summons.

Leaving as much space as possible between herself and their bench, she walked towards the road. It would have been good to know what they were talking about, but not worth the risk of getting near enough for either of them to recognize her. All she caught through the rattling of the wind was her own name, spat out in tones of absolute contempt.

She stopped, took some more photographs from behind them both, and was back in chambers by half past one.

Lunch over and Bettina's problems easily solved, Trish used her mobile to call James Rusham.

'Now we're not in any kind of professional relationship,' she began, 'I'd like to meet for a drink. Could you get to the Cork & Bottle by six?'

'We *are* in a professional relationship, Trish,' he said with a rich chuckle. 'We're about to make you the best-paid barrister in London.'

'Nonsense,' she said, thinking of Antony Shelley's gigantic fees. Even when she became a QC – if it ever happened – she'd be unlikely to catch up. 'In any case, "about to" isn't the same thing as being.'

'Don't be such a Jesuit.'

'*Can* you meet me? It's important.'

'All right. Why the Cork & Bottle? I haven't been there in twenty years.'

'It's convenient. I like it. And our colleagues don't use it. See you there.'

Only a few days, she thought. Can I get everything I need before Steve accepts the brief from Henton, Maltravers?

She checked the photographs she'd taken this morning. All but one were clear as clear and showed everything she wanted. Gazing down at the full-length, full-frontal picture of Guy Bait, she thought of another way she could use it, one that might help Sam too. Printing it and a few of the others took no time.

Computers really have made life easier now, she thought,

remembering childhood waits of a week or more for her photographs to be developed at the chemist. She put the photographs in her bag, along with one of the newsletters put out by Cecilia's company, which showed photographs of all the senior loss adjusters.

'I'm off again, Bettina. If I don't get through everything in time to come back today, I'll see you on Monday. Happy with your brief now?'

She nodded, then remembered to thank Trish for lunch and for the advice.

Trish grabbed her own brief and took it to Steve: 'This looks fine, and I will have time for it. Even if we do come to an agreement with Henton, Maltravers and QPXQ, that won't come to court for months.'

'If ever,' Steve said smugly. 'Now you've found the cause of the Arrow's cracking, the engineers will have to settle.'

'You'd have thought so, wouldn't you? But litigants do the oddest things. I'm off. See you tomorrow.'

'Where—'

She didn't wait to answer. He signalled his pleasure in her latest triumph by refraining from the usual Churchillian quotation. Sometimes she thought his stock must be running low, but so far he'd always managed to find a new one for each time she annoyed him.

The walk to Somerset House took twelve minutes precisely. Today only a few skaters were making a mess of the courtyard's elegant proportions. Children were back at school and everyone else must be either trying to work or still fighting post-Christmas depression under their duvets. The striped tent containing the snack bar was virtually empty too, except for the staff and a lone man reading a paper with a steaming cup in front of him.

Trish asked for hot chocolate and handed over some money. The woman behind the till barely looked at her as she accepted the coins, which was disappointing. Taking the cardboard cup to a table near the transparent side of the tent, Trish sat down and waited. Soon enough a young blonde woman with a cloth made her way along the row of tables, mopping spillages and scattered sugar, picking up rubbish and straightening the salt and pepper pots.

When she reached Trish's table, she smiled and walked on to the next. Trish lifted her cup, saying: 'It's fine. Do mine, too.'

'Is okay,' the waitress said in a heavily accented voice. Trish, who wouldn't have been able to recognize anything but French, German or Spanish, assumed this one was from somewhere in Eastern Europe. That would square with the high cheekbones and wheat-blonde hair.

'Have you been working here long?' Trish asked, making each syllable as clear as she could without sounding absurd.

'Since the skating opens, before Christmas.'

'Ah. Good. I'm looking for a man who said he often comes here. I met him at a Christmas party and he promised to phone me.' Trish shuffled through the prints she'd made.

The waitress's smile, at once sympathetic and relieved, was encouraging.

'Could you have a look to see if you recognize him?'

A shrug was followed by another smile, then a hand was held out. Trish put the full-frontal photograph of Guy Bait into it and sipped her chocolate.

'I don't know . . . Maybe . . . One minute.'

Before Trish could protest, the woman had dumped her cloth on the table, flung her handful of rubbish into a bin by the exit and skipped out of the tent, still holding the print. The older woman behind the till called out, 'Hey! Where you going?' But the younger one didn't stop. The man reading his paper by the entrance looked up in surprise. Trish was relieved to see he was a total stranger. It would be inconvenient to have someone who might recognize her as a witness to this frolic.

She waited. She'd finished her chocolate and wished she'd

brought a paper so that she too could have an excuse for loitering. Then the blonde woman reappeared, clumping up the temporary steps in her heavy black boots and accompanied by someone who could have been her twin.

'Litka is working in skating hire now. Before Christmas she was here also. We think he did come. But not often. We have not seen him like today or yesterday.'

'She means we haven't seen him recently,' Litka said, in a much less heavily accented voice.

'Have you any idea when you saw him?' Trish asked without much hope.

Both women looked blank.

'Was he with anyone?' Trish hoped she'd put the right, half-angry yearning expression on her face to confirm her story of a lonely woman in search of a man who'd shown a few signs of fancying her.

Litka nodded. Her expression was full of sympathy. 'A woman. She was very pregnant and very angry.'

It was hard to keep the satisfaction from showing, but Trish tried to look rueful. 'It must have been his wife.'

She took out the newsletter and flicked through to find a photograph of Cecilia. 'Was it this woman?'

'I think. Yes.'

'Did you hear what she was saying?'

'It was more him.' Litka looked at her friend for confirmation and received a vigorous nod. 'He said: "You're pregnant with my baby but you're prepared to ruin my life."'

Shit. Trish almost said it aloud. Then she asked Litka to repeat the quotation.

'Are you sure that's what he said?'

'Yes.'

'Was it "You are pregnant" or "You were pregnant"?' This time she didn't enunciate so carefully.

'Say again, please.'

Trish produced the alternatives once more. Then again, more clearly.

'I don't know. It could be either.'

'Fine. Thank you. And you have no idea when this was?'

'Before Christmas. Some time before.' The two looked at each other again, talking in their own language. 'We think maybe soon after the skating opened. We were still learning what we have to do.'

Another burst of staccato talk, then Litka added: 'The pregnant woman had been first with the man who talked to us. Older, taller.'

'Talked to you? What do you mean?'

'In our language. Czech. This is why we remember. It does not happen often.'

'I can imagine. What did he talk about?'

Litka glowed in the warmth of her memories. 'Just where we're from, how we like London, and can they have more coffee.'

'Fantastic. Thank you both very much. Was the shorter man with the two of them?'

'No, no. He was waiting until the older man went. She went out with him and the shorter man looked worried, but she leave her coat on her chair, so he wait near it. Then she came back and he sit at her table.'

'Did she seem surprised?' Trish asked.

'I don't know.' Litka checked her memory against her friend's, but the answer was the same.

'And did you see whether he had gloves with him?' Trish said, thinking of Gina's reference to fingerprints.

They shrugged. Again Litka spoke for them both. 'Many people have gloves in winter. I did not look to see.'

Still, they had produced a lot more than Trish had expected. She thanked them both, found two ten-pound notes and handed them over, discreetly folded. She no longer had any real suspicion of Dennis Flack, but just to be certain she reopened the loss adjusters' newsletter and showed them his photograph.

'Did you ever see him here with the woman?'

The two of them peered, exchanged glances and comments in Czech, then Litka said: 'We think maybe, but we are not sure. He is quite like this other one, but older. But we are sure we have seen this other one that day.'

'That's great. Thanks. When does the skating finish? Will you still be able to work here in Somerset House after that?' Trish said.

'No. At the end of the month we have to find other work.'

'Okay. So maybe I won't see you again. But thank you.'

As soon as Litka had returned to her post in the skate-hire tent and her friend had picked up the dirty cloth again, with a quick apology Trish took her mobile from her pocket and rang the Royal Courts of Justice, checking her watch as she did it.

'Mrs Mayford?' she said, when the judge's clerk had admitted that her boss was available and connected them. 'It's Trish here. May I ask you a question that will sound a bit weird?'

'Of course, Trish.'

'You told me about Andrew Suvarov. I realize he must have Russian ancestry. Does he happen to speak the language?'

'Absolutely.'

'Any others?'

'French, Polish, Czech, as far as I know. Probably others too.'

'Thank you very much. I won't take up any more of your time.'

'Trish—'

She clicked off the phone. Caro was never going to believe any of this but Frankie Amis might. Trish had put Frankie's office number in her diary and she dialled it before leaving the tent with a backwards wave of thanks and farewell.

'Frankie, are you busy or could I drop in for a minute or two?'

Chapter 19

That was embarrassing, Trish thought as she made her precarious way down the spiral staircase that led to the Cork & Bottle.

She was only just early enough to secure the least favoured table, beside the entrance to the loos, but it had room for no more than two, which meant no one could try to join them. And with the noise of the Australian cricket tour coming from the television above the bar, they were unlikely to be overheard. Another blonde, East European waitress appeared to take her order. Knowing she had to spend in order to keep her moral right to the table in a place as popular as this, Trish ordered a glass of one of the recommended red wines of the month. Its name meant little to her, but the description of complex fruitiness was enticing.

By now she had bought herself a newspaper and was happy to wait as long as James Rusham kept her dangling. It was hard to concentrate, though, with memories of the short sharp meeting in Frankie's office tweaking at her.

Trish had laid out everything she had, explaining the connections between Guy Bait and Cecilia, his responsibility for the catastrophic mistake at the heart of the case she was fighting for Leviathan, his encounter with her after the session with her father at the Somerset House ice rink, and the possibility that she – upset by her argument with Guy – had taken a taxi across the river to her husband's studio.

'So,' Trish had finished, 'if Guy Bait followed her, wanting to have one more go at trying to make her suppress what she'd worked out about the Arrow's cables, he could have got into the studio because the door hadn't clicked properly. If they quarrelled then he could've grabbed one of Sam's sculpting hammers and . . . well, we know what happened.'

'It's a very interesting little drama you've scripted here,' said Frankie, 'but I don't understand why you're telling me. I know I asked why you're so sure my client is innocent, and it's good to know you're still convinced, but none of this is going to prove it.'

'Except by throwing reasonable doubt on the prosecution's claims,' Trish said, clicking open her briefcase to take out the prints. She found the ones she'd taken from behind the bench. 'Look at Bait's tight, round, short-haired head. Remember what Sam Foundling looks like. Don't you think the witness in the studios might have mistaken this for Sam, in a place where she expected to see him? I mean, if she saw him unlocking the front door, she must have been behind him. She could have mistaken this man's back view for Sam's. Most people see what they're expecting, even when it's not actually there.'

'Possibly. But, as you know, we've briefed Jake Kensal. Don't you think he's capable of protecting our client?' Frankie laughed. 'He's the hottest criminal silk right now. None of his defendants has gone down for murder in the last five years. You've never done much crime, have you?'

Trish felt her cheeks flush again at the memory. She'd rarely been so ruthlessly told to mind her own business and let the experts get on with it.

That made her think of Jess and so of Caro. Were they ever going to be on the old, easy, affectionate terms again?

'Trish! Thought I'd never find you.' James Rusham swung his thick navy overcoat off his shoulders and hung it on the pegs just above her. She felt it hit the back of her head as it swung down to rest against the wall. 'This is such an unlikely place for you.'

'I love it. No fuss, and a fantastic wine list.'

'I seem to remember Gordon's used to be your choice of basement drinking hole, troglodyte that you are.'

'I still quite like it, but slightly higher ceilings and more light have their attraction, even to troglodytes. What would you like to drink, James?'

'I'd better buy it,' he said with a mocking laugh. 'That way you can't be thought to be touting for business.' He leaned round to catch the eye of the waitress, while flicking through the long wine list. 'What's that you're drinking, Trish?'

She told him and he ordered a couple more glasses, adding: 'And bring us something to eat. D'you still have that cheese and ham pie?'

The waitress smiled. 'For two?'

Trish was about to protest when James said one portion would be fine, but he'd like two sets of cutlery.

'Now, Trish. Explain the mystery.'

'I want to talk to you about Malcolm Jensen and his conspiracy against George.'

'Conspiracy? What on earth do you mean?' For once all the easy humour had gone out of James's voice and his back had stiffened.

'I think Malcolm manufactured the whole conflict-of-interest thing.' Seeing him frown, Trish added: 'Did anyone at QPXQ Holdings actually talk to *you* about their fear of a conflict of interest? Or did it all come to you via Malcolm?'

James shifted in his chair as though it had suddenly grown bumps under him.

'Without wanting to be rude, Trish, that's none of your business. And in any case, why are you agitating now? It's all over. QPXQ want you briefed on their case against the consulting engineers, so whatever they may have thought in the past, they know you're on the level now.'

'I need to know exactly what happened, when and why. Listen . . .'

The waitress put two brimming glasses of wine on the table. James took a gulp and swallowed without even tasting it. He wouldn't look at Trish.

'Look, did you know that Malcolm is close friends with one of the consulting engineers who was probably involved in what went wrong with the Arrow? One of the men against whom you – and possibly I – will now be acting on behalf of QPXQ?'

James looked a little less cocksure. 'Are you the reason I got a call from the managing director of QPXQ today, Trish?'

'I don't know what you're talking about.'

'It happened this morning. She wanted to know who gave me the impression QPXQ wanted George out of the office for the duration of the case.' James paused and drank some more, this time with less drama. He stuffed one hand through his bleached hair, making it stand on end and look even more bizarre than usual. 'She was positively stuttering with rage. Have you been stirring her up?'

'I have never spoken to her.'

'Really?' Now James was openly sneering. 'I was beginning to think she must be a fellow member of this knitting-circle thing you legal women have.'

Trish stared him down as she decided what to say next. He had to be referring to SWAB, the Society of Women at the Bar, which had been set up twenty-odd years ago by a group of senior women lawyers, for a mixture of pleasure and networking, a kind of counterbalance to the Old Boys like him, who'd had everything their own way for so long. Not exactly secret, membership of SWAB was still a matter for discretion. The few women who added it to the list of their attainments in *Who's Who* were frowned on by the rest.

'As I said, James, I know nothing about her. But I have come to know rather more about Malcolm Jensen, and—'

'Then I hope you've got some evidence. I'm not going to listen to unsubstantiated garbage about one of my partners.'

'You listened to Malcolm's unsubstantiated garbage about George.'

'So that's what this is really about, is it? You're being the good little woman defending her bloke.' James's sneer had been taken over by the more familiar laughter. 'How sweet!'

Trish smiled back and reached in her bag. She put the photographs on the table in front of him, explained who Guy Bait was, then flicked open the digital camera, which showed the date and time of each photograph.

'I took these at lunchtime today. It's evidence of collusion, if not actual corruption. QPXQ ought to see them if you're planning to keep Malcolm as one of your partners. They may want to dig into the relationship and find out whether it had anything to do with Malcolm's attempt to get me off the Arrow case.'

James looked sick.

'Why do you women have to be so bloody aggressive?' he said at last, pushing away his empty wine glass. When he stood up, his powerful thighs knocked against the small table and threatened to push it over.

Trish laughed. 'In my early days at the Bar, the cry was always that women would never hack it in the big grown-up male world because we were too gentle and lacking in killer instinct. Sort it out, James.'

He left with insulting speed, forgetting his determination to pay for their wine or the cheese and ham pie that hadn't yet been delivered. Trish gave him time to force his way through the heaving crowd, then finished her first glass of wine, left the one he'd ordered for her and went to pay for everything.

She was halfway home on foot, glad the wind had dropped, when she pulled out her phone. Leaning against the parapet of Waterloo Bridge, gazing at the dome of St Paul's, which looked even more comforting than usual, she rang Frankie Amis's office number and was automatically invited to leave a message.

'Hi. It's Trish Maguire. I should have said while I was with you that the last thing I wanted to do was tread on Jake Kensal's toes. I know he'll get a not-guilty verdict in the end. All I'm concerned with is saving Sam from the anguish of a year on bail. Thank you for seeing me.'

Sam's studio was on her way home by this route. She called him to ask if she could drop in and was greeted with real warmth.

Felicity was lying in her carrycot near the stove, sucking her thumb and wrapped in what looked like a pile of white cobwebs.

'She looks lovely,' Trish said. 'And much happier than she ever did with me.'

Sam grinned. Something had loosened in him. Had it come with relief at having been charged so that at least something was clear? Or because he'd been given bail so he knew he'd have several months with his daughter, whatever happened at the trial?

'I like her blanket-thing,' she said when the silence had gone on too long and he'd begun to stare at her.

'Gina gave it to her. It was Cecilia's.' His cheerfulness faded, but not the air of freedom.

'I hope I'm not disturbing your work?'

'I've done enough today and was beginning to make mischief.'

Trish frowned, but before she could ask a question, he'd rushed into explanation.

'Sometimes you go on hacking at a piece, taking away what's actually good. It's better to stop as soon as the warmth goes. D'you understand?'

'Not really. What are you working on?'

'A head. It's for the Prix Narcisse.'

'I've never heard of it; is it for self-portraits? That's what it sounds like.'

The grin came back, charmingly impudent again. Trish thought she could see the gleeful small boy – a kind of *Just William* boy – Sam had never been allowed to be.

'Quite right. I started on me as I am now and produced a gargoyle. It's a good example of what I meant. I went on and on, only making it worse. Cloddy and horrible. But starting again – with Felicity here . . .' He pointed to the carrycot. 'Something clicked and . . .'

He turned away. Clearly this was the end of the conversation. Trish longed to ask whether she could see the work in progress, but dared not. She could see only the lump under a pile of old-fashioned checked tea towels. Maybe it was the head's progress that had given him his new cheerfulness.

'What can I do for you, Trish? It's great to see you, but you're not a natural dropper-in so you must have an ulterior motive.'

'I just wondered whether I could take a photograph of your back view.'

He didn't have to put his question into words. His expression said everything. She tried to forget Frankie's dislike of interference.

'I have a theory, you see, that the witness who says she saw you here could've mistaken someone else's back view for yours. Would you mind?'

'Whose back view?'

Discretion, Trish reminded herself. Don't give Sam a target for all the fury that's subsided now.

'The killer's. I had this theory – although it's none of my business – that if the police could be shown a whole gallery of photographs of men of your build and colouring, taken from behind, they could see how their witness couldn't possibly have identified you securely.'

'Good idea.' His eyes sparkled again. 'Do we do it in here or shall I pose outside the door?'

'Outside sounds best. Let's go.'

Delicious scents of mushrooms and something citrus greeted her as she opened the door of her flat. Inside she saw a perfect tableau. None of the main lights was on, so the four lamps around the big black sofas made a golden pool in the darkness. George and David were in the centre of it, hanging over the Scrabble board. Paul Robeson sang 'The Volga Boatmen's Song' in the great, warm, rolling bass George had so signally failed to match in his bath. Something had gone right today. Maybe he'd found a way to see his time off as a bonus not a humiliation.

She heard the urgent thumping beat of his mobile phone and watched him reach for it with a lazy ease he'd never shown in the past. Had her determination to get him back to work been the biggest mistake of their lives together? Was Caro right, and was her tendency to interfere only the cause of unnecessary trouble to everyone?

'James?' he said, with an exhilaratingly teasing edge in his voice. 'What're you calling *me* for? You haven't gone and got yourself into a mess already, have you?'

Trish quietly closed the door behind her and watched his face in the low light. David looked up, caught her eye and winked. Maybe she hadn't screwed up. Maybe George would refuse James Rusham's inevitable invitation to make peace; maybe he wouldn't. Either way, she'd given him back his power.

Now all she had to do was find a way to make Caro start listening to her again. That was likely to be a lot harder.

Chapter 20

'Oh, Miss Maguire.' The trainee clerk's voice stopped Trish on her way into chambers after a cheerful weekend, filled with all David's favourite activities. She paused. Sally came out into the corridor, as though she wanted to say something out of earshot of Steve and the other clerks. Amused all over again by the formality of her black suit after the post-Christmas pink mini-skirt, Trish walked a few steps with her, then asked what she wanted.

'It was just that a while ago you were asking about that woman, Maria-Teresa Jackson, on remand in Holloway. D'you remember?'

'Yes.' Trish smiled encouragement.

'I happened to be speaking to her solicitor the other day and she said Jackson's trial is on at the Bailey now. It's going pretty fast, apparently. I thought you might like to know.'

'Thanks, Sally.'

'It's an awful case,' she added with a shiver. 'Have you heard what she and her bloke did to that baby?'

Trish shook her head.

'I was told the body was hardly recognizable as human by the time they'd finished with it.'

'I think that's all I need to know,' Trish said quickly. Her days of having to learn every detail of the unspeakable things parents did to their children were long over. However difficult it might be to absorb the facts and theoretical principles necessary for any big commercial case, it was easy in comparison.

Sally looked disappointed, so Trish thanked her again for the information about the trial and sent her off a little happier.

Do I tell Sam? she wondered, then put the question aside until later. She had more urgent decisions to make. All night she'd kept waking beside the peacefully sleeping George with new ideas for trying to get evidence to show Sam was innocent. Even in the drowsy half-light of dawn they'd seemed like phantasmagoria. Now, in control of her imagination and back in her proper sphere, she put adjectives to them in tones of the most contemptuous defence counsel: Machiavellian; Baroque; Jacobean.

Other helpful words, she decided, were stupid, illegal, and counter-productive. Fantasize though she might about using kindness and sympathy to inveigle Guy Bait into confessing, she knew perfectly well any such attempt would screw up the faintest hope she had of seeing him convicted for bribing someone at the ASP to change the data on the Arrow extranet, which she was sure he'd done, or being charged with Cecilia's murder, which was still very much in doubt.

She couldn't even approach him without risking a charge of interfering with a witness in one case or the other. And she still had no evidence.

Jake Kensal would probably manage to get Sam acquitted – after all, the evidence against him still wasn't very strong – but that wouldn't be enough unless someone else took his place in the dock. With no other suspect, Sam would always be considered guilty by enough people to matter. And as the years went on, someone would tell Felicity her father had killed her mother. What kind of life could she have with him then?

The only person who could go after Guy Bait was Caro, and she had cut herself off behind the wall of fury and obstinate certainty of Sam's guilt. Faced with it, Trish could understand some of the emotion that must have driven the Assistant Commissioner's pre-Christmas outburst against the rituals and flummery of trial by jury in the criminal courts.

'Are you all right?' Bettina sounded frightened.

Trish remembered her pupil was due to conduct her first solo case today and needed all the confidence-building available, so she smiled and nodded. 'How's the preparation going?'

'Okay, I think,' Bettina said. 'I was practising in front of the mirror this morning. I think I've got it all straight. I'm due at the Mags by two.'

'You'll be fine,' Trish said and watched her pupil's face relax a little. 'And the euphoria you'll feel afterwards is worth all this angst, I promise.'

Trish waited until Bettina had gone, leaving at least twice as much time as necessary to get to the magistrates' court, before embarking on her own search for more personal information about Guy Bait. If there were something – anything – in his past that might correspond with Sam's traumas, it could help to persuade Caro to disregard the psychologists' predictions about the abused turning abuser. All the resources of the internet were available at the touch of a few keys.

She already knew Guy had been at Brunel University and she had the details of his public school in no time. It was going to be harder to find something in his past or character to counterbalance Sam's violent and violated childhood.

Guy had never married, she reminded herself. Maybe there was something there that might help. He'd once been engaged to Cecilia, but the relationship hadn't outlasted her abortion. Was there something fundamental in his character that made all his relationships fail?

The internet soon provided the names of his parents and grandparents, as well as the address of a house in Devon, where his parents had lived when he was born. They hadn't sold it until four years ago. A few more strokes of the keyboard brought up a map with a red circle around the house.

Set in a small village, it couldn't be hard to find. And if they'd lived there so long, they must have left other inhabitants with useful memories of them and their only son. Trish phoned home to hear George tell her he and David had plans to go swimming first thing after school, then to the cinema, unless she needed them at home.

'That's fine,' she said. 'I've got some work to do, so I probably won't be back till late tonight anyway. Okay?'

'Sure. I can stick around and sleep in Southwark, so take your time. Hope the work goes well. Bye.'

Trish printed off the map and directions, turned off the computer, told Steve she wouldn't be back till tomorrow, and legged it out of chambers. Fetching the car would take about twenty minutes, she thought, and the drive perhaps three and a half or even four hours. It could be a wasted trip, but it had to be worth making. And she was bound to find out more than she'd get with any cold-calling on the phone.

Traffic in central London wasn't too bad and she was soon free and batting down the M4 towards Bristol, with a Bob Dylan CD playing. She'd switch to the M5 at Bristol, then turn off just after the county boundary between Somerset and Devon.

By the time she reached her target, the daylight had gone and the dusk after it. She'd forgotten how dark the country could be. Only the beam of her headlights and a few friendly gleams through the curtains of the row of white cob cottages gave her any help. There was a tiny church in the village, with a small graveyard beside it, an old-fashioned red phone box, and that was it. No post office, no shop, no pub.

Feeling a fool for her suburban assumption that every village had something of the infrastructure she'd known in the small Buckinghamshire town of her childhood, she wondered how anyone could bear to live in a place so isolated. She also wondered how the inhabitants would take to a stranger knocking on their doors after dark. She'd planned to take her seat in the local pub and fall into conversation. As it was, she'd have done better to stick with the internet and save herself the 300-mile round trip.

A knock on the nearside window made her jump. She flicked on the inside light and saw an elderly woman peering in at her. Pressing the button that lowered the window, Trish leaned across the empty passenger seat to smile and heard the sound of more than one dog, worrying at something in the grass verge.

'Are you all right?' asked the woman in commanding tones more familiar from the bench than anywhere else. Trish smiled.

'I'm absolutely fine, thank you. Just lost. I've been going round and round looking for a village called Oakleigh.'

'You've reached it. Who d'you want?'

'No one in particular. I'm doing some research into a family who were here for generations, and I assumed there'd be a way of looking up the parish records. But the church is locked, and there doesn't seem to be a vicarage or anything.'

'We've been part of a group parish for ages and the vicar's based elsewhere. Which family are you after? The Chards? They're the only truly long-standing lot hereabouts.'

'Actually no. It's a family called Bait. The latest ones living here were Alan and Miriam.'

The woman stiffened and her voice was much sharper as she said: 'I don't know who sent you here, but, whoever they are, they've given you rotten information.'

Trish's back and arms felt as though she was being racked, stretched as she was across the car and looking up into the woman's face. So she switched off the light and got out. One of the black Labradors sniffed interestedly at her shoes, while the other barked.

'Shut up, Dougal,' said the woman, who had a strong-featured face under a puff of white hair as soft and round as a dandelion seedhead. Trish wasn't surprised to see the animal shrink apologetically against the brown cord trousers his mistress was wearing under her torn green Barbour.

'My information is that they were here for at least thirty years.'

'No time at all in this part of the country.'

'Were you yourself here then? I mean, did you know them?'

'I did. But I doubt if I could be much help, even if I wanted to be. I've never had much time for snoopers.'

'I suppose it must seem as though I'm snooping,' Trish said with a careful smile, 'but my motives are pure. May I tell you why I'm here?'

She got no direct encouragement, but launched into a more-or-less true account of her determination to help the police avoid a miscarriage of justice.

'Perhaps you could tell me which the Baits' house was,' she added when she saw a slight softening in the other woman's expression.

'There. The cottage at the end; the one with the ugly conservatory wrapped round it. They'd never get planning permission these days. Hideous, isn't it?'

Trish wondered whether the woman's increasingly full responses suggested she might have some problems with the village's isolation and be in need of a friendly chat herself.

'I'd planned to find someone who could help me and then offer them a drink,' she said with a less tentative smile, 'but there doesn't seem to be anywhere round here that could provide such a thing. Might I drive you – and the dogs, of course – somewhere that could?'

'Better come to my cottage,' said the woman. 'It's right up here. Leave the car. It'll be quite safe. No one drives this way after dark – which is why I was sure you were distressed and came down with the boys to see what we could do.'

'The boys?'

She gently kicked her Labrador with a muddy brogue. 'The boys. Come along. I'll give you a whisky. One won't do you any harm.'

Reluctant to leave the car unlit at the edge of such a small road,

Trish took a surreptitious swipe at the rear reflectors as she passed, to clear off any mud that might stop them gleaming at an oncoming vehicle.

'By the way,' said her hostess over her shoulder, 'I'm Margaret Woods.'

'And I'm Trish Maguire. This is very kind of you.'

'Still a few of us who stick to the old country ways. Here we are. Give your feet a good scraping or you'll tramp mud into the house.'

There was a kind of grating beside the door. Trish obediently rubbed her shoes first one way, then the other, and stepped across the threshold. She'd expected to see dusty antiques, Persian rugs and faded chintz, and gaped as she took in the sleek glass-and-steel shelves and the ice-white leather blocks of sofa and chairs.

A rich laugh rumbled all round her. 'I know. Astonishing, isn't it? When my husband died, I decided I'd spent long enough stroking family furniture, polishing silver, and darning his mother's rugs. The one and only good thing to come out of being left on your own is being able to have everything as *you* want it at last. Here.'

She handed Trish a plain heavy tumbler with half an inch of whisky in it.

'Do sit down. The leather's more robust than it looks.'

'Thanks.' Trish laughed too. 'You're a most surprising woman to find at the end of a trip I was beginning to think had been a stupid mistake.'

'What is it you want to know? Here, boys. Come along.' The dogs rubbed themselves against her brown trousers and put up their faces to be caressed.

'Did you like the Baits?' Trish asked.

'He was all right, Alan. She was mad, poor thing.'

'Mad, how?'

'Towards the end they started calling it Bipolar Affective Something-or-other.'

'Ah. Yes. Tricky for the neighbours in a place as small as this.'

'Worse for the family. Whenever there was any nonsense talked about the boy, I reminded the tittle-tattlers that plenty of us had wanted to brain her over the years. I'm glad it's me who found you. You might have got some pre-tty nas-ty non-sense out of some of the others,' she said, giving the words unusual emphasis by dividing them in the middle.

'It doesn't sound as though my journey was wasted,' Trish said, sitting up like a pointer. 'What happened?'

'He attacked her one day, the boy. He was eleven or twelve, I suppose, and she was on the way down. Always at her worst then. When she was in the depths of despair, poor thing, she was really rather likeable. But halfway down, she was a devil. She said things then that could make a grown man cry. What they did to her son, I hate to think.'

'What happened?'

There was a long pause. Margaret Woods busied herself with an excessively thorough examination of her dogs' ears. Trish knew better than to try to break through her loyalty until she was ready.

'No one ever knew for certain. Poor old Alan came back from work, parked his car, and found the boy white as a sheet and vomiting, and Miriam lying on the kitchen floor with a great dent in her head and blood and sugar everywhere. Brown sugar, of the kind that goes hard in the cupboard. Luckily the wound wasn't serious. They got the doctor out and he put in a couple of stitches. They gave him some story about her tidying the cupboards and pulling the sugar down on her own head. Of course it looked to everyone who knew them as though the boy—'

'Guy?'

'That's it. Guy. It looked as though he'd lost his temper and started to belabour her head with the nearest thing to hand. Unfortunately for everyone, it happened to be a pound of sugar gone as hard as a rock.'

'Were the police involved?'

'No. Alan took the view – he explained it all to me later – that she'd done enough damage to the boy already. He admitted it, you see. There was no question of any kind of lunacy on his part; he'd been driven to it. They sent him to a very good boarding school for troubled children. Up in the north somewhere; Yorkshire, I think. Must have cost them all they had, but it worked. And after a few years – three or four – he moved on to a normal school, and there was no more trouble.'

Trish had been hating Guy Bait for days. Now, with this possibly crucial part of his history laid out for her, she couldn't help seeing another side. It no longer surprised her that a professional engineer might have been frightened of admitting he'd overlooked a serious mistake. Any child growing up with a parent whose illness led her to endless switching between being a needy dependant and a tyrant shouting at him for real and imagined failings could find it almost impossible to face up to what he'd done.

But would it have made him a killer too? Trish asked herself.

It didn't seem likely. Thousands of children grew up with manic-depressive mothers and hardly any turned violent. But she did wonder whether Guy might be found to have a damaged MAOA gene on the X chromosome.

'You look bothered,' said Margaret Woods, 'and you haven't drunk your whisky. What were you expecting to hear when you came?'

Trish shook her head, took a small sip of burning spirit. 'I was going to ask whether you'd met any of Guy's girlfriends, but it's not relevant now. There is one thing: can you remember what Guy did in his spare time? What were his hobbies?'

'He wasn't an out-of-doors type. Read a lot. And once he got his computer he was more or less glued to that. Became pretty well expert. They used to say in the village that he could write a program for anything he wanted the bally machine to do.'

Trish tried to hide her satisfaction. None of this was evidence,

but it did provide helpful background to how he'd known enough
to bribe the geek at the ASP. If he had.

'What's happened to his parents?'

'Miriam died nearly five years ago now, and Alan struggled on
in the cottage on his own, getting frailer and frailer, until one day
we began to notice that we hadn't seen him for a few days. And
Chard, he's the local farmer, broke in and we found the poor old
chap had had a massive stroke.' She wrinkled her nose. 'Mercy,
really. He can't have known anything about it. We should all be so
lucky.'

'Maybe. You've been very kind and I ought to get going now.'

'Far to go?'

'London,' she said before she thought.

'Long way to come to hear a story about misery and a bag of
bloody sugar.'

'Worth it, though.'

Had he followed Cecilia, Trish wondered, after she refused to
listen to him, pushed his way into the studio and tried again to
persuade her to help him with his cover-up? Tired, worried and
angry, she'd have refused, perhaps adding something cutting in an
unconscious echo of his mother's ferocious criticisms. Could that
have made him grab the nearest weapon, only to find it wasn't a
bag of sugar but a hammer?

Or had he followed her and been trying to reason with her, perhaps grabbing her by the arms, or breaking down and weeping in
her lap as she lay on the sofa, and been disturbed by Sam?

Already angry with the woman in prison, how would Sam have
reacted then? Was it impossible to believe that he'd forced Guy to
leave and then set about Cecilia's head with the hammer himself?
But if so, why wouldn't Guy have said anything when Caro interviewed him?

Halfway back down the motorway, her eyes burning with the
strain of concentrating on the lights ahead and in her mirror, Trish
found the answer to her own question. If Guy had been disturbed

by Sam while he was wrapped around Cecilia, pleading with her, he'd never tell Caro or anyone else because he'd have to explain why he'd been there. Which would uncover the mistake he'd been so desperate to conceal.

If he could somehow be confronted with evidence to prove his involvement in altering codes in the extranet, would he then give a statement about what had really happened that day in Sam's studio?

Chapter 21

The incident room would have closed now and Caro's role would be restricted to answering questions from the Crown Prosecution Service when they got round to their case preparation. She could already be involved in at least one other murder enquiry.

Trish had to make her call first thing this morning, before she was once more professionally involved in the Arrow case – and before the CPS became so entrenched in their determination to prosecute Sam that no amount of new evidence from Caro or anyone else would move them.

Not sure where Caro would be physically, Trish used her mobile number again.

'I'm busy,' Caro said, without waiting for any greeting. 'Please don't bang on about your certainty that Sam Foundling is innocent. I don't need to hear it again.'

'I know.' Trish made her voice gentle to avoid strengthening Caro's resistance. 'I need to show you something. Can we meet?'

'I'm very busy.'

'Of course you are. And I know you're angry with me, but unless we're going to chuck all these years of friendship down the drain, we're going to have to meet some time. Let it be now. Please? I won't take up much time.'

There was a sigh. 'Oh, all right. D'you want to come to me, to the flat? Or shall I come to you?'

'George and David will be in Southwark. Let me come to you. What time?'

'Six. I *could* be home by six today.'

'Great. I'll see you then.'

As soon as Caro had rung off, Trish phoned Frankie again.

'Thanks for your message,' Frankie said, sounding friendlier. 'Don't worry about Jake Kensal. I haven't told him anything about your ideas.'

'That's probably wise. Look, I'm sorry to bother you again, but I wanted to ask whether you've still got the CCTV tapes from Somerset House.'

'I have.'

'Could I borrow them?'

'Of course not. They're evidence.'

'You said they were a duplicate set, copies.'

'That's true. Even so, I can't hand them out to you.'

'Then may I come and have another look in your office? Last time I was searching the wrong bit of tape, the wrong time.'

'I suppose so.'

'Great. Now? I haven't much time.'

Trish was soon back in the graceful building in Lincoln's Inn, sitting in a windowless room in the basement, watching the tapes on a dusty television with an integral video player.

She found the part where Cecilia was walking towards the camera with her father, then rewound, stopping every few seconds until she saw a short stocky man. She hit the pause button. Peering through the horizontal lines on the screen, trying to match his features with those in her photographs of Guy Bait, she knew she'd got the wrong man. She pressed the rewind button again.

Nearly thirty minutes later, she had two almost certain sightings of Guy and noted the time, which was shown in white figures at the bottom right of the screen. The first was nearly twenty minutes before Cecilia arrived at Somerset House; the second only two minutes after she left.

Trish thought of skipping out of the building with the tape in her bag, but decided it wasn't worth the risk of pissing off Frankie as well as Caro, so she took the tape back to the solicitor's office and hurried back to chambers to organize her material as carefully as though she was about to go into court.

Caro opened the door of the flat she shared with Jess, looking anything but welcoming. She was still dressed in one of the dark suits she habitually wore to work, and her thick fair hair was tightly suppressed with matt wax so that it added to the severity she'd once have shed before they met.

'Hi,' Trish said as breezily as she could. 'Thanks for this.'

'Do you want a drink?'

There had never been a less enthusiastic invitation, Trish thought as she said, 'I'd rather show you what I've brought first.'

'Suit yourself.' Caro produced a constricted smile, as though trying to make up for her brusqueness. 'I'm not sure I want to see it, whatever it is. But you're so damn stubborn I know you'll make me look, one way or another.'

Sensing a small thaw, Trish laughed. 'Come on, old thing. I'm on your side, you know.' She led the way to the grey sofa, opening her bag as she went.

There was a pile of Jess's magazines on the coffee table, as well as a row of cuboid glass vases stuffed with red and purple tulips cut off just under the flowers. They looked glorious, but they were in the way. Trish carefully slid them backwards, then laid out her photographs in their place.

'Look, Caro,' she said. 'Here's Sam Foundling . . .'

'I told you I didn't want to hear this.'

'I know. But you have to look. If you can't see what I mean, I'll take myself and my ideas away, and I won't bother you again. But you have to look. You're too fair-minded to refuse that much.'

'Flattery . . .'

'*Please*, Caro. Don't play games. You sent me photographs of

Cecilia's wounds to remind me why you feel as you do. I looked at your pix; you ought to look at mine. Here's Sam Foundling in the position in which your witness must have seen him. Okay?'

'Yes.'

'And here's a photograph I took of Guy Bait's back view earlier in the day yesterday.'

There was a long pause. At last Caro looked up. Suspicion fought doubt in her suddenly expressive face.

'Aren't you taking a risk here, Trish? This is what Sam's defence will produce at his trial. Handing it to me on a plate like this is . . .'

'Going to make you tell the CPS to withdraw the charge, I hope,' she said, determined to put everything else on the plate too. 'This isn't the only thing. If you take another look at the CCTV tapes from Somerset House, you'll see that a man who looks extraordinarily like Guy arrived there fifteen minutes before Cecilia and left only two minutes after her.'

'If his back view looks so like Foundling's,' Caro said with all the old chill, 'what makes you think the man on the film couldn't be Foundling?'

'Because the front views aren't so alike and because Sam was with me. I know I haven't got specific times for his arrival at chambers or his departure, but he couldn't have been at Somerset House at 11.30 and then killed Cecilia, *and* been with me in the Temple for as long as he was that day. Not physically possible.'

She laid another print of the photograph of Guy Bait and Malcolm Jensen on the table, pushing the rest back.

'I know you found Guy Bait convincing, but this encounter is evidence that he's not straight.'

Before Caro could dismiss her, Trish explained the whole saga she'd already used to convince James Rusham. Caro didn't give in so easily, but eventually she ran out of reasons to protest.

Trish then described her trip to Devon and what she'd learned of Guy's childhood and tendency to violence.

'I wish I could use it all, along with my knowledge of Cecilia, to persuade Guy to talk,' Trish said, 'maybe even to confess he begged her to hide the evidence of his mistake over the Arrow's outer cables when they met in Somerset House, using their old closeness to put emotional pressure on her, but I can't. I'm too deeply involved in the insurance case. So *you've* got to do it.'

Caro didn't speak.

'Look, Caro, it all fits together. You'd heard rumours of a stalker, of whom there's been no evidence. I no longer think it was Dennis; Guy's a much more likely candidate. I suspect Cecilia thought he was trying to resuscitate their old relationship, when all he wanted was to make sure she hadn't discovered his mistake or planned to expose it. When she did discover it—'

'How would he know she had?' Caro said with a snap like a trap.

'Because of the back door I think he opened in her computer,' Trish said gently. 'We know the attack came from a computer at his firm, although we haven't got any evidence to prove it was he who operated it. He's just much the likeliest person to have done it. And it seems he has the expertise.'

'You'd better carry on then.' All the expressiveness had left Caro's face, along with every scrap of the warmth and affection Trish had once known.

'I think he also picked up the texts she and Professor Suvarov exchanged via her BlackBerry when they arranged to meet in Somerset House that last day. Witnesses have said that Guy hung about waiting until Suvarov had gone, then talked to Cecilia. I think he told her he knew she knew what he'd done, and pleaded with her to help him hide it and save his professional life.'

'This is all getting very complicated. And it's all speculation in any case.'

'Bear with it a little longer. Cecilia would have refused at once. I know she would. But it's possible the encounter so troubled her that she rushed – probably by taxi – to her husband's studio,

phoning him on the way and leaving the message you found.'
Trish paused, then added: 'You've never told me what she said.'

'I don't suppose he has either, which is hardly surprising given
how bad it makes him look. It went something like this: "Sam,
Sam! Why didn't you come home last night? I need to talk to you.
Please pick up the phone if you're there. Please. I need to see you.
I'm on my way. Please don't be angry with me."' Caro's voice was
detached, emotionless. 'She sounded frightened, Trish.'

'So she might, having just had the encounter with Guy Bait. I
don't know whether he threatened her, or whether she was just
scared of his fury . . .'

'If she was as frightened as you're suggesting, why would she
have let Guy Bait into the studio, supposing he really did follow
her?' Caro was still not looking friendly, but at least she was taking
the propositions seriously enough to argue now.

'This is only guesswork,' Trish said, 'but it could have been
because there's no spyhole in the door, or chain, so she wouldn't
have known it was him until she opened the door. Or—'

'I told you she was attacked while she was lying on the sofa,'
Caro reminded her. 'She wouldn't have gone back to lie on it if
she'd found a furious enemy on the doorstep.'

'Or,' Trish went on as she'd planned all along, 'because the latch
hadn't clicked properly. I saw that happen myself the day you
found me scrubbing the floor.'

'What then? What's the next scene in this mental movie of
yours?'

'He tries again,' Trish said, wondering why Caro looked so
blank, almost as though half her mind was somewhere else,
'hoping to persuade her. When she refuses to help, he grabs one
of the sculpting hammers and attacks her. Or maybe he doesn't
even try to persuade her. Maybe he pushes his way in, through
the unlatched door. She's lying on the sofa, assuming the incomer
is Sam. By the time she's realized it isn't and has managed to push
herself up – I saw how long that took even with a table to lean

on – he's there, holding one of Sam's hammers in his gloved hand.'

'How d'you know he had gloves?'

'In the CCTV the man who looks just like him has his gloves on. And when I photographed him by the river, he had to take off his gloves – black leather – to eat his sandwich. Unlike Sam, Guy's a man who habitually has gloves with him.'

Trish wanted to plead with Caro, threaten her, beg her. She knew she mustn't. All she could do was sit in silence, while Caro fought the loathing and whatever else had been keeping her so stubborn and so angry all these weeks.

A key sounded in the front door, then Jess's light footsteps announced her arrival. She took one look at the two of them, then backed away. Caro raised her head. Her eyes looked even bleaker than during their angriest encounters.

'Leave it with me.'

'Will you—'

'Don't push it, Trish. What is it you're always saying to me? It's better that nine guilty men should go free than that a single innocent one be convicted?' Caro's eyes widened as she spoke, clearly seeing too late that she'd just made Trish's argument for her.

'Don't push me,' Sam said into the phone, picturing his agent's foxy face. 'I've enough pressure at the moment without this. And I don't work well under pressure.'

'Of course I know you're under pressure, Sam. And you know how much I sympathize over . . . over everything that's happened. But you told me not to get mawkish or make you talk about Cecilia. So I'm trying to stay businesslike. And I need to remind you there isn't much time, and you may not get another invitation to submit a piece for the Narcisse. Don't forget, receiving the invitation is like being put on an ordinary long list in itself.'

'I know, I know. Only ten sculptors worldwide get to put in an

entry and the prize only happens once every five years,' Sam
rattled off like a child with a well-learned but ill-understood
poem. 'I know.'

'So, how's it going?'

Sam looked at the head and couldn't prevent a smile forming.
He damped it down, not wanting it to sound in his voice, which
might give his agent an excuse to come round, invading his studio
and making comments that couldn't possibly help at this stage.

The head had two sides, like a Janus. One showed the naive boy
Sam had fought so long. Hoping, yearning, allowing himself to
believe there were good people in the world, his eye looked out
with eagerness and his half of the mouth smiled. The other side of
the face was the fighter: bitter, without hope, older-looking and
yet obviously not older in years.

It scared Sam to see himself so exposed, but there was satisfaction in having got it right. And there was no one left to take
advantage of what it betrayed.

'Sam. Sam.' The voice in his ear had been shouting at him for
a while, he realized.

'Yes? What?'

'I asked how the head is going.'

'Not too bad.'

'Don't forget you've only got another week. Will you have it
done by then?'

Sam looked at his faces. 'Yes.'

Chapter 22

'And so, sir, I think we ought to pull him in and hear what he has to say,' Caro said, standing in front of the chief superintendent.

'Why are you doing this to me? You had weeks to find this man and interview him in the ordinary way. Now, you've stirred up the press, charged someone else, and handed the files to the CPS. Are you trying to make us look incompetent as well as ridiculous?' He glared at her like a basilisk, the mythical serpent that could kill with a breath or a glance. 'Is this the way you expect to make career progress?'

'Believe me, sir, it's the last thing I wanted to do. I've fought the battle every which way, night after night.'

'You do look as though you've not been sleeping.' He sounded a little kinder.

'It has to be better that we look fools at this stage than that we go through the whole performance of a trial with a defendant we're not convinced is guilty, when there's another potential one out there, quite possibly destroying evidence while we dilly-dally. And maybe going on to kill the next person who gets in his way.'

'You're not seriously trying to persuade yourself he hasn't already got rid of every single thing that could betray him, are you? If – *if* mind you – he did kill your victim, he'll have destroyed any evidence the day he did it.'

Caro's phone rang. She wanted to leave it, but he gestured

angrily at it. She picked it up and saw Trish's name on the screen, shook her head and put it down again.

'Take it,' he said. 'I need time to think.'

'This is not a good moment,' Caro said into the phone.

'Sorry.'

Trish didn't sound remotely apologetic, Caro thought; more smug.

'I've had a thought. He must have been blood-spattered after the attack. I know Sam keeps spare clothes in the studio, so Guy could've stripped off his own clothes and put them in the stove. Did you find any evidence of burned textiles there?'

'You can't expect me to answer that.'

'Which means you did. Why not go to Guy and ask him to provide you with the clothes he can be seen wearing in the Somerset House CCTV?'

'There are plenty of reasons why he might not still have them.' Caro kept watch on the chief superintendent.

'It's a thought, though, isn't it? A way into questioning him, making him feel unsafe enough to need to talk. And if you search his flat, you might find some clothes of Sam's, something he took from the studio. And Sam might be able to tell you what's missing from his clothes there.'

'Unlikely. It wasn't that kind of wardrobe. Thanks for calling.' That ought to be enough to make Trish realize there was someone in the room with her, who shouldn't be party to the conversation.

The chief super wheeled round and stood with his back to the window. 'All right, Caro. I don't like it, but I can see where you're coming from. Clear it with the CPS and then go in. But kid gloves. Even more than last time. And don't give Foundling's defence team – or Mrs Justice Mayford – any idea of what you're doing.'

'And if Guy Bait goes to the press? What then?'

'It's a gamble, but from what you've said, he sounds unlikely to want publicity. Go for it. You can have Glen Makins and a DC. More later, if you turn up anything that convinces me.'

'Thank you, sir.'

He was half out of the door before he looked back.

'Pray you're right. Otherwise I can't see any good end to this, Caro. And I'd be sorry to see you brought down before you've even begun.'

I will kill Trish if she's messing me about this time, Caro thought, keeping her face free of every expression beyond mild, confident gratitude.

The chief super nodded and left.

Trish felt George stir beside her. She hadn't been able to sleep yet, running over and over everything she'd done, in case there'd been any gaps she should have filled. From here there was no going back. She'd risked all sorts of professional trouble, as well as the friendship that meant so much to her. It could still all go horribly wrong. Cecilia's killer might get away with it. And Sam might never be free of suspicion that it was him.

George's hand landed on her thigh and he moved his thumb in a gentle, circular motion against her skin.

'Can't sleep?' he said.

'No.' She rolled her head to smile at him in the darkness. 'Mind like a rat in a trap, thrashing about to no good purpose.'

He slid his hand up, past her hipbone, into the dip before her ribs, then over them, letting his fingers bump a little over each bone, so near the surface of her skin. She flattened her body, to give him better access and saw the shadow of him leaning over her against the thicker blackness beyond. She stretched her free arm towards the light.

'Don't turn it on,' he murmured, his lips now moving softly across her breast, their dryness rough against her skin. 'Let it be all one sensation, not muddled up with what you can see.'

Trish lay back and did her best. But George's intentions were too obvious. She loved making love with him, but being the passive recipient of sex-as-therapy wasn't the same.

After a few minutes, she stroked his hair. 'I'm sorry, George. I've lost it.'

'Pity,' he said. His erection brushed her thigh as he rolled away from her and she felt mean, ungrateful, but unable to fake anything with him. Suddenly she wondered whether the outpouring of physical affection just after Christmas had been a way of blunting anxiety for him. Maybe this move too had been made out of his need, not hers, in which case she had to do something to help.

'George, I . . .'

'It's okay. Don't explain. I hope you sleep. 'Night.'

Gina Mayford switched on her light to look at the clock she'd had since childhood. Its illuminated numbers had long since faded.

'Four thirty,' she muttered aloud, and half turned to beat her pillows into submission. The twist made two vertebrae grind together. For a second she thought she'd damaged her spine and lay back in terror, waiting for the pain to recede.

Did Sam do it? she asked herself for the thousandth time. Will I ever know? What happens to my faith in my work if we go through the trial and I still don't know for sure by the time it's over?

Don't be so self-centred. It's more important to worry about what happens to Felicity. Whether Sam's around to bring her up or in a cell somewhere, serving a life sentence, she'll suffer. If he isn't convicted people will always whisper. How old will she be before someone tells her Sam probably killed her mother?

It had been hard enough growing up with the knowledge that her own mother had died of cruel natural causes soon after she'd given birth, but at least Gina had always had her father: loved, admired, relied on. Trusted. Who would Felicity have?

Half past four. Too late for a sleeping pill. She'd never be able to stay awake on the bench if she took one now, and she had some tricky arguments to disentangle in court. There was no point lying fretting like this, making herself feel worse, so she got up to make a cup of tea and read through the notes she'd made of the evidence she'd heard so far.

An empty lorry crashing over a hole in the road outside the studio woke Sam with its rattling doors. He lay for a moment, wondering why Felicity hadn't been disturbed, until the familiar mewling began. Sticking his short legs out from under the duvet on the sofa, he shuddered in the cold and hurried to chuck some briquettes in the stove. The flaring light from the open door must have reassured Felicity. When he turned to pick her out of her Moses basket, she smiled at him.

Astonished, he squatted by her side, gazing down. She waved her arms above the shawl and began to drum her legs on the mattress.

'Hey!' he said, recognizing a person for the first time.

She smiled again, a broad, gummy, dribbly expression of delighted familiarity. The kicking of her legs became more frenzied. He slid his hands under her body and picked her out, to swing her up to his shoulder.

'This is going to make night feeds a lot more interesting,' he told her and heard a friendly sucking sound as she nipped his bare shoulder with her amazingly tough little gums.

No more vehicles passed the building. And there were no sounds except Felicity's sucking and the soft splutter of the stove. They could have been alone at the end of the world.

Cecilia should've been allowed to have this too, he thought.

Felicity looked up from her bottle, distracted by the cold droplet that had fallen onto her cheek. He muttered an apology and wiped her warm skin dry, turning his face so that no more tears fell on her.

Never again, he thought. I'll never wake to see Ceel smiling at me in the early morning, hair in a tangle, covering her mouth with her hand because she's terrified of her own early morning breath. I'll never hang above her, watching as she bunches up just before she comes, then lets everything go and looks up at me with sleepy-eyed smiles.

I'll never see her rattled and trying not to snap, holding back from the kind of remark she now knows I can't take. I'll never hear her words with that tiny slur as she finishes the third glass of wine, or fight my fury as she misdirects me for the fourth time on a long journey. Or watch as she lights up with friends when idle talk over food suddenly lifts into a celebration of everything she most values. Or hold her against my shoulder when all that strength and courage abandons her to tears and tiredness.

His mood shifted with a hateful lurch as his mind produced the last thought: or listen to her rip into me with an idle comment that shows how little she thinks of me.

He had to wipe Felicity's head again and tried to forget the times when Cecilia had looked at him like an enemy and he'd hated her so much he'd have happily heard of her death in a terrorist attack or a car crash.

Felicity sneezed. Her forehead and nose were glistening with his tears. He had to put her down to wash his own horrible face at the sink and deal with the disgusting snot. Had it been those few wicked times, when he'd let his subconscious hate take over everything he'd wanted to feel, that had led to Cecilia's murder? Had his occasional fantasies of her death tempted the fates to make it happen?

The baby's angry cries wrenched him back to the present and his responsibilities and something that was almost sanity. At least, he hoped it was.

Caro had slept much better than she expected, as though finally accepting the possibility that Trish could be right had freed her in some weird way. Wearing her best suit, a Max Mara sale buy that made the most of her long legs and gave her a feeling of authority she needed today, she sat at her desk, waiting for her officers to bring Guy Bait for interview.

She had all the information Trish had supplied summarized in front of her. She had a warrant ready to seize all the computers to which Guy had had access. She'd already spoken to Mrs Woods in Oakleigh and had confirmation of everything Trish had reported of Guy Bait's childhood. She'd traced the therapeutic establishment he'd attended in Yorkshire and had got them to fax through the final report sent to his parents when he'd been assessed as fit for normal school again.

There was a phone number under the printed address at the top of the report. She rang it and asked to speak to the head.

'Is there anyone on your staff who would remember Guy Bait?' she asked when she'd explained who she was and given the woman a chance to check her records.

'I'm afraid not,' said the head. 'He left at the age of fourteen, nearly twenty years ago.'

'What about records of his time with you?'

'That's a little difficult, Chief Inspector,' said the head. 'I would have to have a court order to release them.'

'I'll get it,' Caro said. 'In the meantime, could you just tell me whether there's any mention of a repetition of the incident that persuaded his parents to send him to your school in the first place?'

There was a pause easily long enough to tell Caro her suspicions were right.

'I'm afraid I cannot tell you anything,' said the head at last. 'I will be happy to release the files on the proper authority, but I can't do anything without it.'

'You've been most helpful. Thank you.' Caro put down the phone and drummed her fingers on the edge of her desk. The nails were short and clean. She knew by the end of the day they'd be grimed with the blackness London always managed to produce.

Confession evidence on its own would never be enough, but they had plenty of circumstantial stuff to support it. Trish was right: apart from everyone's gut feeling that he'd done it and the

well-known statistics about spousal abuse, the case against Sam
Foundling could end up weaker than the one that might be made
against Guy Bait.

'He's here, guv,' said the young DC, putting her head round
Caro's door. 'And he doesn't want a brief.'

'How does he seem?'

'Calmly puzzled. Ready to help in any way he can.'

'So you didn't need to arrest him?'

The DC shook her red head. 'We just asked him if he could
accompany us to the station in true *Dixon of Dock Green* style, and
he came like a lamb.'

'Still talking like a gentle uncle to a frightened child?'

'More or less.'

Caro stiffened her shoulders and stood up without touching her
desk or chair. She was strong enough to tackle this interview. She
just hoped she'd be subtle enough. Trish's exasperating confidence
mocked her own doubts.

'Let's go,' she said with a smile and a brisk delivery.

Guy Bait stood as she came into the room, which surprised her,
and held out his hand for shaking, which made her wonder
whether he was unaware of his status as a suspect or merely trying
to make her uncomfortable.

'Good morning, Chief Inspector Lyalt,' he said, as though
greeting a valued client. 'It's really good to see you again. How can
I help you this time?'

'I wanted to ask you some more questions. Haven't you been
offered the chance to have a solicitor?'

He laughed. 'Of course. But that doesn't seem necessary.'

'Maybe not, but I must caution you.' She recited the familiar
words and watched his expression darken. 'Do you understand?'

'I entirely understand the caution,' he said, 'but not why you feel
it necessary to apply it to me. Am I a suspect of some kind now?'

She looked into his clear eyes and saw nothing. His lips didn't
tremble, nor his hands twitch. He smiled.

'Chief Inspector? I imagine the rules say you do have to tell me if you suspect me of something. Don't they?'

'I have to tell you if I'm going to charge you, sir. And I have to caution you before I question you. My suspicions may fall on all kinds of people.'

'Then you'd better fire away. I have a busy day. Luckily my first meeting isn't until twelve, but I will have to be gone by half eleven to be sure of getting there in time.'

And I can't hold you unless I arrest you, Caro thought.

'Can you tell me again where you were on the morning of Monday December the sixth?'

He leaned back in his chair, giving himself plenty of room to cross his legs. 'I've already explained. I freely offered you a list of my movements that morning, when I had my diary and my secretary there to confirm it. All I can rely on now is my memory.'

'You did not mention then the fact that you were in Somerset House.'

A delighted smile creased his face. 'Didn't I? How silly of me. You remember how I told you I'd bought Christmas cards? That's where I found them. The news about poor Cecilia Mayford probably put it right out of my head. I'd been all along the Strand, looking for some cards I could bear to send out and nothing seemed quite right. Then I saw the board announcing the Courtauld Institute shop and I nipped in and bought them there.'

'What were you wearing?'

His brows twitched and his eyes narrowed. 'A suit, of course. I had a lunch to go to and an afternoon of client meetings.'

'Could you provide us with the suit?'

'Certainly. You'd have to come to my flat.'

'Has it been cleaned recently?'

'The flat?'

This bastard is playing games, Caro thought, finding it easier to dislike him. Maybe I *will* get him.

'The suit. Could you describe it?'

As he ran through a description that could probably have been applied to most of the suits in his wardrobe, a hint of satisfaction made his mouth curl up at the corners. He flicked a glance at the clock on the wall. Caro couldn't help following and saw she had less than an hour and a half before she would have to arrest him or allow him to leave for his meeting. There wouldn't be much choice.

'Did you see Cecilia Mayford while you were there?'

'I can't say I did. Was she there at the same time? Buying Christmas cards too?'

'No. Have a look at this.'

Caro swung round and slid the CCTV tape into the video player. He watched politely, apparently quite unworried.

'Did you do much acting at university?' she said suddenly and had the satisfaction of seeing him look genuinely surprised.

'No. Why?'

'Just a thought. Right, we have established to our mutual satisfaction that you were there. But we still disagree on why you went.'

'I told you . . .'

'I know you did. But it seems too much of a coincidence, particularly after the email Cecilia Mayford sent to Leviathan Insurance's solicitors when she was working late the evening before.'

'I don't know what you're talking about.'

'Mr Bait, we could go on playing games all morning, but it seems a little childish. Our experts will be examining the computer that is awaiting recycling in your offices to gather physical evidence – probably DNA from sweat or skin fragments – to show that it was you who used it to open the back door in Ms Mayford's system.'

She paused to allow him to comment, but he kept his mouth shut and his expression bland.

'A back door that gave you access to everything she typed,' Caro went on. 'We know you saw the email she sent asking for copies of all the documents relating to the cables that were used at the corners of the London Arrow to keep it upright.'

Still he said nothing. He didn't even look worried. Frustration grabbed at Caro's gut, along with a scary question: had Trish's imagination run away with them both?

'And, I suspect you also picked up the text messages to and from her BlackBerry,' she said steadily, hoping she showed no sign of doubt. 'The ones arranging a meeting at Somerset House that morning.'

There was nothing in his face or posture to suggest he had any idea he knew what she was talking about.

'Knowing what you and I both know, you must have realized she had at last uncovered the mistake you made – or overlooked – when your firm was putting the architect's original vision for the London Arrow into practical shape.'

He uncrossed his legs and leaned towards Caro. 'Please don't take this the wrong way, Chief Inspector, but you have completely lost your marbles. I have no need of a solicitor to protect me against questions concerning the appalling murder of Cecilia Mayford, but I and my firm would need one if I'm to talk about anything to do with the London Arrow. There are court cases pending, as I'm sure you know. I can't say any more until my lawyers are here.'

Chapter 23

'Caro Lyalt says it was you, Trish.' Gina Mayford's voice was warm as well as shaky. 'I don't know what to say, how to thank you.'

'You don't need to say anything,' Trish told her.

'I think I do. I've spent so long harbouring very unfair thoughts, wishing I'd never opened the door to your . . . your . . .'

'My interference?'

Gina's laugh, which Trish hadn't heard for months, echoed down the phone. 'Exactly. But you've done everything I could have wanted. More than I ever expected.'

'How's Sam?'

'A little stand-offish, but that's hardly surprising. He knows I suspected him. I can't think why he hasn't said anything to you yet.'

'He and Felicity are coming round for a celebration high tea this afternoon. I expect he's keeping it till then. Would you like to join us?'

'I'd better not, Trish. I need to step lightly round him for a while. I think I'll wait until he feels able to bring her back to live at home instead of camping in the studio.'

That might never happen, Trish thought, but it seemed better not to say it. She put down the phone, wondering how Guy Bait's arrest would affect the way the consulting engineers tackled their legal problems now. They'd have to settle with QPXQ, which would mean she'd be without a big case. Still, there'd be large brief fees to come, and Steve was showing signs of continuing approval, which suggested he'd find her something else soon.

She smiled at the thought of George, at home in her flat now cooking all kinds of illicit treats for the afternoon's celebration. He'd decided to take only half the proposed sabbatical, thus giving everyone a reasonable amount of face. Malcolm Jensen had shown signs of resisting the suggestion that he might be happier working for a different firm, but once the police had visited him to ask for information about his dealings with Guy Bait, and his partners had asked how this had affected his accusations against George, he had gone to ground. Presumably he was trying to find another job before he formally departed from Henton, Maltravers.

One day Trish would ask George whether Jensen's CV had included the years she was sure he must have spent at the school for troubled boys in Yorkshire, but George's wounds had only just skinned over and she didn't want to risk that healing by talking too much too soon.

David was happy too, secure in the knowledge that he'd managed to meet his few distant British relations and come safely home to Trish, welcomed and wanted. Soon, she'd have to tackle the continuing problem of their father, Paddy Maguire, charming, feckless, but affectionate when he was allowed to be. George might have become David's father in everything but name, but she was sure it was important for children to know their genetic parents.

There was a knock at the door. Bettina twitched. Trish called, 'Come in,' and saw Sally Elliott, the trainee clerk.

'I've just had a call from Maria-Teresa Jackson's solicitor,' she said.

'Yes?'

'Like I said, her trial's on at the Bailey at the moment. Remembering your interest, she thought you might like to know, the judge was to start summing up first thing today.'

It was an easy walk to the Old Bailey and a good day for it, with the air soft and the light almost as creamy as Trish had seen it in

Venice once. A few of the daffodils were even showing yellow tips in the window boxes of King's Bench Walk as she strolled up towards Mitre Court. Emerging into Fleet Street gave her the usual sensation of crossing into a quite different world, and she pushed her way through the crowds down towards Ludgate Circus. Across at the lights, trying not to inhale too many of the exhaust fumes, up Ludgate Hill, then she passed the entrance to Seacole Lane and so into Old Bailey itself.

Most of the criminal courts were now housed in a modern concrete block beside the older building. Queues were waiting outside the entrance to the public galleries, but Trish had the right of entry and was soon past security and checking which court she needed. A quick word with one of the ushers saw her pushing open the door, bowing to the judge, and finding a seat. From here, she could see only the backs of Maria-Teresa and her husband, as they stood in the dock, but she could see the jury's faces.

They were the usual collection of mostly middle-aged men and women, with little to distinguish them from each other or a thousand of their predecessors, except that they looked hostile, all of them, as they stared towards the dock. Did they hate Maria-Teresa in the same way as the woman Sam had described, who'd attacked her in Holloway?

The judge, robed and bewigged, addressed them with an unpatronizing straightforwardness Trish admired.

'The prosecution have shown that Melvin Briggs was in the house throughout the evening when the child died,' he said, so Trish realized she'd missed all the harrowing details of exactly what had been done to the toddler, as well as the familiar instructions on how the jury must arrive at a verdict. 'And his counsel has not disputed that.

'The prosecution have accepted that Maria-Teresa Jackson was out for part of the evening, attending her art-appreciation lessons at the local college of further education. Her counsel has brought as witnesses to that fact not only fellow members of the class but

also the tutor. They have shown by means of the evidence of the
bus driver who recognized her as one of his passengers that night,
and of various closed-circuit television cameras, that she could not
have reached home until ten thirty, at the very earliest. Now, the
pathologist told you it is possible that the baby, Daniel, was still
alive at that time, although he believes death is more likely to have
taken place earlier. It is for you to decide.'

Several of the jurors shifted in their benches, as though the
responsibility made them uncomfortable. As well it might, Trish
thought, knowing how accustomed many jurors had become to
the certainties of pathologists in television series, which were rarely
reproduced in real life.

'The pathologist's evidence has shown that some of the bruises
on the child's neck and ankles fit the size and shape of Melvin
Briggs's hands. He has also stated that there were other bruises
with less defined boundaries, which cannot be matched to the fingers of either defendant. DNA from both defendants was
recovered from the child's body. When defence counsel asked
whether this could have been left during normal contact, he
agreed that it could.

'You have heard Melvin Briggs testify on oath that his son was
alive and crying when Maria-Teresa Jackson returned and that
she lost her temper with his crying and picked him up, shook
him and slammed his head against the wall. He has further
stated that the only time he gripped his son, making the bruises
described by the pathologist, was when he tried to take the child
from his mother.

'She, however, gave contrary evidence that when she reached the
house her husband was asleep and smelling of alcohol and that the
baby was lying in a pool of blood, not breathing. She stated that
she phoned the emergency services and asked for an ambulance,
evidence that has been corroborated by the London Ambulance
Service's records.'

He took a careful breath, to Trish's eyes sharing most judges' distaste for this kind of defence, which was known in the profession as 'cut throat', with each defendant blaming the other and insisting on their own innocence. Now he had to explain to the jury what the law allowed them to do. She watched them, waiting to assess their reaction to it.

'If you are sure that both defendants are guilty of the murder of their son, then that is the verdict you must bring. If you believe both are innocent, your verdict must be not guilty. If you are sure one is guilty but not the other, that too is a simple matter. However, members of the jury, if you decide that only one is guilty but you cannot decide – on the evidence, and on the evidence alone – which one that is, you must bring in a verdict of not guilty for both of them.'

He went on to explain the difference between murder and manslaughter and how they must make their choice between the two, adding: 'Take your time assessing the evidence you have heard. Do not hesitate to tell the jury bailiff if you would like to ask any questions on points of law or if you would like to be reminded of any of the evidence you have heard, and I will do my best to help. Now, go with the jury bailiff, who will show you the room that has been set aside for you and wait until you are ready to return.'

The jury filed out, still moving awkwardly. One or two looked back at either the judge or the dock, with expressions of doubt rather than rage, which suggested to Trish that the evidence had been fairly presented and none of the barristers had exerted undue charisma over the proceedings. She'd seen more than one jury go against all the evidence because of a brilliantly presented defence by a dashing and witty silk.

Everyone else in court rose, the judge departed, and the two defendants were taken down the stairs that led from the dock to the cells beneath the court. Trish had visited them often enough in her early days at the Bar to know what bleak little rooms they were, with their tiled walls and minimal furniture.

The jury were likely to be out for some time, so Trish decided to go to the canteen for coffee.

'Hey, Trish!' called one of the more junior members of her chambers, as she emerged from court. 'What are you doing here? You're not coming to pick up a few tips on how to run a successful fraud prosecution, are you?'

'I'm sure if I'd thought of it I would have,' she said, laughing at his insult, even though she felt too depressed by what she'd heard for real amusement. 'I'm interested in the Briggs/Jackson case. I thought I'd be in time for the meat of the summing-up today, but I didn't get much more than the awful warning to the jury and an explanation of the cut-throat rules.'

'They're running that, are they? Pretty optimistic, if what I heard in the mess at lunchtime was accurate. You know, it's lucky jurors are still not allowed to know defendants' full records. They'd convict both at the drop of a hat if they knew the whole story.'

'Maria-Teresa too?'

'That sounds as though you know her,' he said, pulling her out of the way of a clutch of lawyers and defendants' families. He took off his wig and gave his short hair a vigorous rub to put it back in order, tucking the wig under his arm.

'I don't know her,' Trish said. 'I've just heard a bit about her. Everything I've heard suggests she's been the victim of a string of brutal men.'

He wagged his head from side to side in a gesture that seemed to express bottomless scepticism.

'I heard at lunch today that it's only four years since she got off a serious assault charge. She put her common-law husband – this same bloke – in hospital with a broken leg and ferocious burns. It was alleged that she'd tipped the chip pan over him and he'd flung himself downstairs, breaking one leg, as he tried to get away from the boiling oil.'

'What was the defence?'

'Didn't hear any details,' he said, 'but whatever it was, it must have been bloody clever, and her counsel must have been shit-hot for her to get off.'

'And that, dear boy,' Trish said, 'is precisely why the jury are not allowed to hear about the defendants' past. You don't know she was guilty; she was in fact acquitted; it's just your prejudice that makes you think she was.'

'Prejudice?' he said, looking down at her from his four-inch superiority. 'Or experience, Trish? You know as well as I that a fair proportion of women in refuges have been the perpetrators, not the victims, of domestic violence. Don't ever let yourself believe women are not quite as revolting as men. I've got to go; closing speech to prepare. See you.'

She'd lost her appetite, even for coffee. Not knowing anything that had gone on before the judge's summing-up, she had no idea how long the jury was likely to be out and she didn't want to miss the verdict. It seemed absurd, given that she could easily find out later, but her brief moments of sympathy for Maria-Teresa Jackson in Holloway and then as she read the letters in the Foundling Museum made her want to stay to hear the jury's decision in real time.

She went out to buy a couple of newspapers, then returned to sit on one of the benches outside the court, waiting for the bailiff to announce the jury's return.

Here we go again, Caro thought as she looked at Guy Bait's impassive face. For this session, she had Glen Makins beside her and Guy had his solicitor as usual.

'I'd like to talk about the shares you sold just over a year ago,' Caro began, reaching for a piece of paper from the pile in front of her. 'Fifty thousand pounds' worth. What did you do with the money?'

The solicitor leaned towards Guy, who immediately said he didn't wish to comment.

'We have had access to your bank accounts,' Caro went on, 'and to your tax records. Your capital gain was very properly reported, but there's no record of any subsequent acquisition. What did you spend the money on?'

She got no answer and casually took another piece of paper.

'The stock brokers have provided us with details of the bank in Leicester that accepted the settlement cheque,' she said, looking down as though she was reading from the sheet. 'They said it was used to open an account, through which there has only ever been one other transaction. Forty-nine thousand was converted into Euros; one thousand remained.'

'I never opened any account in Leicester,' Guy said before his solicitor could stop him.

Caro looked up to smile at him, trying to banish all loathing and suspicion from her expression and make it show warmth, even affection.

'No,' she agreed, 'your young friend from the extranet ASP did that. We'll find him, you know, Guy, and he'll explain what you wanted him to do to the locked computer files containing the original designs for the building known as the Arrow, and how you paid him, and what he did with the money.'

Guy said nothing, and his face barely changed, but for the first time Caro could sense in him the kind of pressure-cooker rage that would make sense of Trish's suspicions and all the evidence her officers had managed to collect.

'We've got lots more, already,' she said in a cheerfully confiding tone. 'A witness who will identify you as the man she saw pushing at the unlatched door of Sam Foundling's studio just before she heard screams from Cecilia. We have the labs working now on the ashes of the clothes you burned in the stove. I'm pretty sure we will manage to recover some of your DNA. It's over, Guy. You don't need to go on fighting. We understand what happened. And we understand why. We know how Cecilia's criticisms and refusal to help you reminded you of your mother, and the time when you smashed her head in with the solidified sugar, and she—'

'Stop it.' It wasn't the solicitor who spoke, but Guy. Caro sat back in her chair and waited. She knew he'd talk now.

QPXQ Holdings had announced record profits, Trish noticed as she skimmed the financial pages. That should help them fund the reconstruction of the Arrow, even if they didn't get the full costs back from the engineers' professional indemnity insurers.

She wondered how Caro was getting on with Guy Bait and whether the case against him would hold.

'Jury's coming back,' she heard, and shook out the paper to fold it back on itself into a small enough bundle to tuck under her arm.

This has to be a guilty verdict for at least one of the defendants, she thought. No jury comes back after less than an hour with an acquittal on any grounds, unless they hate the prosecution or the defence is especially brilliant. None of the jury had looked engaged enough for either of those to be true.

The defendants re-emerged, separated by uniformed prison officers. Neither looked at the other. The judge's clerk preceded him into court and then the jury filed back in.

'Members of the jury,' said the clerk of the court, as soon as the foreman had announced herself by standing up, 'have you reached a verdict on which you are all agreed?'

'We have,' she said, revealing an Australian twang.

'Is your verdict in respect of Melvin Briggs guilty or not guilty of murder?'

'Guilty.'

The broad shoulders Trish could see from her bench slumped forwards.

'Is your verdict in respect of Maria-Teresa Jackson guilty or not guilty of murder?'

'Not guilty.'

I wish I'd heard the evidence, Trish thought, even though the summing-up had been pretty clear.

She barely heard him announcing the mandatory life sentence of murder for Melvin Briggs, but the familiar words 'take him down' made her look towards the dock.

'Maria-Teresa Jackson, you have been found not guilty of the charge of murder and you are free to go.'

'All rise.'

Getting to her feet with the rest, Trish saw Maria-Teresa Jackson look round the court, as though in search of someone to tell her what to do. Her gaze slid past Trish's face, showing no sign of recognition. The prison officer with her murmured something, then opened the door of the dock. Maria-Teresa took a tottery step out of it, still looking hunted. Her solicitor walked towards her with a broad smile.

'It's over, Maria-Teresa,' she said, well within Trish's hearing.

'What do I do?'

'You can go home now. And rebuild your life.'

'You mean I just go out into the road? Now?'

'That's right. We can call you a taxi.'

'I don't know what to do.'

'Come on outside anyway,' said the solicitor kindly. 'And we'll talk about it.'

Trish followed them at a discreet distance, wondering whether she ought to go over and say something. It was easy to imagine the sense of bemused anxiety that would stop Maria-Teresa feeling any kind of triumph after the ordeal of this kind of trial. She'd had no family or supporters in court with her.

You can't take her on, Trish reminded herself. So any friendliness now would be unfair. She's got her solicitor there. She'll be all right. She's not your responsibility.

They'd reached the outside now. There were no journalists or photographers here. The case hadn't been reported and no one was particularly interested in a scraggy untidy woman who hadn't killed her two-year-old son.

A strong hand came down on Trish's shoulder and she whirled

round in shock to see Sam Foundling. The baby was lying against his chest, suspended in her dark-blue sling.

'Were you in court?' he said. 'They wouldn't let me in with Felicity and I didn't have anyone to leave her with.'

'I was there.' She told him what the verdicts were.

'I know. I've just heard. I'll do my best to be back for our celebration tea,' he said, 'but I've got to go with her now.'

Trish opened her mouth to ask if he had taken the DNA test.

'Whoever she is,' he said quickly. 'Whatever she's done. She shouldn't be alone now.'

He didn't wait for Trish's nod, just walked towards Maria-Teresa with one hand held out. Her solicitor barked a question, but Maria-Teresa took his hand between both of hers and spoke rapidly. Trish moved closer to listen, then knew it was none of her business. From where she stood she could see Sam unmistakably dismissing the solicitor and hailing a taxi. He took the arm of the woman who might be his mother and escorted her to the cab, holding the door for her, then getting in himself.

The court had declared Maria-Teresa innocent, and the CPS had dropped all charges against Sam. But no one knew whether they were right. Only these two knew the truth.

Trish stood in the street, wondering how it would end for them. Once she'd yearned for final answers, neat endings, certainty. Now she knew nothing could ever be neat, neither the start nor the end of any story. All of them had roots that spread far beyond the lives of any of the parties, and they would go on involving these two and their children and their children's children.

There was no point going back to chambers now so she turned down New Bridge Street for her usual walk across the Thames at Blackfriars. Most of the light had gone, but it was nowhere near real darkness. Spring would come soon and then summer, with all the plans David and George had been making for a month-long trip to the States. George's descriptions of Cape Cod in July had entranced them both and they were determined to walk along pale golden sands and gaze out at horizons where sea and sky merged in one glorious blaze of blue.

Her phone buzzed in the pocket of her trousers when she was halfway across the bridge. She flipped it open and heard Caro's voice.

'Trish, I thought you should know: we got a confession.'

'From Guy Bait?' she asked, leaning against the parapet, looking west towards the National Theatre and the London Eye.

'Yup. His solicitor was here. He signed the statement. It's all on the level. He killed Cecilia Mayford, just as you thought, not after a plan but in an excess of frustration when she wouldn't agree to hide what she knew about the building he'd ruined with his mistake in the diameter of the cables.'

It didn't seem right to congratulate Caro or express any kind of relief, so Trish produced a complicated, non-specific murmuring sound.

'We'd never have got there without you,' Caro said. 'I . . . I'm too played out to say it right now. We've been at it all weekend as well as today. But I'm sorry. For the things I said and even more for the ones I thought.'

'I know. Don't worry,' Trish said, feeling the lids slide over her eyes. 'I'm just glad to know he really did do it.'

'So you *weren't* sure?' Caro said. 'You always managed to sound pretty confident.'

'Sure? I don't know what that means any more. You can want something to be true so much that you can't let yourself believe it isn't; and you can be so afraid it's not that your subconscious paints pictures of the very thing you most dread, until you can't remember what's real and what's not.' She paused, wondering why the relief didn't make her feel any better. The street lights came on, casting a warm yellow light over the dusk. 'I wish Cecilia hadn't died.'

'Thanks to you, her child will grow up with her father, unlike Cecilia herself – or you or me,' Caro said, generous again now they'd lost the huge obstacle that had grown big enough to block their friendship. 'There should be some comfort in that.'

'I suppose there is.'

'Good. Oh, and by the way, I don't know whether it's of interest to you, but Sam Foundling asked us for a copy of the DNA fingerprint we took while he was with us.'

And Maria-Teresa was tested too, Trish thought, so maybe he does know who she is.

'So shall we meet?' Caro said down the phone. 'We never did have that lunch.'

They made a date and Trish walked on, home to George and David, and her own life.

Epilogue

Gina Mayford was drafting the judgement she was due to give next week when her clerk brought in a cup of ginger-and-lemon tea. The slice of ginger was so perfectly peeled and shaped Gina knew it was an expression of sympathy in itself. She glanced up to smile her gratitude. The clerk nodded, looked as though she was about to speak, then backed away. Gina tried to concentrate on her judgement, but there were other things she had to do, and there wasn't much time. She saw her rolly suitcase out of the corner of her eye and checked her watch. There was just under half an hour before she had to leave to pick up Sam and Felicity.

They were all off to Paris by Eurostar so that she could babysit while Sam was presented with the Prix Narcisse for his *Head of a Boy*, with all the formality and glamour the Parisians did so well.

A batch of photographs he'd taken of Felicity lay beside the phone. Gina reached for one and had to smile again at the sight of the small pudgy face, already so individual it barely reminded her of Cecilia's in babyhood. She pulled out a sheet of paper from the box, found her old fountain pen, shook some ink down into the nib and wrote:

Dear Andrew,
  I think it's time we . . .

She paused, still not sure how to put it, and stared unseeingly at the tall oak bookshelves opposite her desk. They held all the legal texts that had formed and buttressed her life for the past thirty-six years. After a moment she started to write again, but the ink had dried. Shaking the pen this time, she dropped a huge blot on the paper. When she'd screwed it into a ball and flung it into the wastepaper basket, she tried once more.

My dear Andrew . . .

POCKET
BOOKS

A Poisoned Mind
Natasha Cooper

When a chemical explosion rips through quiet fields in the
North of England, it destroys much more than the innocent life
of the man who farmed them. In her grief his widow, Angie,
turns on the company responsible. Enter hotshot barrister
Trish Maguire, who finds herself in turmoil when she is
called on to defend not the ruined and heartbroken
Angie, but the multinational company instead.

As the case develops, Trish comes to believe the explosion
can't possibly have been pure accident. Which leads her
to ask who stood to gain most from such a
dangerous act of sabotage . . .

At the same time, Trish faces emotional explosions at
home. Her adopted son David has a new school friend in the
damaged and volatile Jay. When Jay's mother is found brutally
beaten, Trish knows she has to help. But in doing so, she finds
herself embroiled in two major battles – one for everything she
has worked for, and one for everything she believes is right . . .

ISBN 978–0-7432–9547–5
PRICE £17.99

POCKET
BOOKS

Gagged & Bound
Natasha Cooper

**Sticks and stones can break my bones,
but words can never hurt me . . .**

London is awash with secret information and vicious rumour.
A politician fights for his reputation. Gangs of organized
criminals poison the streets with their lesson that greed
and violence pay. Some of those who hunt them bend the
rules; others take their money. A whistleblower
goes in fear of her life.

Trish Maguire and her close friend, DI Caro Lyalt of the Met,
will have to disentangle fact from fiction if they are to protect
the innocent and pin down the guilty. But their actions
bring danger horrifyingly close to home . . .

**ISBN 978–0–7434–9533–2
PRICE £6.99**

POCKET
BOOKS

Keep Me Alive
Natasha Cooper

Who is the man beaten to death in a Kentish field? How will
his story affect barrister Trish Maguire and her client Will
Applewood as she fights his case against a giant supermarket
chain? And what will happen to Inspector Caro Lyalt, half-
dead with food poisoning after a meal she cooked for Trish?

Breaking new ground in this novel, Natasha Cooper takes
Trish Maguire beyond her usual world of legal London and
confronts her with the grimmest side of human nature and
some exceptionally nasty crimes.

ISBN 978–0-7434–4987–8
PRICE £6.99

**POCKET
BOOKS**

This book and other **Natasha Cooper** titles are available from your local bookshop or can be ordered direct from the publisher.

Please send cheque or postal order for the value of the book, **free postage and packing within the UK**, to
SIMON & SCHUSTER CASH SALES
PO Box 29, Douglas Isle of Man, IM99 1BQ
Tel: 01624 677237, Fax: 01624 670923
Email: bookshop@enterprise.net
www.bookpost.co.uk

Please allow 14 days for delivery. Prices and availability subject to change without notice